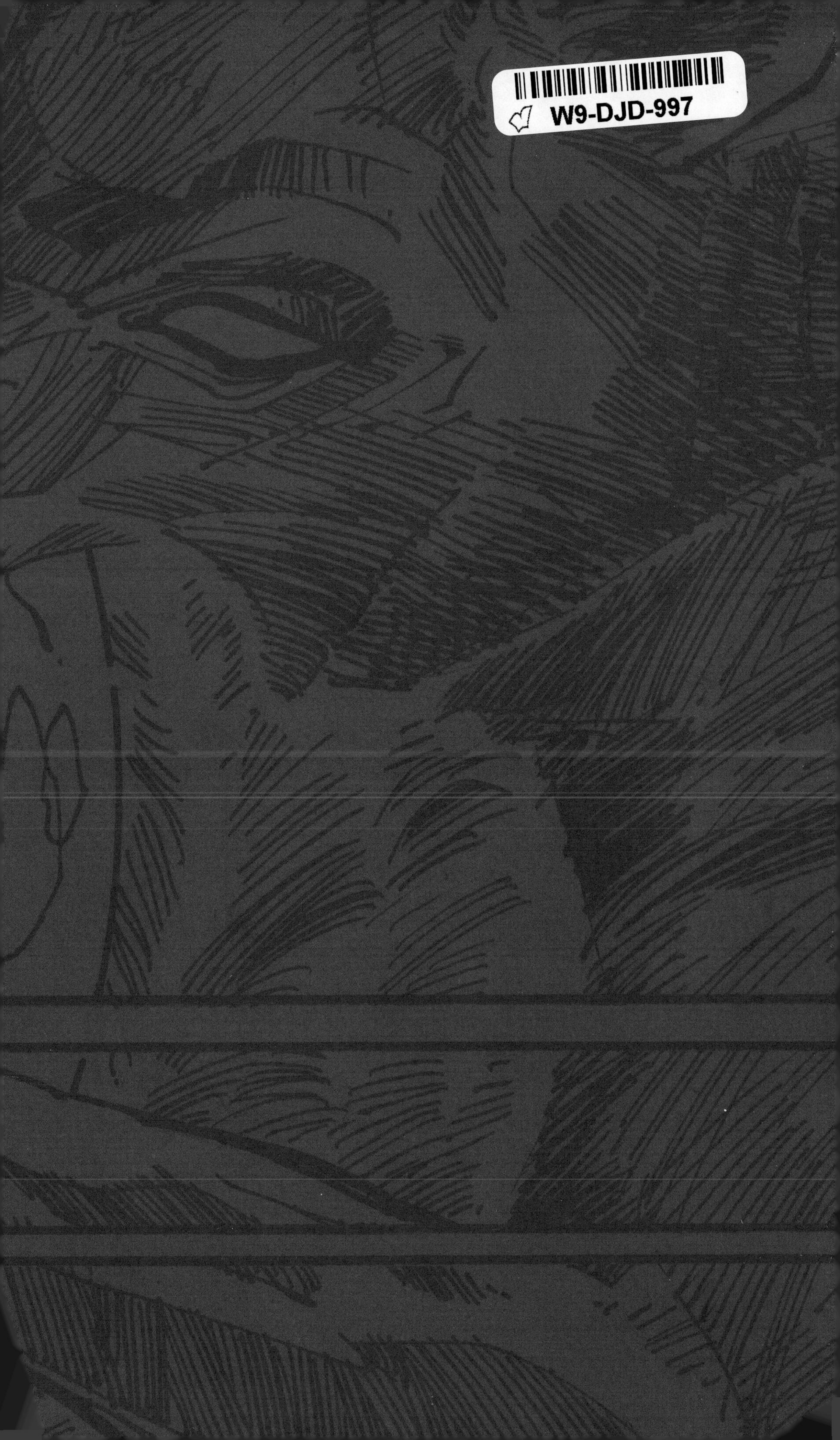

RAGNARÖK

VOL. THREE: THE BREAKING OF HELHEIM

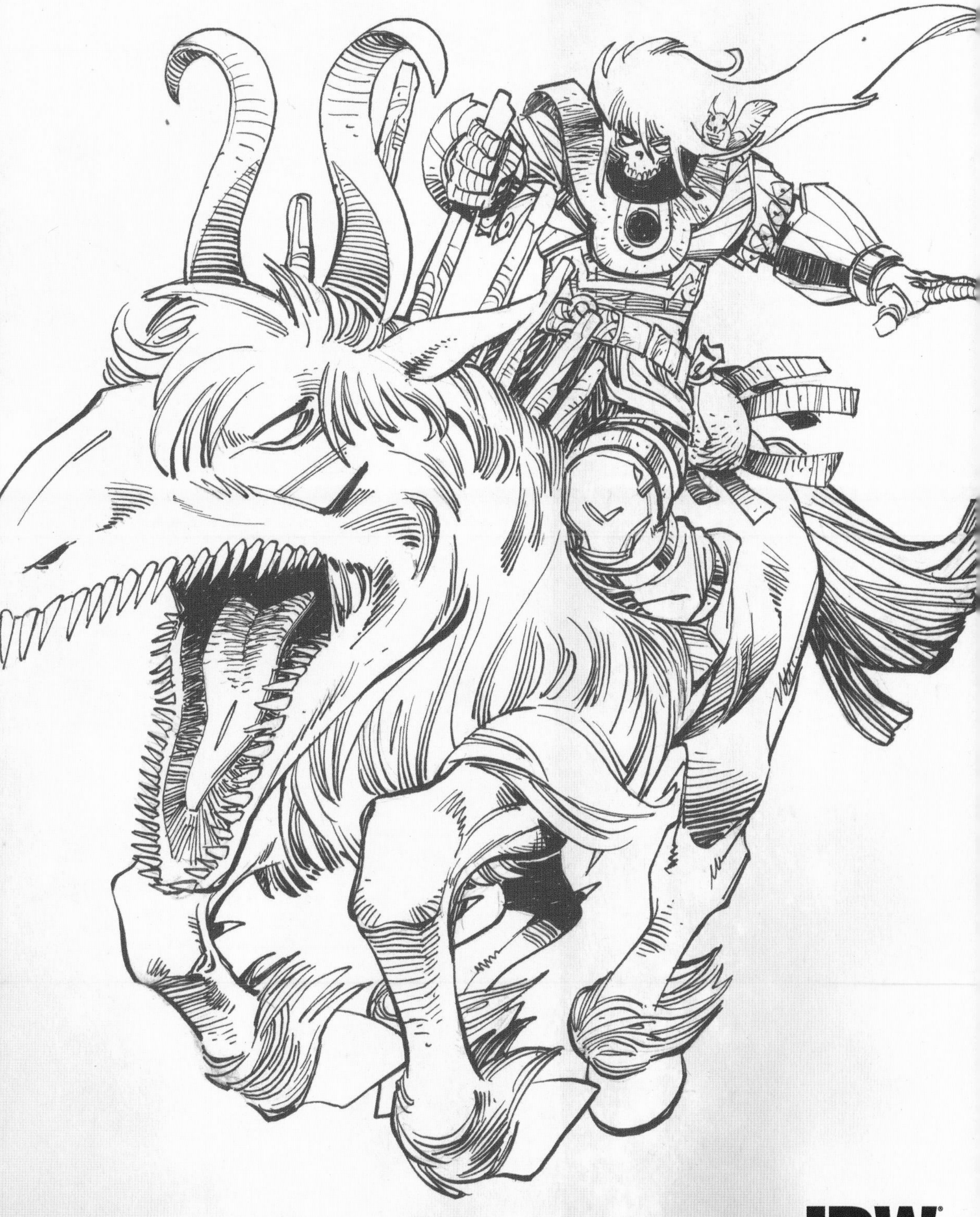

IDW

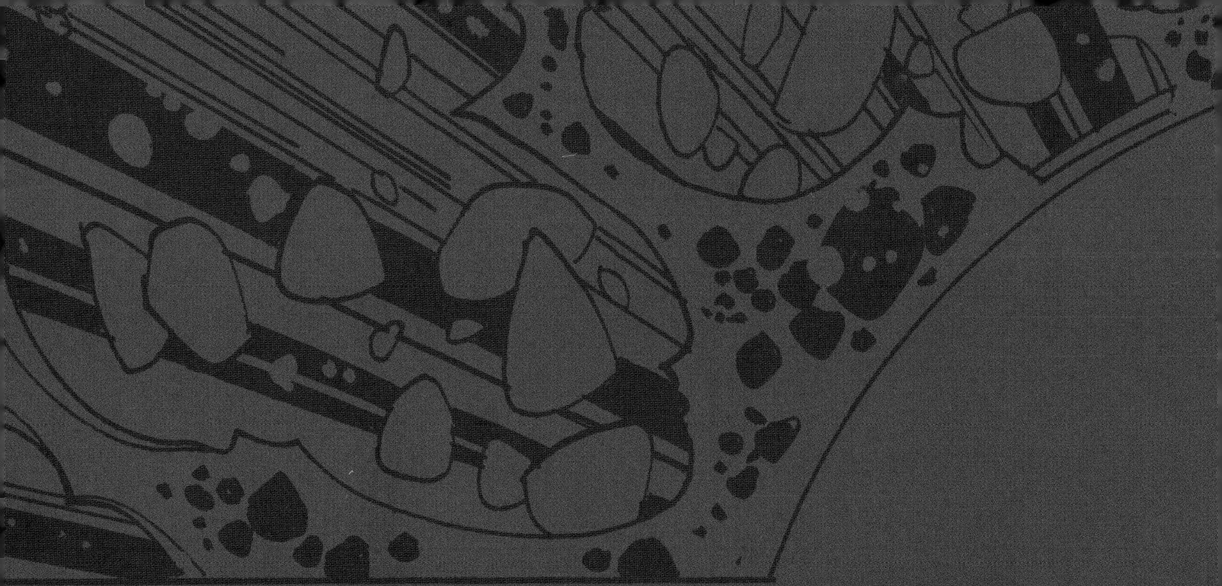

Special thanks and appreciation to Louise Simonson, Lillian Laserson, and Jean Scrocco of Spiderwebart Gallery.

www.idwpublishing.co

ISBN: 978-1-68405-713

23 22 21 20 1 2 3
Printed in Chi

PROOFREAD BY SCOTT TIPTO
PRODUCTION ASSISTANCE BY SHAWN L
EDITED BY SCOTT DUNBI

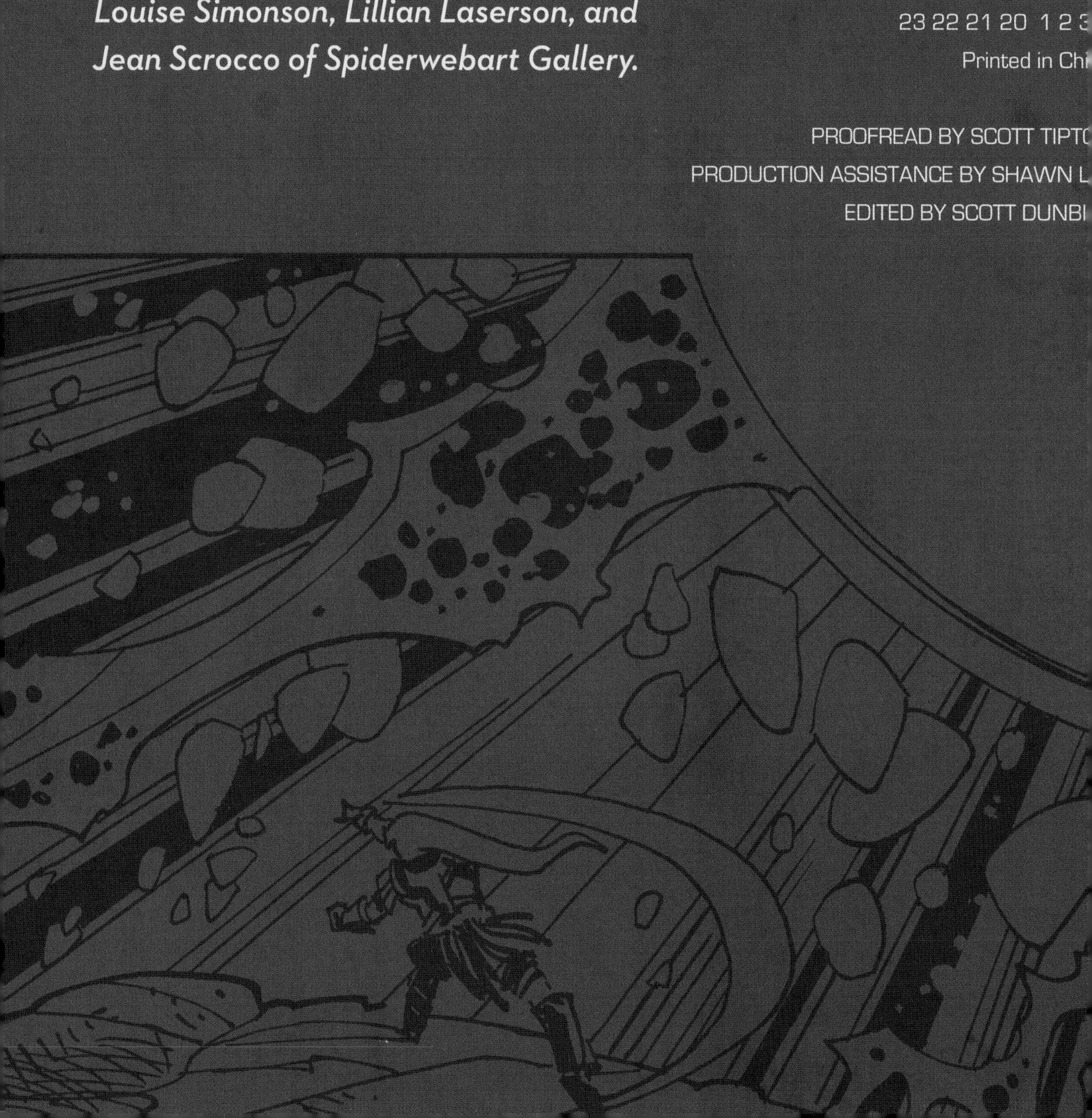

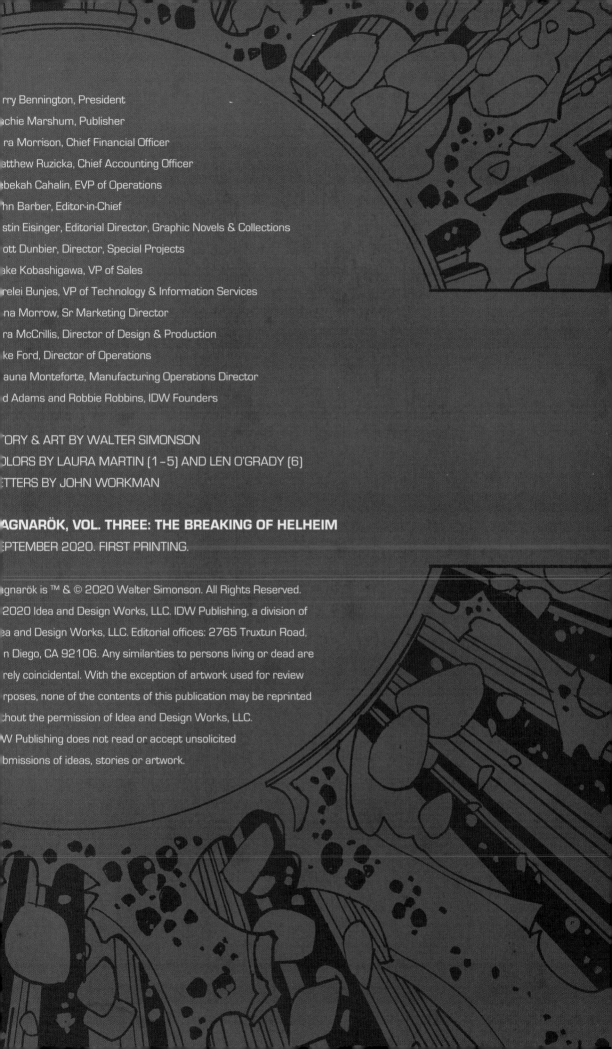

TORY & ART BY WALTER SIMONSON

OLORS BY LAURA MARTIN (1–5) AND LEN O'GRADY (6)

ETTERS BY JOHN WORKMAN

AGNARÖK, VOL. THREE: THE BREAKING OF HELHEIM

EPTEMBER 2020. FIRST PRINTING.

agnarök is ™ & © 2020 Walter Simonson. All Rights Reserved.

2020 Idea and Design Works, LLC. IDW Publishing, a division of

ea and Design Works, LLC. Editorial offices: 2765 Truxtun Road,

n Diego, CA 92106. Any similarities to persons living or dead are

rely coincidental. With the exception of artwork used for review

rposes, none of the contents of this publication may be reprinted

thout the permission of Idea and Design Works, LLC.

W Publishing does not read or accept unsolicited

bmissions of ideas, stories or artwork.

INTRODUCTION

On *The Breaking of Helheim*…

The stories in the mythologies the world round are not structured like comic-book continuity. No big surprise. Comics share many of the same tropes; they have borrowed a lot from mythology and legends and storytelling traditions down through the ages. But for all the lovely stories and heroics and tragedies related in myths, their purpose is quite different from that of myths. Comics are meant to entertain and occasionally enlighten us. Mythologies are an attempt to come to grips with some of the deepest questions of our existence, with meaning, with life and death, and with humanity's place in the universe. Myths live at the edges of these great questions, and the questions themselves are often more important than the answers. The answers aren't always clear, they're often metaphorical, and they don't dot every "I" and cross every "T" as comic-book continuity often tries to do. The questions give myths their power. The stories in comics generally supply questions. Fortunately, as a writer and drawer of comic books, nobody expects me to answer the great questions which are clearly well beyond my scope of my powers. Yet the very existence of those questions that mythology wrestles with gives a storyteller a place to begin. This is particularly true with Norse mythology.

The Breaking of Helheim originated, as have many of my tales in Ragnarök, in the incompleteness of the Norse myths as they have come down to us.

Scandinavian myths in the surviving texts are wonderful and fascinating, but many are clearly incomplete or unknown to us today. Some stories, to be sure, are presented in relatively finished forms as the Vikings themselves might have heard them a thousand years ago. But there are many stories that are only partially known, and in some cases, there are merely fragments or even simply allusions to events of which we know nothing other than the allusions themselves. It's frustrating in the sense that I would love to have been able to read the complete corpus of Viking mythology. On the other hand, this very incompleteness has left me a lot of room for invention as a storyteller.

So with this volume, I decided to explore the realm of the dead as described in the Norse literature, and wrestle with one of the great-unanswered questions.

If one doesn't die in glorious battle and get chosen by a Valkyrie to be carried off to Valhalla or Folkvang, one ends up in Hel—a realm of the dead. At least this is the common understanding. Because the myths aren't as concerned with continuity as comic books are, they don't really supply quite such a specific answer. The actual source material suggests a rather more complex relationship between life and death with perhaps even more realms in play, but for this story, the common understanding will suffice.

Hel is ruled by Loki's daughter, likewise named Hel. She is half living and half dead although the myths aren't clear about exactly how the halves are divided up. There is some evidence to suggest that she was a fairly late addition to the mythology, a personification of the place itself—hence the same name. Hel, the realm, is described in various ways, but for my purposes, I see it as a fairly dreary place in which to end up. It isn't the equivalent of the Christian Hell, a realm of eternal damnation and punishment. It seems more to me like a dampish, somewhat unpleasant location but not a place of torment. However, it is a place you wouldn't mind leaving if you could.

Nevertheless, I have structured Hel geographically with a nod to Dante's *Inferno*. While I haven't made explicit use of Dante's Circles of Hell, I have incorporated the idea of Hel as an enormous canyon or meteor crater with descending layers that bottom out eventually. I have also changed the name of the realm slightly to avoid confusion. In the literature, "Hel," the place, is occasionally referred to as "Helheim." It's not common, but I have used it in my story so as to distinguish more easily between "Hel," the ruler, and "Helheim," her kingdom. "Heim" in several Northern European languages means "home," so that seemed appropriate.

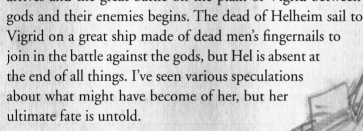

Hel herself, one of Loki's children, was flung into Helheim by Odin early on and has ruled there since. As far as I know, she isn't mentioned in the original Norse source material once Ragnarök arrives and the great battle on the plain of Vigrid between the gods and their enemies begins. The dead of Helheim sail to Vigrid on a great ship made of dead men's fingernails to join in the battle against the gods, but Hel is absent at the end of all things. I've seen various speculations about what might have become of her, but her ultimate fate is untold.

Seizing on the opportunity, I decided I wanted to know about Hel's fate during and after Ragnarök. What DID become of her?

You hold at least one answer in your hands.

Walter Simonson
New York
2020

DEDICATION

For the late Anne Murphy…

Anne was the wife of Archie Goodwin. Between them, they helped keep me fed in my very early days in comics in New York City, with frequent invitations to dinner. Archie gave me my professional career by offering me "Manhunter," and Anne introduced me to Louise Jones, whom I would eventually marry. In their apartment on Broadway on the West Side, my personal and professional lives were born, gifts I can only pay forward.

And of course, as with all things, for Weezie…

CONTENTS

Ragnarök—The Breaking of Helheim #1   Page 9

Ragnarök—The Breaking of Helheim #2   Page 31

Ragnarök—The Breaking of Helheim #3   Page 53

Ragnarök—The Breaking of Helheim #4   Page 75

Ragnarök—The Breaking of Helheim #5   Page 97

Ragnarök—The Breaking of Helheim #6   Page 119

RAGNARÖK ART GALLERY   Page 142

Ragnarök—The Breaking of Helheim #1
& Usagi Yojimbo #1 Variant Jam cover   Page 144,145
Art by Stan Sakai and Walter Simonson

Ragnarök—The Breaking of Helheim #1
& Usagi Yojimbo #1 Variant Jam cover   Page 146,147
Art by Stan Sakai and Walter Simonson, colors by Laura Martin

Ragnarök #1 cover inks   Page 148

Ragnarök #1 cover colors   Page 149
Art by Walter Simonson, colors by Laura Martin

Ragnarök #2 cover inks   Page 150

Ragnarök #2 cover colors   Page 151
Art by Walter Simonson, colors by Laura Martin

Ragnarök #3 cover inks   Page 152

Ragnarök #3 cover colors   Page 153
Art by Walter Simonson, colors by Laura Martin

Ragnarök #4 cover inks   Page 154

Ragnarök #4 cover colors   Page 155
Art by Walter Simonson, colors by Laura Martin

Ragnarök #5 cover inks   Page 156

Ragnarök #5 cover colors   Page 157
Art by Walter Simonson, colors by Laura Martin

Ragnarök #6 cover inks   Page 158

Ragnarök #6 cover colors   Page 159
Art by Walter Simonson, colors by Laura Martin

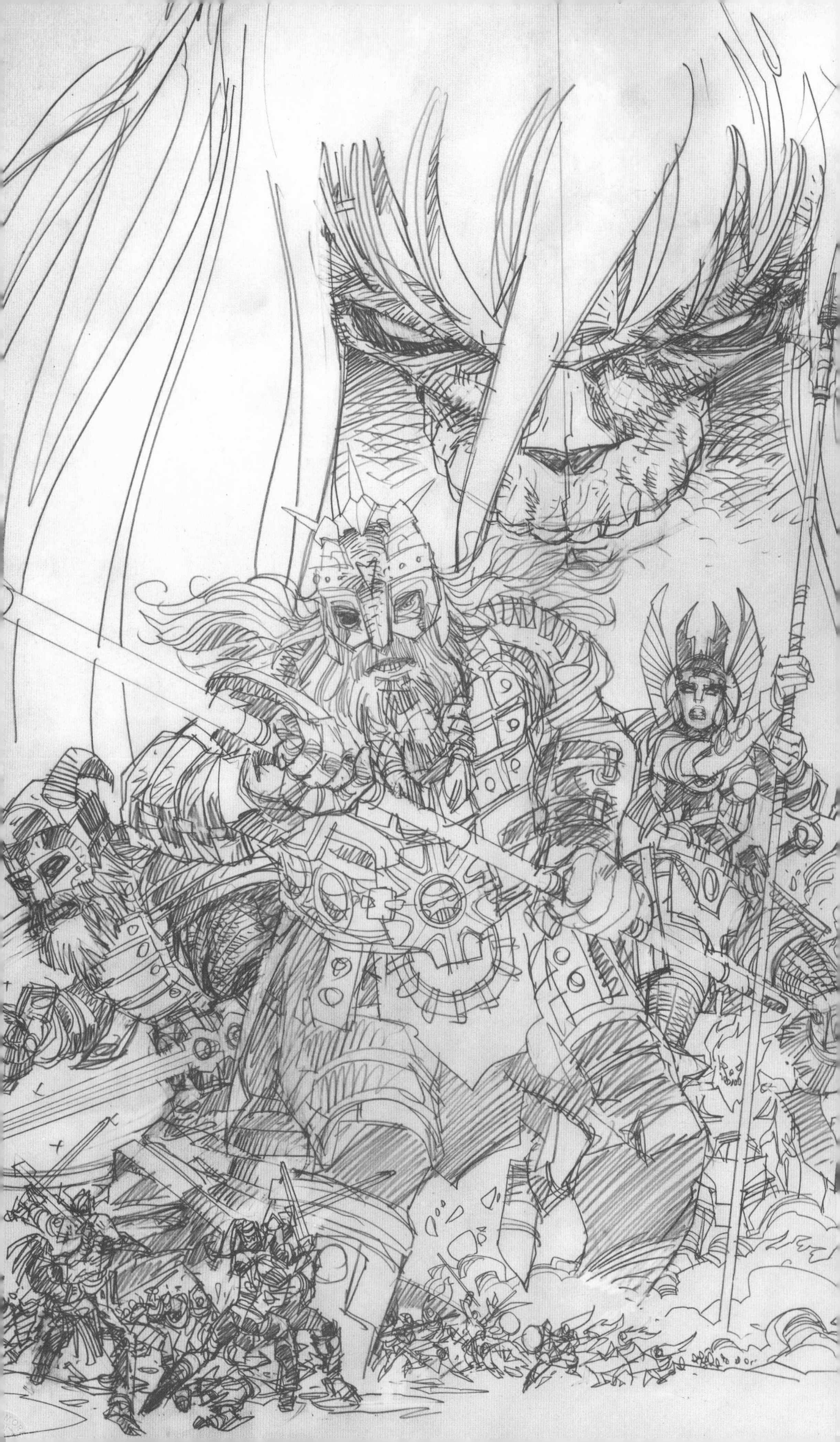

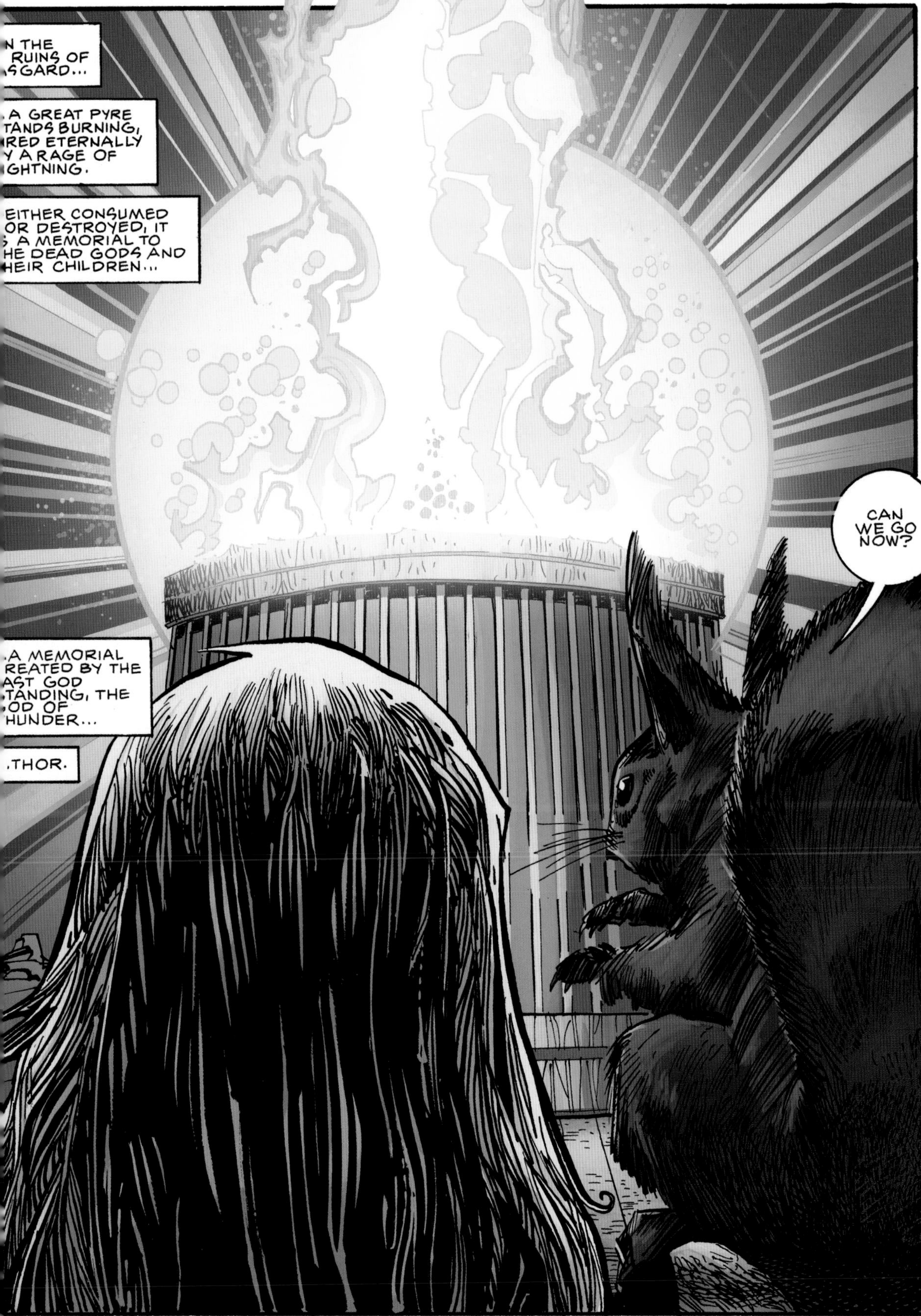
N THE RUINS OF SGARD...
. A GREAT PYRE TANDS BURNING, IRED ETERNALLY Y A RAGE OF GHTNING.
EITHER CONSUMED OR DESTROYED, IT S A MEMORIAL TO HE DEAD GODS AND HEIR CHILDREN...
CAN WE GO NOW?
. A MEMORIAL REATED BY THE AST GOD TANDING, THE OD OF HUNDER...
.THOR.

HE DOOM OF THE POWERS

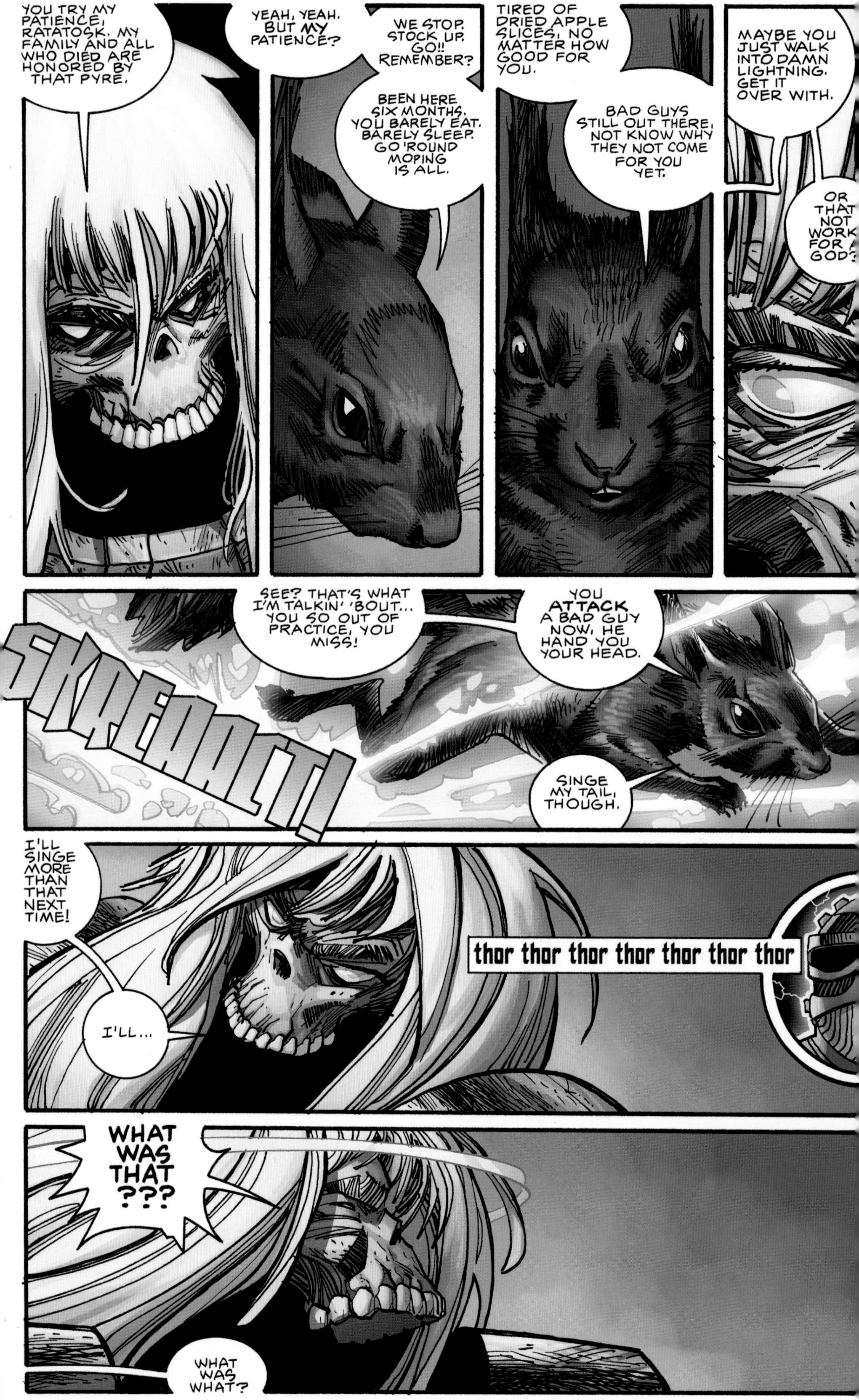
YOU TRY MY PATIENCE, RATATOSK. MY FAMILY AND ALL WHO DIED ARE HONORED BY THAT PYRE.
YEAH, YEAH. BUT MY PATIENCE?
WE STOP. STOCK UP. GO!! REMEMBER?
BEEN HERE SIX MONTHS. YOU BARELY EAT. BARELY SLEEP. GO 'ROUND MOPING IS ALL.
TIRED OF DRIED APPLE SLICES, NO MATTER HOW GOOD FOR YOU.
BAD GUYS STILL OUT THERE, NOT KNOW WHY THEY NOT COME FOR YOU YET.
MAYBE YOU JUST WALK INTO DAMN LIGHTNING, GET IT OVER WITH.
OR THAT NOT WORK FOR A GOD?
SKREAACT!!
SEE? THAT'S WHAT I'M TALKIN' 'BOUT... YOU SO OUT OF PRACTICE, YOU MISS!
YOU ATTACK A BAD GUY NOW, HE HAND YOU YOUR HEAD.
SINGE MY TAIL, THOUGH.
I'LL SINGE MORE THAN THAT NEXT TIME!
I'LL...
thor thor thor thor thor thor thor
WHAT WAS THAT???
WHAT WAS WHAT?

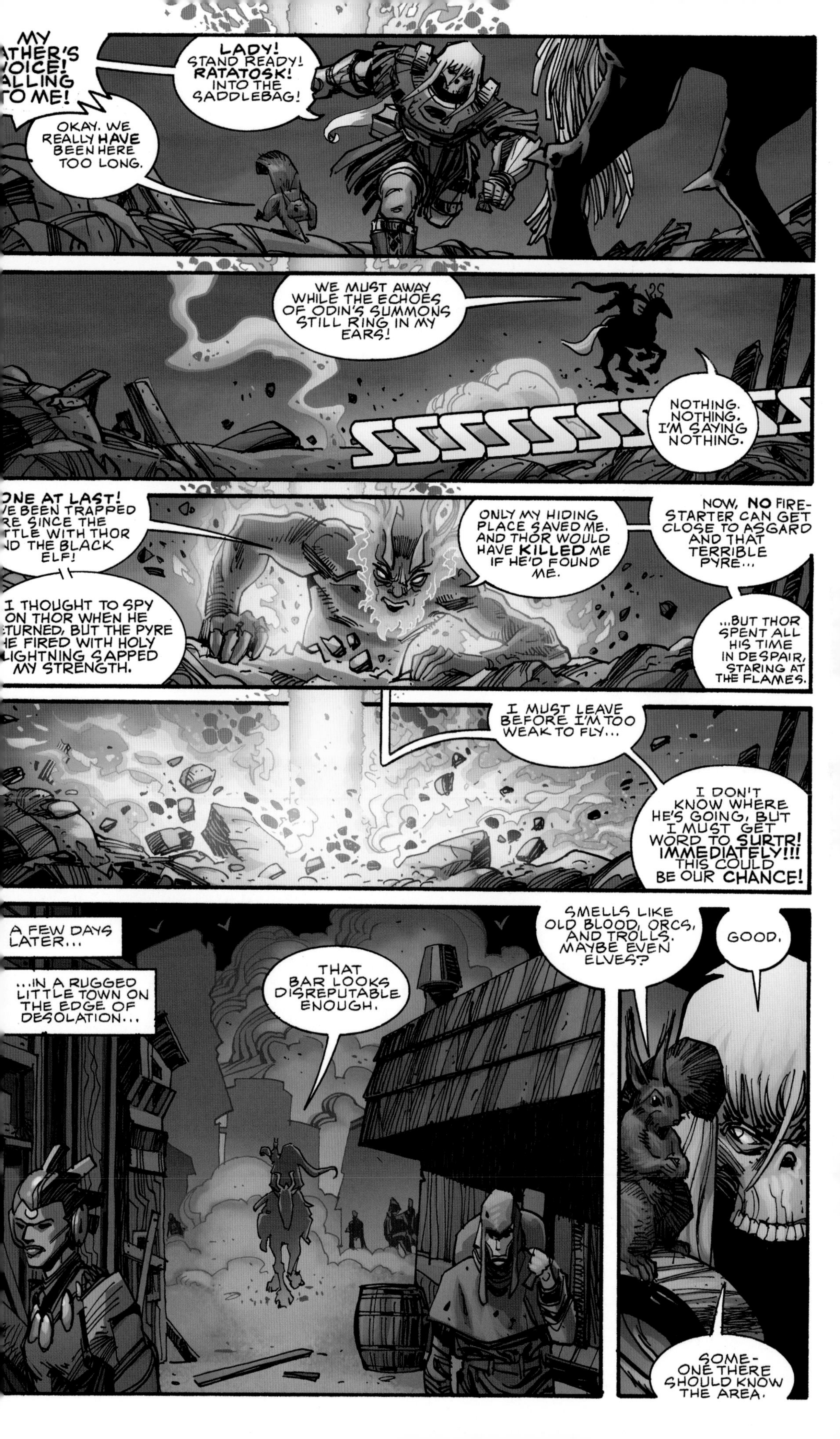
MY
ATHER'S
OICE!
ALLING
TO ME!
LADY! STAND READY! RATATOSK! INTO THE SADDLEBAG!
OKAY. WE REALLY HAVE BEEN HERE TOO LONG.
WE MUST AWAY WHILE THE ECHOES OF ODIN'S SUMMONS STILL RING IN MY EARS!
SSSSSSSSSS
NOTHING. NOTHING. I'M SAYING NOTHING.
ONE AT LAST!
VE BEEN TRAPPED
RE SINCE THE
TTLE WITH THOR
ND THE BLACK
ELF!
I THOUGHT TO SPY
ON THOR WHEN HE
ETURNED, BUT THE PYRE
HE FIRED WITH HOLY
LIGHTNING SAPPED
MY STRENGTH.
ONLY MY HIDING PLACE SAVED ME. AND THOR WOULD HAVE KILLED ME IF HE'D FOUND ME.
NOW, NO FIRE-STARTER CAN GET CLOSE TO ASGARD AND THAT TERRIBLE PYRE...
...BUT THOR SPENT ALL HIS TIME IN DESPAIR, STARING AT THE FLAMES.
I MUST LEAVE BEFORE I'M TOO WEAK TO FLY...
I DON'T KNOW WHERE HE'S GOING, BUT I MUST GET WORD TO SURTR! IMMEDIATELY!!! THIS COULD BE OUR CHANCE!
A FEW DAYS LATER...
...IN A RUGGED LITTLE TOWN ON THE EDGE OF DESOLATION...
THAT BAR LOOKS DISREPUTABLE ENOUGH.
SMELLS LIKE OLD BLOOD, ORCS, AND TROLLS. MAYBE EVEN ELVES?
GOOD.
SOME-ONE THERE SHOULD KNOW THE AREA.

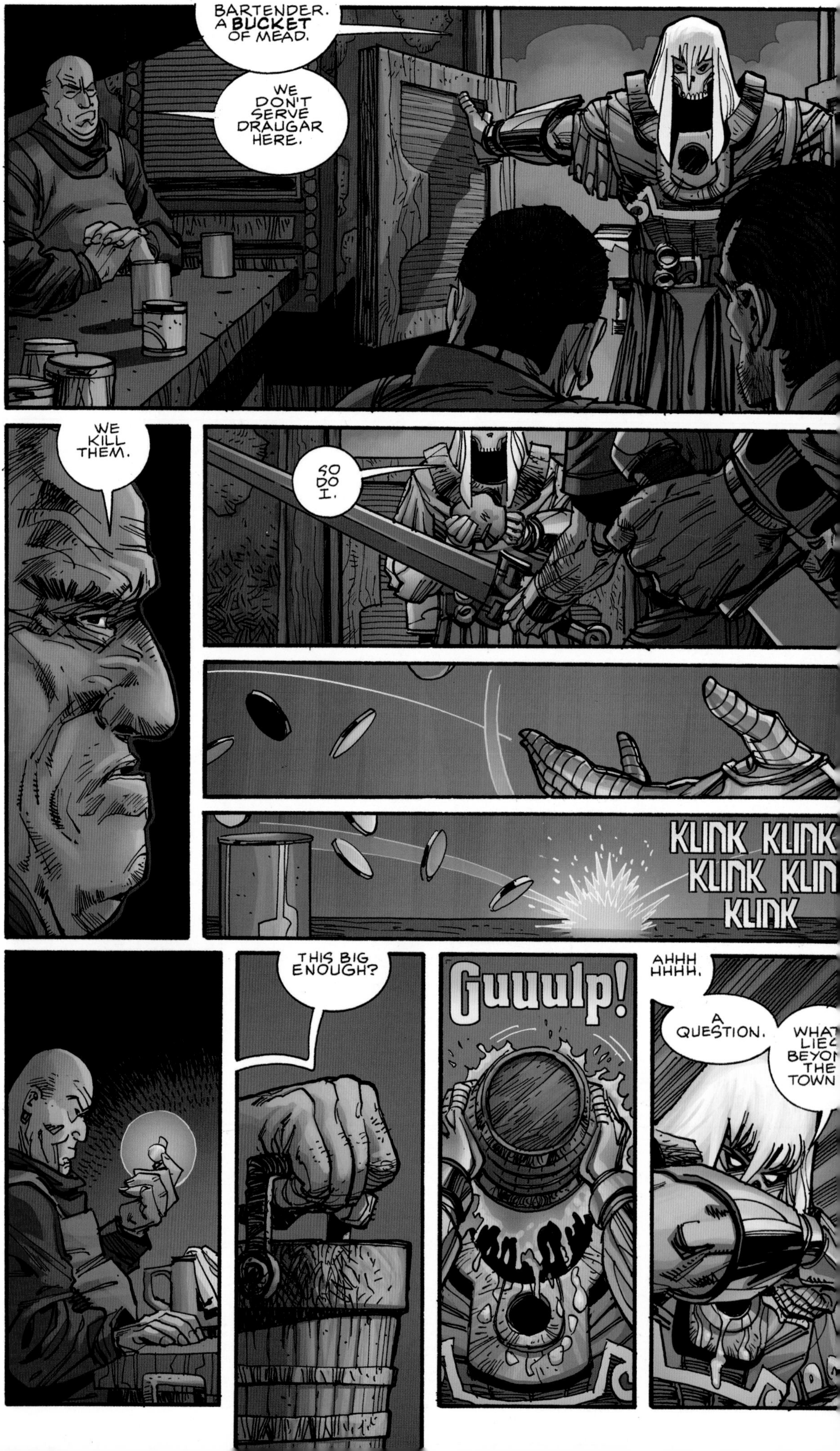
BARTENDER. A BUCKET OF MEAD.
WE DON'T SERVE DRAUGAR HERE.
WE KILL THEM.
SO DO I.
KLINK KLINK KLINK KLIN KLINK
THIS BIG ENOUGH?
Guuulp!
AHHH HHHH.
A QUESTION.
WHAT LIES BEYON THE TOWN

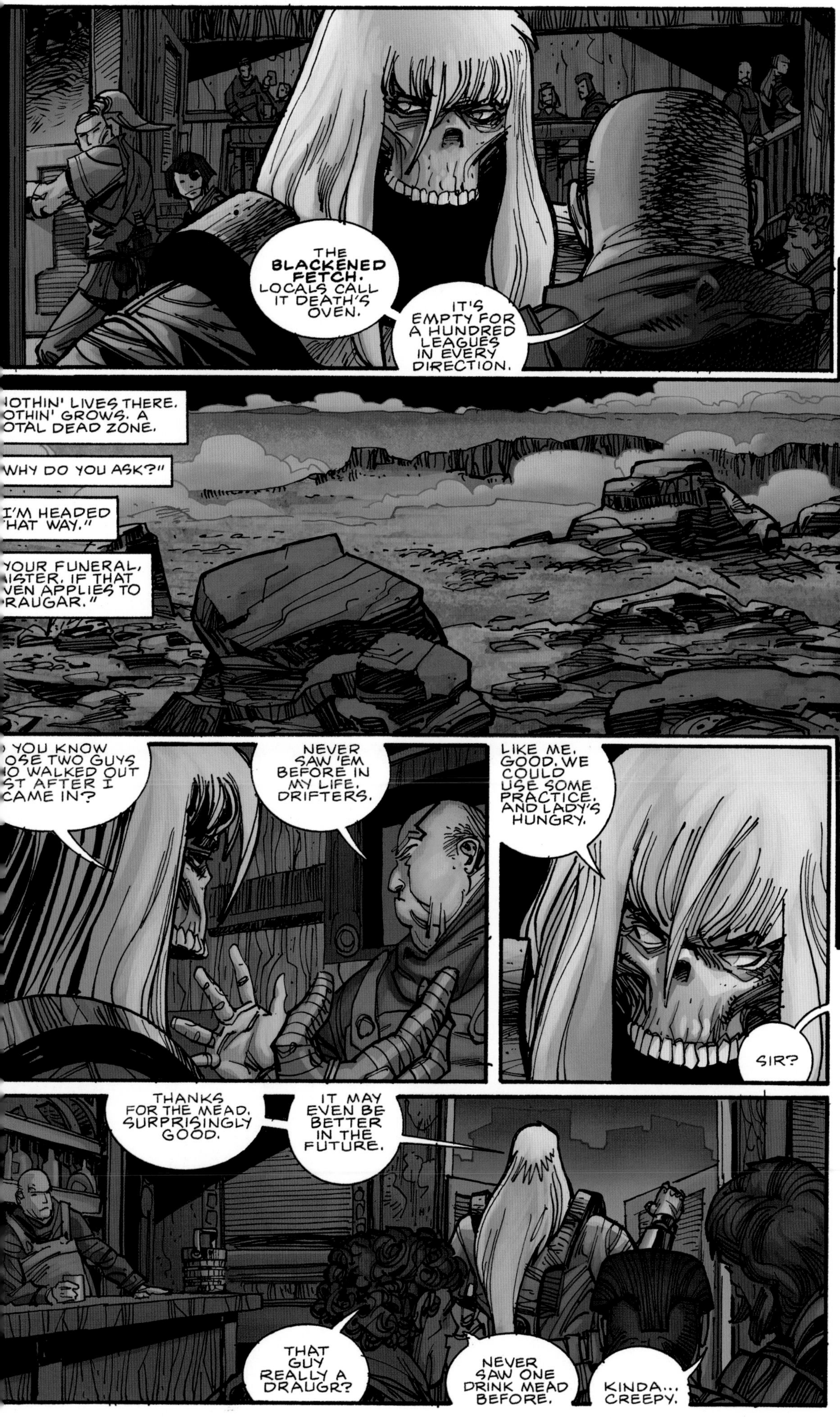
THE BLACKENED FETCH. LOCALS CALL IT DEATH'S OVEN.
IT'S EMPTY FOR A HUNDRED LEAGUES IN EVERY DIRECTION.
NOTHIN' LIVES THERE. OTHIN' GROWS. A OTAL DEAD ZONE.
WHY DO YOU ASK?"
I'M HEADED HAT WAY."
YOUR FUNERAL, MISTER. IF THAT VEN APPLIES TO RAUGAR."
YOU KNOW OSE TWO GUYS IO WALKED OUT ST AFTER I CAME IN?
NEVER SAW 'EM BEFORE IN MY LIFE. DRIFTERS.
LIKE ME. GOOD. WE COULD USE SOME PRACTICE. AND LADY'S HUNGRY.
SIR?
THANKS FOR THE MEAD. SURPRISINGLY GOOD.
IT MAY EVEN BE BETTER IN THE FUTURE.
THAT GUY REALLY A DRAUGR?
NEVER SAW ONE DRINK MEAD BEFORE.
KINDA... CREEPY.

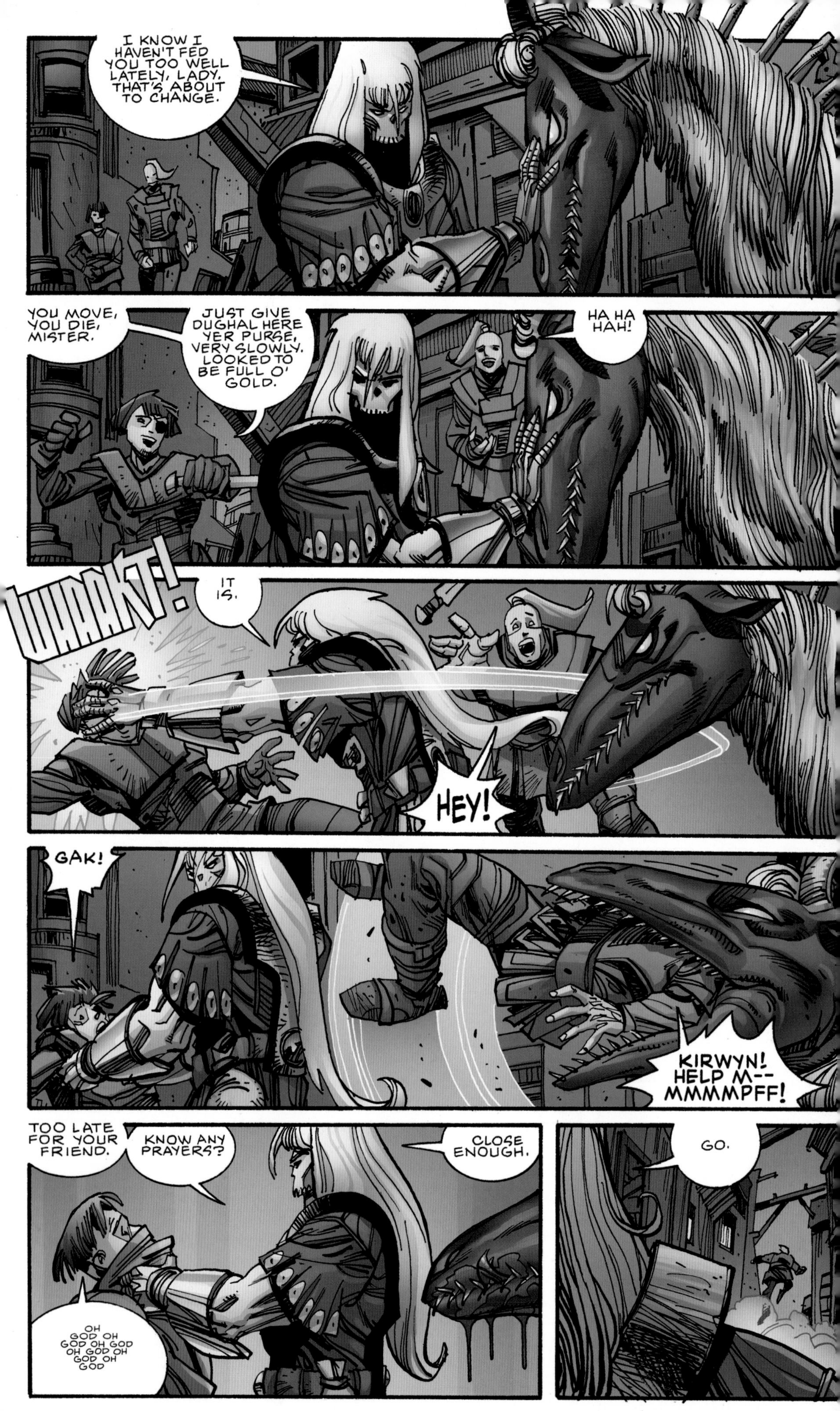
I KNOW I HAVEN'T FED YOU TOO WELL LATELY, LADY. THAT'S ABOUT TO CHANGE.
YOU MOVE, YOU DIE, MISTER.
JUST GIVE DUGHAL HERE YER PURSE, VERY SLOWLY. LOOKED TO BE FULL O' GOLD.
HA HA HAH!
WHAKT!
IT IS.
HEY!
GAK!
KIRWYN! HELP M-- MMMMPFF!
TOO LATE FOR YOUR FRIEND.
KNOW ANY PRAYERS?
CLOSE ENOUGH.
OH GOD OH GOD OH GOD OH GOD OH GOD OH GOD
GO.

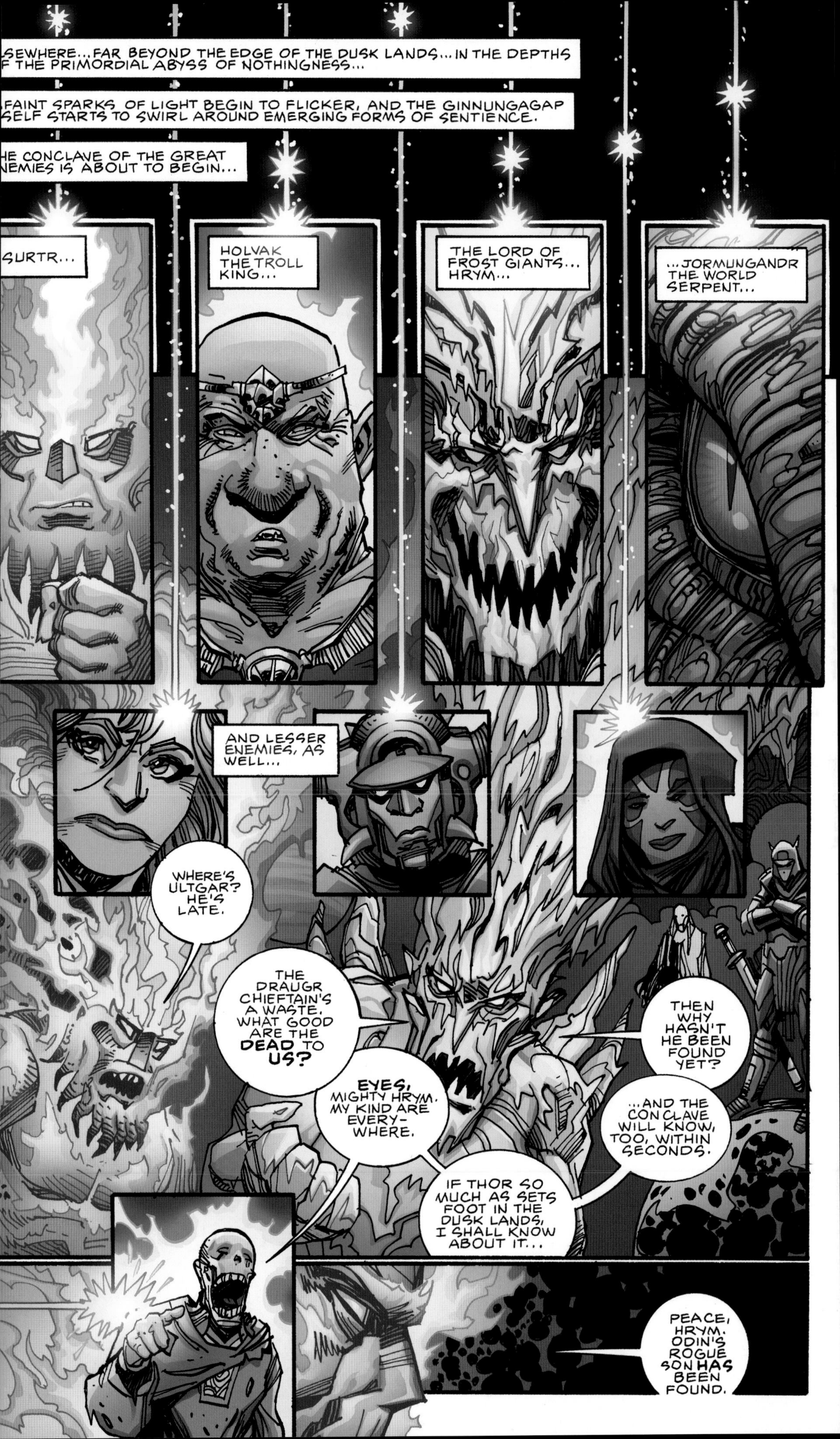
SEWHERE... FAR BEYOND THE EDGE OF THE DUSK LANDS... IN THE DEPTHS F THE PRIMORDIAL ABYSS OF NOTHINGNESS...
FAINT SPARKS OF LIGHT BEGIN TO FLICKER, AND THE GINNUNGAGAP SELF STARTS TO SWIRL AROUND EMERGING FORMS OF SENTIENCE.
HE CONCLAVE OF THE GREAT NEMIES IS ABOUT TO BEGIN...
SURTR...
HOLVAK THE TROLL KING...
THE LORD OF FROST GIANTS... HRYM...
...JORMUNGANDR THE WORLD SERPENT...
AND LESSER ENEMIES, AS WELL...
WHERE'S ULTGAR? HE'S LATE.
THE DRAUGR CHIEFTAIN'S A WASTE. WHAT GOOD ARE THE DEAD TO US?
THEN WHY HASN'T HE BEEN FOUND YET?
EYES, MIGHTY HRYM. MY KIND ARE EVERY-WHERE.
...AND THE CONCLAVE WILL KNOW, TOO, WITHIN SECONDS.
IF THOR SO MUCH AS SETS FOOT IN THE DUSK LANDS, I SHALL KNOW ABOUT IT...
PEACE, HRYM. ODIN'S ROGUE SON HAS BEEN FOUND.

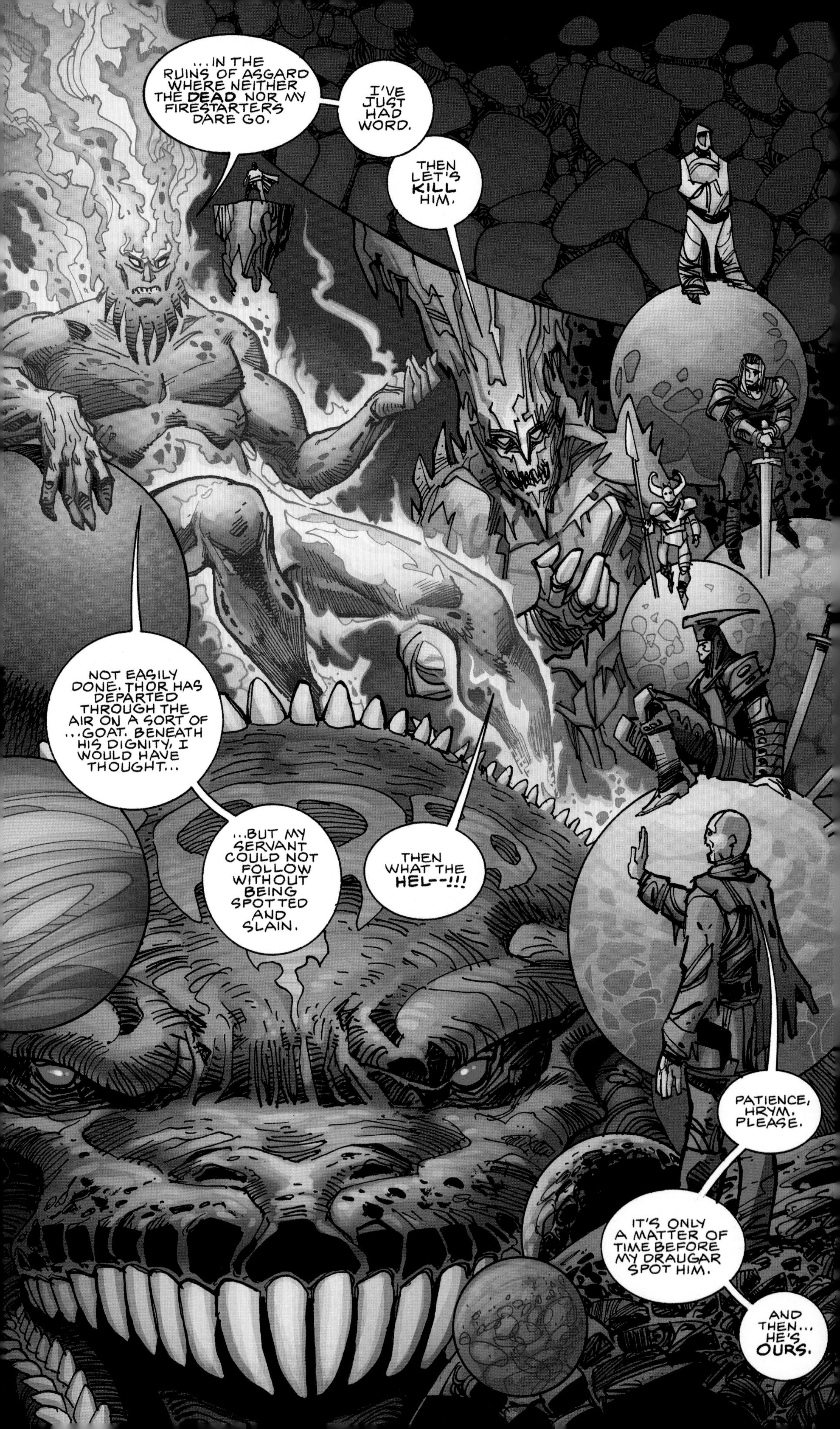
...IN THE RUINS OF ASGARD WHERE NEITHER THE **DEAD** NOR MY FIRESTARTERS DARE GO.
I'VE JUST HAD WORD.
THEN LET'S **KILL** HIM.
NOT EASILY DONE. THOR HAS DEPARTED THROUGH THE AIR ON A SORT OF ...GOAT. BENEATH HIS DIGNITY, I WOULD HAVE THOUGHT...
...BUT MY SERVANT COULD NOT FOLLOW WITHOUT BEING SPOTTED AND SLAIN.
THEN WHAT THE **HEL--!!!**
PATIENCE, HRYM. PLEASE.
IT'S ONLY A MATTER OF TIME BEFORE MY DRAUGAR SPOT HIM.
AND THEN... HE'S **OURS.**

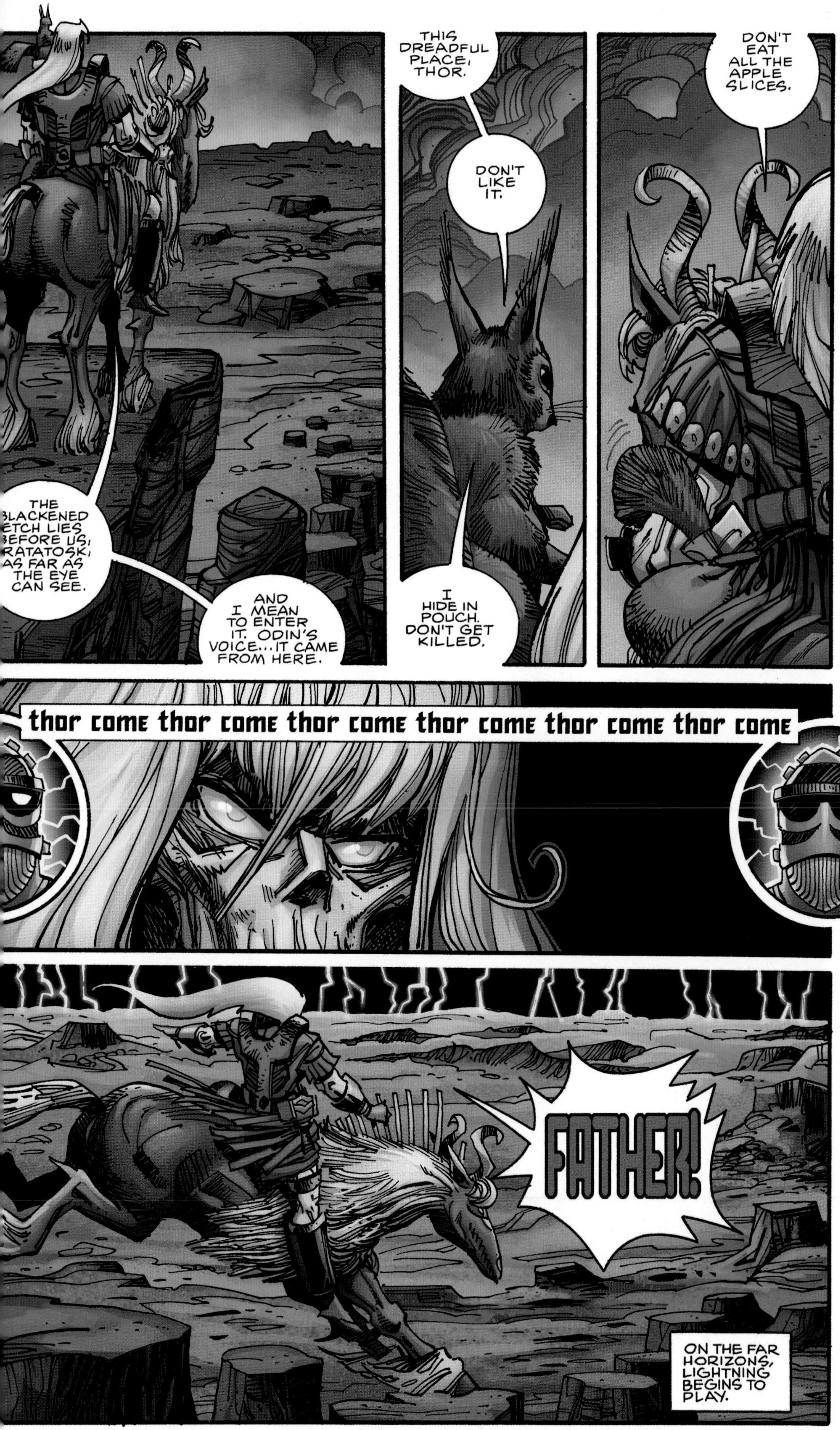
THE BLACKENED ETCH LIES BEFORE US, RATATOSK, AS FAR AS THE EYE CAN SEE.
AND I MEAN TO ENTER IT. ODIN'S VOICE... IT CAME FROM HERE.
THIS DREADFUL PLACE, THOR.
DON'T LIKE IT.
I HIDE IN POUCH. DON'T GET KILLED.
DON'T EAT ALL THE APPLE SLICES.
thor come thor come thor come thor come thor come thor come
FATHER!
ON THE FAR HORIZONS, LIGHTNING BEGINS TO PLAY.

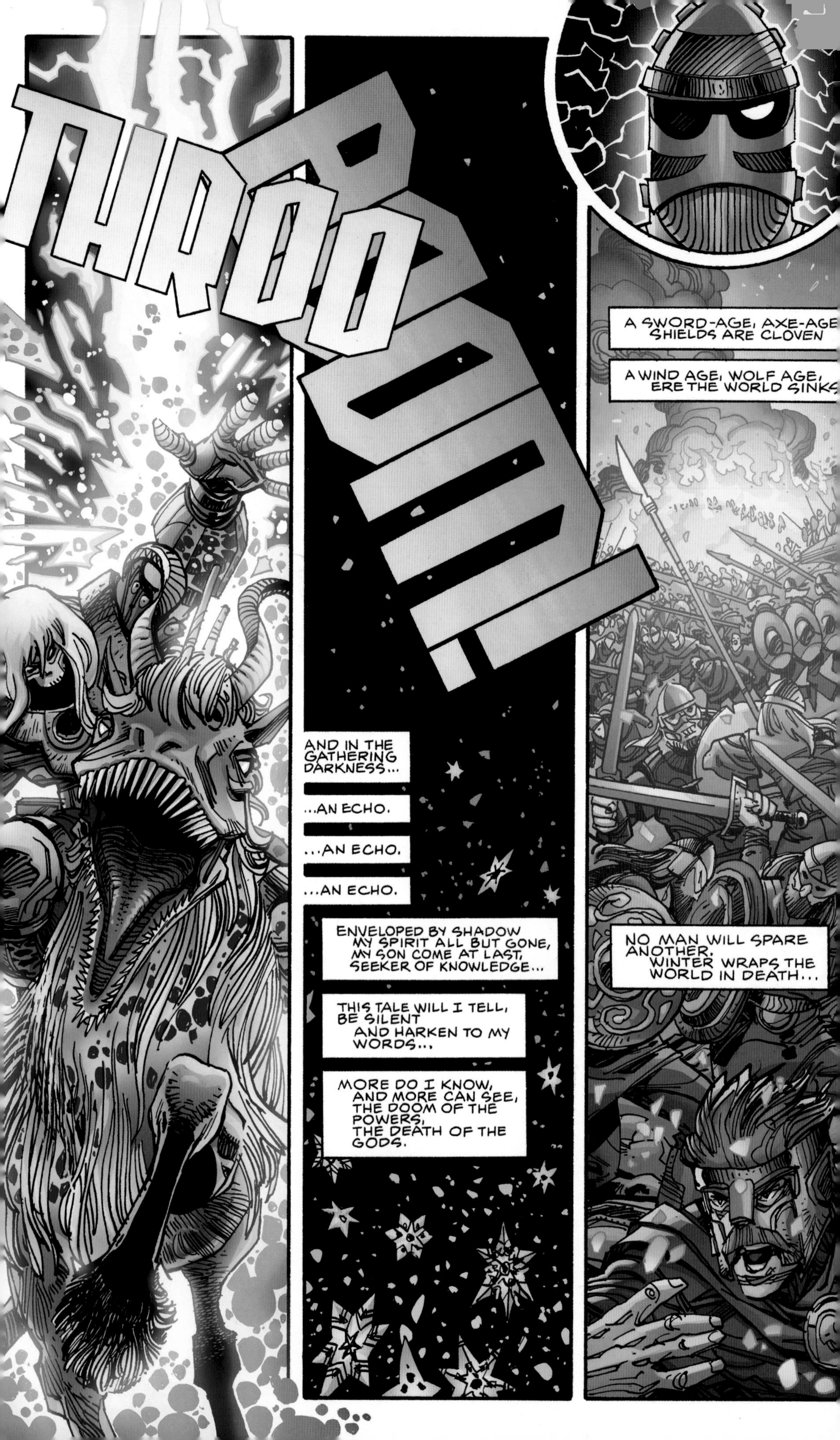
THROOOM!
AND IN THE GATHERING DARKNESS...
...AN ECHO.
...AN ECHO.
...AN ECHO.
ENVELOPED BY SHADOW MY SPIRIT ALL BUT GONE, MY SON COME AT LAST, SEEKER OF KNOWLEDGE...
THIS TALE WILL I TELL, BE SILENT AND HARKEN TO MY WORDS...
MORE DO I KNOW, AND MORE CAN SEE, THE DOOM OF THE POWERS, THE DEATH OF THE GODS.
A SWORD-AGE, AXE-AGE SHIELDS ARE CLOVEN
A WIND AGE, WOLF AGE, ERE THE WORLD SINKS
NO MAN WILL SPARE ANOTHER. WINTER WRAPS THE WORLD IN DEATH...

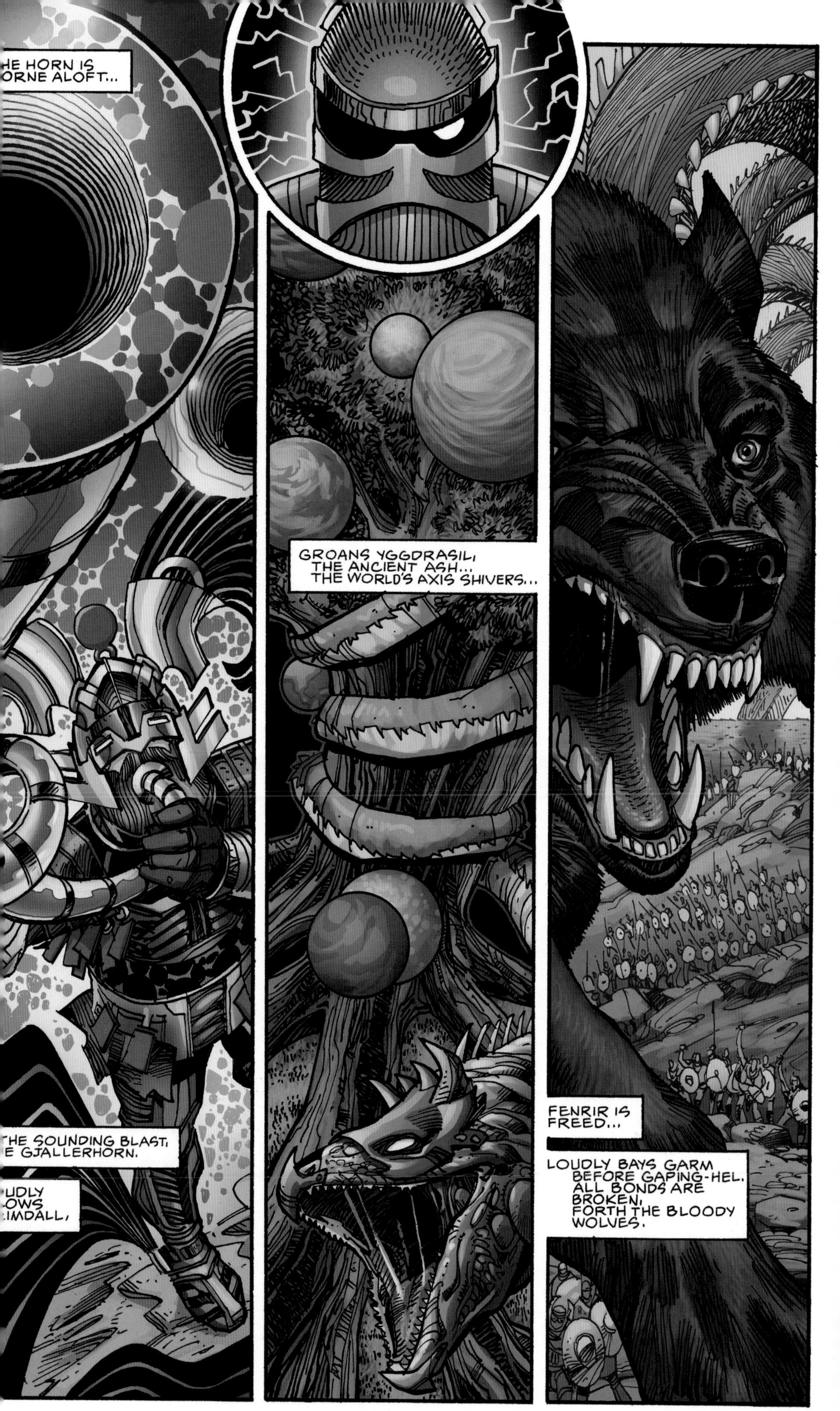
HE HORN IS
ORNE ALOFT...
THE SOUNDING BLAST,
E GJALLERHORN.
UDLY
OWS
IMDALL,
GROANS YGGDRASIL,
THE ANCIENT ASH...
THE WORLD'S AXIS SHIVERS...
FENRIR IS
FREED...
LOUDLY BAYS GARM
BEFORE GAPING-HEL.
ALL BONDS ARE
BROKEN,
FORTH THE BLOODY
WOLVES.

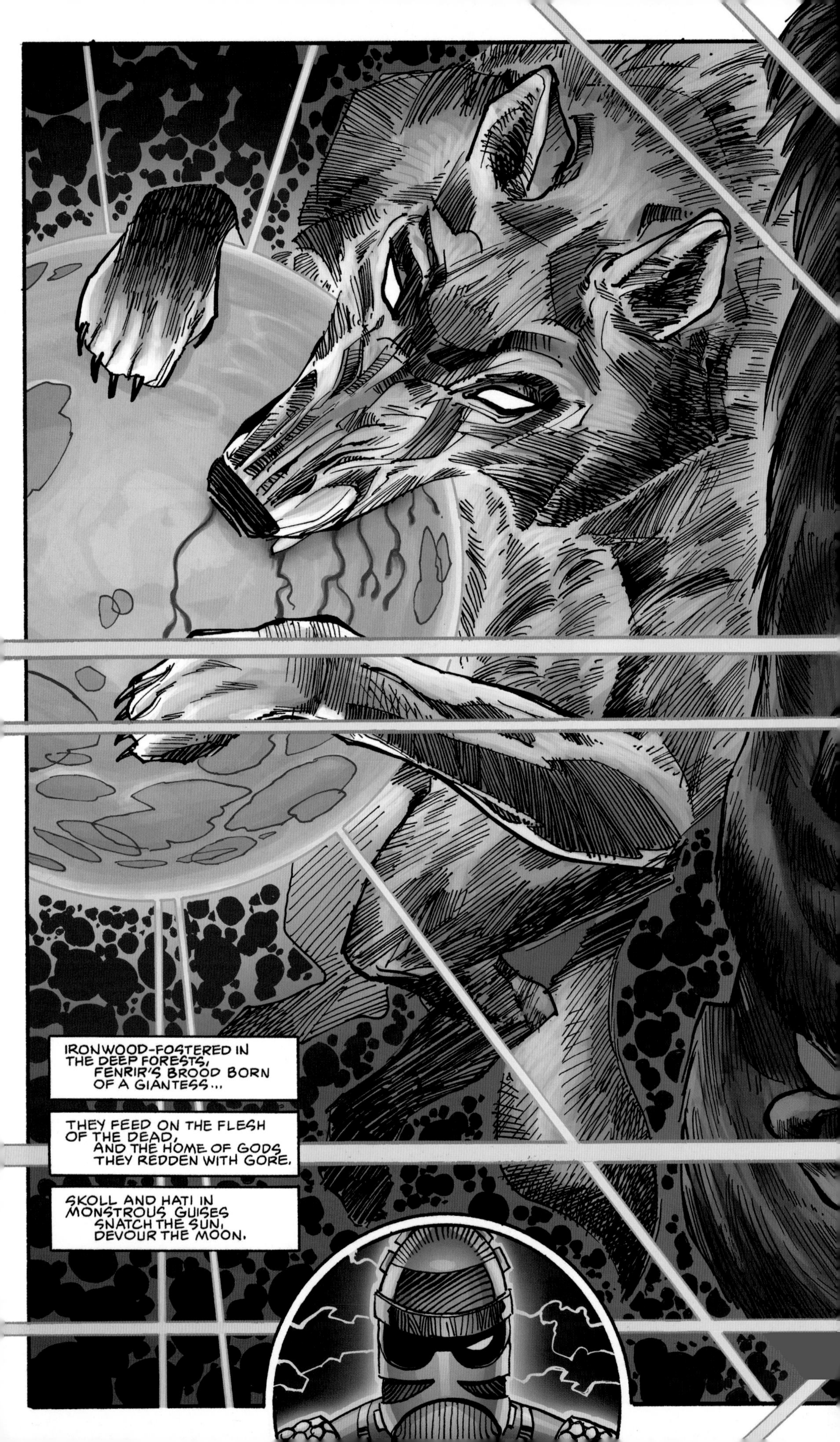
IRONWOOD-FOSTERED IN THE DEEP FORESTS, FENRIR'S BROOD BORN OF A GIANTESS...
THEY FEED ON THE FLESH OF THE DEAD, AND THE HOME OF GODS THEY REDDEN WITH GORE.
SKOLL AND HATI IN MONSTROUS GUISES SNATCH THE SUN, DEVOUR THE MOON.

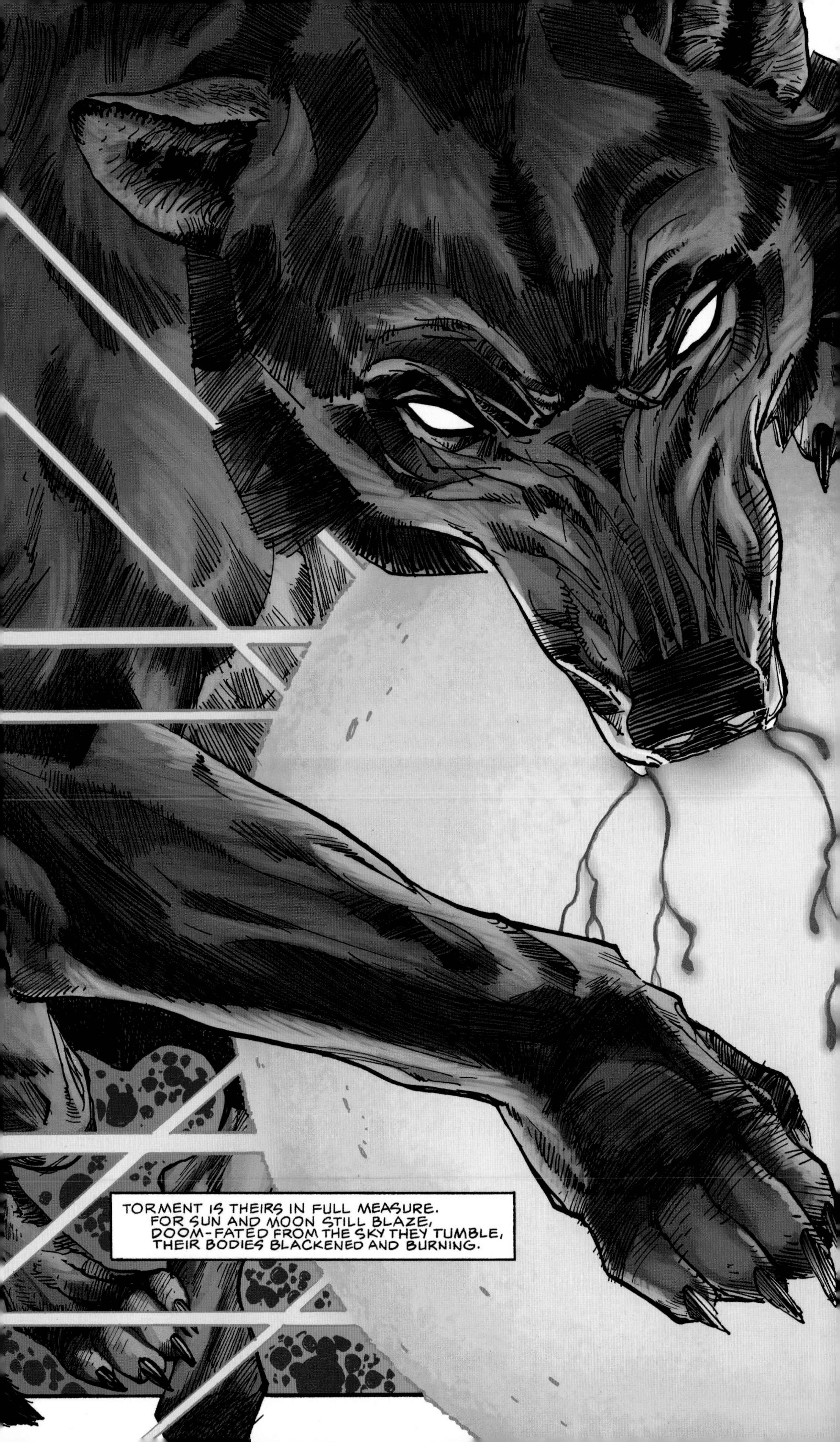

TORMENT IS THEIRS IN FULL MEASURE.
FOR SUN AND MOON STILL BLAZE,
DOOM-FATED FROM THE SKY THEY TUMBLE,
THEIR BODIES BLACKENED AND BURNING.

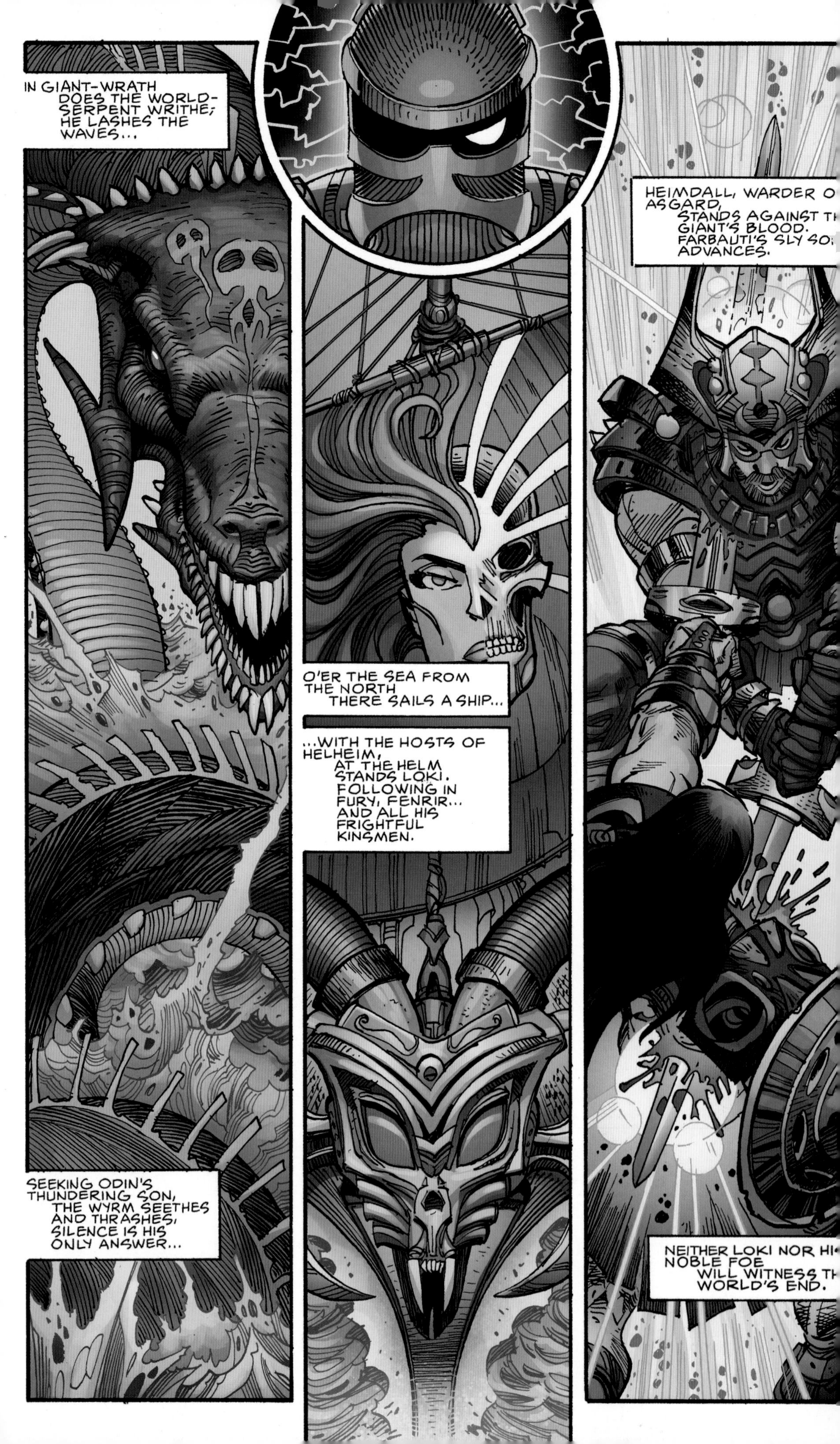
IN GIANT-WRATH DOES THE WORLD-SERPENT WRITHE; HE LASHES THE WAVES...
SEEKING ODIN'S THUNDERING SON, THE WYRM SEETHES AND THRASHES, SILENCE IS HIS ONLY ANSWER...
O'ER THE SEA FROM THE NORTH THERE SAILS A SHIP...
...WITH THE HOSTS OF HELHEIM, AT THE HELM STANDS LOKI. FOLLOWING IN FURY, FENRIR... AND ALL HIS FRIGHTFUL KINSMEN.
HEIMDALL, WARDER O ASGARD, STANDS AGAINST T GIANT'S BLOOD. FARBAUTI'S SLY SO ADVANCES.
NEITHER LOKI NOR HI NOBLE FOE WILL WITNESS T WORLD'S END.

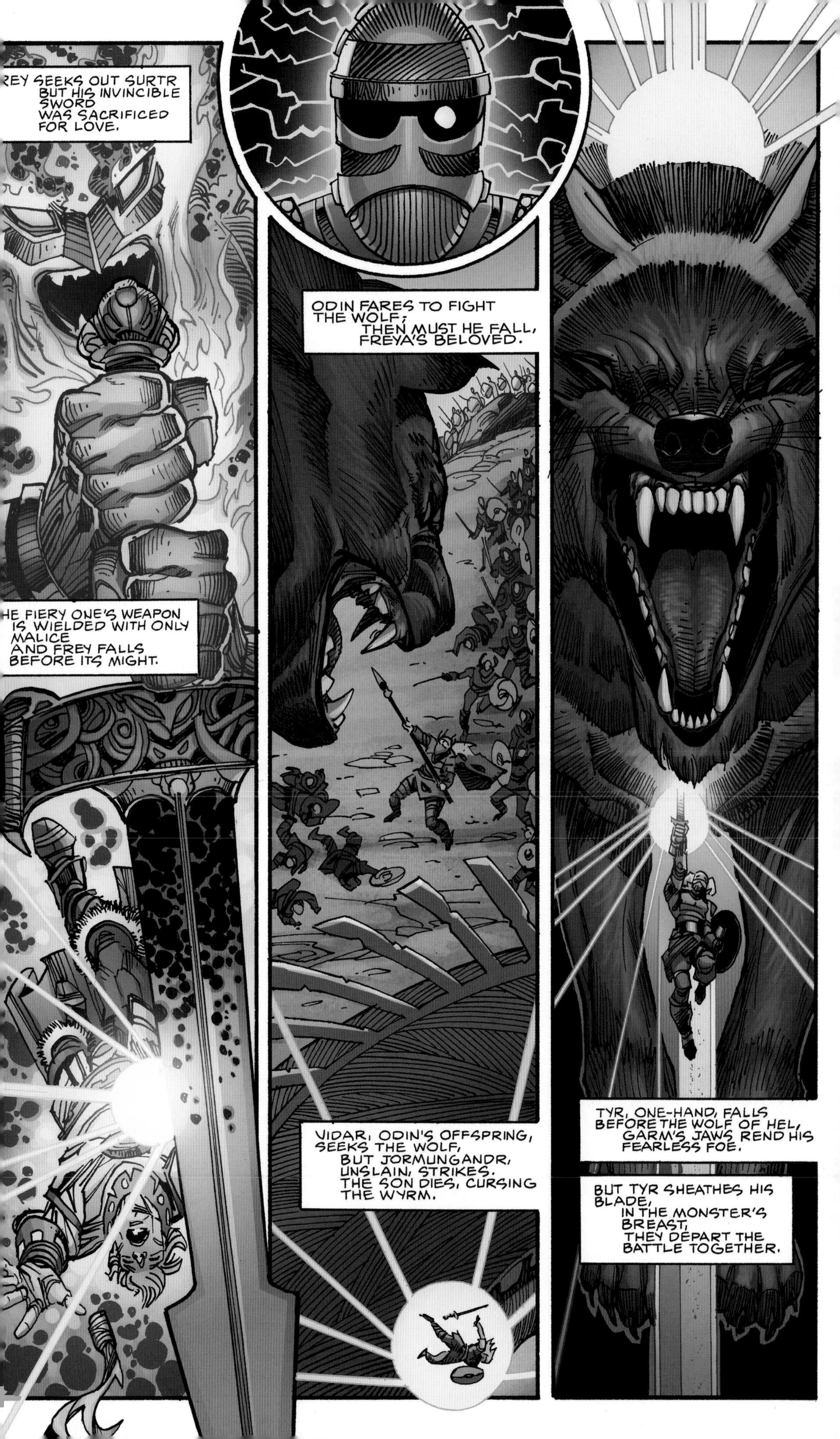
REY SEEKS OUT SURTR BUT HIS INVINCIBLE SWORD WAS SACRIFICED FOR LOVE.
HE FIERY ONE'S WEAPON IS WIELDED WITH ONLY MALICE AND FREY FALLS BEFORE ITS MIGHT.
ODIN FARES TO FIGHT THE WOLF; THEN MUST HE FALL, FREYA'S BELOVED.
VIDAR, ODIN'S OFFSPRING, SEEKS THE WOLF, BUT JORMUNGANDR, UNSLAIN, STRIKES. THE SON DIES, CURSING THE WYRM.
TYR, ONE-HAND, FALLS BEFORE THE WOLF OF HEL, GARM'S JAWS REND HIS FEARLESS FOE.
BUT TYR SHEATHES HIS BLADE, IN THE MONSTER'S BREAST, THEY DEPART THE BATTLE TOGETHER.

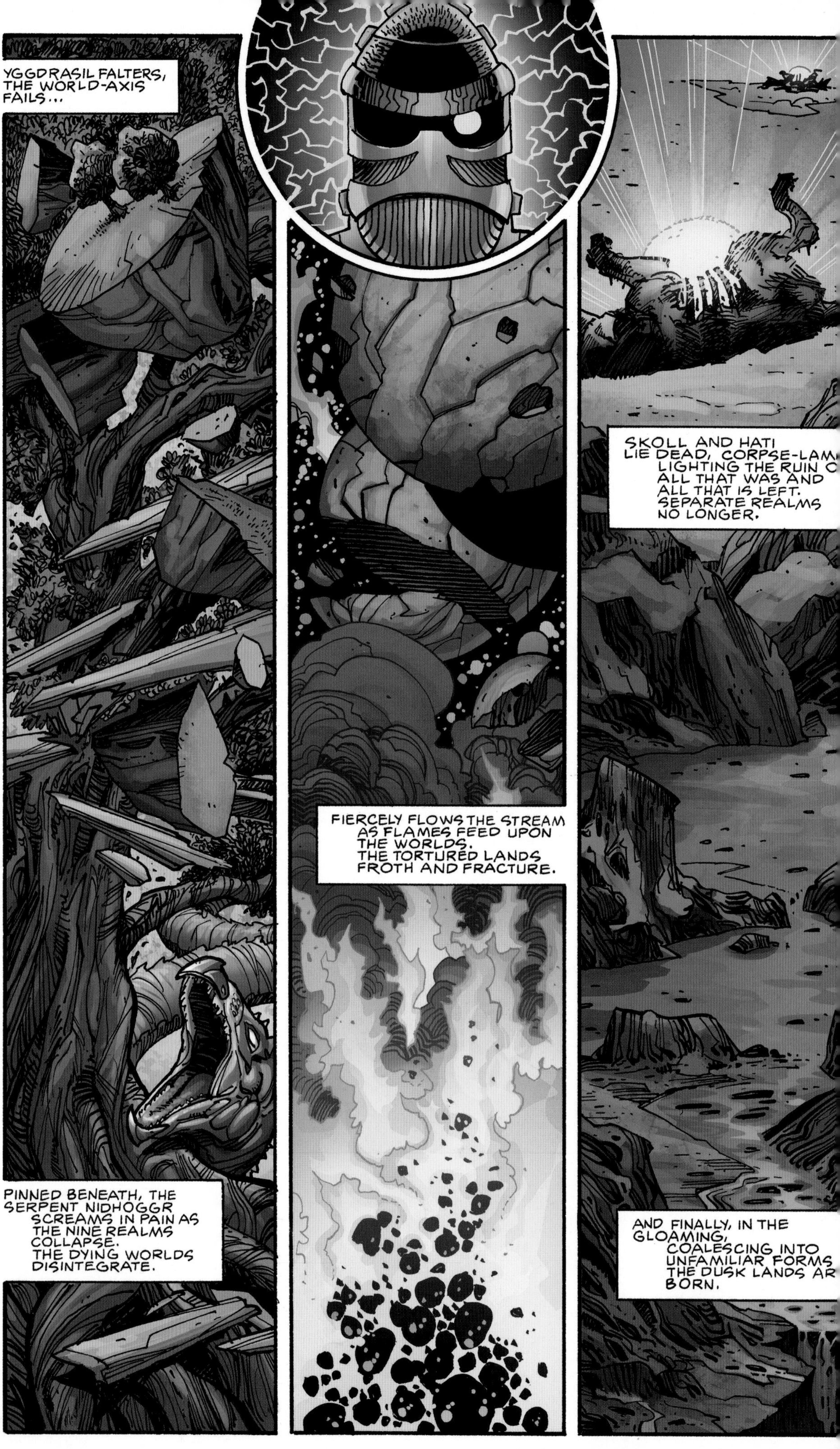
YGGDRASIL FALTERS, THE WORLD-AXIS FAILS...
PINNED BENEATH, THE SERPENT NIDHOGGR SCREAMS IN PAIN AS THE NINE REALMS COLLAPSE. THE DYING WORLDS DISINTEGRATE.
FIERCELY FLOWS THE STREAM AS FLAMES FEED UPON THE WORLDS. THE TORTURED LANDS FROTH AND FRACTURE.
SKOLL AND HATI LIE DEAD, CORPSE-LAM LIGHTING THE RUIN O ALL THAT WAS AND ALL THAT IS LEFT. SEPARATE REALMS NO LONGER.
AND FINALLY, IN THE GLOAMING, COALESCING INTO UNFAMILIAR FORMS THE DUSK LANDS AR BORN.

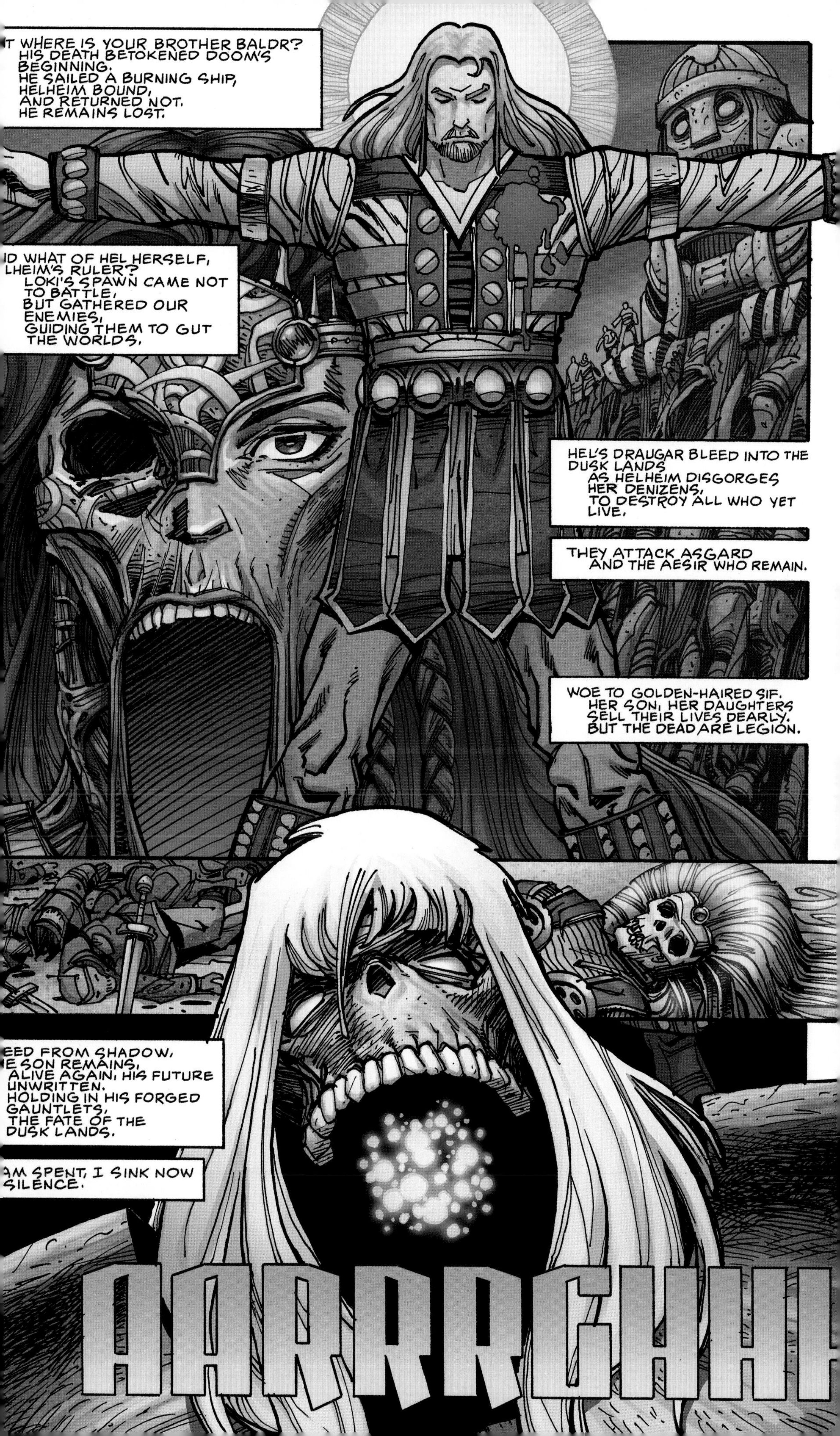
T WHERE IS YOUR BROTHER BALDR? HIS DEATH BETOKENED DOOM'S BEGINNING. HE SAILED A BURNING SHIP, HELHEIM BOUND, AND RETURNED NOT. HE REMAINS LOST.
D WHAT OF HEL HERSELF, LHEIM'S RULER? LOKI'S SPAWN CAME NOT TO BATTLE, BUT GATHERED OUR ENEMIES, GUIDING THEM TO GUT THE WORLDS.
HEL'S DRAUGAR BLEED INTO THE DUSK LANDS AS HELHEIM DISGORGES HER DENIZENS, TO DESTROY ALL WHO YET LIVE.
THEY ATTACK ASGARD AND THE AESIR WHO REMAIN.
WOE TO GOLDEN-HAIRED SIF. HER SON, HER DAUGHTERS SELL THEIR LIVES DEARLY. BUT THE DEAD ARE LEGION.
EED FROM SHADOW, E SON REMAINS, ALIVE AGAIN, HIS FUTURE UNWRITTEN. HOLDING IN HIS FORGED GAUNTLETS, THE FATE OF THE DUSK LANDS.
AM SPENT, I SINK NOW SILENCE.
AARRRGHH

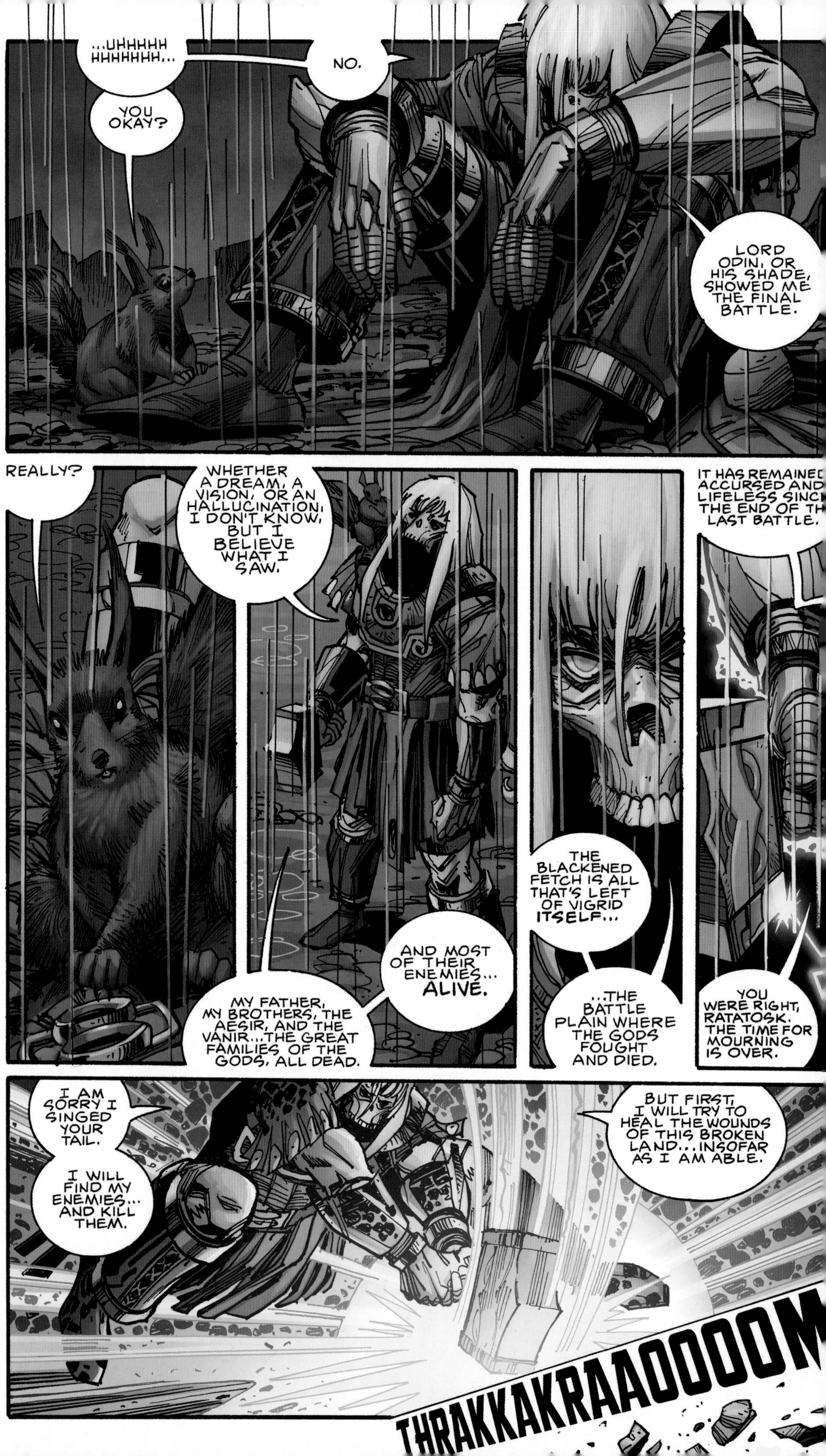
...UHHHHH HHHHHHH...
NO.
YOU OKAY?
LORD ODIN, OR HIS SHADE, SHOWED ME THE FINAL BATTLE.
REALLY?
WHETHER A DREAM, A VISION, OR AN HALLUCINATION, I DON'T KNOW, BUT I BELIEVE WHAT I SAW.
MY FATHER, MY BROTHERS, THE AESIR, AND THE VANIR...THE GREAT FAMILIES OF THE GODS, ALL DEAD.
AND MOST OF THEIR ENEMIES... ALIVE.
THE BLACKENED FETCH IS ALL THAT'S LEFT OF VIGRID ITSELF...
...THE BATTLE PLAIN WHERE THE GODS FOUGHT AND DIED.
IT HAS REMAINED ACCURSED AND LIFELESS SINC THE END OF TH LAST BATTLE.
YOU WERE RIGHT, RATATOSK. THE TIME FOR MOURNING IS OVER.
I AM SORRY I SINGED YOUR TAIL.
I WILL FIND MY ENEMIES... AND KILL THEM.
BUT FIRST, I WILL TRY TO HEAL THE WOUNDS OF THIS BROKEN LAND... INSOFAR AS I AM ABLE.
THRAKKAKRAAOOOOM

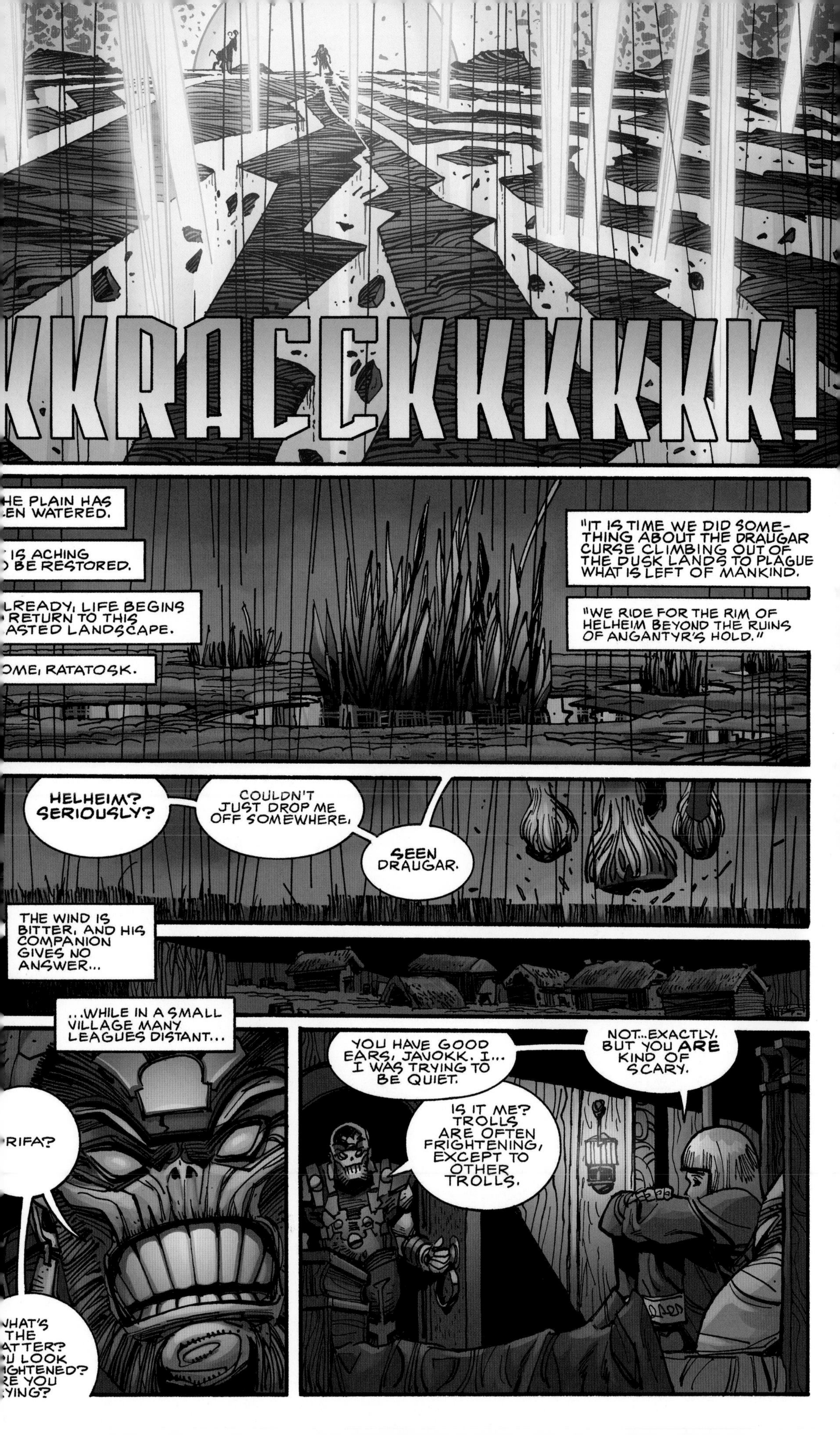
KKRACCKKKKKKK!
HE PLAIN HAS
EN WATERED.
IS ACHING
BE RESTORED.
LREADY, LIFE BEGINS
RETURN TO THIS
ASTED LANDSCAPE.
OME, RATATOSK.
"IT IS TIME WE DID SOMETHING ABOUT THE DRAUGAR CURSE CLIMBING OUT OF THE DUSK LANDS TO PLAGUE WHAT IS LEFT OF MANKIND.
"WE RIDE FOR THE RIM OF HELHEIM BEYOND THE RUINS OF ANGANTYR'S HOLD."
HELHEIM? SERIOUSLY?
COULDN'T JUST DROP ME OFF SOMEWHERE.
SEEN DRAUGAR.
THE WIND IS BITTER, AND HIS COMPANION GIVES NO ANSWER...
...WHILE IN A SMALL VILLAGE MANY LEAGUES DISTANT...
RIFA?
HAT'S THE ATTER? U LOOK IGHTENED? RE YOU YING?
YOU HAVE GOOD EARS, JAVOKK. I... I WAS TRYING TO BE QUIET.
NOT...EXACTLY. BUT YOU ARE KIND OF SCARY.
IS IT ME? TROLLS ARE OFTEN FRIGHTENING, EXCEPT TO OTHER TROLLS.

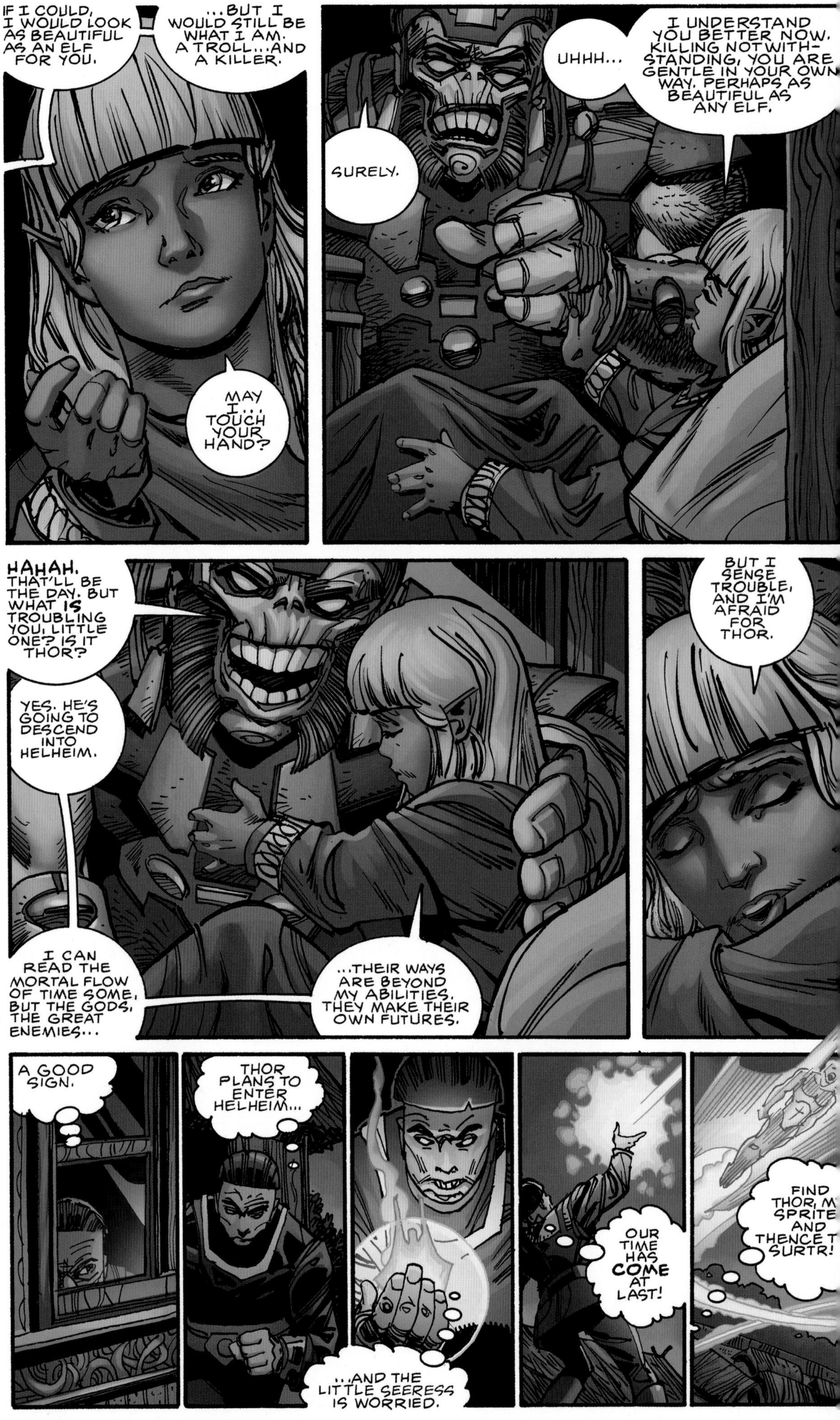
IF I COULD, I WOULD LOOK AS BEAUTIFUL AS AN ELF FOR YOU.
...BUT I WOULD STILL BE WHAT I AM. A TROLL...AND A KILLER.
MAY I... TOUCH YOUR HAND?
UHHH...
I UNDERSTAND YOU BETTER NOW. KILLING NOTWITH-STANDING, YOU ARE GENTLE IN YOUR OWN WAY. PERHAPS AS BEAUTIFUL AS ANY ELF.
SURELY.
HAHAH. THAT'LL BE THE DAY. BUT WHAT IS TROUBLING YOU, LITTLE ONE? IS IT THOR?
YES. HE'S GOING TO DESCEND INTO HELHEIM.
I CAN READ THE MORTAL FLOW OF TIME SOME, BUT THE GODS, THE GREAT ENEMIES...
...THEIR WAYS ARE BEYOND MY ABILITIES. THEY MAKE THEIR OWN FUTURES.
BUT I SENSE TROUBLE, AND I'M AFRAID FOR THOR.
A GOOD SIGN.
THOR PLANS TO ENTER HELHEIM...
...AND THE LITTLE SEERESS IS WORRIED.
OUR TIME HAS COME AT LAST!
FIND THOR, M SPRITE AND THENCE T SURTR!

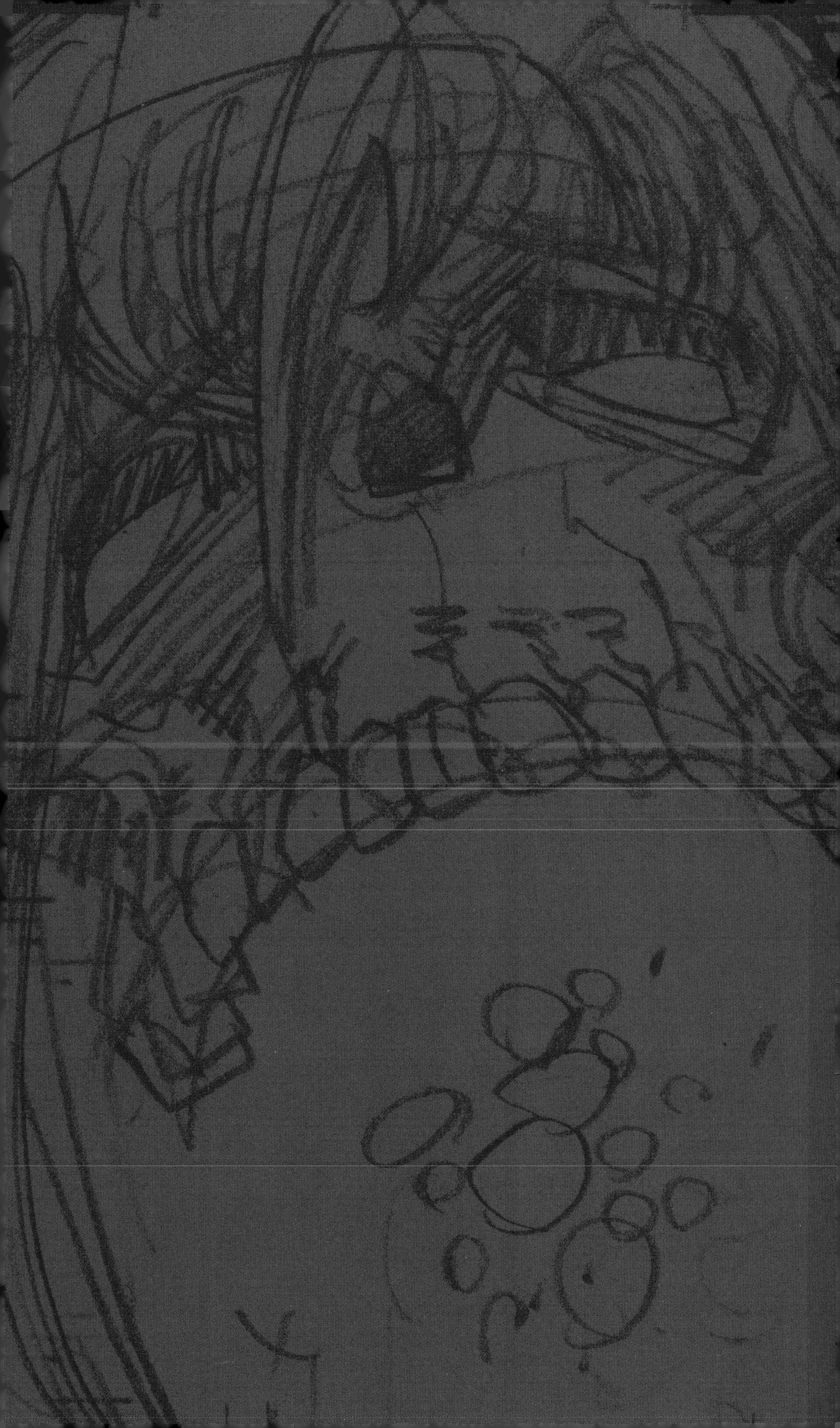

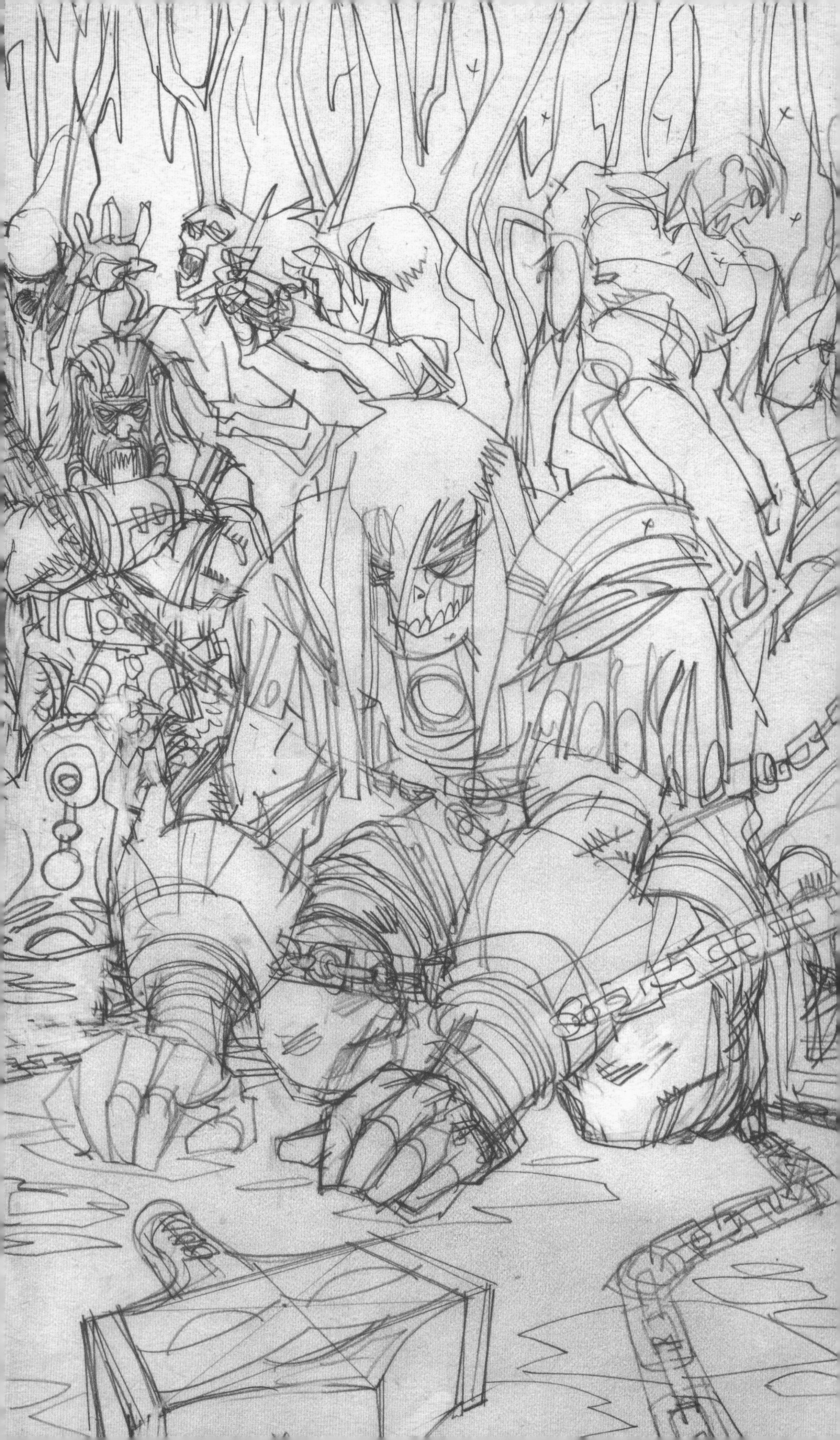

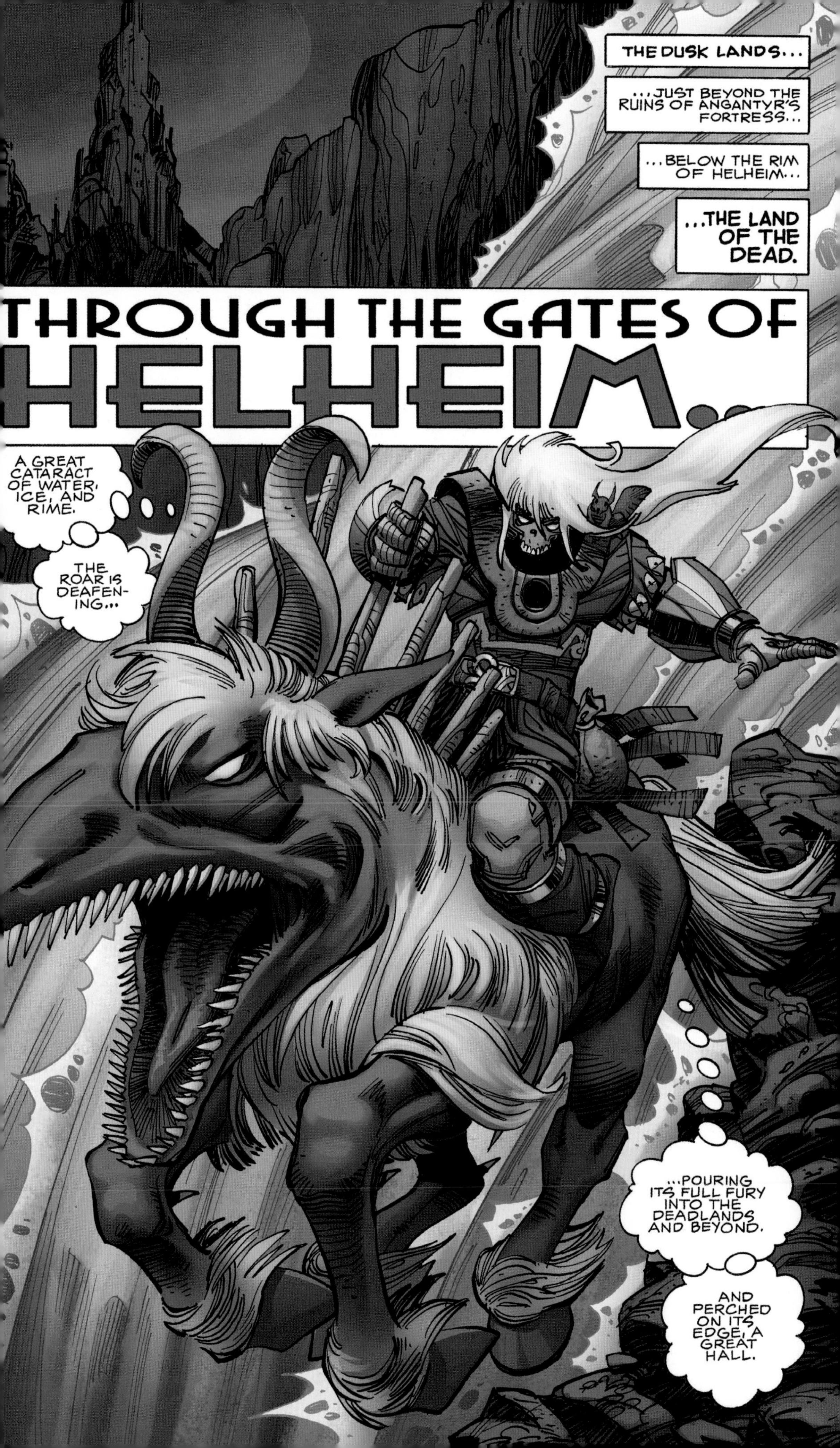
THE DUSK LANDS...
...JUST BEYOND THE RUINS OF ANGANTYR'S FORTRESS...
...BELOW THE RIM OF HELHEIM...
...THE LAND OF THE DEAD.
THROUGH THE GATES OF HELHEIM...
A GREAT CATARACT OF WATER, ICE, AND RIME.
THE ROAR IS DEAFEN-ING...
...POURING ITS FULL FURY INTO THE DEADLANDS AND BEYOND.
AND PERCHED ON ITS EDGE, A GREAT HALL.

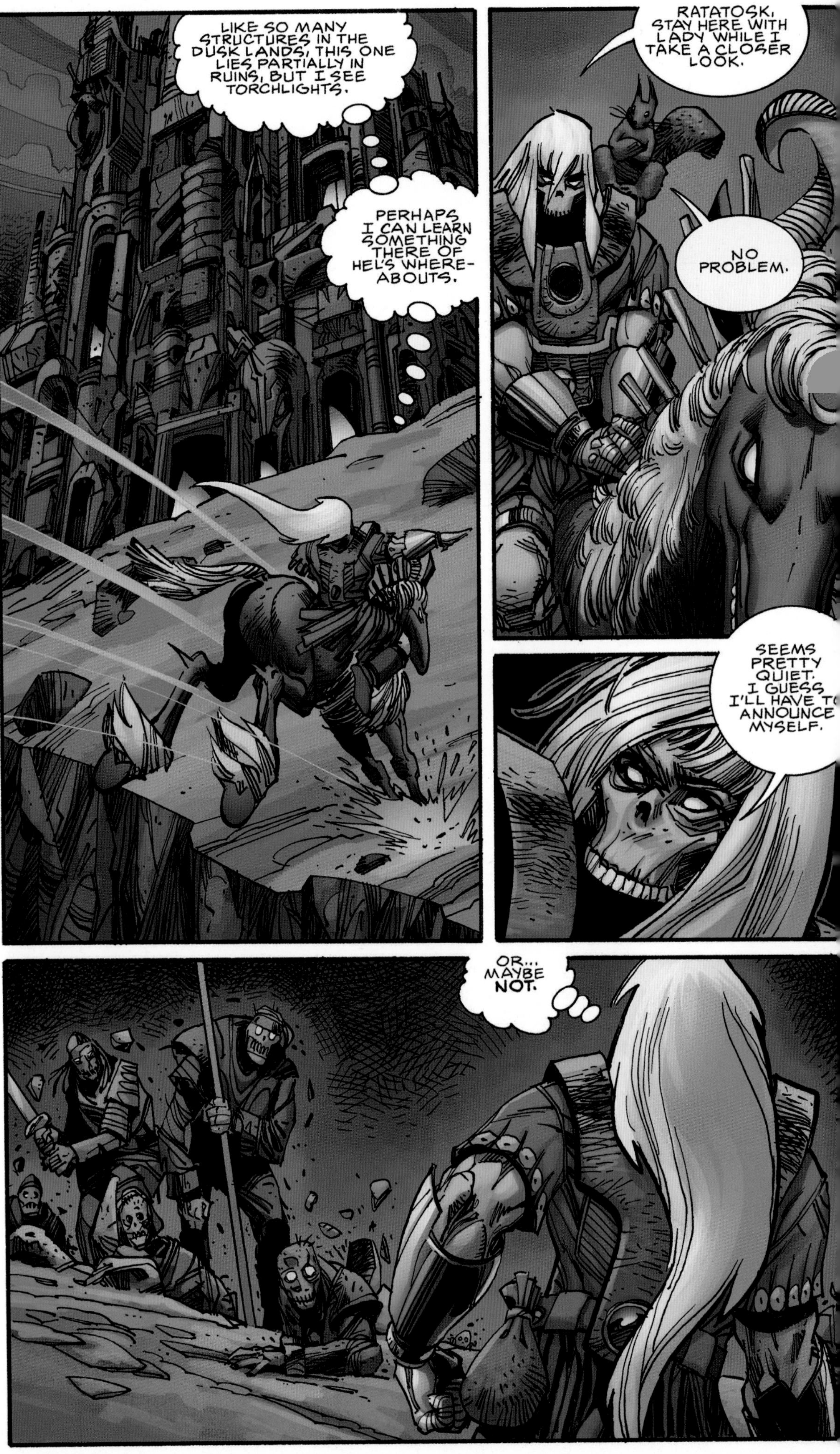
LIKE SO MANY STRUCTURES IN THE DUSK LANDS, THIS ONE LIES PARTIALLY IN RUINS, BUT I SEE TORCHLIGHTS.
PERHAPS I CAN LEARN SOMETHING THERE OF HEL'S WHEREABOUTS.
RATATOSK, STAY HERE WITH LADY WHILE I TAKE A CLOSER LOOK.
NO PROBLEM.
SEEMS PRETTY QUIET. I GUESS I'LL HAVE TO ANNOUNCE MYSELF.
OR... MAYBE **NOT.**

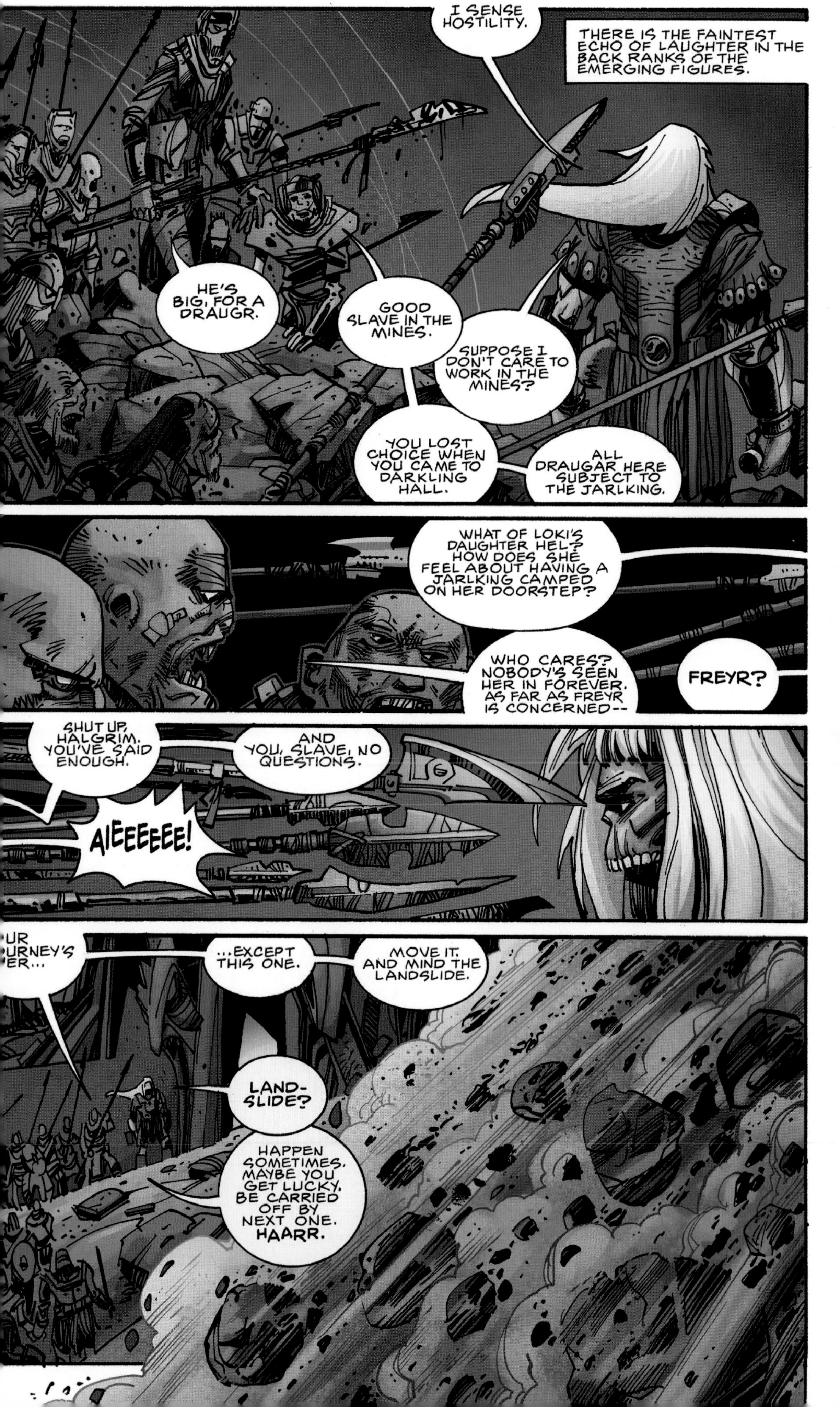
I SENSE HOSTILITY.
THERE IS THE FAINTEST ECHO OF LAUGHTER IN THE BACK RANKS OF THE EMERGING FIGURES.
HE'S BIG, FOR A DRAUGR.
GOOD SLAVE IN THE MINES.
SUPPOSE I DON'T CARE TO WORK IN THE MINES?
YOU LOST CHOICE WHEN YOU CAME TO DARKLING HALL.
ALL DRAUGAR HERE SUBJECT TO THE JARLKING.
WHAT OF LOKI'S DAUGHTER HEL? HOW DOES SHE FEEL ABOUT HAVING A JARLKING CAMPED ON HER DOORSTEP?
WHO CARES? NOBODY'S SEEN HER IN FOREVER. AS FAR AS FREYR IS CONCERNED--
FREYR?
SHUT UP, HALGRIM. YOU'VE SAID ENOUGH.
AND YOU, SLAVE, NO QUESTIONS.
AIEEEEEE!
UR URNEY'S ER...
...EXCEPT THIS ONE.
MOVE IT. AND MIND THE LANDSLIDE.
LAND-SLIDE?
HAPPEN SOMETIMES. MAYBE YOU GET LUCKY. BE CARRIED OFF BY NEXT ONE. HAARR.

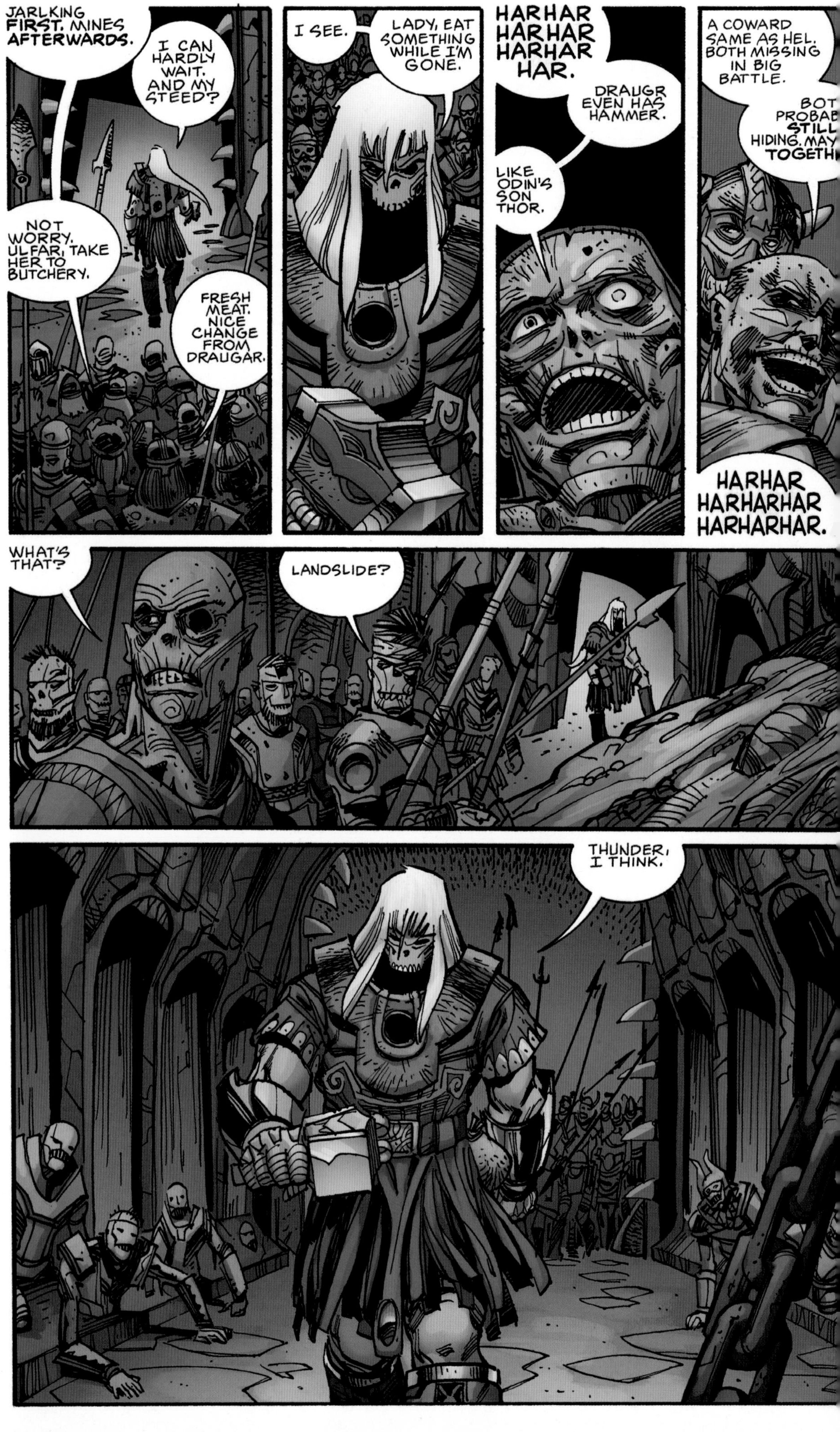
JARLKING FIRST. MINES AFTERWARDS.
I CAN HARDLY WAIT. AND MY STEED?
NOT WORRY. ULFAR, TAKE HER TO BUTCHERY.
FRESH MEAT. NICE CHANGE FROM DRAUGAR.
I SEE.
LADY, EAT SOMETHING WHILE I'M GONE.
HARHAR HARHAR HARHAR HAR.
DRAUGR EVEN HAS HAMMER.
LIKE ODIN'S SON THOR.
A COWARD SAME AS HEL. BOTH MISSING IN BIG BATTLE.
HARHAR HARHARHAR HARHARHAR.
WHAT'S THAT?
LANDSLIDE?
THUNDER, I THINK.

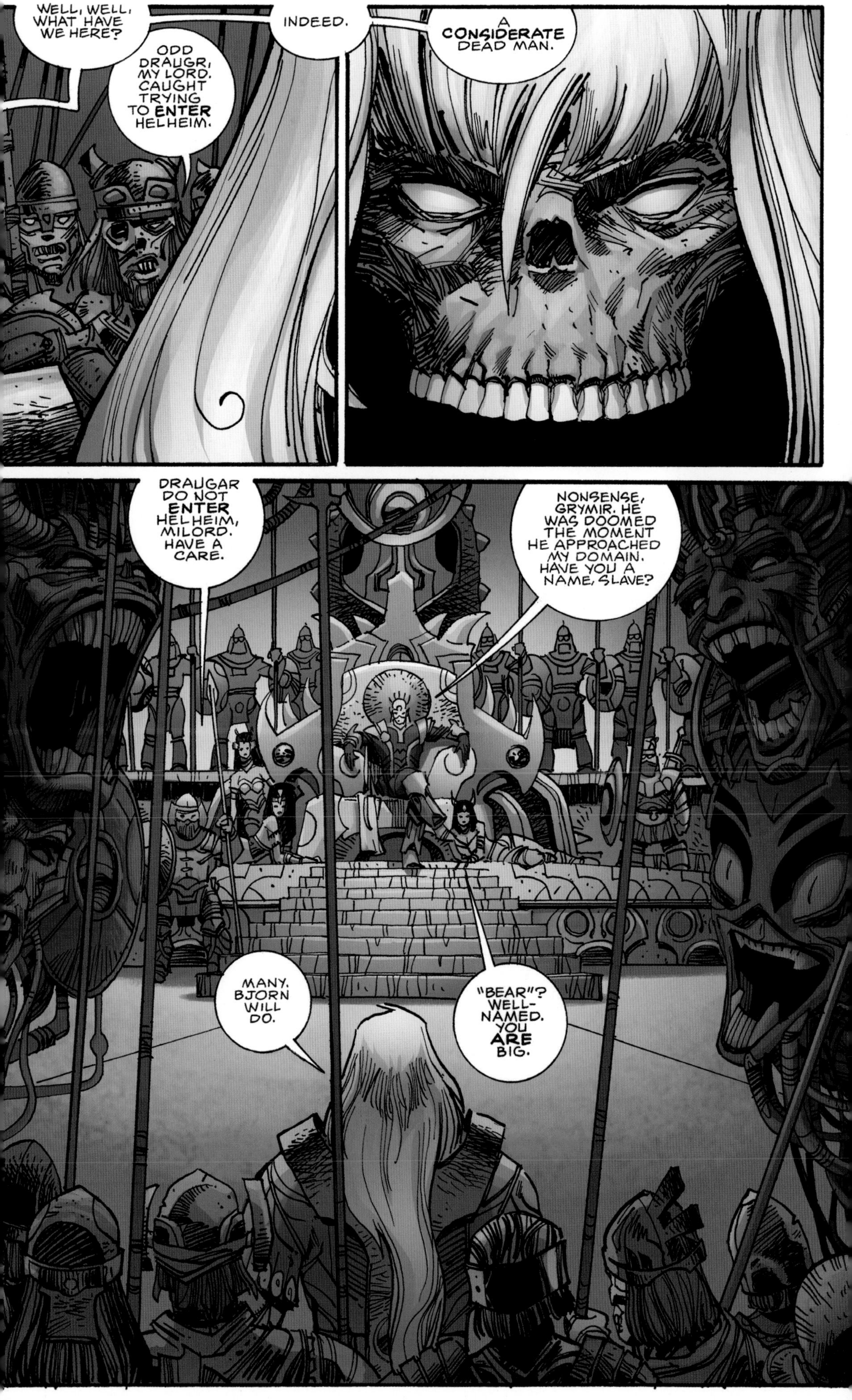
WELL, WELL, WHAT HAVE WE HERE?
ODD DRAUGR, MY LORD. CAUGHT TRYING TO ENTER HELHEIM.
INDEED.
A CONSIDERATE DEAD MAN.
DRAUGAR DO NOT ENTER HELHEIM, MILORD. HAVE A CARE.
NONSENSE, GRYMIR. HE WAS DOOMED THE MOMENT HE APPROACHED MY DOMAIN. HAVE YOU A NAME, SLAVE?
MANY. BJORN WILL DO.
"BEAR"? WELL-NAMED. YOU ARE BIG.

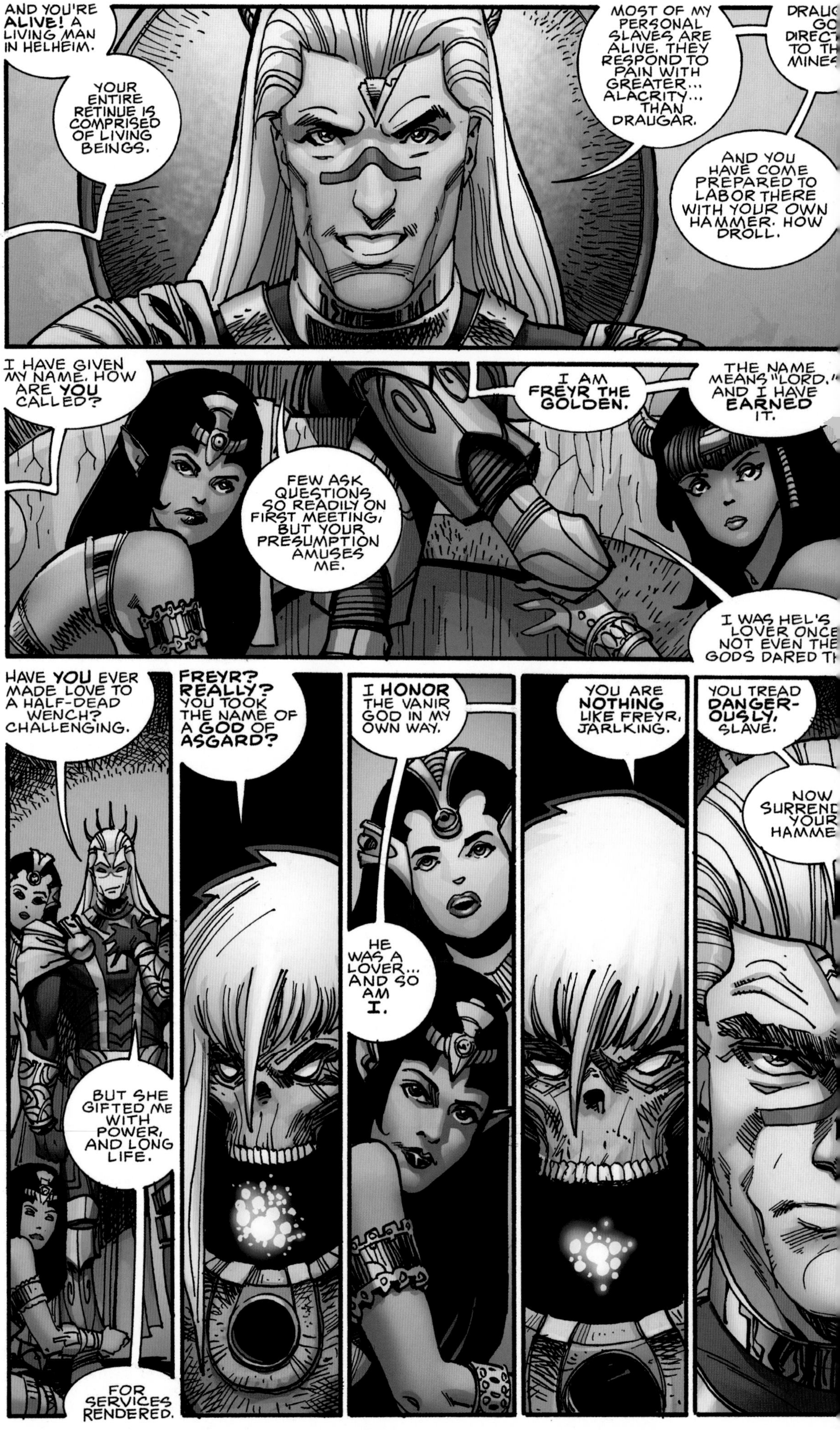
AND YOU'RE **ALIVE!** A LIVING MAN IN HELHEIM.
YOUR ENTIRE RETINUE IS COMPRISED OF LIVING BEINGS.
MOST OF MY PERSONAL SLAVES ARE ALIVE. THEY RESPOND TO PAIN WITH GREATER... ALACRITY... THAN DRAUGAR.
DRAUG GO DIREC TO TH MINES
AND YOU HAVE COME PREPARED TO LABOR THERE WITH YOUR OWN HAMMER. HOW DROLL.
I HAVE GIVEN MY NAME. HOW ARE **YOU** CALLED?
FEW ASK QUESTIONS SO READILY ON FIRST MEETING, BUT YOUR PRESUMPTION AMUSES ME.
I AM **FREYR THE GOLDEN.**
THE NAME MEANS "LORD." AND I HAVE **EARNED** IT.
I WAS HEL'S LOVER ONCE NOT EVEN THE GODS DARED T
HAVE **YOU** EVER MADE LOVE TO A HALF-DEAD WENCH? CHALLENGING.
BUT SHE GIFTED ME WITH POWER, AND LONG LIFE.
FOR SERVICES RENDERED.
FREYR? REALLY? YOU TOOK THE NAME OF A **GOD** OF **ASGARD?**
I **HONOR** THE VANIR GOD IN MY OWN WAY.
HE WAS A LOVER... AND SO AM **I.**
YOU ARE **NOTHING** LIKE FREYR, JARLKING.
YOU TREAD **DANGER-OUSLY,** SLAVE.
NOW SURREND YOUR HAMME

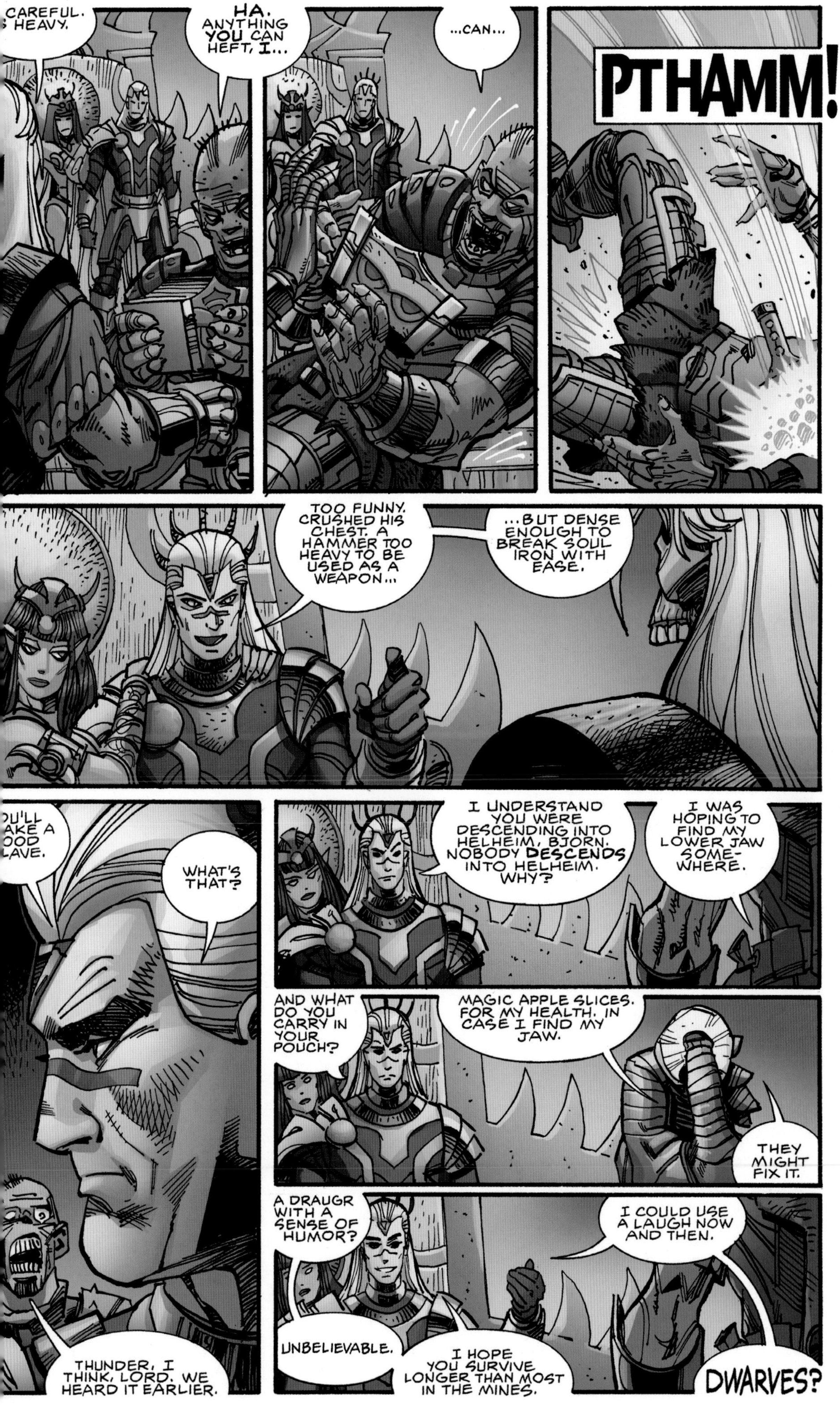
CAREFUL.
S HEAVY.
HA. ANYTHING YOU CAN HEFT, I...
...CAN...
PTHAMM!
TOO FUNNY. CRUSHED HIS CHEST. A HAMMER TOO HEAVY TO BE USED AS A WEAPON...
...BUT DENSE ENOUGH TO BREAK SOUL IRON WITH EASE.
OU'LL AKE A OOD LAVE.
WHAT'S THAT?
THUNDER, I THINK, LORD. WE HEARD IT EARLIER.
I UNDERSTAND YOU WERE DESCENDING INTO HELHEIM, BJORN. NOBODY DESCENDS INTO HELHEIM. WHY?
I WAS HOPING TO FIND MY LOWER JAW SOME-WHERE.
AND WHAT DO YOU CARRY IN YOUR POUCH?
MAGIC APPLE SLICES. FOR MY HEALTH. IN CASE I FIND MY JAW.
THEY MIGHT FIX IT.
A DRAUGR WITH A SENSE OF HUMOR?
I COULD USE A LAUGH NOW AND THEN.
UNBELIEVABLE.
I HOPE YOU SURVIVE LONGER THAN MOST IN THE MINES.
DWARVES?

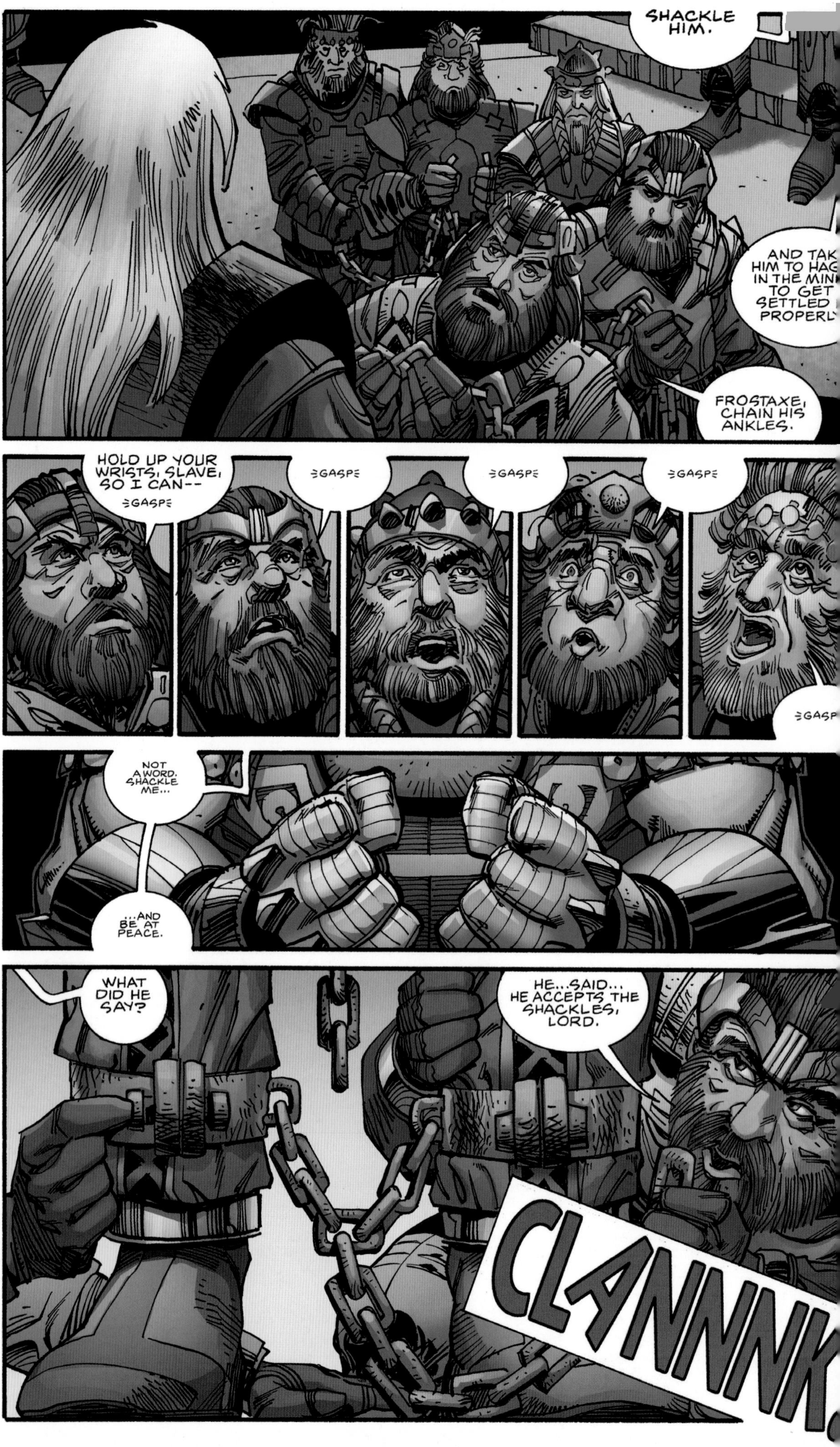
SHACKLE HIM.
AND TAK
HIM TO HAG
IN THE MIN
TO GET
SETTLED
PROPERL
FROSTAXE, CHAIN HIS ANKLES.
HOLD UP YOUR WRISTS, SLAVE, SO I CAN--
≡GASP≡
≡GASP≡
≡GASP≡
≡GASP≡
≡GASP
NOT A WORD. SHACKLE ME...
...AND BE AT PEACE.
WHAT DID HE SAY?
HE...SAID... HE ACCEPTS THE SHACKLES, LORD.
CLANNNK

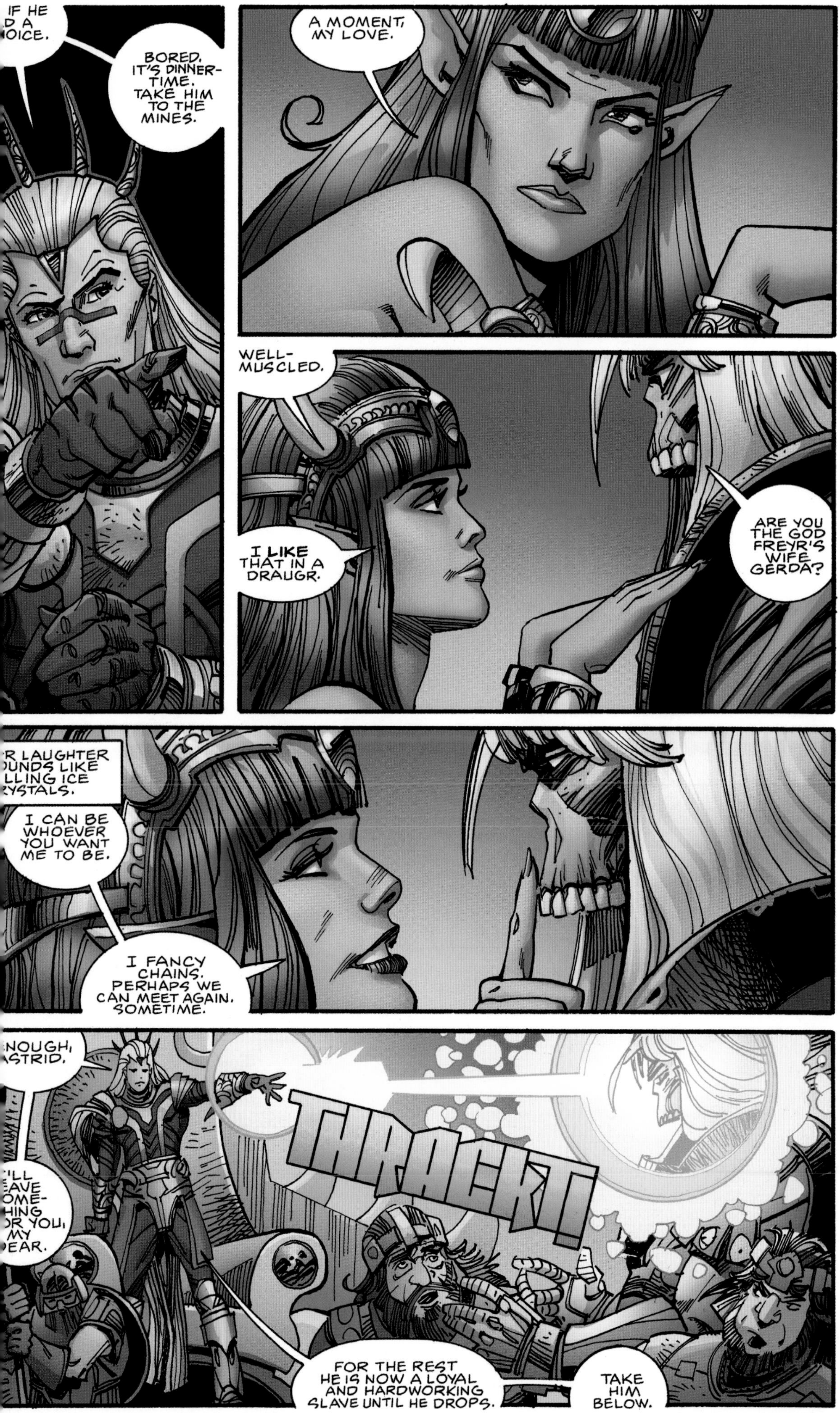
IF HE D A OICE.
BORED. IT'S DINNER-TIME. TAKE HIM TO THE MINES.
A MOMENT, MY LOVE.
WELL-MUSCLED.
I LIKE THAT IN A DRAUGR.
ARE YOU THE GOD FREYR'S WIFE GERDA?
R LAUGHTER UNDS LIKE LLING ICE YSTALS.
I CAN BE WHOEVER YOU WANT ME TO BE.
I FANCY CHAINS. PERHAPS WE CAN MEET AGAIN. SOMETIME.
NOUGH, ASTRID.
THRACK!
'LL EAVE OME-HING OR YOU, MY EAR.
FOR THE REST HE IS NOW A LOYAL AND HARDWORKING SLAVE UNTIL HE DROPS.
TAKE HIM BELOW.

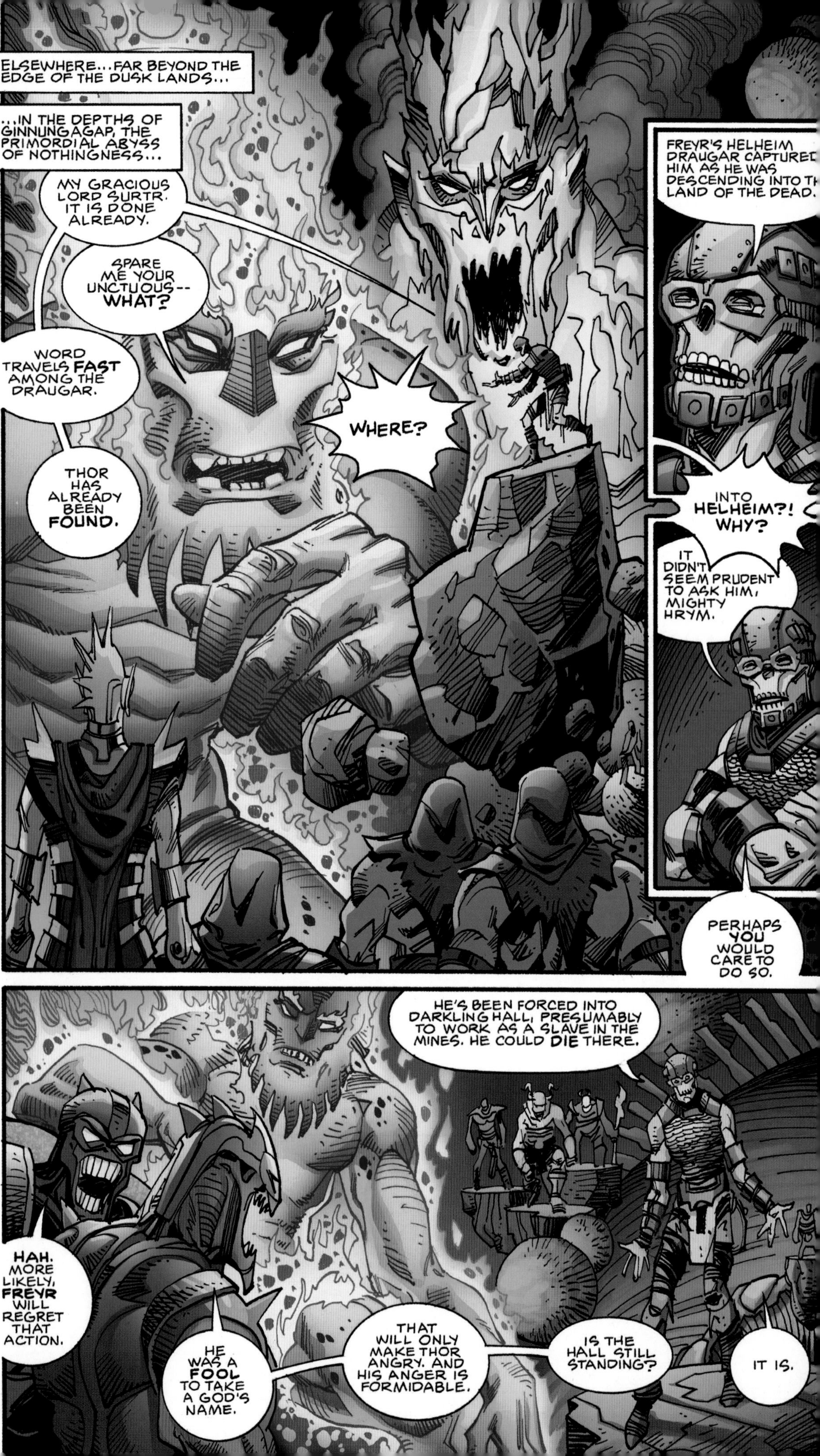
ELSEWHERE...FAR BEYOND THE EDGE OF THE DUSK LANDS...
...IN THE DEPTHS OF GINNUNGAGAP, THE PRIMORDIAL ABYSS OF NOTHINGNESS...
MY GRACIOUS LORD SURTR. IT IS DONE ALREADY.
SPARE ME YOUR UNCTUOUS-- **WHAT?**
WORD TRAVELS **FAST** AMONG THE DRAUGAR.
THOR HAS ALREADY BEEN **FOUND.**
WHERE?
FREYR'S HELHEIM DRAUGAR CAPTURED HIM AS HE WAS DESCENDING INTO THE LAND OF THE DEAD.
INTO **HELHEIM?! WHY?**
IT DIDN'T SEEM PRUDENT TO ASK HIM, MIGHTY HRYM.
PERHAPS **YOU** WOULD CARE TO DO SO.
HE'S BEEN FORCED INTO DARKLING HALL, PRESUMABLY TO WORK AS A SLAVE IN THE MINES. HE COULD **DIE** THERE.
HAH. MORE LIKELY, **FREYR** WILL REGRET THAT ACTION.
HE WAS A **FOOL** TO TAKE A GOD'S NAME.
THAT WILL ONLY MAKE THOR ANGRY. AND HIS ANGER IS FORMIDABLE.
IS THE HALL STILL STANDING?
IT IS.

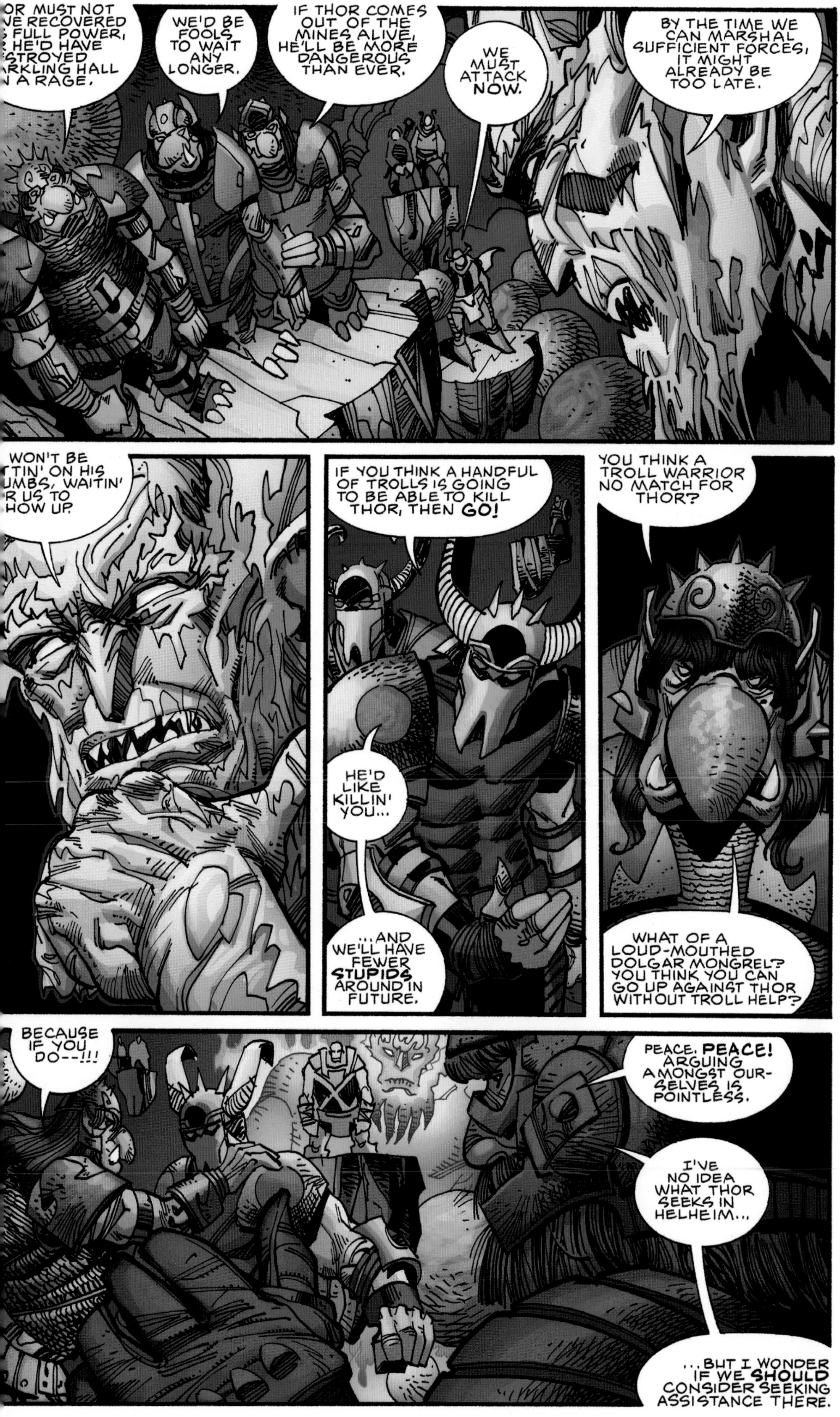
OR MUST NOT VE RECOVERED FULL POWER, HE'D HAVE STROYED ARKLING HALL N A RAGE.
WE'D BE FOOLS TO WAIT ANY LONGER.
IF THOR COMES OUT OF THE MINES ALIVE, HE'LL BE MORE DANGEROUS THAN EVER.
WE MUST ATTACK **NOW.**
BY THE TIME WE CAN MARSHAL SUFFICIENT FORCES, IT MIGHT ALREADY BE TOO LATE.
WON'T BE TTIN' ON HIS UMBS, WAITIN' R US TO HOW UP.
IF YOU THINK A HANDFUL OF TROLLS IS GOING TO BE ABLE TO KILL THOR, THEN **GO!**
HE'D LIKE KILLIN' YOU...
...AND WE'LL HAVE FEWER **STUPIDS** AROUND IN FUTURE.
YOU THINK A TROLL WARRIOR NO MATCH FOR THOR?
WHAT OF A LOUD-MOUTHED DOLGAR MONGREL? YOU THINK YOU CAN GO UP AGAINST THOR WITHOUT TROLL HELP?
BECAUSE IF YOU DO--!!!
PEACE. **PEACE!** ARGUING AMONGST OUR-SELVES IS POINTLESS.
I'VE NO IDEA WHAT THOR SEEKS IN HELHEIM...
...BUT I WONDER IF WE **SHOULD** CONSIDER SEEKING ASSISTANCE THERE.

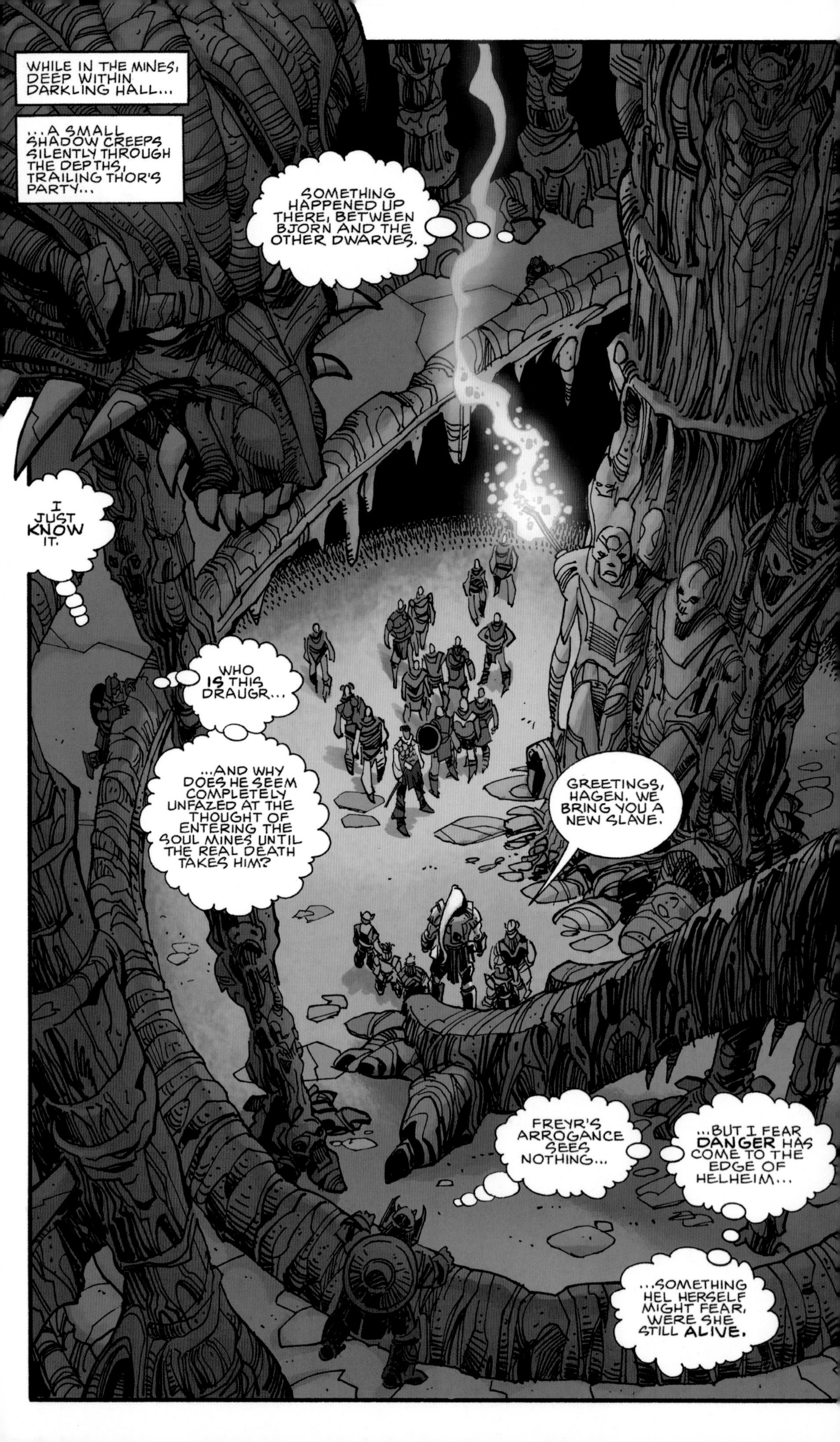
WHILE IN THE MINES, DEEP WITHIN DARKLING HALL...
...A SMALL SHADOW CREEPS SILENTLY THROUGH THE DEPTHS, TRAILING THOR'S PARTY...
SOMETHING HAPPENED UP THERE, BETWEEN BJORN AND THE OTHER DWARVES.
I JUST **KNOW** IT.
WHO **IS** THIS DRAUGR...
...AND WHY DOES HE SEEM COMPLETELY UNFAZED AT THE THOUGHT OF ENTERING THE SOUL MINES UNTIL THE REAL DEATH TAKES HIM?
GREETINGS, HAGEN. WE BRING YOU A NEW SLAVE.
FREYR'S ARROGANCE SEES NOTHING...
...BUT I FEAR **DANGER** HAS COME TO THE EDGE OF HELHEIM...
...SOMETHING HEL HERSELF MIGHT FEAR, WERE SHE STILL **ALIVE.**

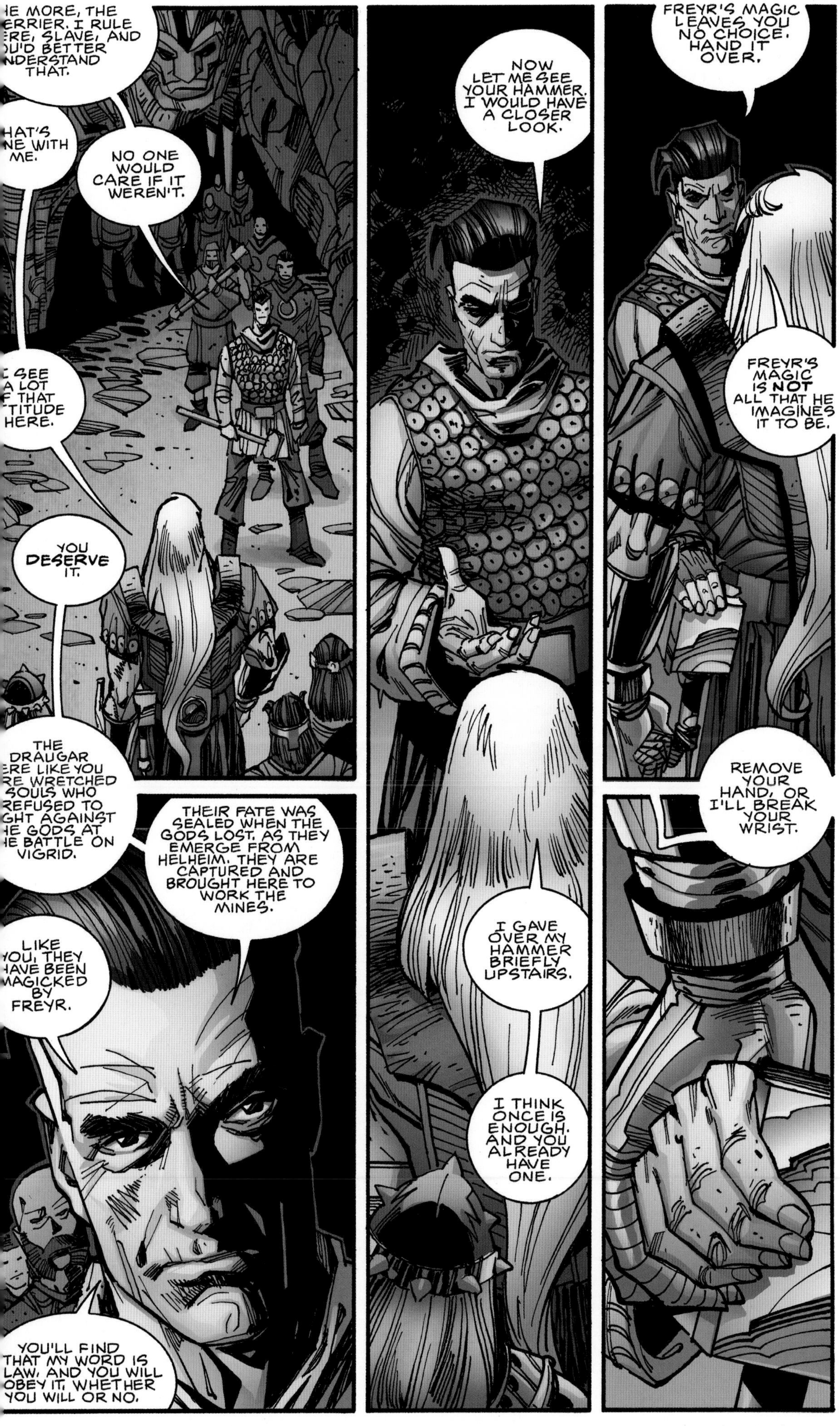

HE MORE, THE ERRIER. I RULE ERE, SLAVE, AND OU'D BETTER NDERSTAND THAT.
HAT'S NE WITH ME.
NO ONE WOULD CARE IF IT WEREN'T.
I SEE A LOT F THAT TTITUDE HERE.
YOU **DESERVE** IT.
THE DRAUGAR ERE LIKE YOU RE WRETCHED SOULS WHO REFUSED TO GHT AGAINST HE GODS AT HE BATTLE ON VIGRID.
THEIR FATE WAS SEALED WHEN THE GODS LOST. AS THEY EMERGE FROM HELHEIM, THEY ARE CAPTURED AND BROUGHT HERE TO WORK THE MINES.
LIKE YOU, THEY HAVE BEEN MAGICKED BY FREYR.
YOU'LL FIND THAT MY WORD IS LAW, AND YOU WILL OBEY IT, WHETHER YOU WILL OR NO.
NOW LET ME SEE YOUR HAMMER. I WOULD HAVE A CLOSER LOOK.
I GAVE OVER MY HAMMER BRIEFLY UPSTAIRS.
I THINK ONCE IS ENOUGH. AND YOU ALREADY HAVE ONE.
FREYR'S MAGIC LEAVES YOU NO CHOICE. HAND IT OVER.
FREYR'S MAGIC IS **NOT** ALL THAT HE IMAGINES IT TO BE.
REMOVE YOUR HAND, OR I'LL BREAK YOUR WRIST.

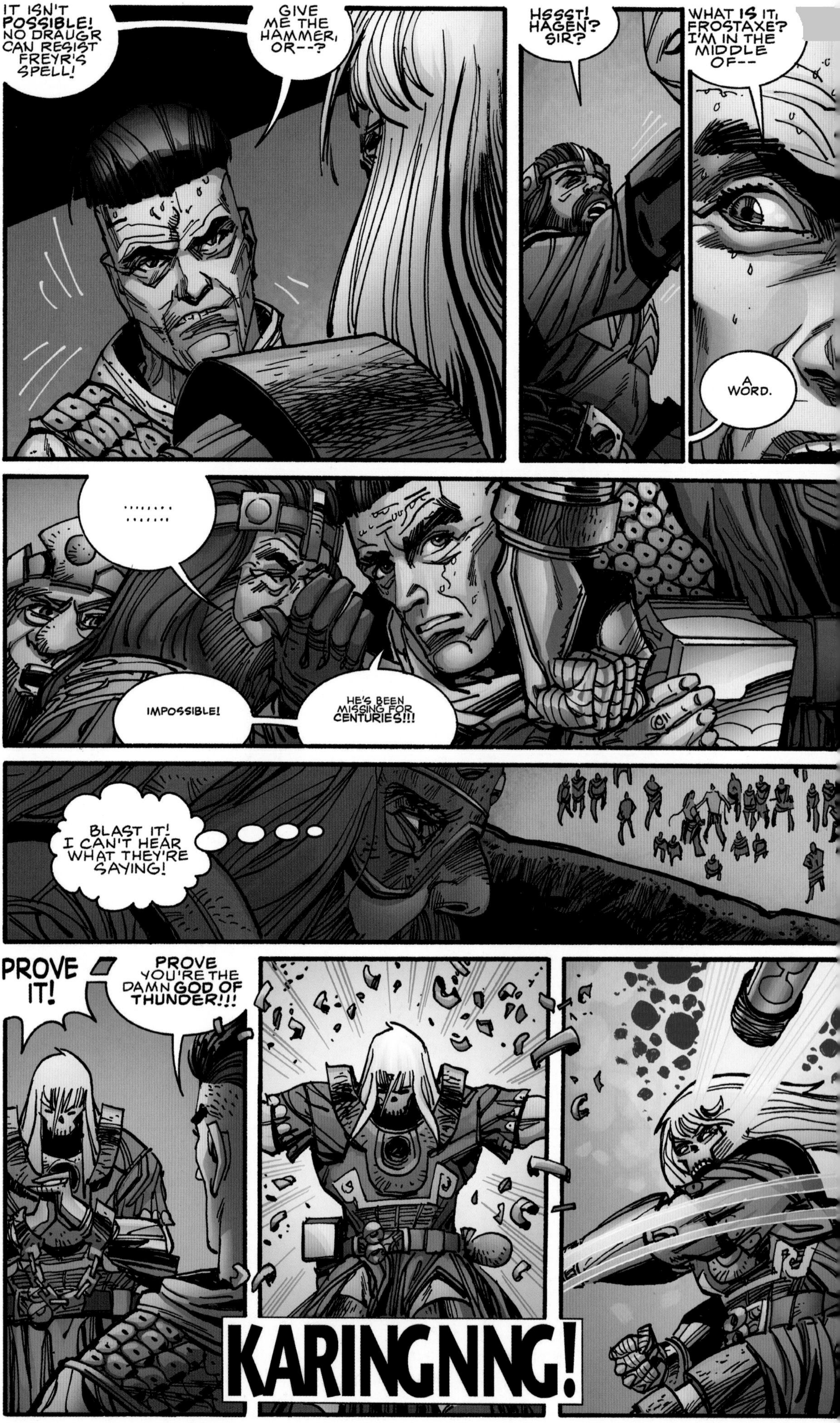
IT ISN'T POSSIBLE! NO DRAUGR CAN RESIST FREYR'S SPELL!
GIVE ME THE HAMMER, OR--?
HSSST! HAGEN? SIR?
WHAT IS IT, FROSTAXE? I'M IN THE MIDDLE OF--
A WORD.
....
....
IMPOSSIBLE!
HE'S BEEN MISSING FOR CENTURIES!!!
BLAST IT! I CAN'T HEAR WHAT THEY'RE SAYING!
PROVE IT!
PROVE YOU'RE THE DAMN GOD OF THUNDER!!!
KARINGNNG!

BKHRACKKK!

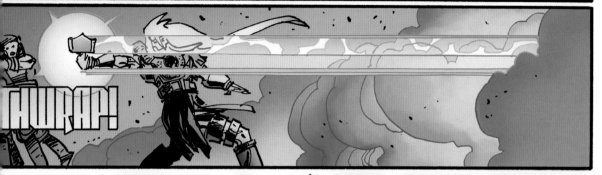

THWRAP!

OOOOKAY. LOOK, I DON'T RECOGNIZE YOU. I'M REALLY SORRY.

...DIDN'T WANT YOUR HAMMER, ANYWAY.

A WISE CHOICE. IT WOULD HAVE BURNED YOUR HAND TO A CINDER.

GOD'S CURSE!

HE'S BACK!

"WE THOUGHT YOU WERE **DEAD!** WHY HAVE YOU NOT REVEALED YOURSELF TO MORTALS IN THE DUSK LANDS BEFORE THIS?"

I AM SORRY. A LONG STORY. I WAS UNABLE TO HELP EVEN MYSELF FOR CENTURIES.

NOW, I INTEND TO MAKE UP FOR LOST TIME.

BUT TELL ME. YOU AND THE OTHERS HERE HAVE CLEARLY **NOT** BEEN MAGICKED.

WHY HAVE YOU NOT REBELLED AGAINST FREYR?

"HE HOLDS OUR WOMEN HOSTAGE AGAINST OUR GOOD BEHAVIOR.

"EACH NIGHT, ONE OF US IS PERMITTED A VISIT TO PROVE THAT HIS WIFE IS ALIVE AND IN GOOD HEALTH.

"HE HAS ALREADY KILLED SEVERAL IN RETALIATION FOR INFRACTIONS,"

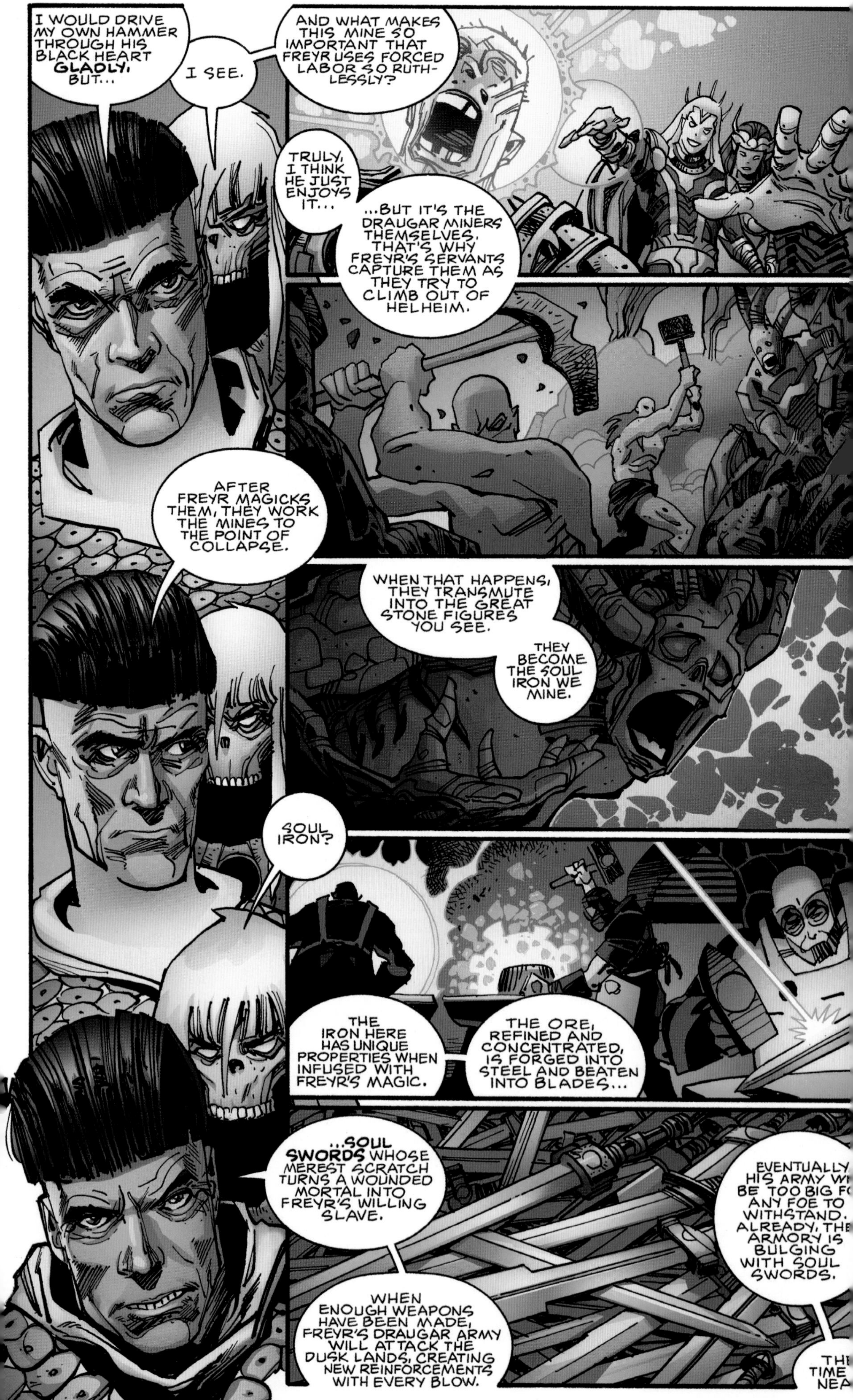
I WOULD DRIVE MY OWN HAMMER THROUGH HIS BLACK HEART GLADLY, BUT...
I SEE.
AND WHAT MAKES THIS MINE SO IMPORTANT THAT FREYR USES FORCED LABOR SO RUTH-LESSLY?
TRULY, I THINK HE JUST ENJOYS IT...
...BUT IT'S THE DRAUGAR MINERS THEMSELVES. THAT'S WHY FREYR'S SERVANTS CAPTURE THEM AS THEY TRY TO CLIMB OUT OF HELHEIM.
AFTER FREYR MAGICKS THEM, THEY WORK THE MINES TO THE POINT OF COLLAPSE.
WHEN THAT HAPPENS, THEY TRANSMUTE INTO THE GREAT STONE FIGURES YOU SEE.
THEY BECOME THE SOUL IRON WE MINE.
SOUL IRON?
THE IRON HERE HAS UNIQUE PROPERTIES WHEN INFUSED WITH FREYR'S MAGIC.
THE ORE, REFINED AND CONCENTRATED, IS FORGED INTO STEEL AND BEATEN INTO BLADES...
...SOUL SWORDS WHOSE MEREST SCRATCH TURNS A WOUNDED MORTAL INTO FREYR'S WILLING SLAVE.
WHEN ENOUGH WEAPONS HAVE BEEN MADE, FREYR'S DRAUGAR ARMY WILL ATTACK THE DUSK LANDS, CREATING NEW REINFORCEMENTS WITH EVERY BLOW.

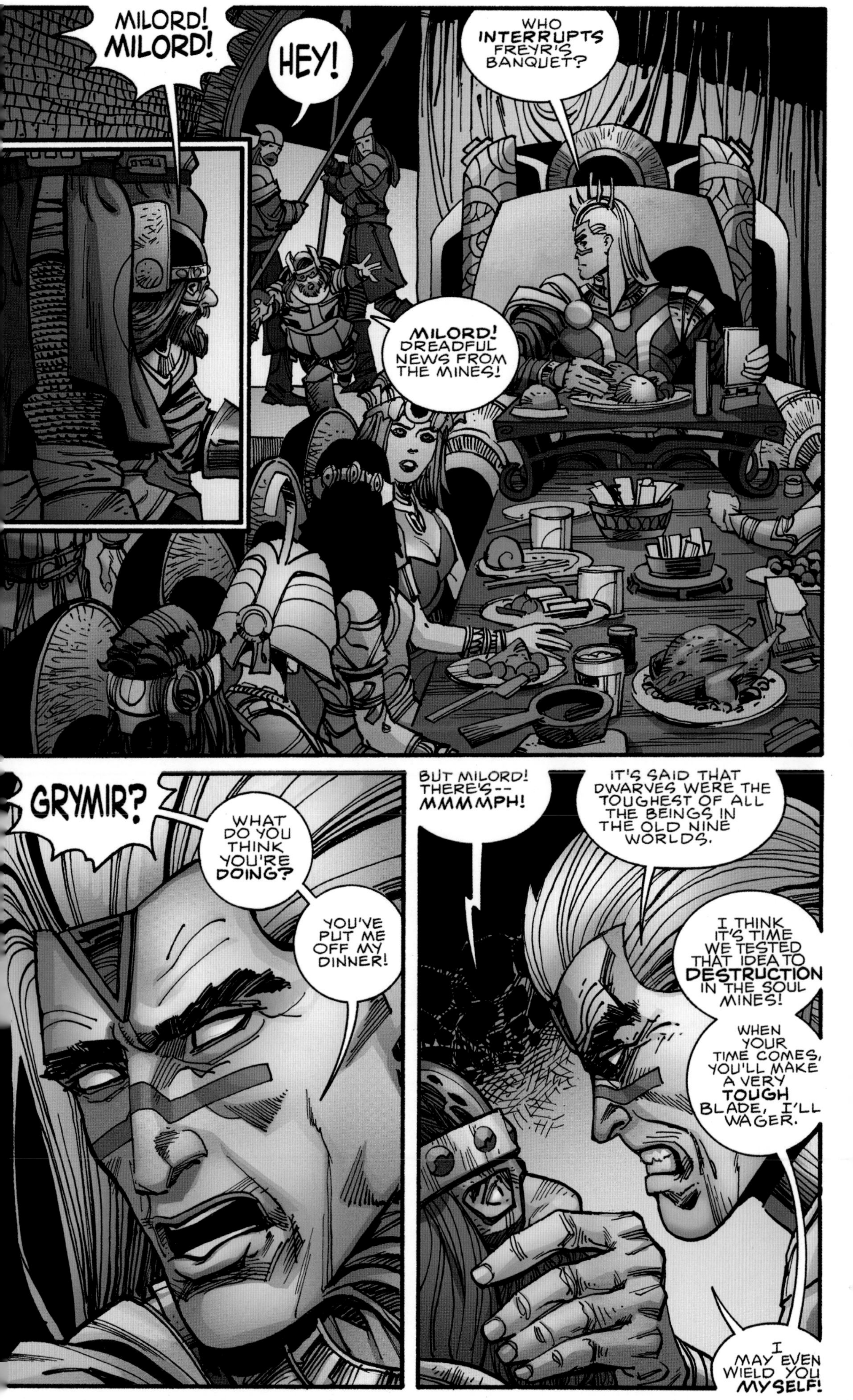
MILORD! MILORD!
HEY!
WHO INTERRUPTS FREYR'S BANQUET?
MILORD! DREADFUL NEWS FROM THE MINES!
GRYMIR?
WHAT DO YOU THINK YOU'RE DOING?
YOU'VE PUT ME OFF MY DINNER!
BUT MILORD! THERE'S-- MMMMPH!
IT'S SAID THAT DWARVES WERE THE TOUGHEST OF ALL THE BEINGS IN THE OLD NINE WORLDS.
I THINK IT'S TIME WE TESTED THAT IDEA TO DESTRUCTION IN THE SOUL MINES!
WHEN YOUR TIME COMES, YOU'LL MAKE A VERY TOUGH BLADE, I'LL WAGER.
I MAY EVEN WIELD YOU MYSELF!

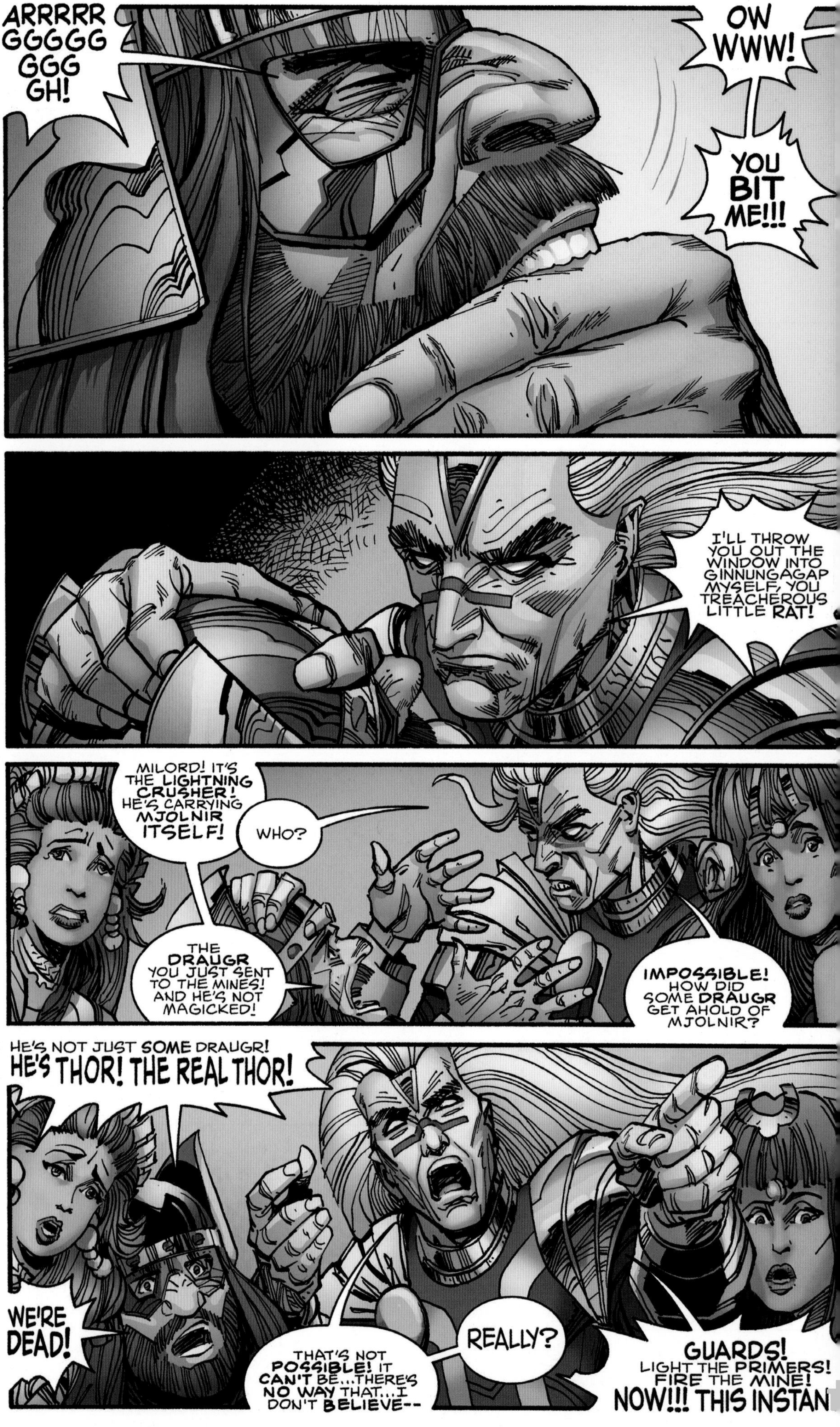
ARRRRR GGGGG GGG GH!
OW WWW!
YOU BIT ME!!!
I'LL THROW YOU OUT THE WINDOW INTO GINNUNGAGAP MYSELF, YOU TREACHEROUS LITTLE RAT!
MILORD! IT'S THE LIGHTNING CRUSHER! HE'S CARRYING MJOLNIR ITSELF!
WHO?
THE DRAUGR YOU JUST SENT TO THE MINES! AND HE'S NOT MAGICKED!
IMPOSSIBLE! HOW DID SOME DRAUGR GET AHOLD OF MJOLNIR?
HE'S NOT JUST SOME DRAUGR! HE'S THOR! THE REAL THOR!
WE'RE DEAD!
THAT'S NOT POSSIBLE! IT CAN'T BE...THERE'S NO WAY THAT...I DON'T BELIEVE--
REALLY?
GUARDS! LIGHT THE PRIMERS! FIRE THE MINE! NOW!!! THIS INSTAN

YOU **KNOW** ANGANTYR IS **DEAD**, HIS FORTRESS IN RUINS?

ORIGINALLY, FREYR WAS THE **ARMORER** FOR THE LORD OF THE DEAD... ANGANTYR...ON HELHEIM'S RIM ABOVE.

BUT THE MORE HE THOUGHT ABOUT IT, THE MORE FREYR WANTED TO BECOME A POWER **HIMSELF**, RULING THE DUSK LANDS.

OH, **WE** KNOW THAT. BUT NO ONE'S TOLD **FREYR**. HE'S ANTICIPATING ANGANTYR GROVELING BEFORE HIM.

SO HE WOULDN'T **THANK** THE MESSENGER WHO BROUGHT HIM WORD OF ANGANTYR'S **DEATH**?

HARDLY. HE'S OBSESSED WITH THE IDEA OF EXPANDING HIS POWER AND TORTURING THOSE HE SEES AS LORDING IT OVER HIM; ANGANTYR MOST OF ALL.

HE'LL BE ANGRY.

I THINK HE TOOK THE NAME FREYR IN HOPES OF ASSUMING, IN SOME WAY, A GOD'S DESTINY.

SINCE THE GODS ARE PRETTY MUCH ALL **DEAD**, I CAN **HELP** WITH THAT.

≶SNIFF≶ ≶SNIFF≶

O YOU MELL OMETHING?

IKE **HOT** ETAL?

IT'S COMING FROM EVERY- WHERE!

OH, **GOD!** IT'S **FREYR!**

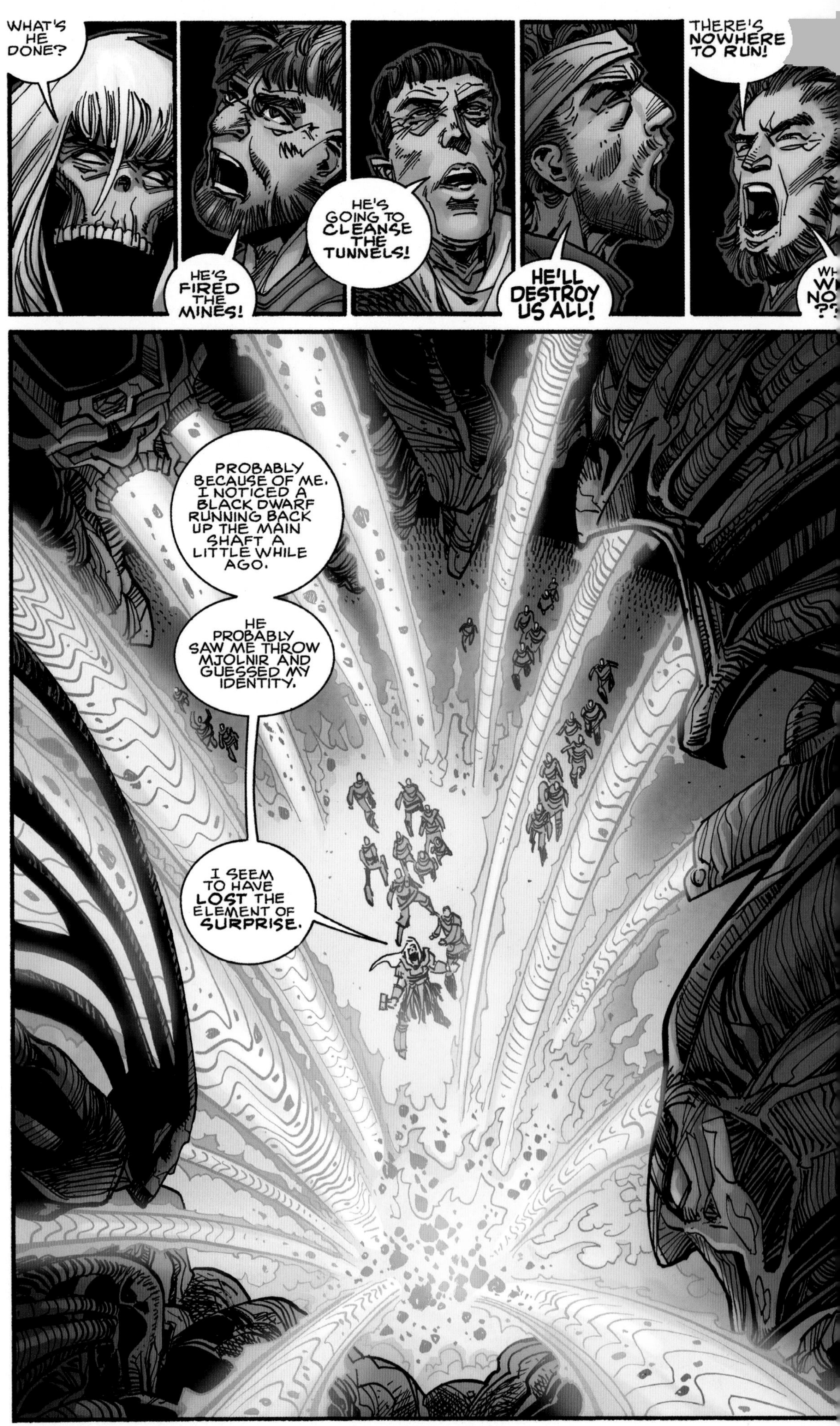
WHAT'S HE DONE?
HE'S FIRED THE MINES!
HE'S GOING TO CLEANSE THE TUNNELS!
HE'LL DESTROY US ALL!
THERE'S NOWHERE TO RUN!
PROBABLY BECAUSE OF ME. I NOTICED A BLACK DWARF RUNNING BACK UP THE MAIN SHAFT A LITTLE WHILE AGO.
HE PROBABLY SAW ME THROW MJOLNIR AND GUESSED MY IDENTITY.
I SEEM TO HAVE LOST THE ELEMENT OF SURPRISE.

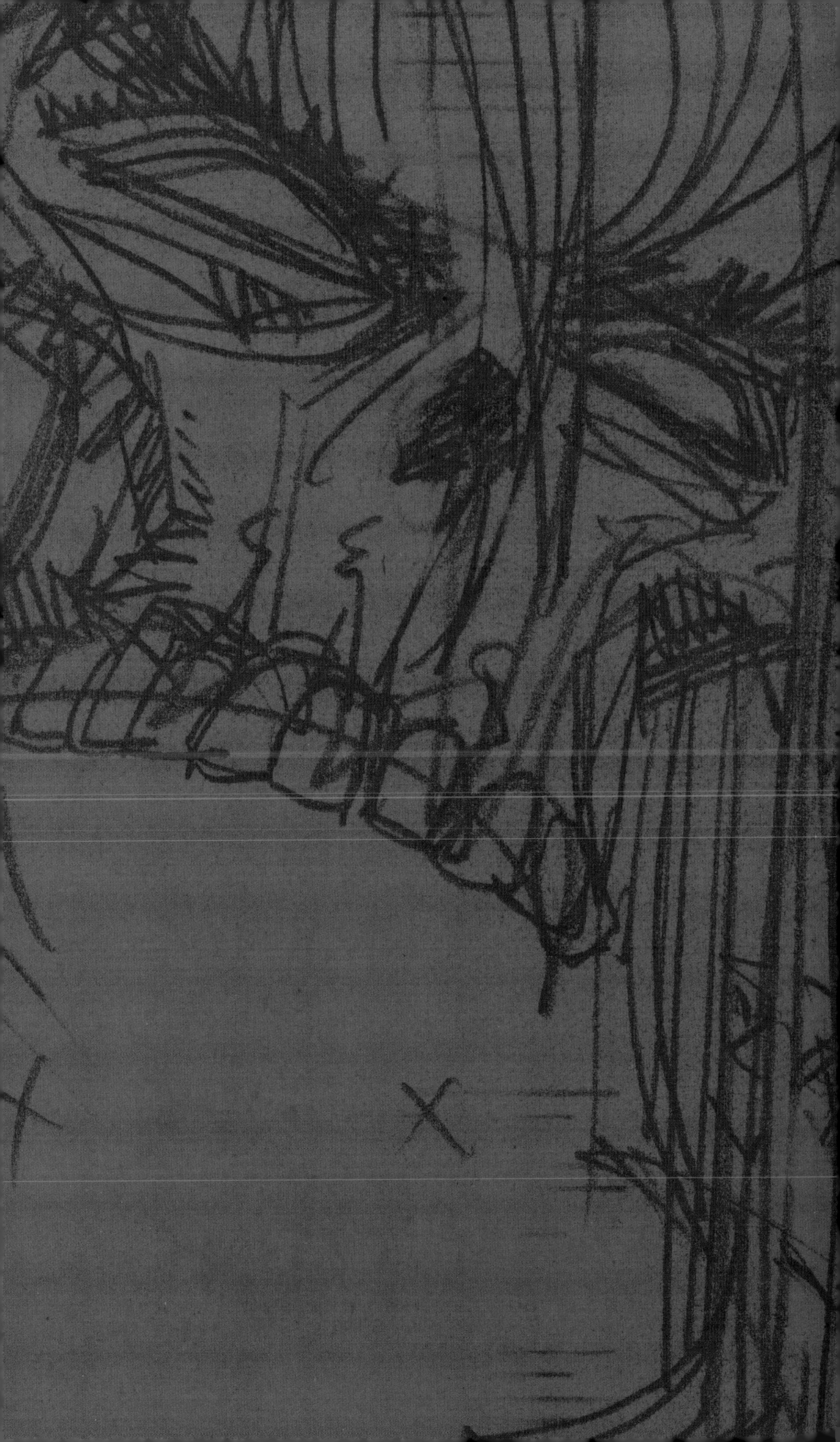

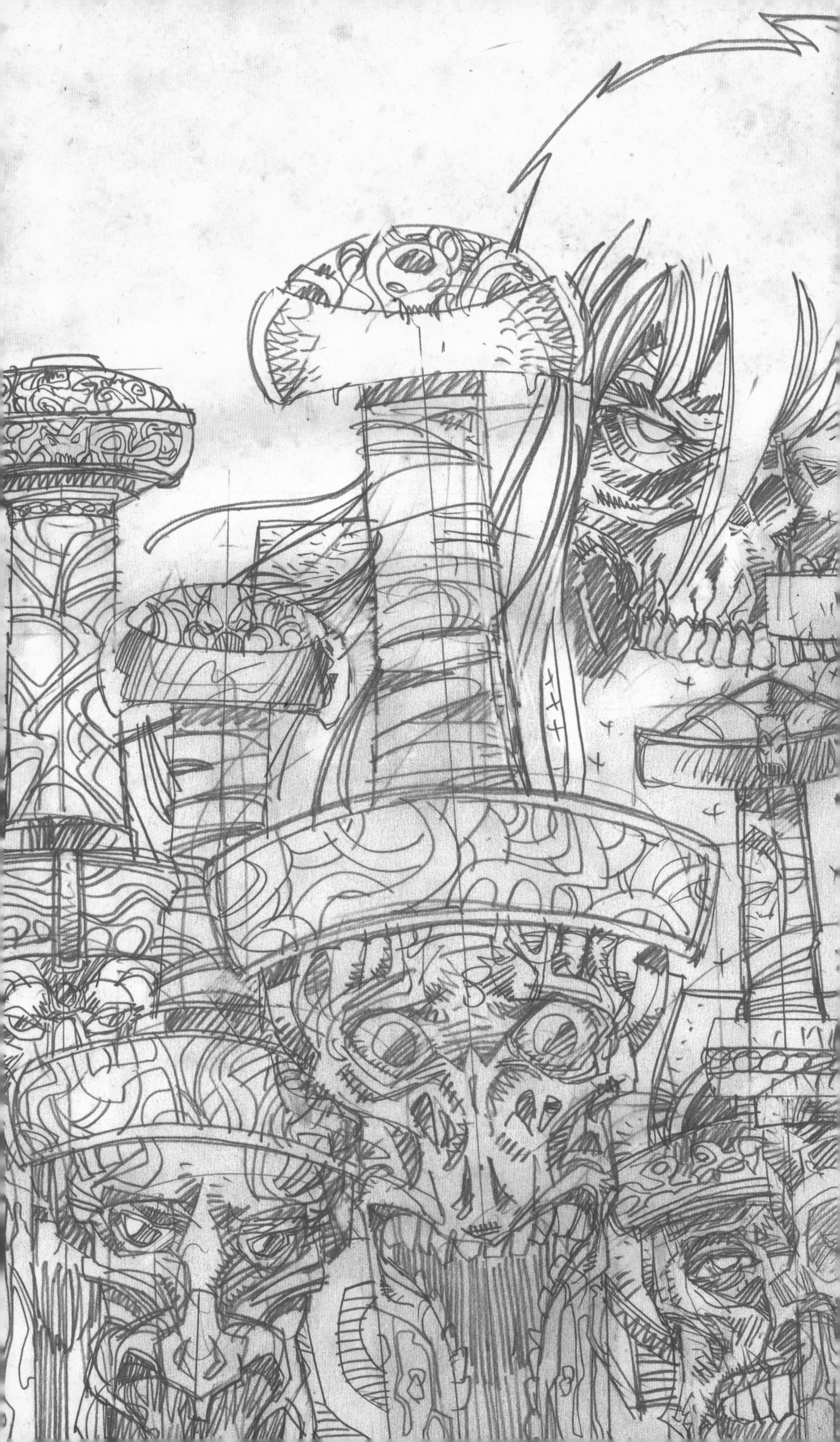

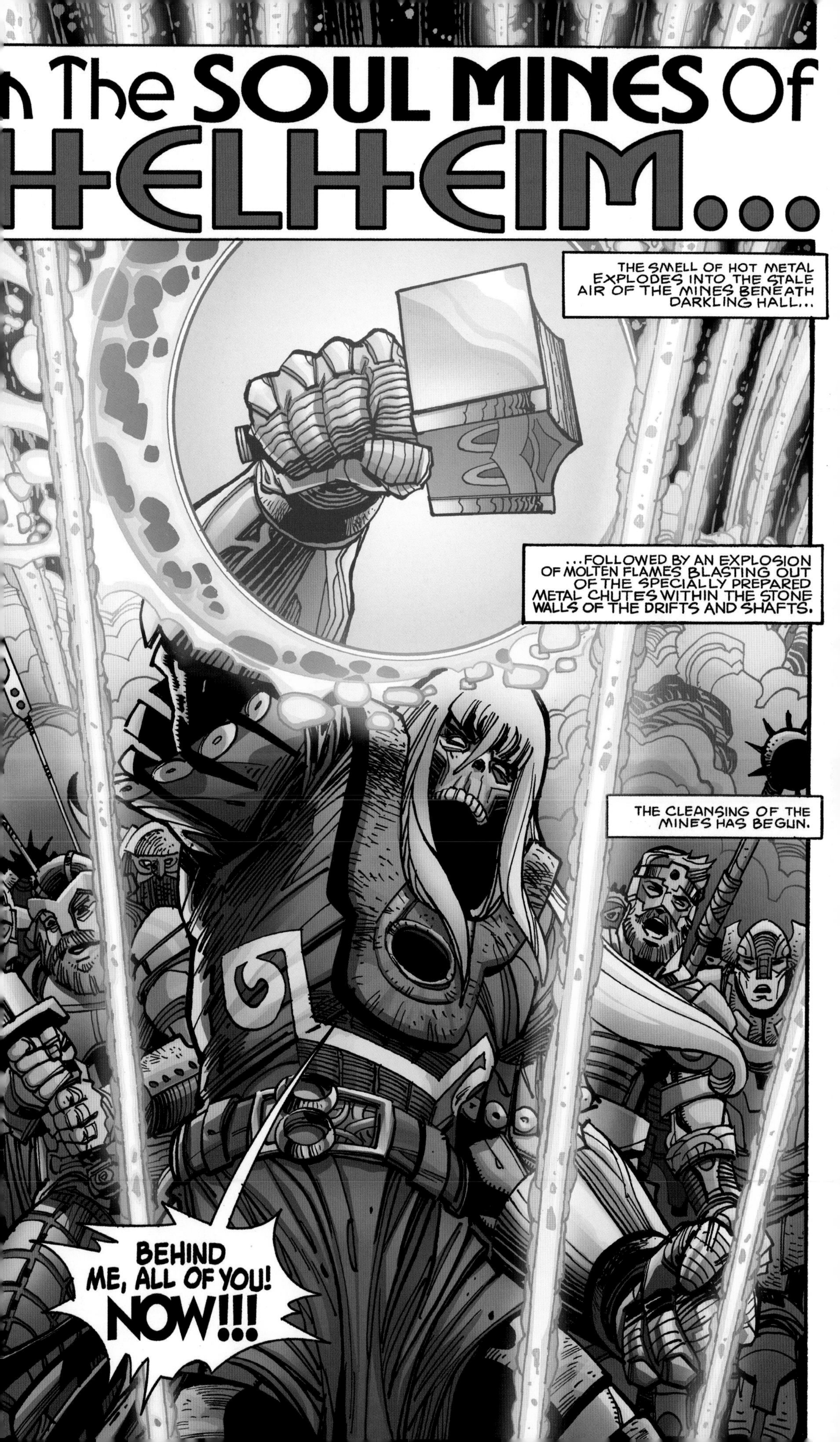
In The SOUL MINES Of HELHEIM...
THE SMELL OF HOT METAL EXPLODES INTO THE STALE AIR OF THE MINES BENEATH DARKLING HALL...
...FOLLOWED BY AN EXPLOSION OF MOLTEN FLAMES BLASTING OUT OF THE SPECIALLY PREPARED METAL CHUTES WITHIN THE STONE WALLS OF THE DRIFTS AND SHAFTS.
THE CLEANSING OF THE MINES HAS BEGUN.
BEHIND ME, ALL OF YOU! NOW!!!

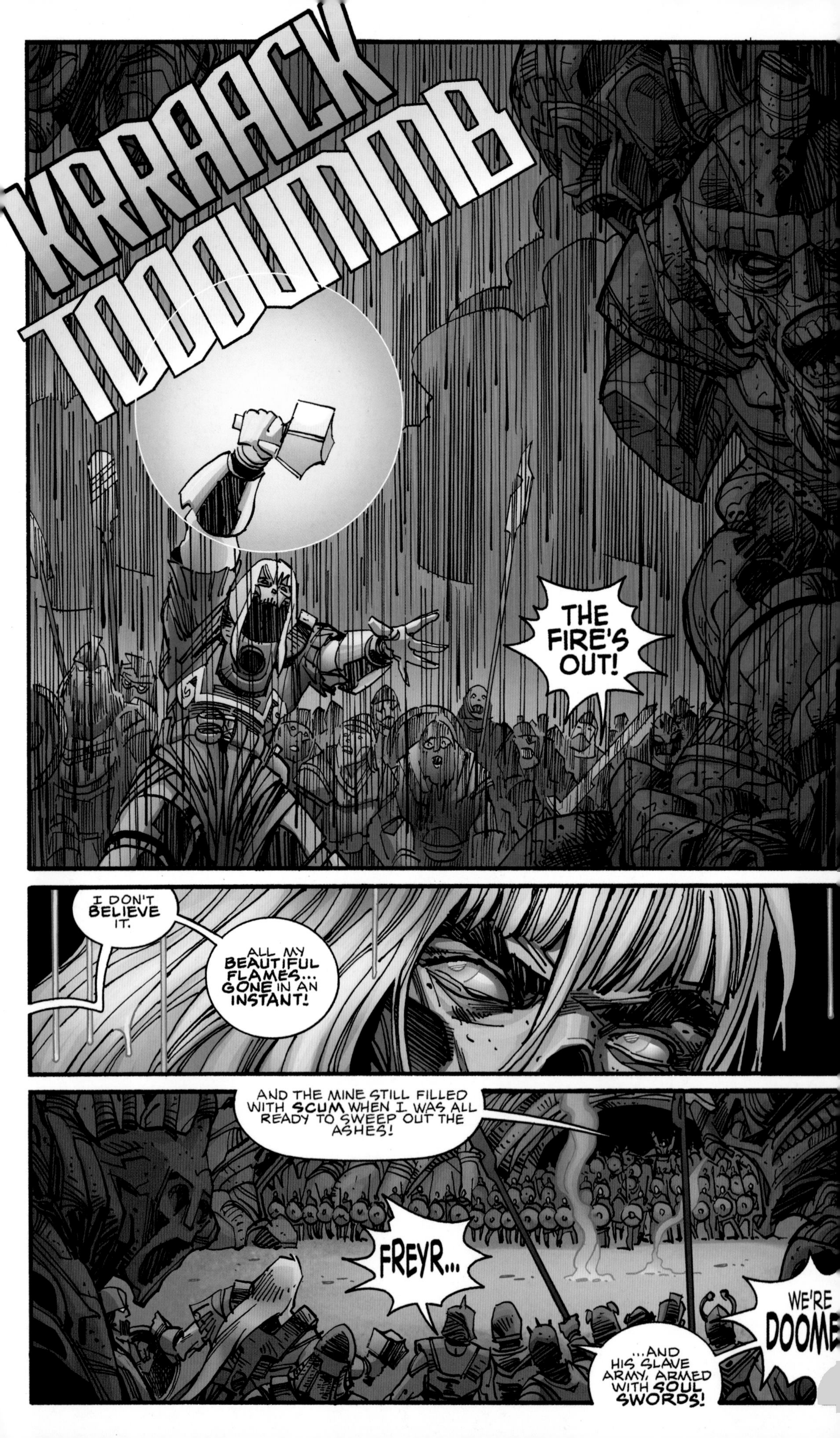
KRRAACK
TOOOUMMB
THE FIRE'S OUT!
I DON'T BELIEVE IT.
ALL MY BEAUTIFUL FLAMES... GONE IN AN INSTANT!
AND THE MINE STILL FILLED WITH SCUM WHEN I WAS ALL READY TO SWEEP OUT THE ASHES!
FREYR...
...AND HIS SLAVE ARMY, ARMED WITH SOUL SWORDS!
WE'RE DOOME

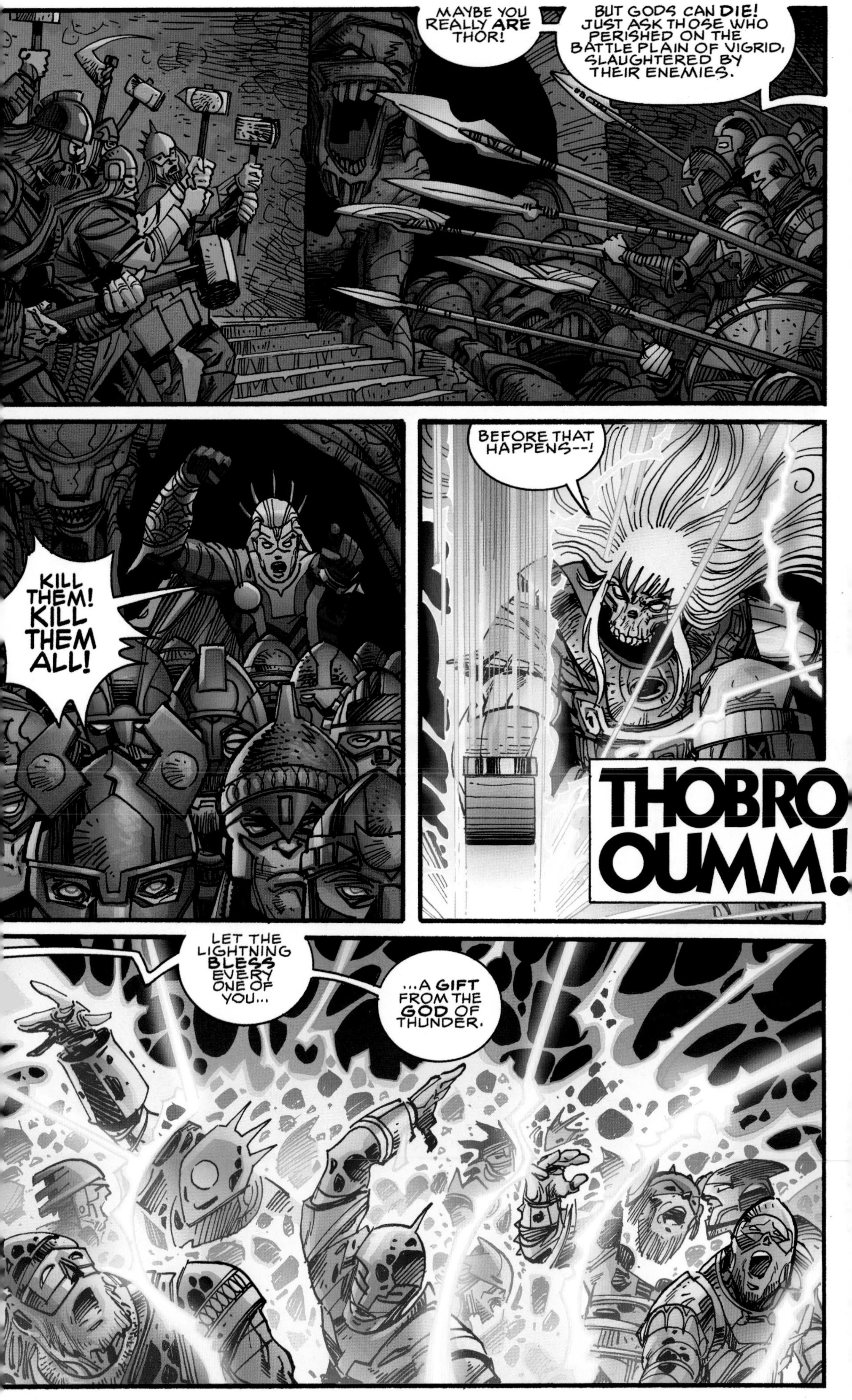
MAYBE YOU REALLY ARE THOR!
BUT GODS CAN DIE! JUST ASK THOSE WHO PERISHED ON THE BATTLE PLAIN OF VIGRID, SLAUGHTERED BY THEIR ENEMIES.
KILL THEM! KILL THEM ALL!
BEFORE THAT HAPPENS--!
THOBROOUMM!
LET THE LIGHTNING BLESS EVERY ONE OF YOU...
...A GIFT FROM THE GOD OF THUNDER.

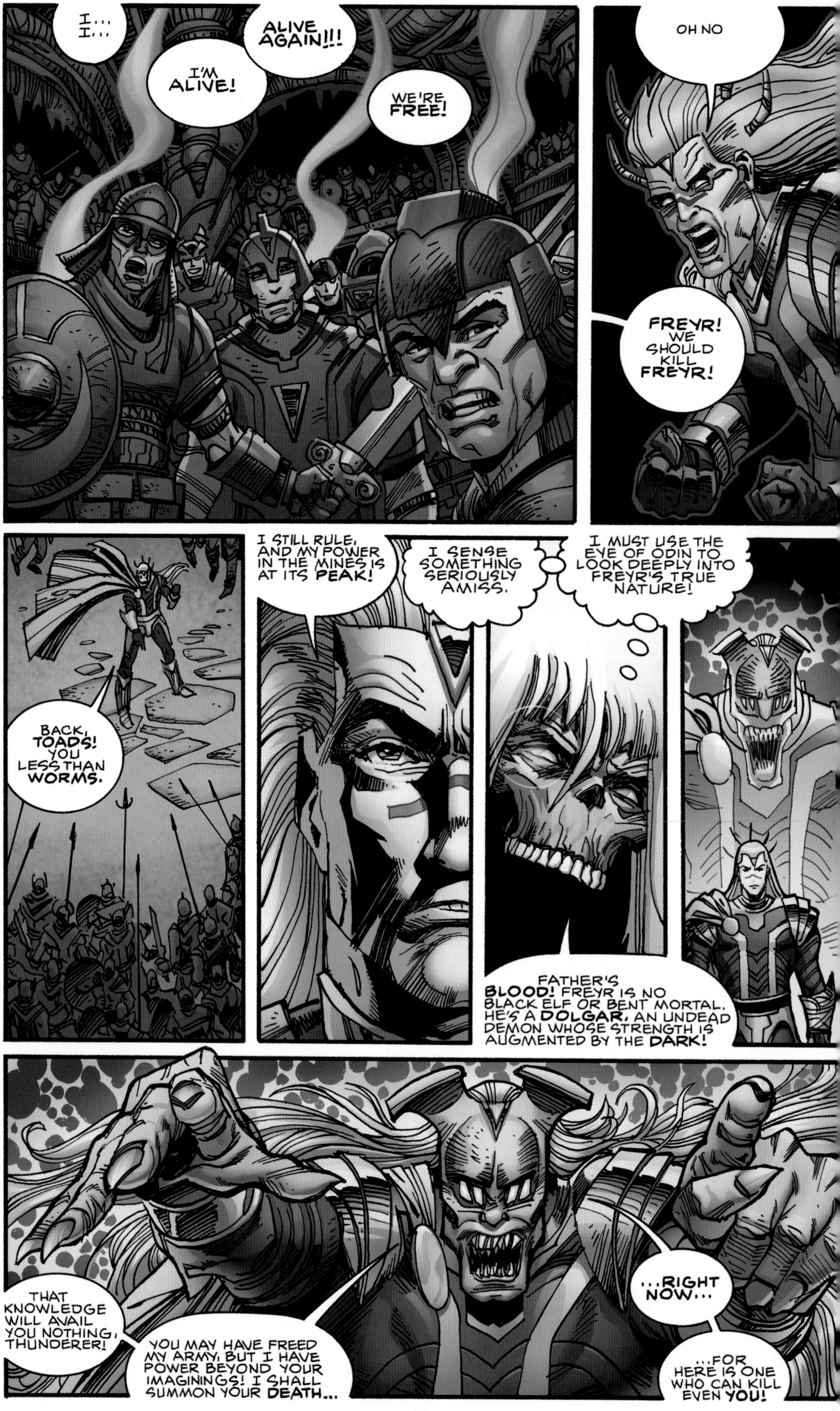
I... I...
I'M ALIVE!
ALIVE AGAIN!!!
WE'RE FREE!
OH NO
FREYR! WE SHOULD KILL FREYR!
BACK, TOADS! YOU LESS THAN WORMS.
I STILL RULE, AND MY POWER IN THE MINES IS AT ITS PEAK!
I SENSE SOMETHING SERIOUSLY AMISS.
I MUST USE THE EYE OF ODIN TO LOOK DEEPLY INTO FREYR'S TRUE NATURE!
FATHER'S BLOOD! FREYR IS NO BLACK ELF OR BENT MORTAL. HE'S A DOLGAR, AN UNDEAD DEMON WHOSE STRENGTH IS AUGMENTED BY THE DARK!
THAT KNOWLEDGE WILL AVAIL YOU NOTHING, THUNDERER!
YOU MAY HAVE FREED MY ARMY, BUT I HAVE POWER BEYOND YOUR IMAGININGS! I SHALL SUMMON YOUR DEATH...
...RIGHT NOW...
...FOR HERE IS ONE WHO CAN KILL EVEN YOU!

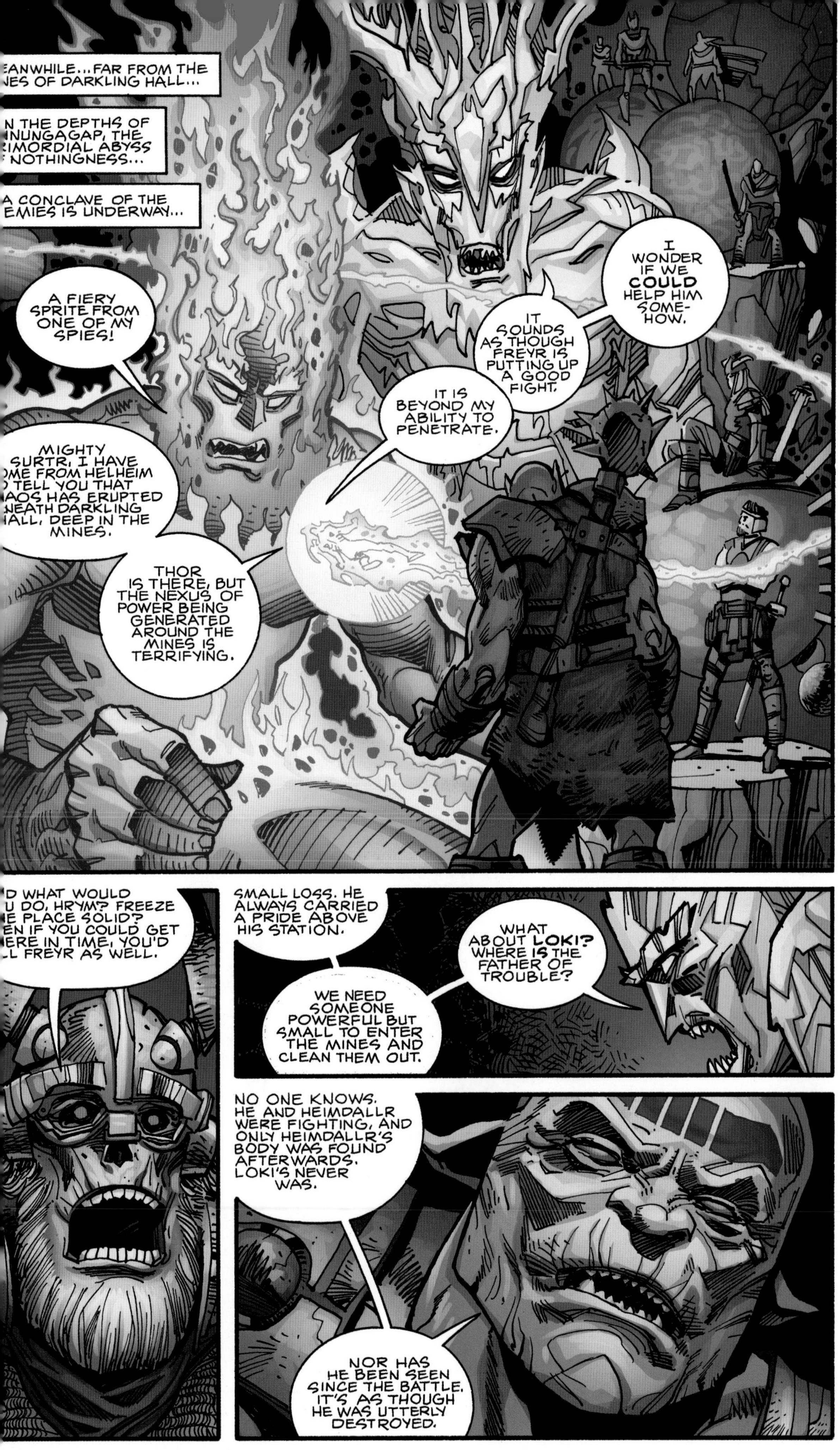

EANWHILE...FAR FROM THE NES OF DARKLING HALL...
N THE DEPTHS OF INUNGAGAP, THE IMORDIAL ABYSS NOTHINGNESS...
A CONCLAVE OF THE EMIES IS UNDERWAY...
A FIERY SPRITE FROM ONE OF MY SPIES!
MIGHTY SURTR, I HAVE OME FROM HELHEIM TELL YOU THAT AOS HAS ERUPTED NEATH DARKLING HALL, DEEP IN THE MINES.
THOR IS THERE, BUT THE NEXUS OF POWER BEING GENERATED AROUND THE MINES IS TERRIFYING.
IT IS BEYOND MY ABILITY TO PENETRATE.
IT SOUNDS AS THOUGH FREYR IS PUTTING UP A GOOD FIGHT.
I WONDER IF WE COULD HELP HIM SOME-HOW.
D WHAT WOULD U DO, HRYM? FREEZE E PLACE SOLID? EN IF YOU COULD GET ERE IN TIME, YOU'D L FREYR AS WELL.
SMALL LOSS. HE ALWAYS CARRIED A PRIDE ABOVE HIS STATION.
WE NEED SOMEONE POWERFUL BUT SMALL TO ENTER THE MINES AND CLEAN THEM OUT.
WHAT ABOUT LOKI? WHERE IS THE FATHER OF TROUBLE?
NO ONE KNOWS. HE AND HEIMDALLR WERE FIGHTING, AND ONLY HEIMDALLR'S BODY WAS FOUND AFTERWARDS. LOKI'S NEVER WAS.
NOR HAS HE BEEN SEEN SINCE THE BATTLE. IT'S AS THOUGH HE WAS UTTERLY DESTROYED.

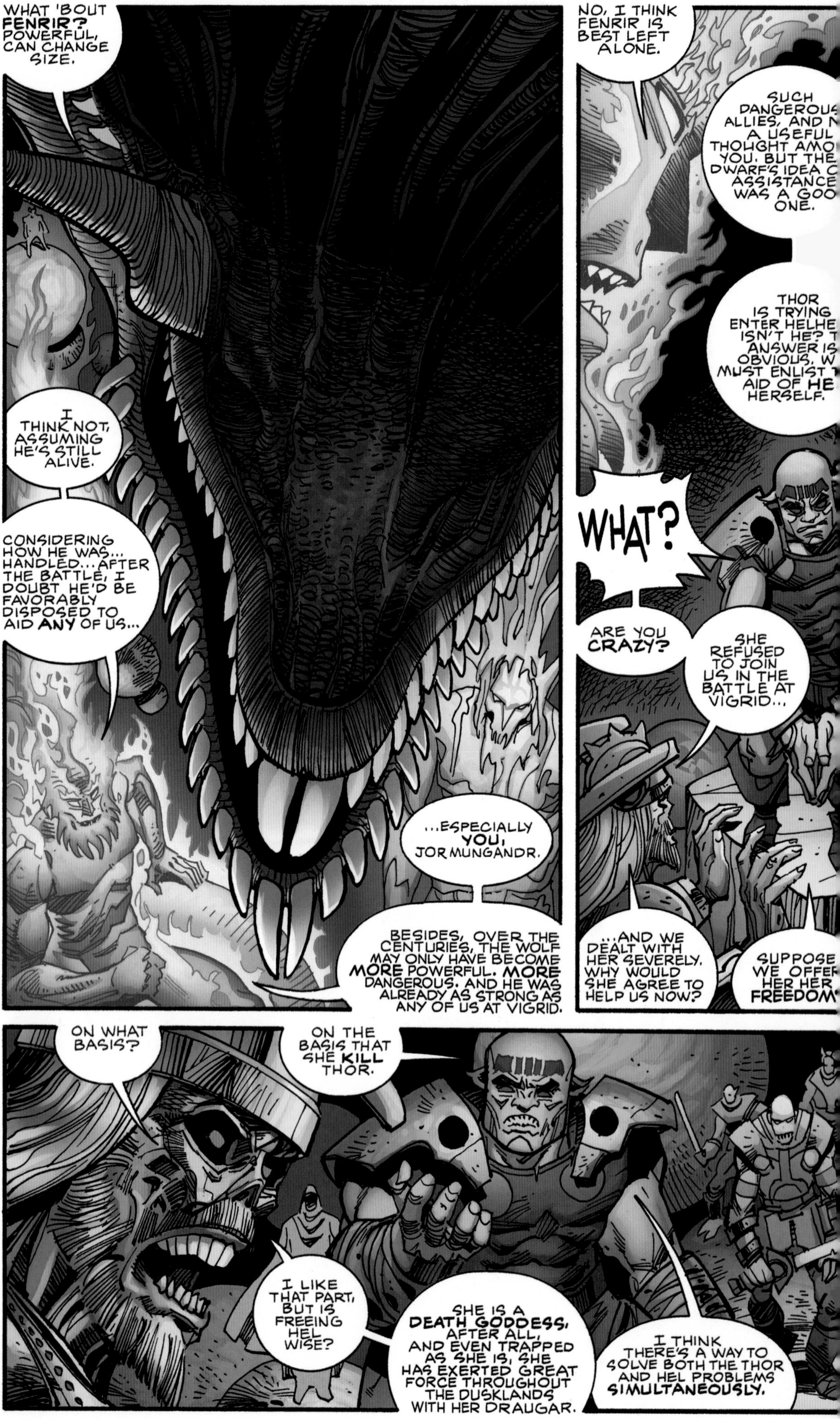

WHAT 'BOUT FENRIR? POWERFUL, CAN CHANGE SIZE.
I THINK NOT, ASSUMING HE'S STILL ALIVE.
CONSIDERING HOW HE WAS... HANDLED... AFTER THE BATTLE, I DOUBT HE'D BE FAVORABLY DISPOSED TO AID ANY OF US...
...ESPECIALLY YOU, JORMUNGANDR.
BESIDES, OVER THE CENTURIES, THE WOLF MAY ONLY HAVE BECOME MORE POWERFUL. MORE DANGEROUS. AND HE WAS ALREADY AS STRONG AS ANY OF US AT VIGRID.
NO, I THINK FENRIR IS BEST LEFT ALONE.
WHAT?
ARE YOU CRAZY?
SHE REFUSED TO JOIN US IN THE BATTLE AT VIGRID...
...AND WE DEALT WITH HER SEVERELY. WHY WOULD SHE AGREE TO HELP US NOW?
ON WHAT BASIS?
ON THE BASIS THAT SHE KILL THOR.
I LIKE THAT PART, BUT IS FREEING HEL WISE?
SHE IS A DEATH GODDESS, AFTER ALL, AND EVEN TRAPPED AS SHE IS, SHE HAS EXERTED GREAT FORCE THROUGHOUT THE DUSKLANDS WITH HER DRAUGAR.
I THINK THERE'S A WAY TO SOLVE BOTH THE THOR AND HEL PROBLEMS SIMULTANEOUSLY.

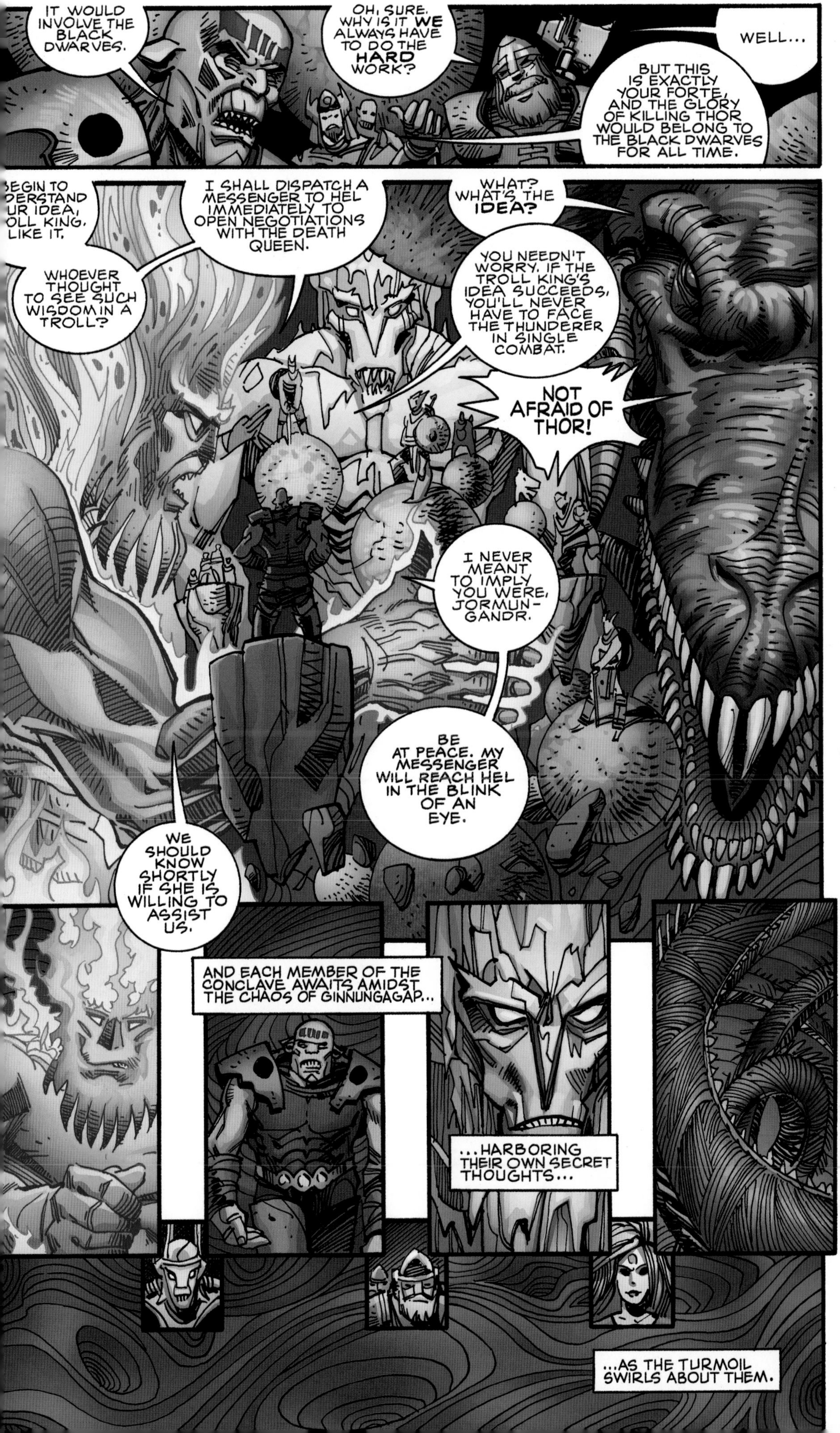

IT WOULD INVOLVE THE BLACK DWARVES.
OH, SURE. WHY IS IT WE ALWAYS HAVE TO DO THE HARD WORK?
WELL...
BUT THIS IS EXACTLY YOUR FORTE, AND THE GLORY OF KILLING THOR WOULD BELONG TO THE BLACK DWARVES FOR ALL TIME.
EGIN TO DERSTAND UR IDEA, OLL KING. LIKE IT.
WHOEVER THOUGHT TO SEE SUCH WISDOM IN A TROLL?
I SHALL DISPATCH A MESSENGER TO HEL IMMEDIATELY TO OPEN NEGOTIATIONS WITH THE DEATH QUEEN.
WHAT? WHAT'S THE IDEA?
YOU NEEDN'T WORRY. IF THE TROLL KING'S IDEA SUCCEEDS, YOU'LL NEVER HAVE TO FACE THE THUNDERER IN SINGLE COMBAT.
NOT AFRAID OF THOR!
I NEVER MEANT TO IMPLY YOU WERE, JORMUN-GANDR.
BE AT PEACE. MY MESSENGER WILL REACH HEL IN THE BLINK OF AN EYE.
WE SHOULD KNOW SHORTLY IF SHE IS WILLING TO ASSIST US.
AND EACH MEMBER OF THE CONCLAVE AWAITS AMIDST THE CHAOS OF GINNUNGAGAP...
...HARBORING THEIR OWN SECRET THOUGHTS...
...AS THE TURMOIL SWIRLS ABOUT THEM.

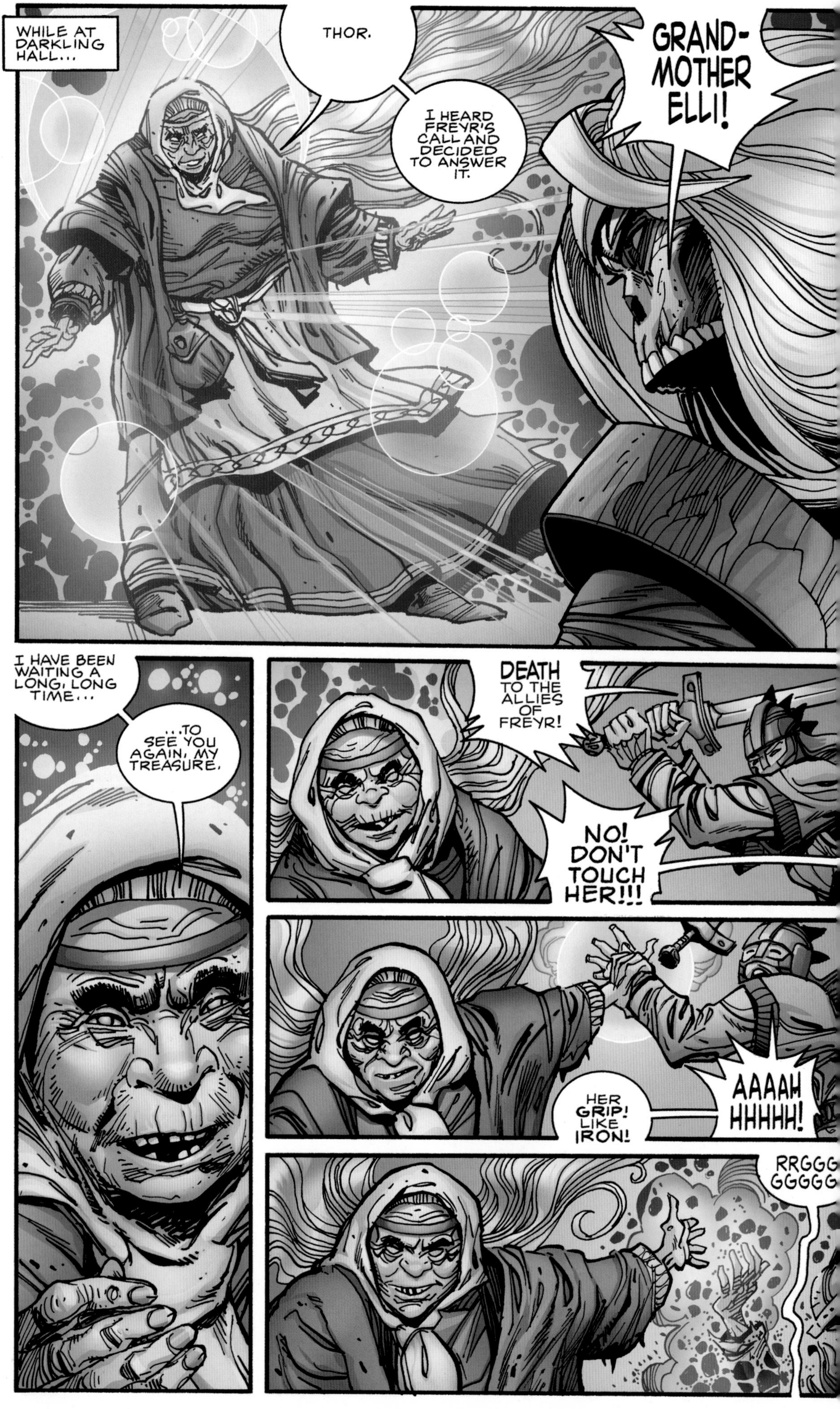
WHILE AT DARKLING HALL...
THOR.
I HEARD FREYR'S CALL AND DECIDED TO ANSWER IT.
GRAND-MOTHER ELLI!
I HAVE BEEN WAITING A LONG, LONG TIME...
...TO SEE YOU AGAIN, MY TREASURE.
DEATH TO THE ALLIES OF FREYR!
NO! DON'T TOUCH HER!!!
HER GRIP! LIKE IRON!
AAAAHHHHH!
RRGGG GGGGG

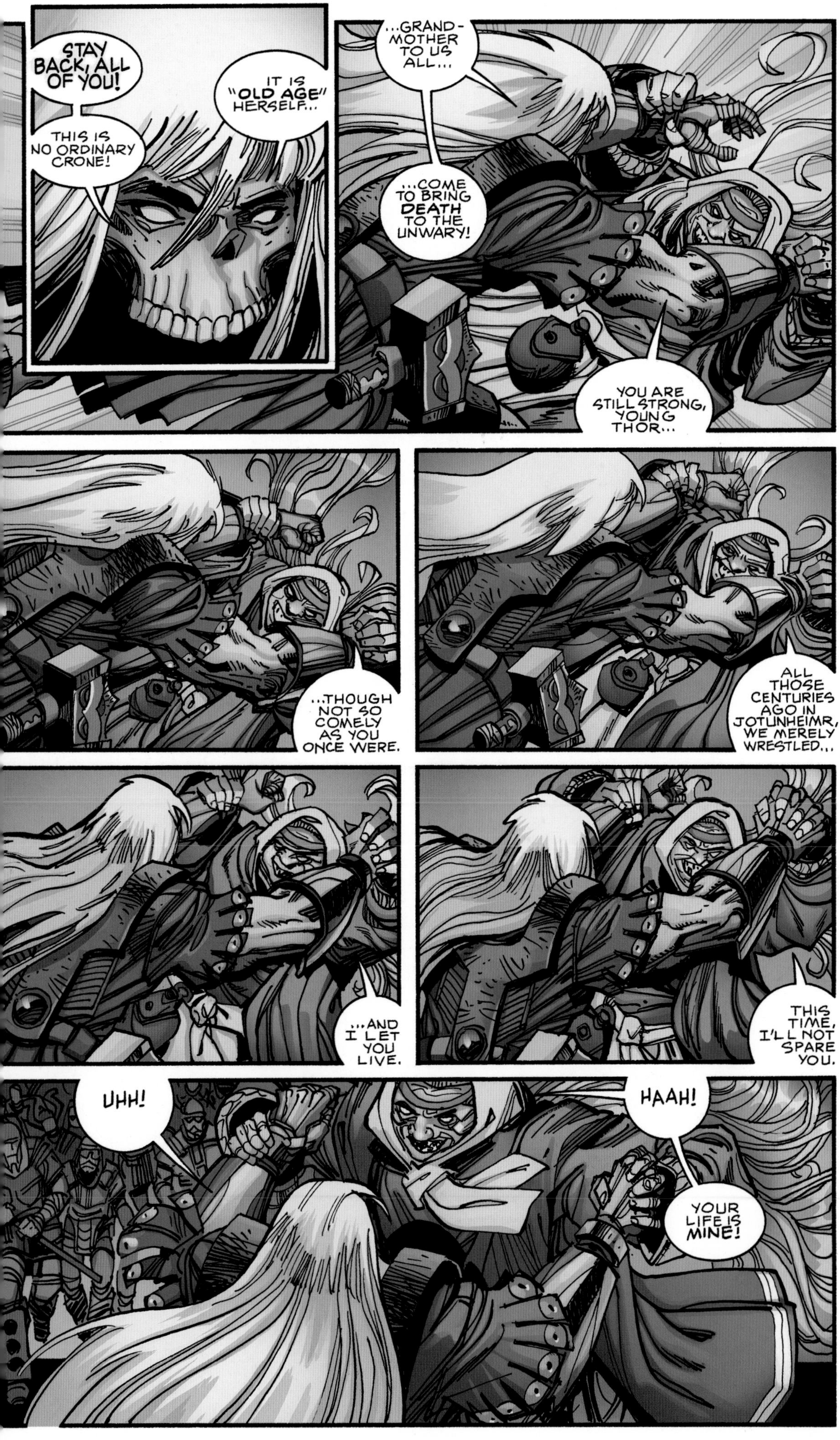
STAY BACK, ALL OF YOU!
THIS IS NO ORDINARY CRONE!
IT IS "OLD AGE" HERSELF...
...GRAND-MOTHER TO US ALL...
...COME TO BRING DEATH TO THE UNWARY!
YOU ARE STILL STRONG, YOUNG THOR...
...THOUGH NOT SO COMELY AS YOU ONCE WERE.
ALL THOSE CENTURIES AGO IN JOTUNHEIMR, WE MERELY WRESTLED...
...AND I LET YOU LIVE.
THIS TIME, I'LL NOT SPARE YOU.
UHH!
HAAH!
YOUR LIFE IS MINE!

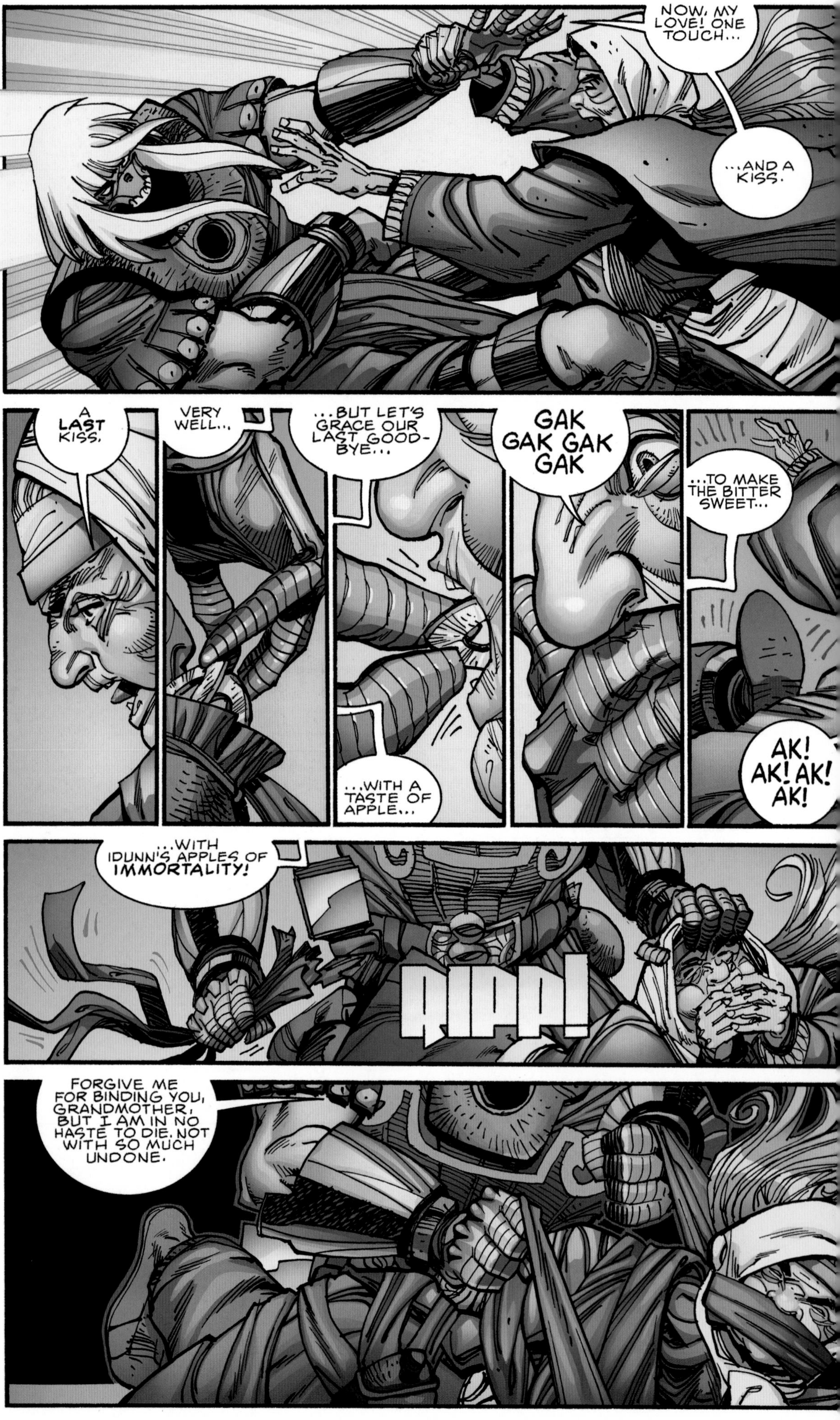
NOW, MY LOVE! ONE TOUCH...
...AND A KISS.
A LAST KISS.
VERY WELL...
...BUT LET'S GRACE OUR LAST GOOD-BYE...
...WITH A TASTE OF APPLE...
GAK GAK GAK GAK
...TO MAKE THE BITTER SWEET...
AK! AK! AK! AK!
...WITH IDUNN'S APPLES OF IMMORTALITY!
RIPP!
FORGIVE ME FOR BINDING YOU, GRANDMOTHER, BUT I AM IN NO HASTE TO DIE. NOT WITH SO MUCH UNDONE.

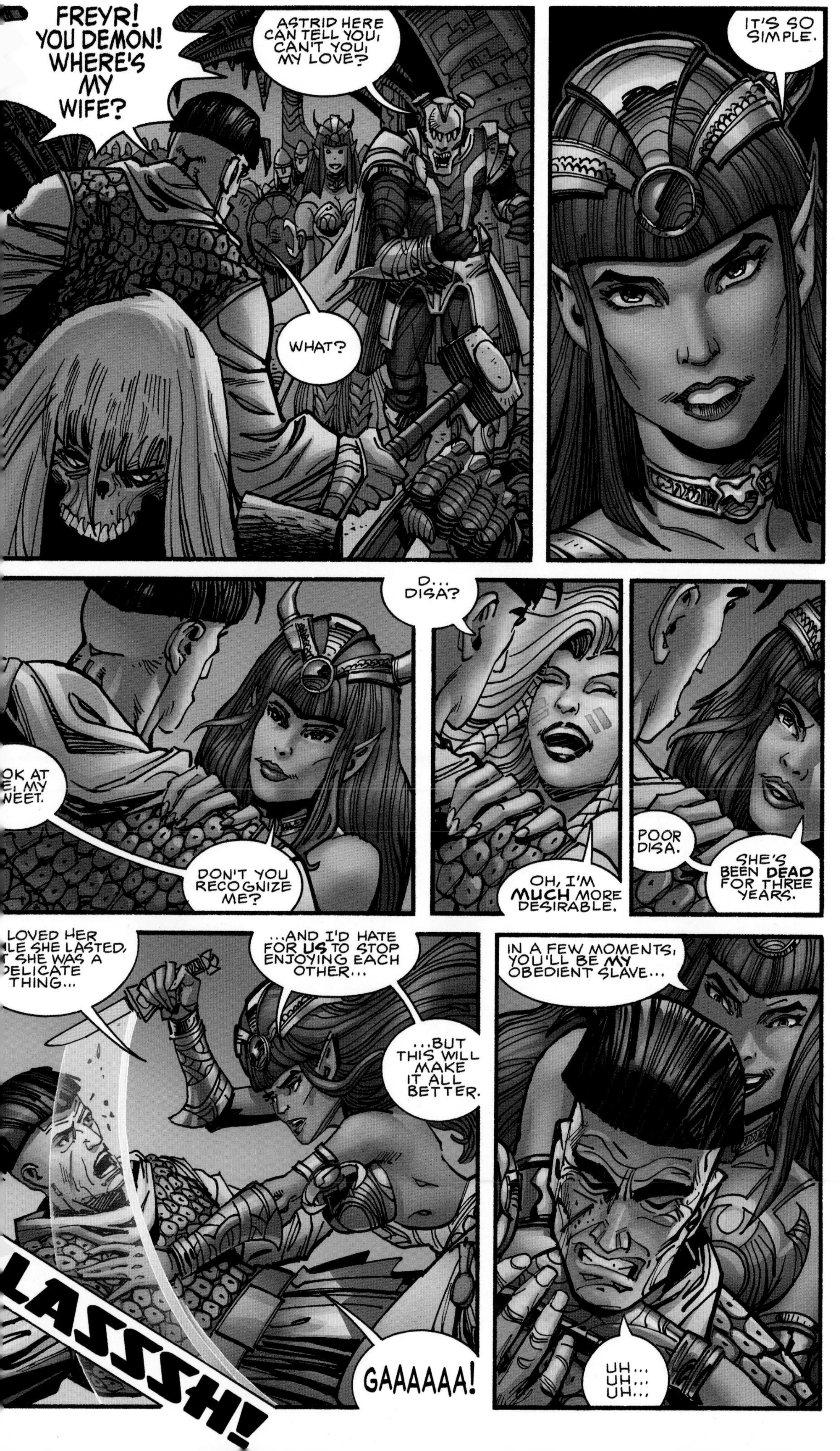

FREYR! YOU DEMON! WHERE'S MY WIFE?
ASTRID HERE CAN TELL YOU, CAN'T YOU, MY LOVE?
WHAT?
IT'S SO SIMPLE.
OK AT E, MY WEET.
DON'T YOU RECOGNIZE ME?
D... DISA?
OH, I'M MUCH MORE DESIRABLE.
POOR DISA.
SHE'S BEEN DEAD FOR THREE YEARS.
LOVED HER ILE SHE LASTED, T SHE WAS A DELICATE THING...
...AND I'D HATE FOR US TO STOP ENJOYING EACH OTHER...
...BUT THIS WILL MAKE IT ALL BETTER.
LASSSH!
GAAAAAA!
IN A FEW MOMENTS, YOU'LL BE MY OBEDIENT SLAVE...
UH... UH... UH...

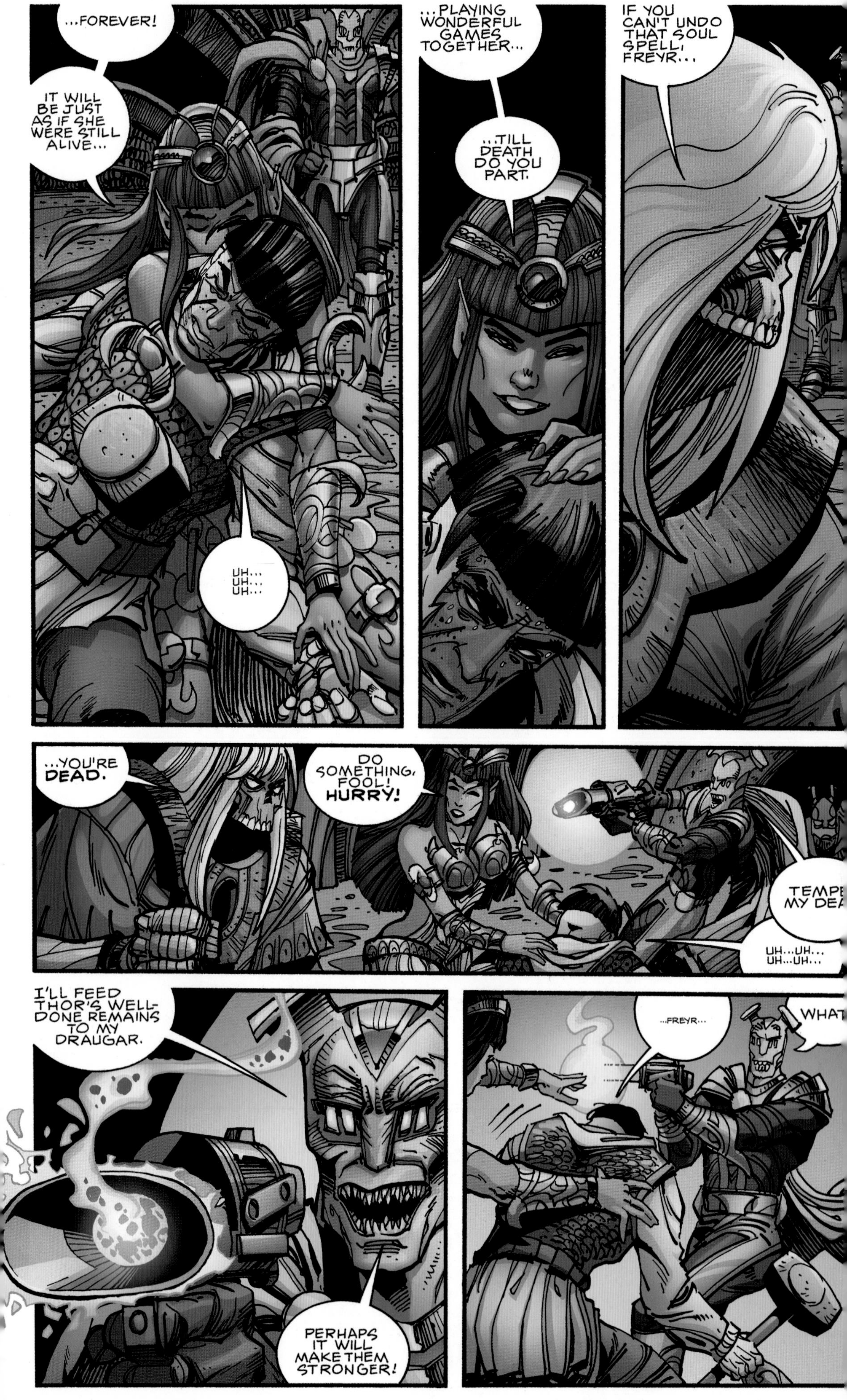
...FOREVER!
IT WILL BE JUST AS IF SHE WERE STILL ALIVE...
UH... UH... UH...
...PLAYING WONDERFUL GAMES TOGETHER...
...TILL DEATH DO YOU PART.
IF YOU CAN'T UNDO THAT SOUL SPELL, FREYR...
...YOU'RE DEAD.
DO SOMETHING, FOOL! HURRY!
TEMPE MY DEA
UH...UH... UH...UH...
I'LL FEED THOR'S WELL-DONE REMAINS TO MY DRAUGAR.
PERHAPS IT WILL MAKE THEM STRONGER!
...FREYR...
WHAT

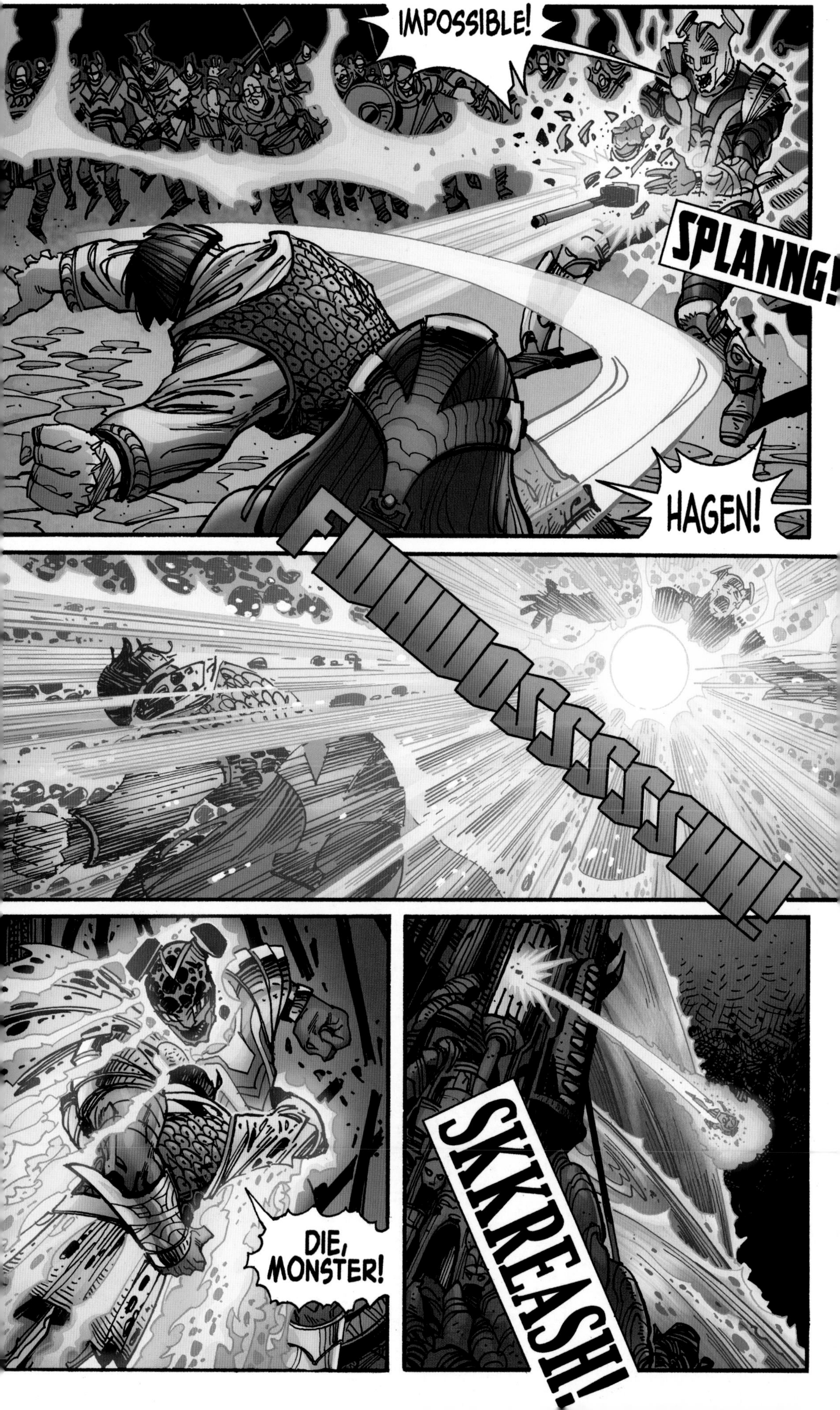
IMPOSSIBLE!
SPLANNG!
HAGEN!
FWHOOSSSSSHH!
DIE, MONSTER!
SKKREASH!

FREYR'S SCREAMS ARE LOST IN THE ROARING SOUNDS OF THE GREAT CATARACT.

GONE. AND BY THE LOOK OF IT, THE FALLS REACH ALL THE WAY DOWN INTO GINNUNGAGAP ITSELF.

SO BE IT. FIRE HAS TAKEN THE REST. MY WORK HERE IS DONE.

NOT QUITE. HAVE YOU FORGOTTEN ME ALREADY?

GRAND-MOTHER!

THAT WAS CLEVER, THOR. THANK YOU.

A GRA MOTH NC LONG

I THINK YOU'VE EARNED ANOTHER DRAW.

BUT YOU WILL BE MINE EVENTUAL ODINSON

YO WILL MINE

FIFFTHHHH!

SHE'S... GONE!

THE HALL STILL STINKS OF BRIMSTONE.

MY LORD? WHY DID YOU NOT PUT THE FLAMES OUT? SAVE HAGEN?

HE WOULD NOT HAVE THANKED ME.

HE VENGED HIMSELF UPON FREYR...

...AND DIED A HERO'S DEATH.

NO WARRIOR COULD ASK FOR MORE.

AND IF THERE IS SOME SORT OF EXISTENCE BEYOND THIS BLEAK WORLD...

HE'LL SURELY BE WELCOMED AMONG THE VALIANT.

MY LORD, WE FOUND THE TREACHEROUS GRYMIR...

...HIDING IN A CORRIDOR.

SHOULD WE NOT KILL HIM, AS WELL?

MERCY, MY LORD THOR! MERCY!

I SWEAR FREYR FORCED ME TO AID HIM.

YOU ARE A LIAR, GRYMIR...

...BUT THERE HAS BEEN A FAIR DAY'S WORTH OF KILLING ALREADY.

GET OUT. LET ME NOT SEE THEE AGAIN UNDER PAIN OF DEATH.

NOW THEN, GENTLEMEN...

...TAKE ME TO THE ARMORY.

I WOULD SEE THIS CACHE OF SOUL BLADES FOR MYSELF.

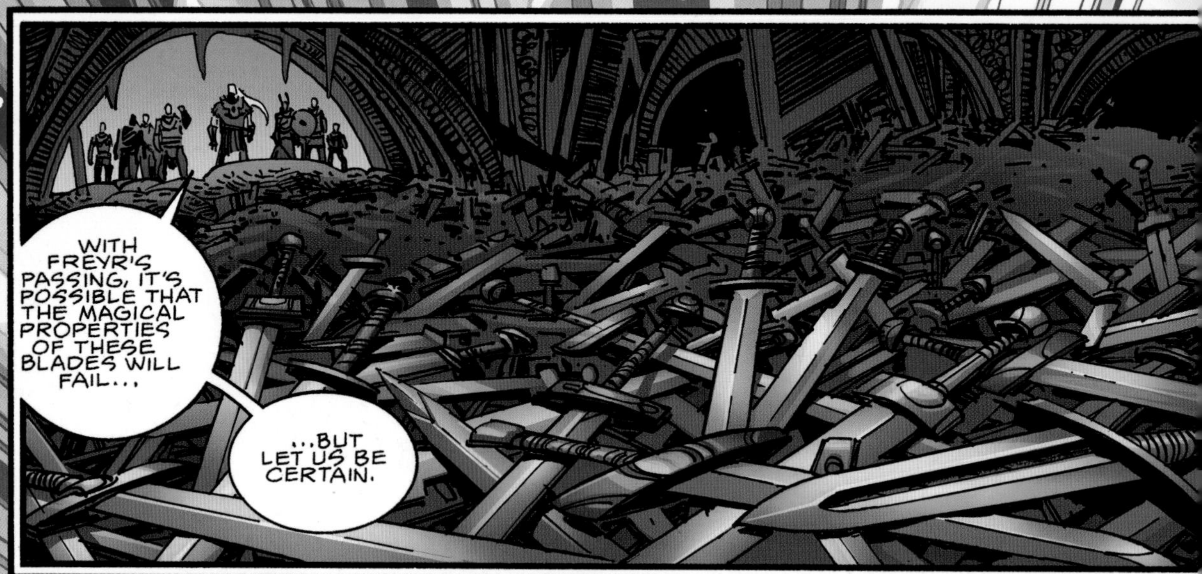
WITH FREYR'S PASSING, IT'S POSSIBLE THAT THE MAGICAL PROPERTIES OF THESE BLADES WILL FAIL...
...BUT LET US BE CERTAIN.

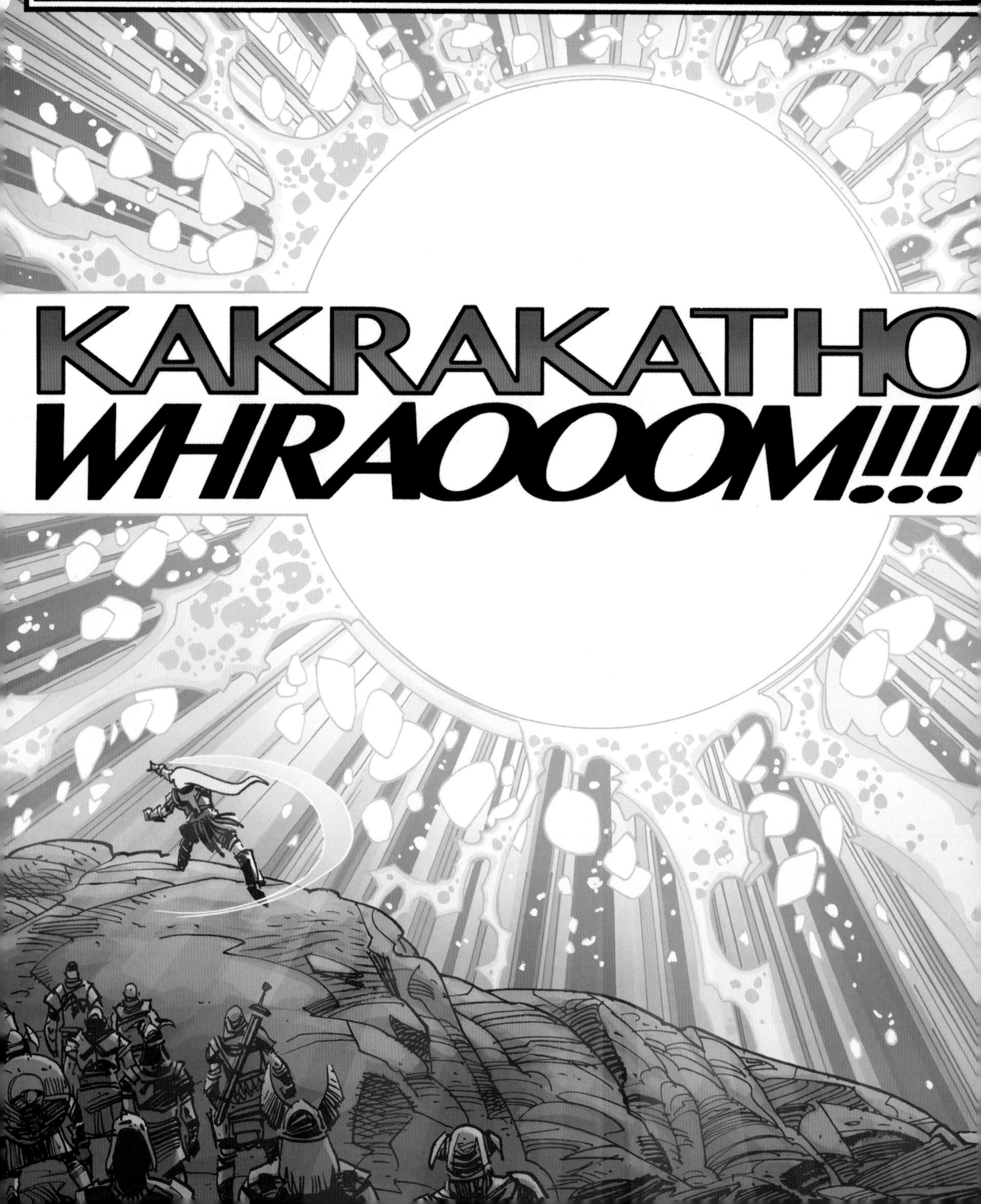
KAKRAKATHO
WHRAOOOM!!!

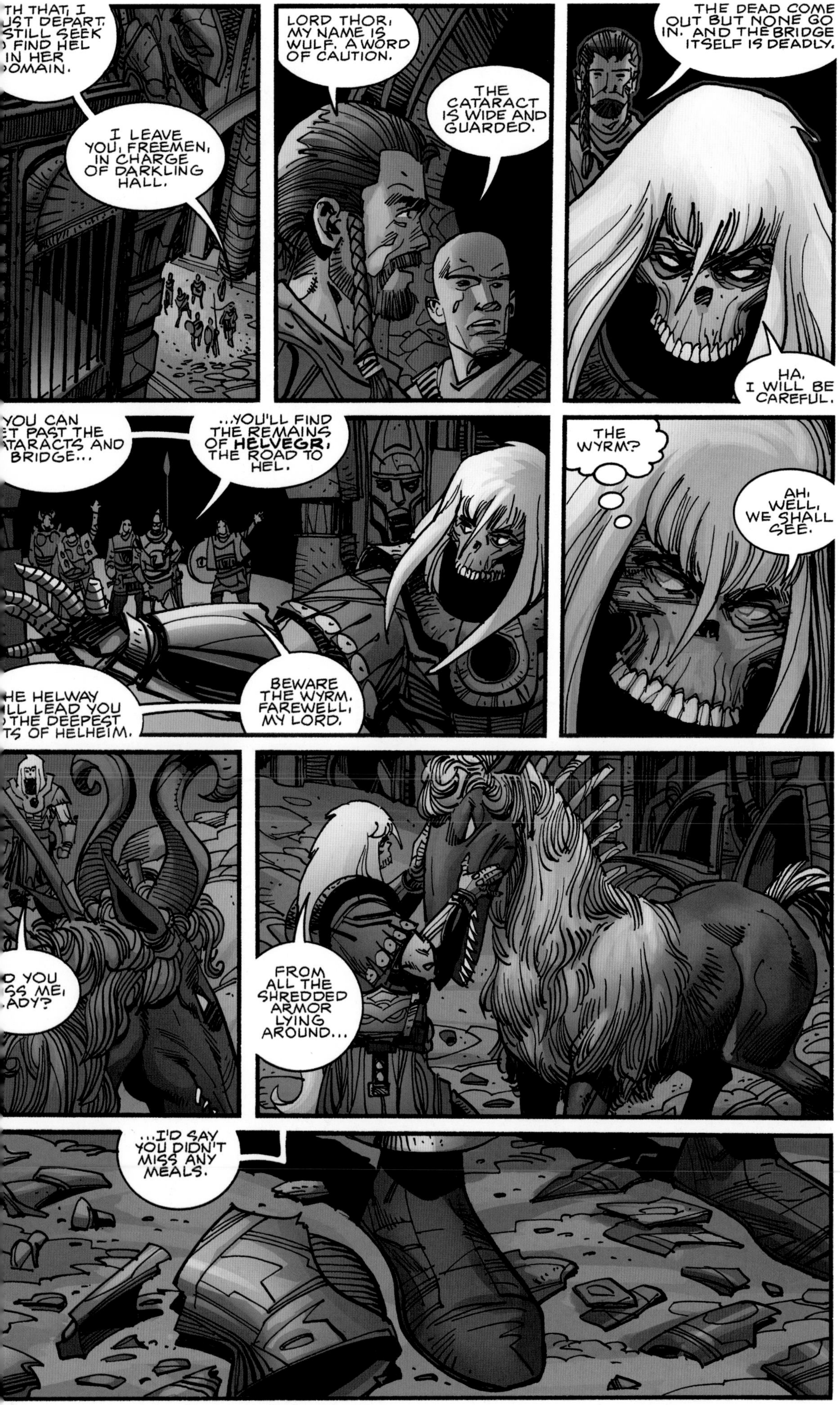
TH THAT, I
UST DEPART.
STILL SEEK
FIND HEL
IN HER
DOMAIN.
I LEAVE YOU, FREEMEN, IN CHARGE OF DARKLING HALL.
LORD THOR, MY NAME IS WULF. A WORD OF CAUTION.
THE CATARACT IS WIDE AND GUARDED.
THE DEAD COME OUT BUT NONE GO IN. AND THE BRIDGE ITSELF IS DEADLY.
HA, I WILL BE CAREFUL.
YOU CAN
T PAST THE
ATARACTS AND
BRIDGE...
...YOU'LL FIND THE REMAINS OF **HELVEGR**, THE ROAD TO HEL.
HE HELWAY
LL LEAD YOU
THE DEEPEST
TS OF HELHEIM.
BEWARE THE WYRM. FAREWELL, MY LORD.
THE WYRM?
AH, WELL, WE SHALL SEE.
D YOU
SS ME,
ADY?
FROM ALL THE SHREDDED ARMOR LYING AROUND...
...I'D SAY YOU DIDN'T MISS ANY MEALS.

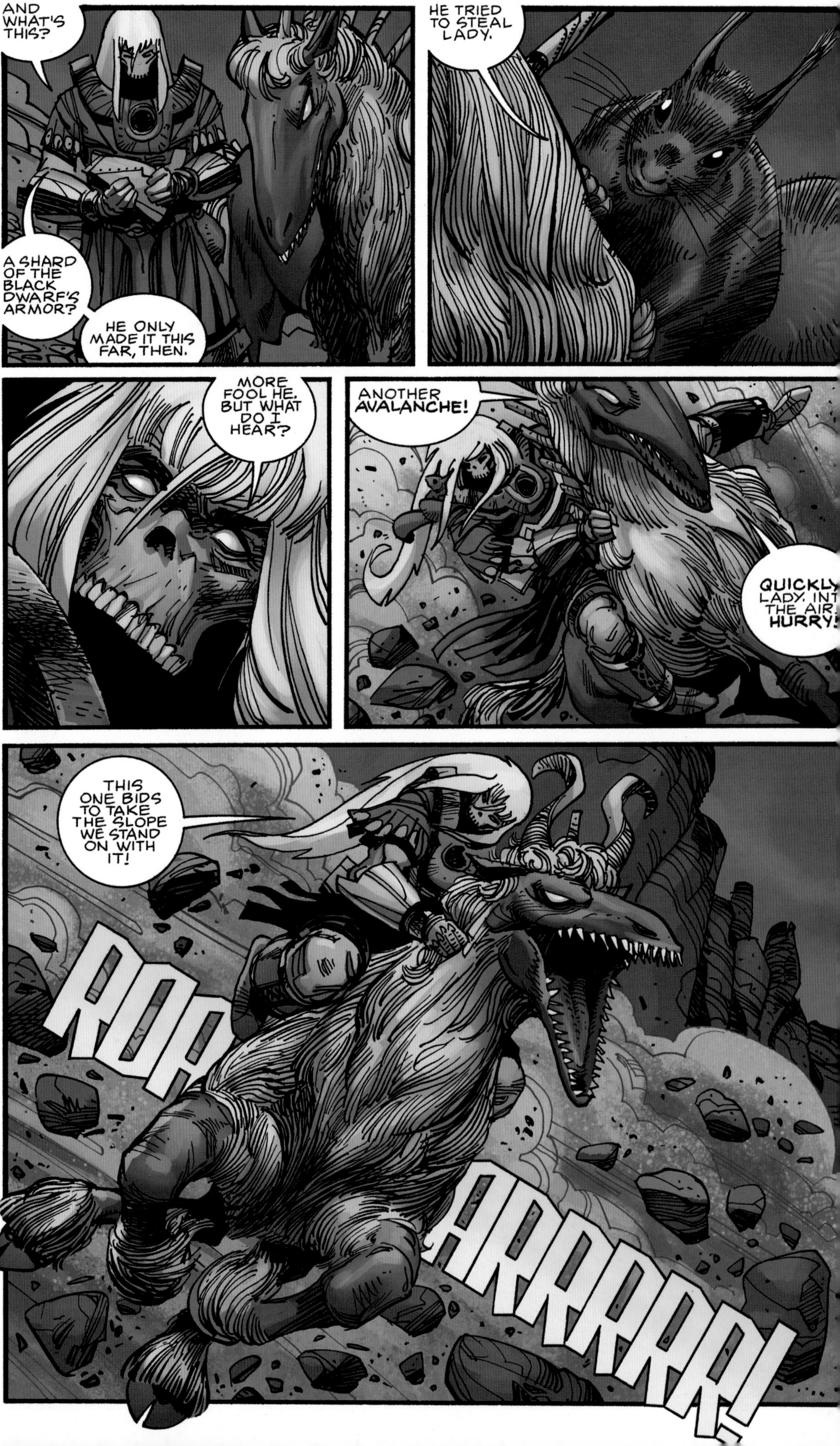
AND WHAT'S THIS?
A SHARD OF THE BLACK DWARF'S ARMOR?
HE ONLY MADE IT THIS FAR, THEN.
HE TRIED TO STEAL LADY.
MORE FOOL HE. BUT WHAT DO I HEAR?
ANOTHER AVALANCHE!
QUICKLY LADY, INT THE AIR! HURRY!
THIS ONE BIDS TO TAKE THE SLOPE WE STAND ON WITH IT!
ROARRRRRR!

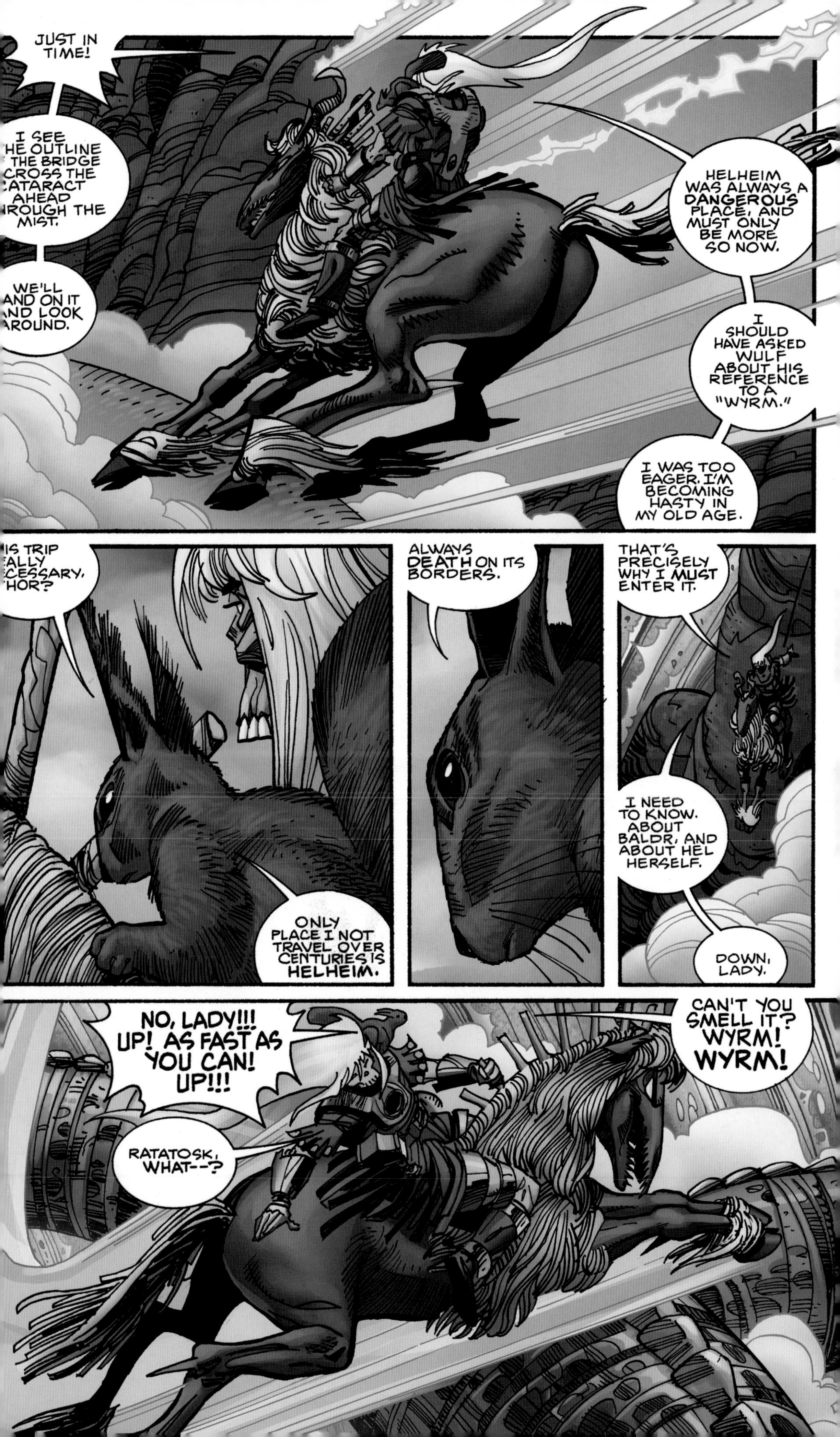
JUST IN TIME!
I SEE HE OUTLINE THE BRIDGE CROSS THE CATARACT AHEAD ROUGH THE MIST.
WE'LL AND ON IT AND LOOK AROUND.
HELHEIM WAS ALWAYS A DANGEROUS PLACE, AND MUST ONLY BE MORE SO NOW.
I SHOULD HAVE ASKED WULF ABOUT HIS REFERENCE TO A "WYRM."
I WAS TOO EAGER. I'M BECOMING HASTY IN MY OLD AGE.
IS TRIP ALLY ECESSARY, THOR?
ONLY PLACE I NOT TRAVEL OVER CENTURIES IS HELHEIM.
ALWAYS DEATH ON ITS BORDERS.
THAT'S PRECISELY WHY I MUST ENTER IT.
I NEED TO KNOW. ABOUT BALDR, AND ABOUT HEL HERSELF.
DOWN, LADY.
NO, LADY!!! UP! AS FAST AS YOU CAN! UP!!!
CAN'T YOU SMELL IT? WYRM! WYRM!
RATATOSK, WHAT--?

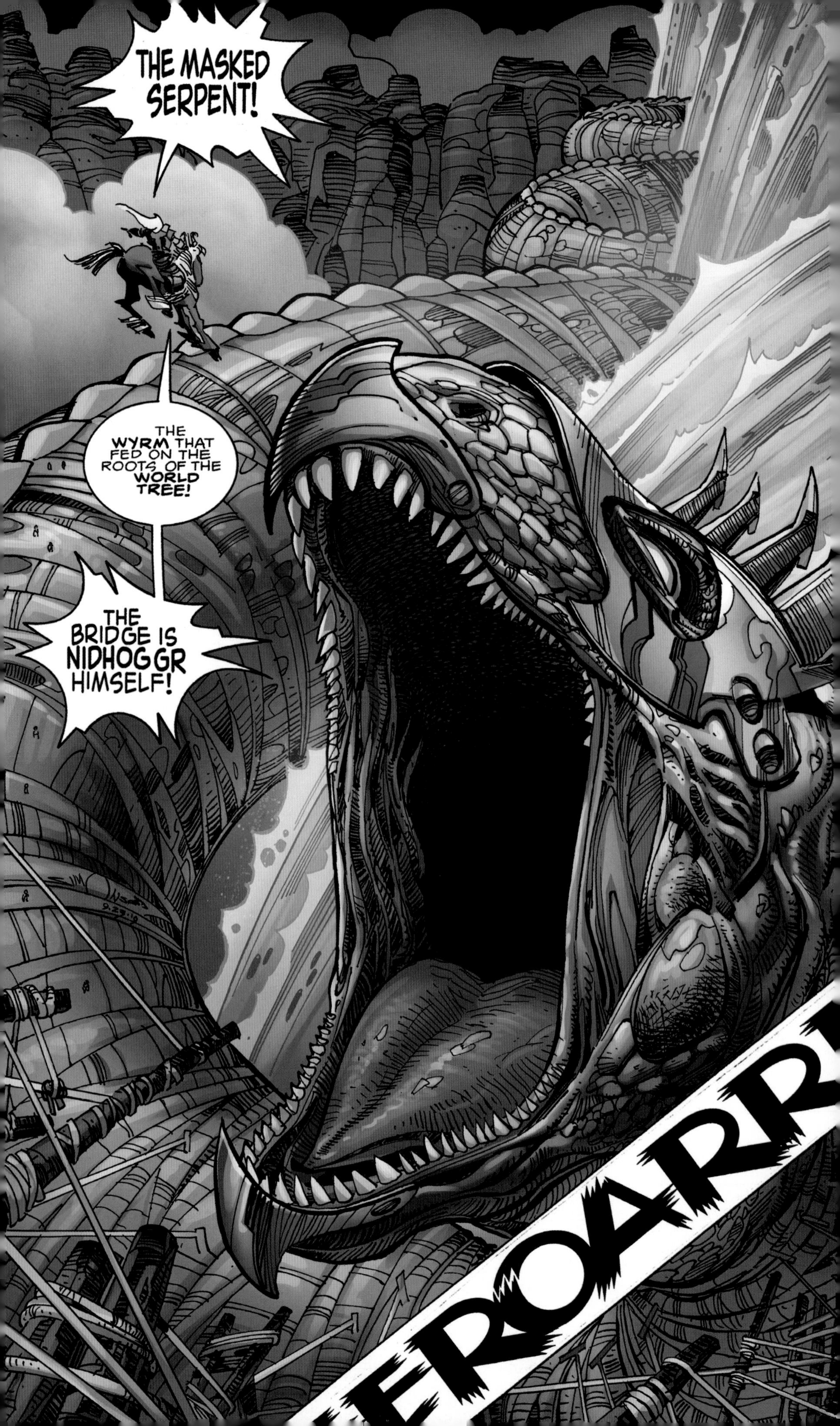

THE MASKED SERPENT!
THE WYRM THAT FED ON THE ROOTS OF THE WORLD TREE!
THE BRIDGE IS NIDHOGGR HIMSELF!
RROARR

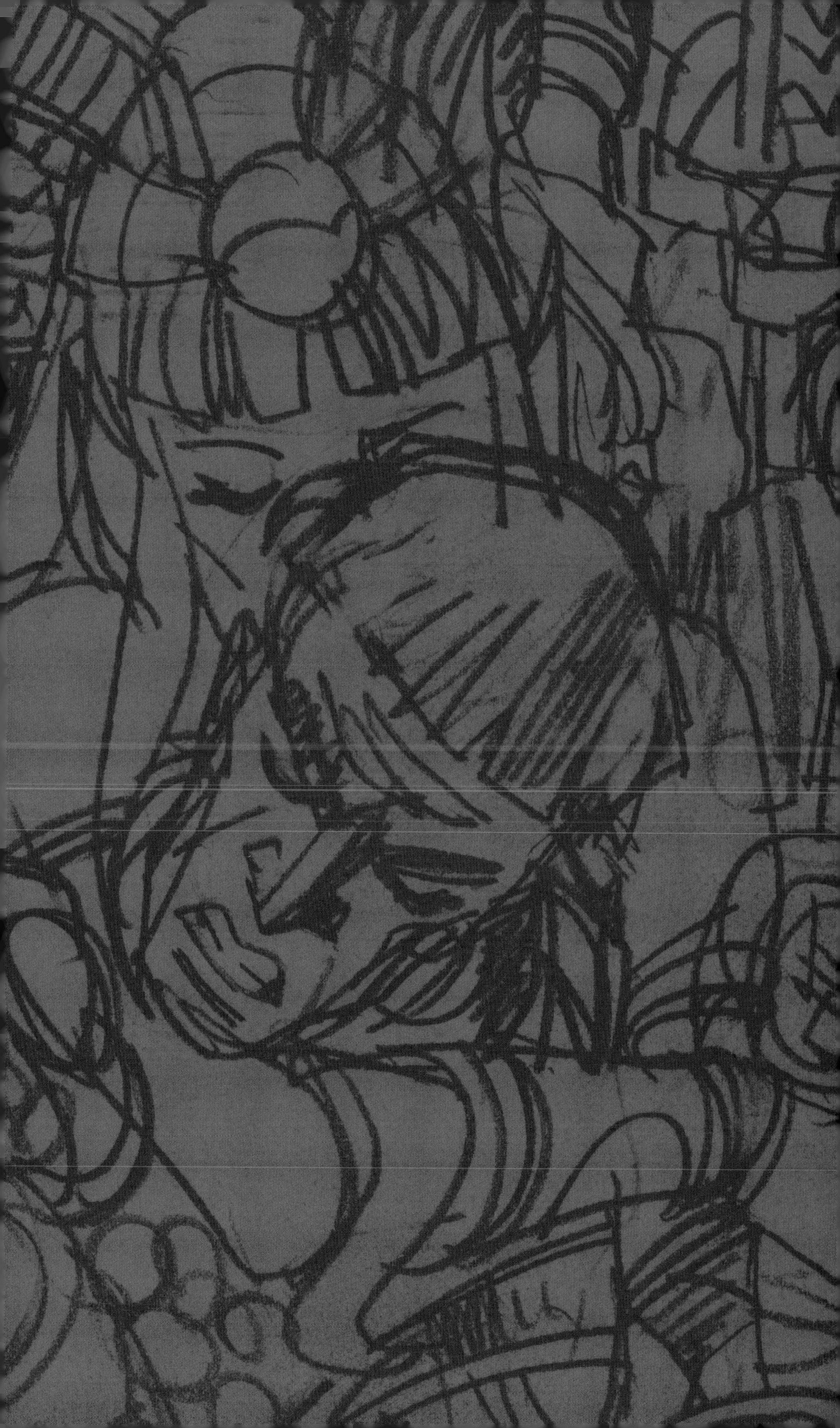

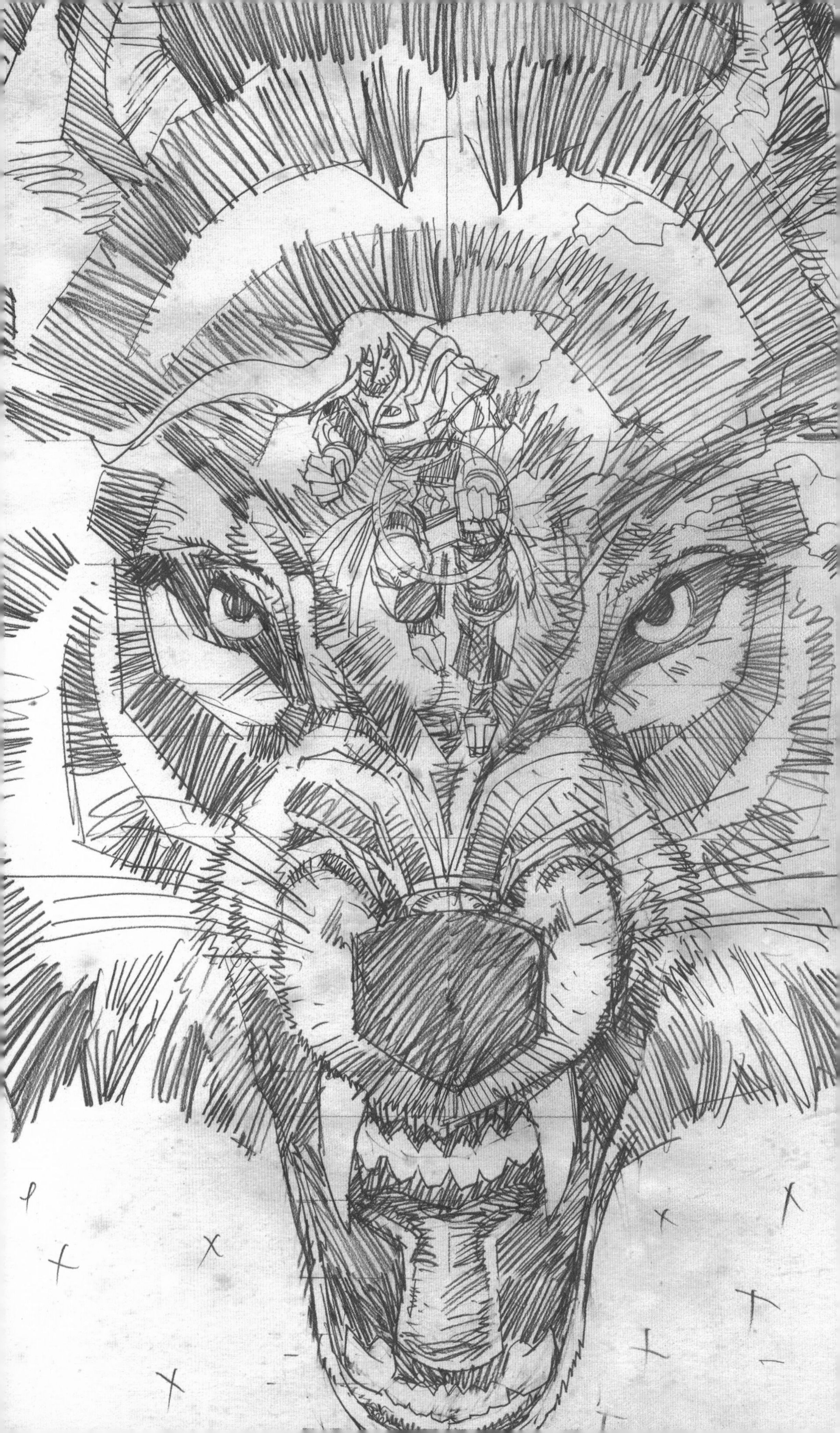

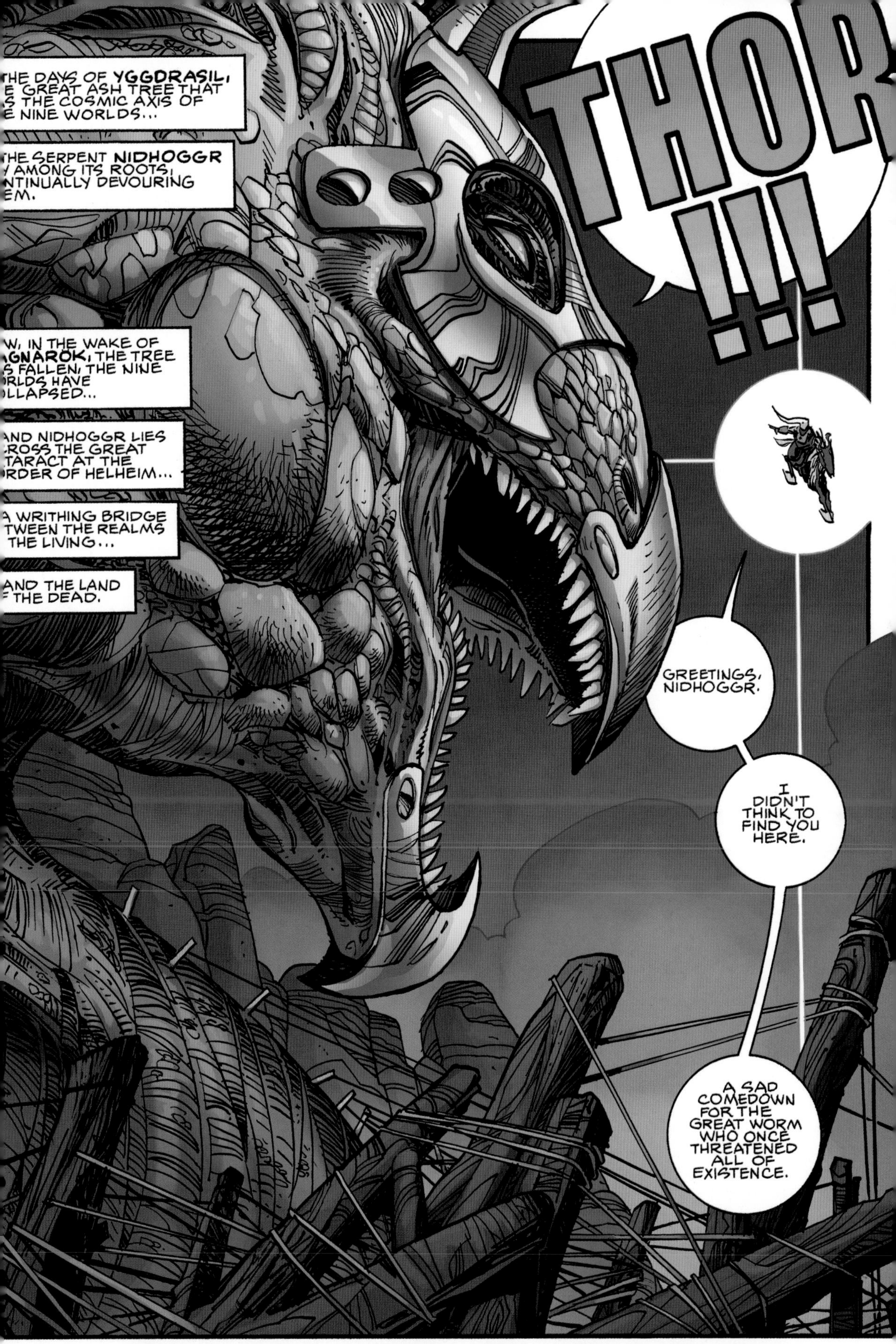
THE DAYS OF YGGDRASIL, E GREAT ASH TREE THAT S THE COSMIC AXIS OF E NINE WORLDS...
THE SERPENT NIDHOGGR Y AMONG ITS ROOTS, NTINUALLY DEVOURING EM.
THOR!!!!
W, IN THE WAKE OF GNARÖK, THE TREE S FALLEN, THE NINE ORLDS HAVE LLAPSED...
AND NIDHOGGR LIES CROSS THE GREAT TARACT AT THE RDER OF HELHEIM...
A WRITHING BRIDGE TWEEN THE REALMS THE LIVING...
AND THE LAND F THE DEAD.
GREETINGS, NIDHOGGR.
I DIDN'T THINK TO FIND YOU HERE.
A SAD COMEDOWN FOR THE GREAT WORM WHO ONCE THREATENED ALL OF EXISTENCE.

The WOLVES of HELHEIM...

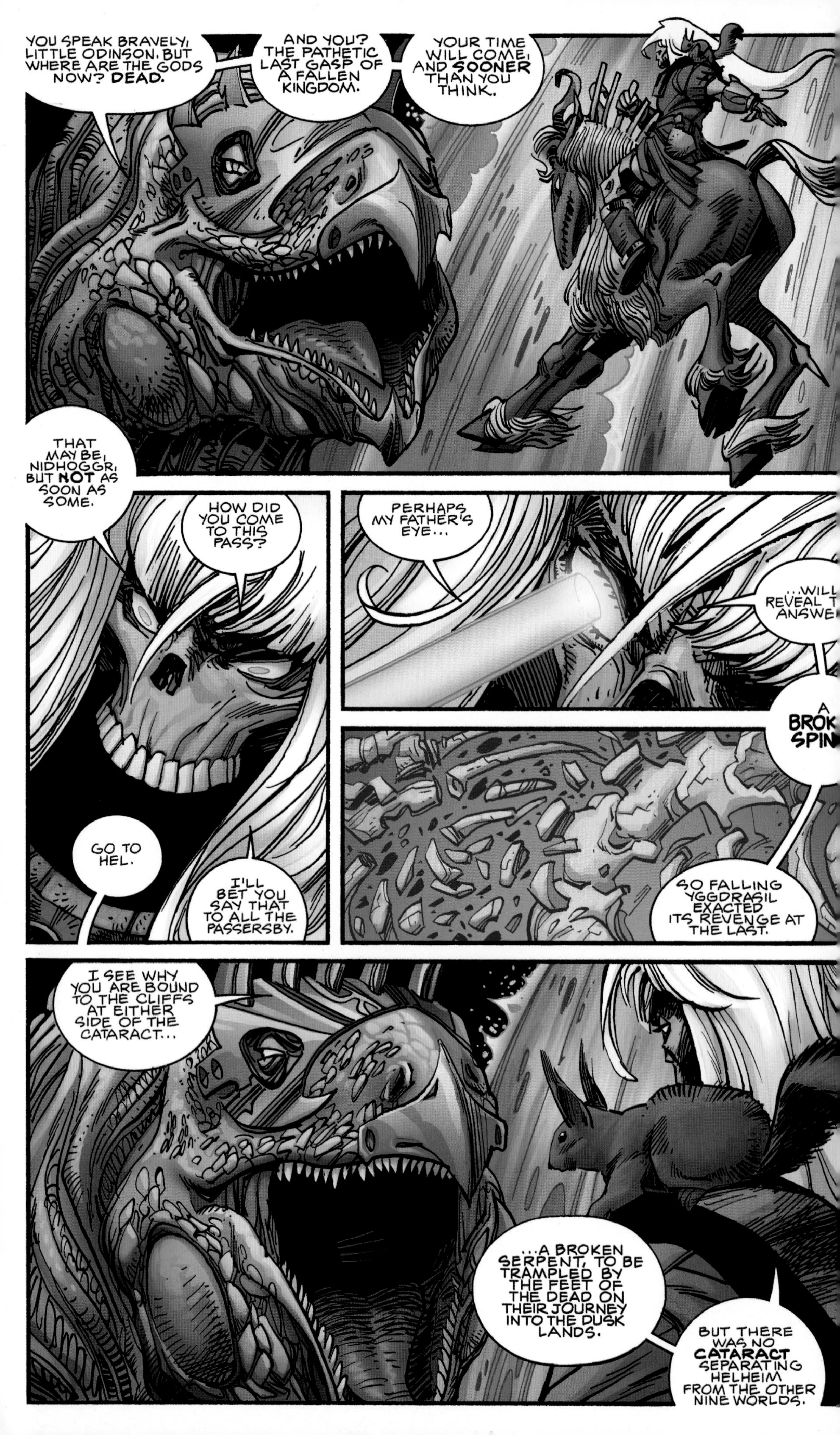

YOU SPEAK BRAVELY, LITTLE ODINSON. BUT WHERE ARE THE GODS NOW? **DEAD.**
AND YOU? THE PATHETIC LAST GASP OF A FALLEN KINGDOM.
YOUR TIME WILL COME, AND **SOONER** THAN YOU THINK.
THAT MAY BE, NIDHOGGR, BUT **NOT** AS SOON AS SOME.
HOW DID YOU COME TO THIS PASS?
PERHAPS MY FATHER'S EYE...
GO TO HEL.
I'LL BET YOU SAY THAT TO ALL THE PASSERSBY.
SO FALLING YGGDRASIL EXACTED ITS REVENGE AT THE LAST.
I SEE WHY YOU ARE BOUND TO THE CLIFFS AT EITHER SIDE OF THE CATARACT...
...A BROKEN SERPENT, TO BE TRAMPLED BY THE FEET OF THE DEAD ON THEIR JOURNEY INTO THE DUSK LANDS.
BUT THERE WAS NO **CATARACT** SEPARATING HELHEIM FROM THE OTHER NINE WORLDS.

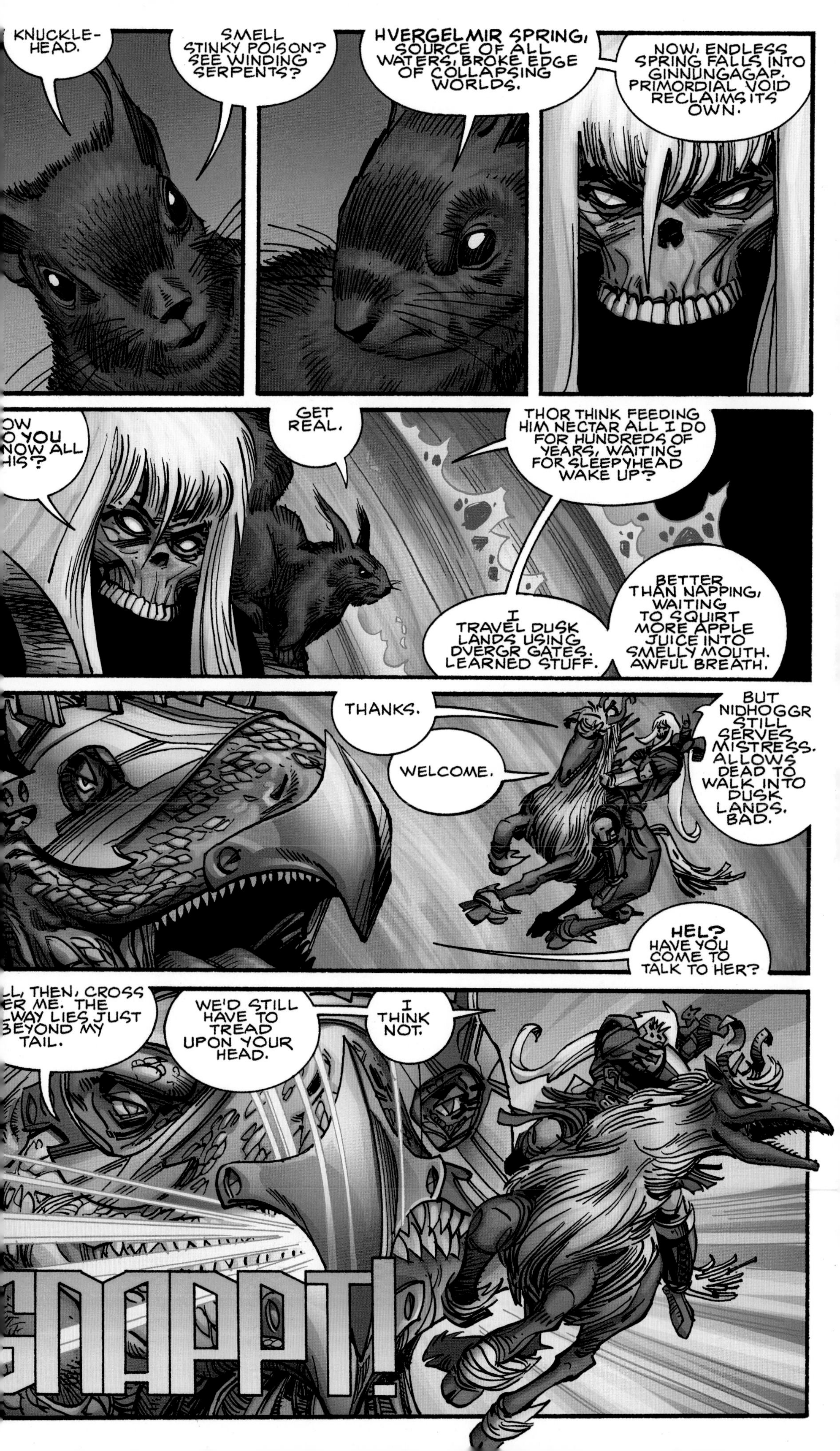
KNUCKLEHEAD.
SMELL STINKY POISON? SEE WINDING SERPENTS?
HVERGELMIR SPRING, SOURCE OF ALL WATERS, BROKE EDGE OF COLLAPSING WORLDS.
NOW, ENDLESS SPRING FALLS INTO GINNUNGAGAP. PRIMORDIAL VOID RECLAIMS ITS OWN.
OW O YOU NOW ALL HIS?
GET REAL.
THOR THINK FEEDING HIM NECTAR ALL I DO FOR HUNDREDS OF YEARS, WAITING FOR SLEEPYHEAD WAKE UP?
I TRAVEL DUSK LANDS USING DVERGR GATES. LEARNED STUFF.
BETTER THAN NAPPING, WAITING TO SQUIRT MORE APPLE JUICE INTO SMELLY MOUTH. AWFUL BREATH.
THANKS.
WELCOME.
BUT NIDHOGGR STILL SERVES MISTRESS. ALLOWS DEAD TO WALK INTO DUSK LANDS. BAD.
HEL? HAVE YOU COME TO TALK TO HER?
LL, THEN, CROSS ER ME. THE LWAY LIES JUST BEYOND MY TAIL.
WE'D STILL HAVE TO TREAD UPON YOUR HEAD.
I THINK NOT.
SNAPPT!

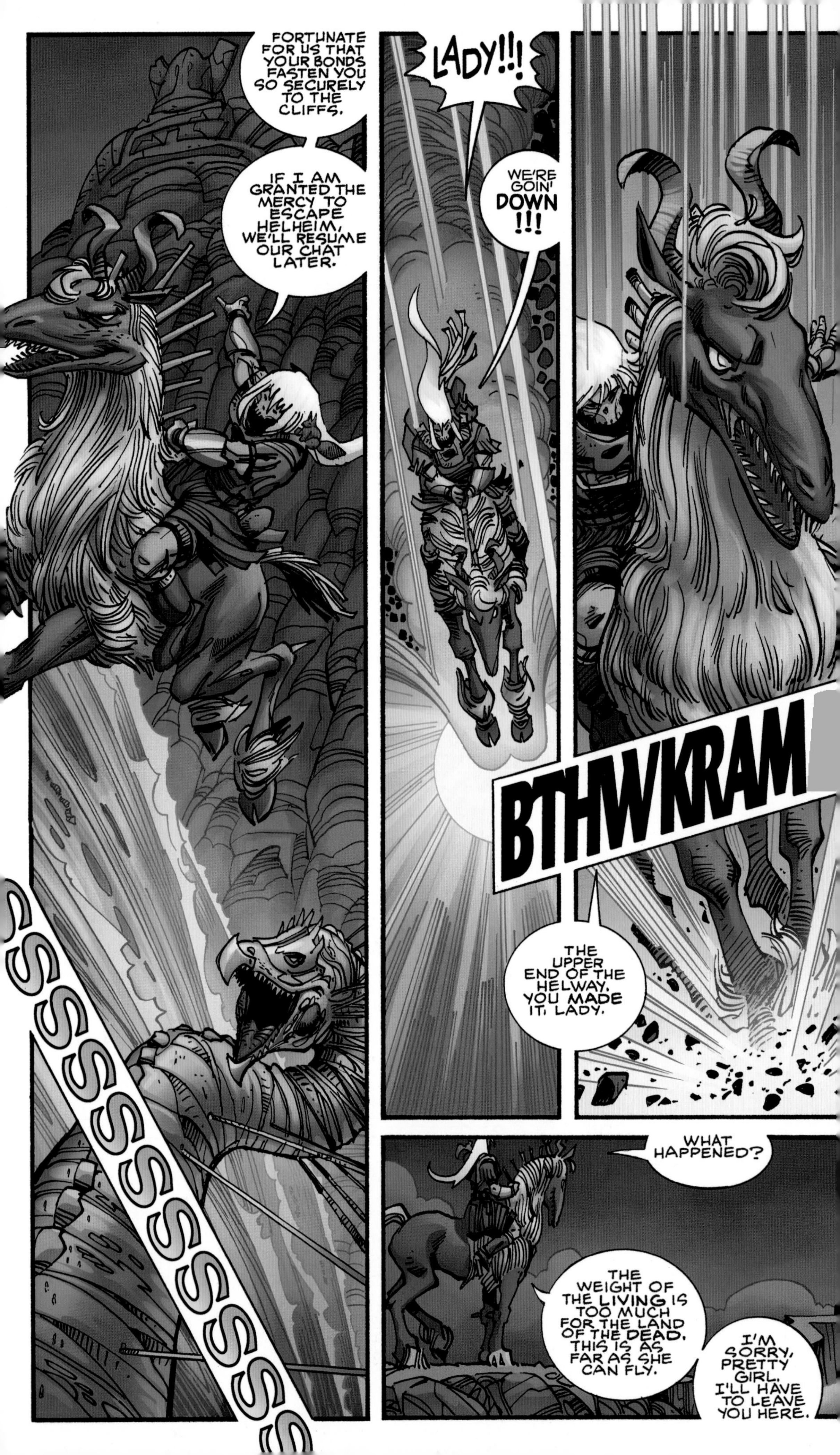
FORTUNATE FOR US THAT YOUR BONDS FASTEN YOU SO SECURELY TO THE CLIFFS.
IF I AM GRANTED THE MERCY TO ESCAPE HELHEIM, WE'LL RESUME OUR CHAT LATER.
SSSSSSSSSSSSS
LADY!!!
WE'RE GOIN' DOWN !!!
BTHWKRAM
THE UPPER END OF THE HELWAY. YOU MADE IT, LADY.
WHAT HAPPENED?
THE WEIGHT OF THE LIVING IS TOO MUCH FOR THE LAND OF THE DEAD. THIS IS AS FAR AS SHE CAN FLY.
I'M SORRY, PRETTY GIRL. I'LL HAVE TO LEAVE YOU HERE.

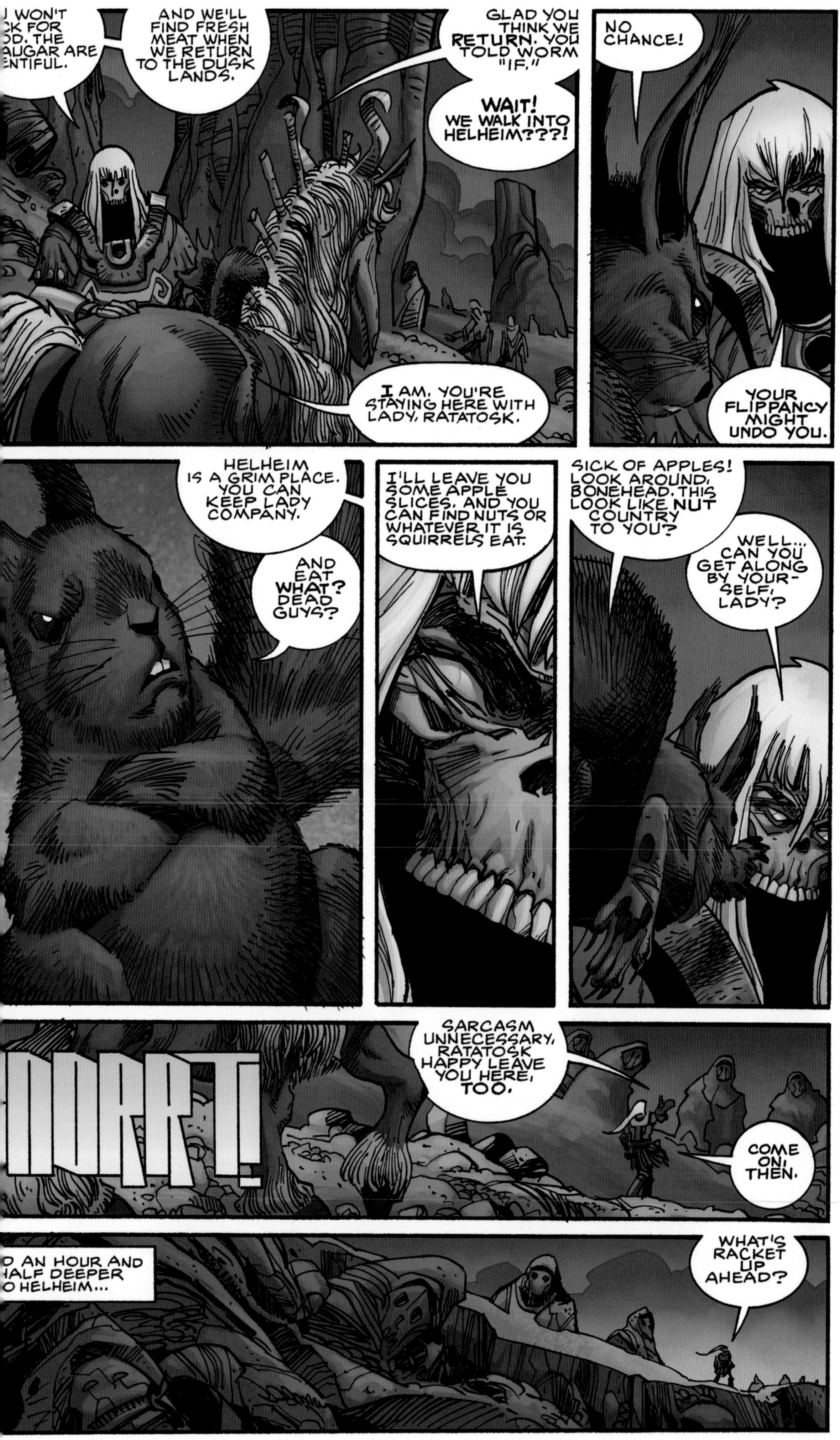

U WON'T CK FOR OD. THE AUGAR ARE ENTIFUL.
AND WE'LL FIND FRESH MEAT WHEN WE RETURN TO THE DUSK LANDS.
GLAD YOU THINK WE RETURN. YOU TOLD WORM "IF."
WAIT! WE WALK INTO HELHEIM???!
I AM. YOU'RE STAYING HERE WITH LADY, RATATOSK.
NO CHANCE!
YOUR FLIPPANCY MIGHT UNDO YOU.
HELHEIM IS A GRIM PLACE. YOU CAN KEEP LADY COMPANY.
AND EAT WHAT? DEAD GUYS?
I'LL LEAVE YOU SOME APPLE SLICES. AND YOU CAN FIND NUTS OR WHATEVER IT IS SQUIRRELS EAT.
SICK OF APPLES! LOOK AROUND, BONEHEAD. THIS LOOK LIKE NUT COUNTRY TO YOU?
WELL... CAN YOU GET ALONG BY YOUR-SELF, LADY?
DORRT!
SARCASM UNNECESSARY. RATATOSK HAPPY LEAVE YOU HERE, TOO.
COME ON, THEN.
D AN HOUR AND HALF DEEPER O HELHEIM...
WHAT'S RACKET UP AHEAD?

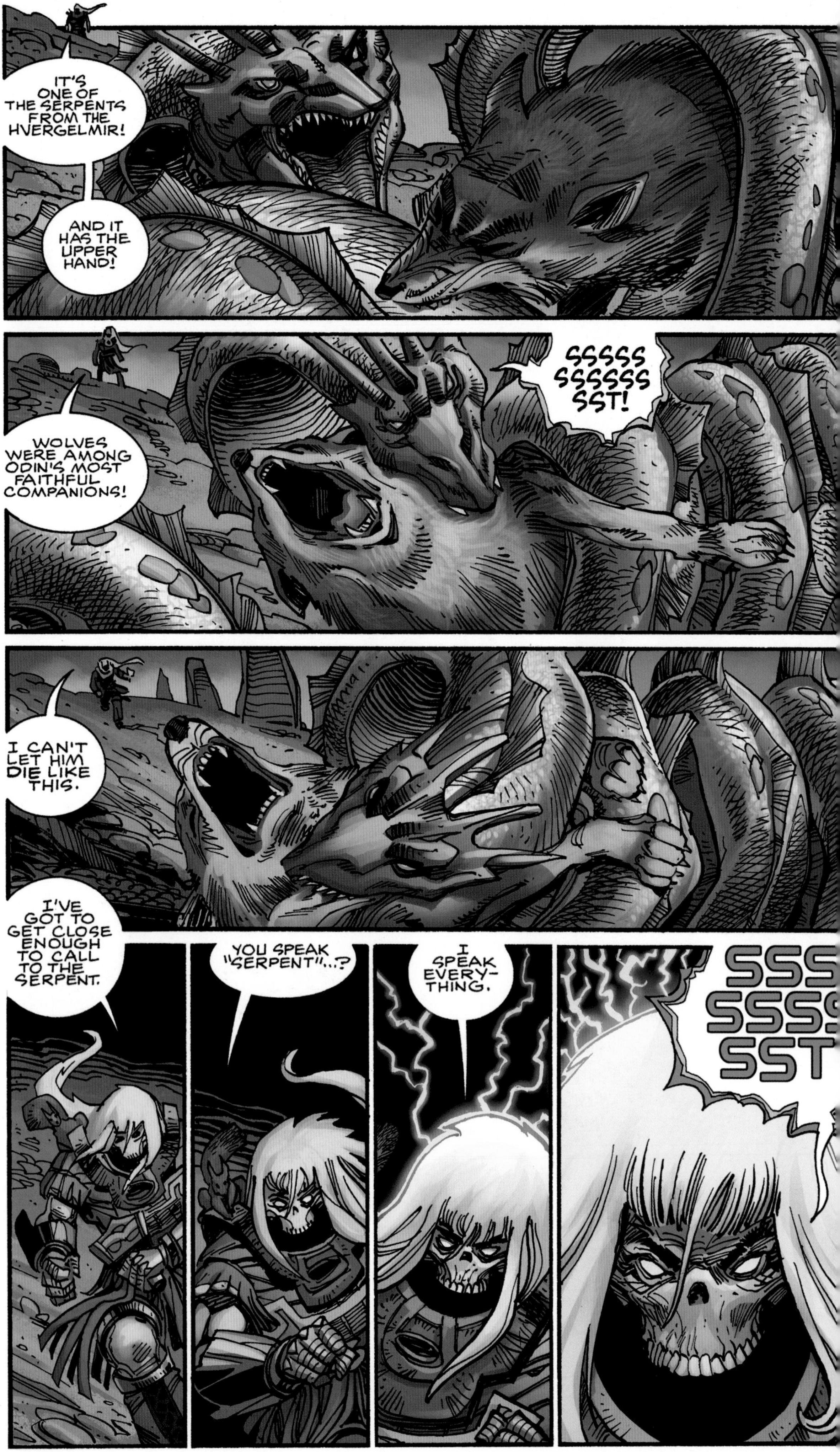
IT'S ONE OF THE SERPENTS FROM THE HVERGELMIR!
AND IT HAS THE UPPER HAND!
WOLVES WERE AMONG ODIN'S MOST FAITHFUL COMPANIONS!
SSSSS SSSSSS SST!
I CAN'T LET HIM DIE LIKE THIS.
I'VE GOT TO GET CLOSE ENOUGH TO CALL TO THE SERPENT.
YOU SPEAK "SERPENT"...?
I SPEAK EVERY-THING.

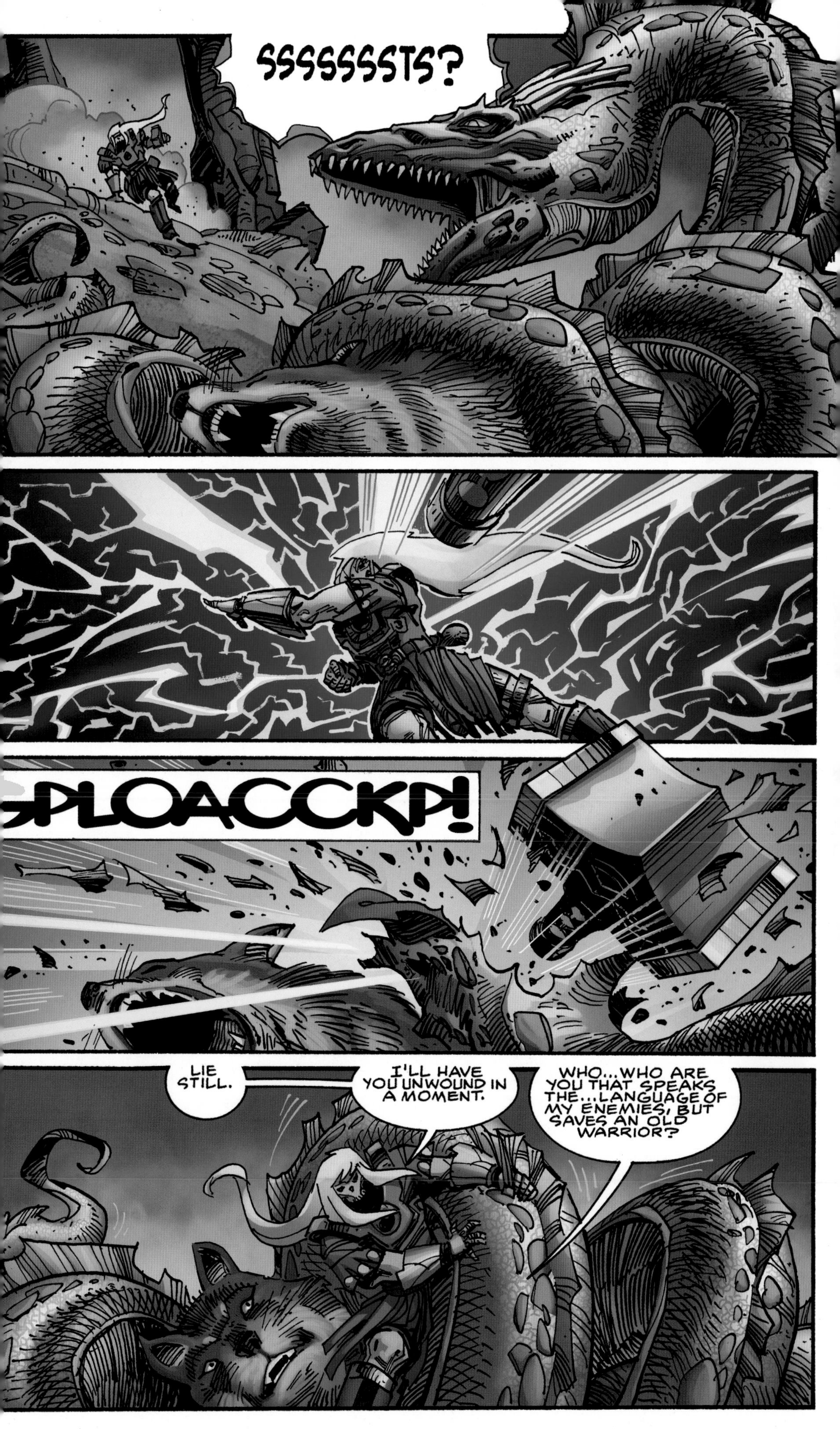
SSSSSSSSTS?
SPLOACCKP!
LIE STILL.
I'LL HAVE YOU UNWOUND IN A MOMENT.
WHO...WHO ARE YOU THAT SPEAKS THE...LANGUAGE OF MY ENEMIES, BUT SAVES AN OLD WARRIOR?

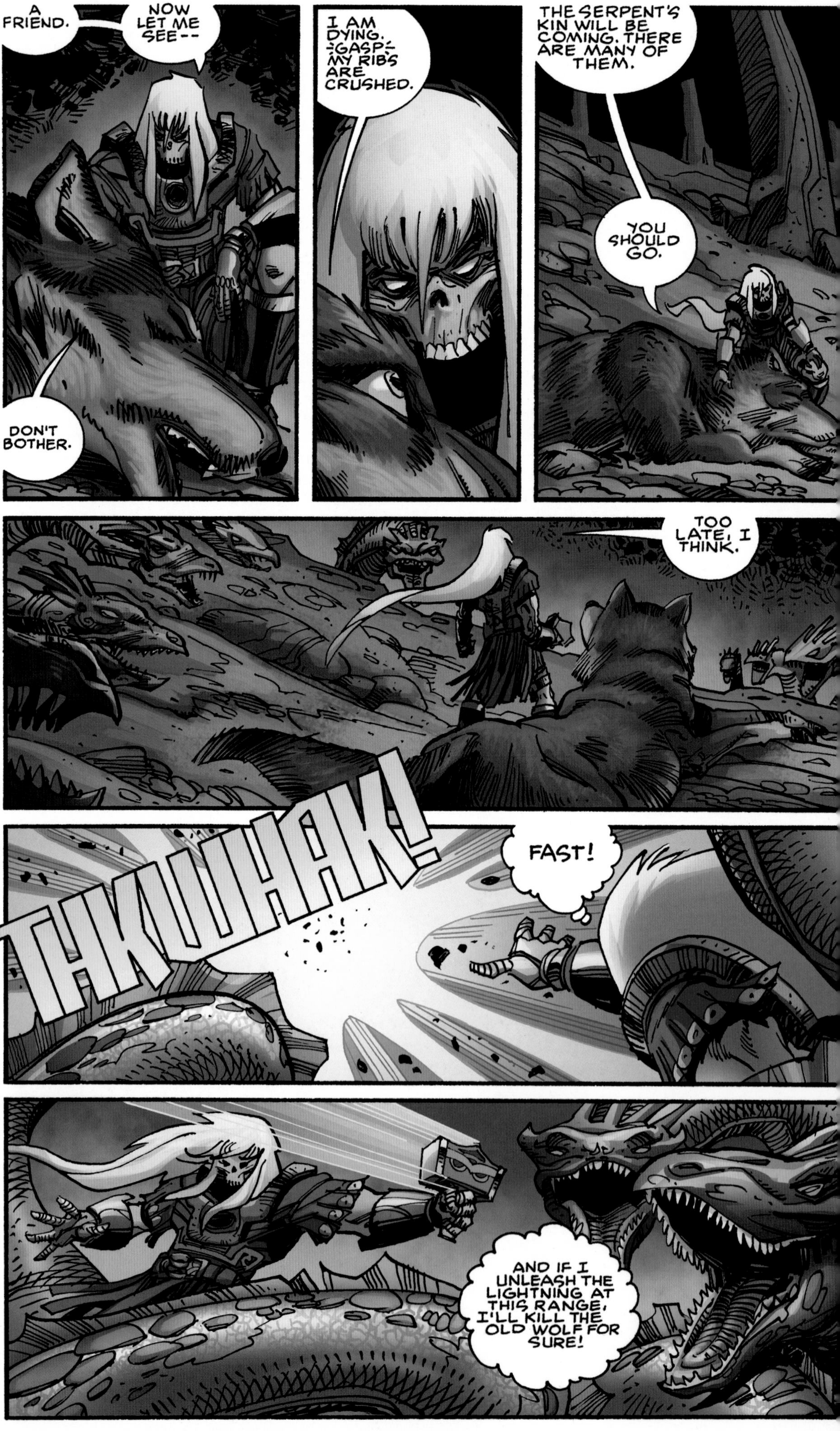
A FRIEND.
NOW LET ME SEE--
DON'T BOTHER.
I AM DYING. -GASP- MY RIB'S ARE CRUSHED.
THE SERPENT'S KIN WILL BE COMING. THERE ARE MANY OF THEM.
YOU SHOULD GO.
TOO LATE, I THINK.
THWAK!
FAST!
AND IF I UNLEASH THE LIGHTNING AT THIS RANGE, I'LL KILL THE OLD WOLF FOR SURE!

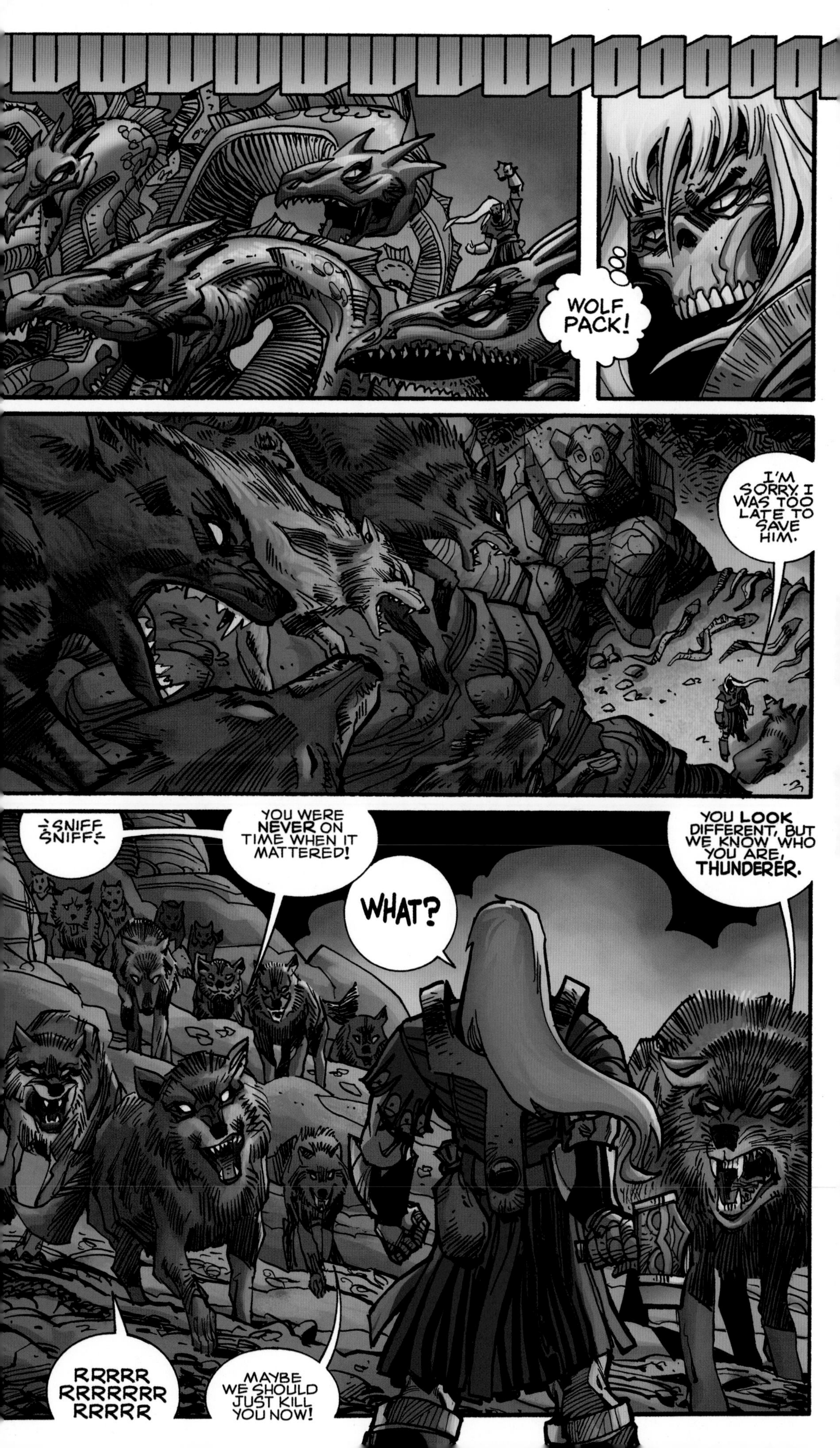
WWWWWWWWWOOOOOO
WOLF PACK!
I'M SORRY. I WAS TOO LATE TO SAVE HIM.
SNIFF SNIFF
YOU WERE NEVER ON TIME WHEN IT MATTERED!
WHAT?
YOU LOOK DIFFERENT, BUT WE KNOW WHO YOU ARE, THUNDERER.
RRRRR RRRRRRR RRRRR
MAYBE WE SHOULD JUST KILL YOU NOW!

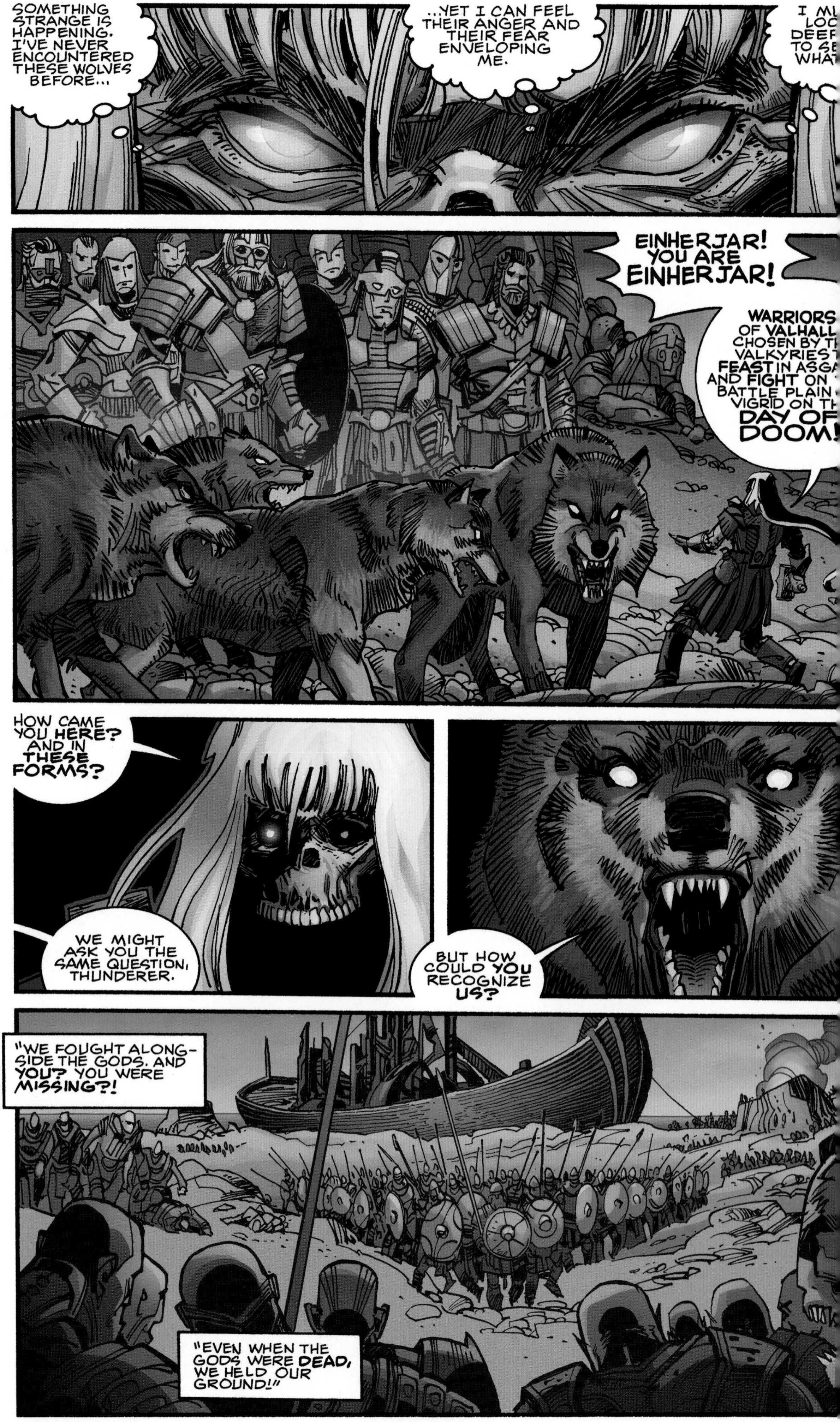
SOMETHING STRANGE IS HAPPENING. I'VE NEVER ENCOUNTERED THESE WOLVES BEFORE...
...YET I CAN FEEL THEIR ANGER AND THEIR FEAR ENVELOPING ME.
EINHERJAR! YOU ARE EINHERJAR!
WARRIORS OF VALHALL CHOSEN BY T VALKYRIES T FEAST IN ASGA AND FIGHT ON BATTLE PLAIN VIGRID ON TH DAY OF DOOM!
HOW CAME YOU HERE? AND IN THESE FORMS?
WE MIGHT ASK YOU THE SAME QUESTION, THUNDERER.
BUT HOW COULD YOU RECOGNIZE US?
"WE FOUGHT ALONGSIDE THE GODS. AND YOU? YOU WERE MISSING?!
"EVEN WHEN THE GODS WERE DEAD, WE HELD OUR GROUND!"

"BUT THERE WAS NO WAY OUT FOR US ACROSS VIGRID.

"BEHIND US, THE GREAT SHIP NAGLFAR RESTED AT ANCHOR, STILL SITTING WHERE SHE HAD DISGORGED HER CARGO OF THE DEAD OF HELHEIM TO ATTACK THE GODS AND THEIR ALLIES.

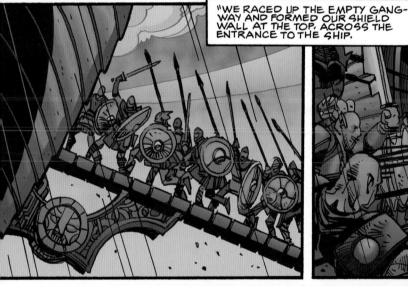

"WE RACED UP THE EMPTY GANG-WAY AND FORMED OUR SHIELD WALL AT THE TOP, ACROSS THE ENTRANCE TO THE SHIP.

"WHEN THEY CAME FOR US, THE WAY WAS TOO NARROW. WE SLAUGHTERED THEM.

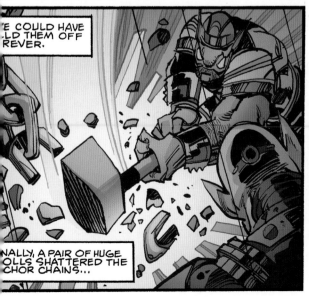

"E COULD HAVE LD THEM OFF REVER.

NALLY, A PAIR OF HUGE OLLS SHATTERED THE CHOR CHAINS...

"...AND SET THE GREAT SHIP ADRIFT.

"NO DOUBT THEY HOPED THE SHIP WOULD FOUNDER IN THE STORMY SEAS, DROWNING US ALL."

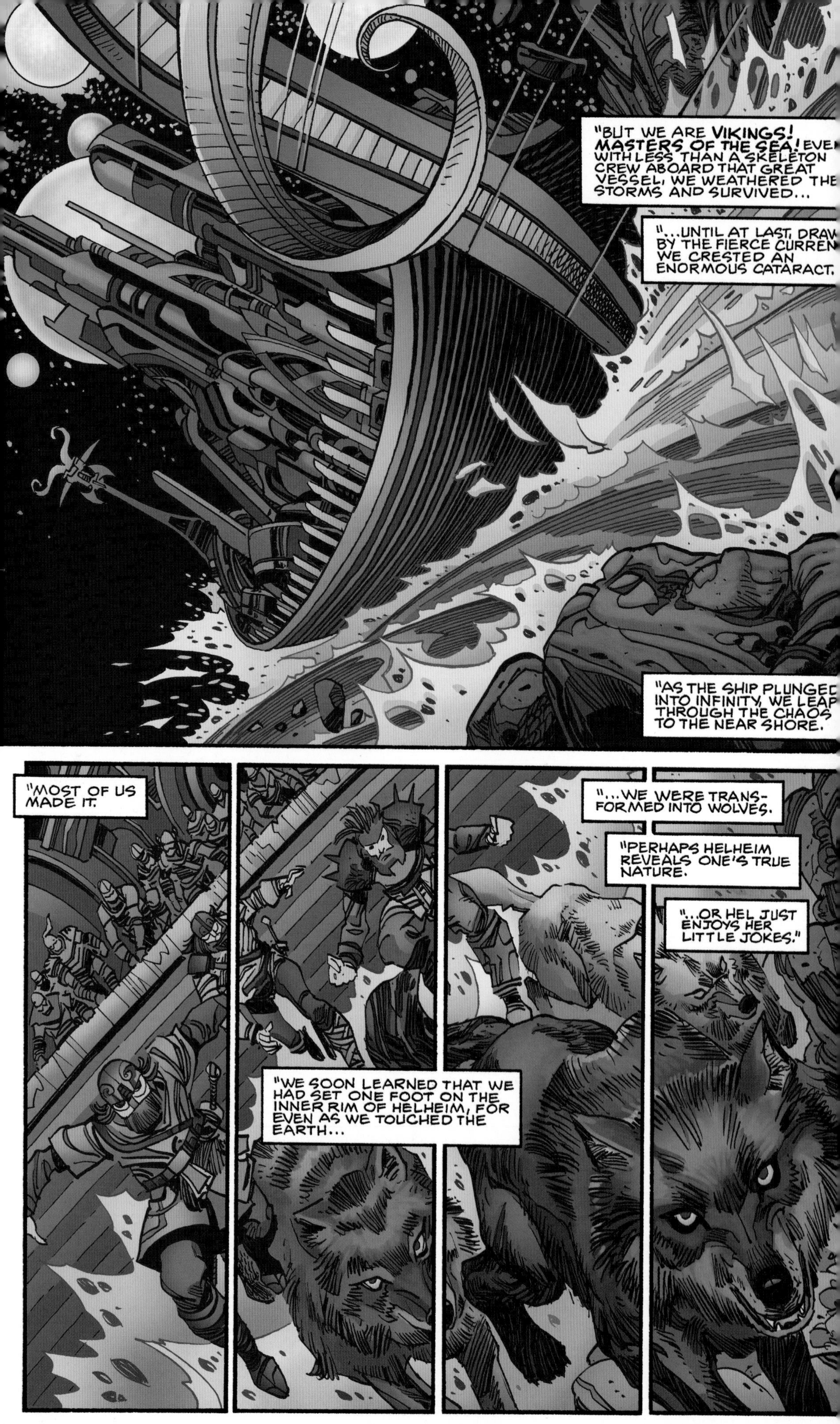

"BUT WE ARE **VIKINGS! MASTERS OF THE SEA!** EVE WITH LESS THAN A SKELETON CREW ABOARD THAT GREAT VESSEL, WE WEATHERED THE STORMS AND SURVIVED...
"...UNTIL AT LAST, DRAW BY THE FIERCE CURREN WE CRESTED AN ENORMOUS CATARACT.
"AS THE SHIP PLUNGED INTO INFINITY, WE LEAP THROUGH THE CHAOS TO THE NEAR SHORE.
"MOST OF US MADE IT.
"WE SOON LEARNED THAT WE HAD SET ONE FOOT ON THE INNER RIM OF HELHEIM, FOR EVEN AS WE TOUCHED THE EARTH...
"...WE WERE TRANS-FORMED INTO WOLVES.
"PERHAPS HELHEIM REVEALS ONE'S TRUE NATURE.
"...OR HEL JUST ENJOYS HER LITTLE JOKES."

SOON ENOUGH, WE FOUND THE WAY OF THINGS HERE IN THE UPPER REACHES OF HELHEIM.

THE POISON SERPENTS OF VERGELMIR SPILL OUT OF THE CATARACT. SOME FALL INTO THE GAP, BUT MANY FALL ONTO THE LOWER REALM.

NIDHOGGR GIVES THEM SAFE PASSAGE TO THE UPPER REALMS.

WE HAVE CHOSEN TO STAY AND SLAY AS MANY AS WE CAN TO PREVENT THEM FROM ENTERING THE DUSK LANDS ABOVE.

WE HAVE SLAIN COUNTLESS THOUSANDS OF THEM, BUT OVER THE CENTURIES, **OUR** NUMBERS HAVE DIMINISHED.

THE TIME WILL COME WHEN THERE WILL NOT BE ENOUGH OF US TO HOLD THEM BACK..."

...AND THE DUSK LANDS WILL BE OVERRUN BY THE SERPENTS AND THE DEAD! THE LEGACY OF THE GODS' DEFEAT AT VIGRID!

AND WHERE WAS **THOR** WHEN HELHEIM BROKE LOOSE AND TORE THE WORLDS APART?

WHERE?!

I DON'T KNOW IF YOU HAVE A PROPER THROAT OR NOT, BUT I'M WILLING TO TEAR OUT WHATEVER YOU HAVE LEFT...

...AND END YOUR MISERABLE EXISTENCE **HERE** AND **NOW!**

ELSEWHERE, IN A SMALL VILLAGE MANY LEAGUES FROM THE RIM OF HELHEIM...

DAMMIT! I CAN'T LOOSEN THE CORD.

THAT STUPID TROLL TIES KNOTS LIKE I'VE NEVER SEEN!

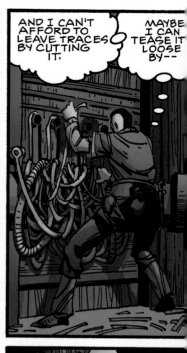

AND I CAN'T AFFORD TO LEAVE TRACES BY CUTTING IT.

MAYBE I CAN TEASE IT LOOSE BY--

??

HELLO, KOLLI.

OH... UH... HI, DRIFA.

I WAS JUST... JUS' MAKING SURE THAT THE DOOR WAS SECURE. GREAT KNOTS.

THAT TROLL DOES SO MUCH FOR THE VILLAGE.

I THOUGHT I COULD MAYBE GIVE HIM A HAND.

I'M SURE JAVOKK WILL BE VERY GRATEFUL.

YOU BET. TIME TO TURN IN. YOU SHOULD GET TO BED NOW, TOO. IT'S LATE.

CREEPY LITTLE SPY. I CAN'T WAIT TO SEE HER CHAINED IN MUSPELHEIM IN TEARS BEFORE GREAT SURTR. HE'LL BREAK HER, ALL RIGHT!

AND PUT HE TALENTS T GOOD US

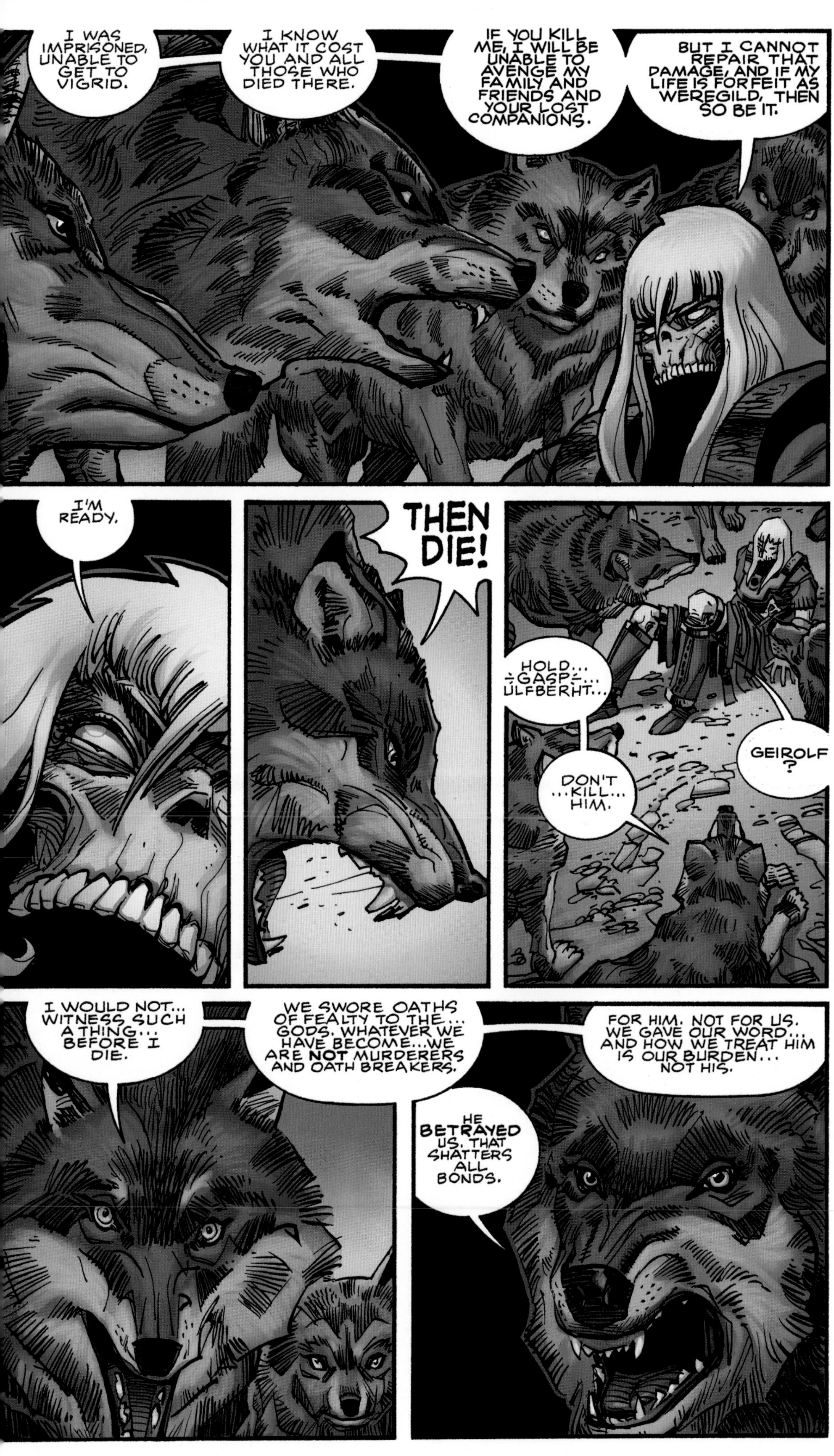
I WAS IMPRISONED, UNABLE TO GET TO VIGRID.
I KNOW WHAT IT COST YOU AND ALL THOSE WHO DIED THERE.
IF YOU KILL ME, I WILL BE UNABLE TO AVENGE MY FAMILY AND FRIENDS AND YOUR LOST COMPANIONS.
BUT I CANNOT REPAIR THAT DAMAGE, AND IF MY LIFE IS FORFEIT AS WEREGILD, THEN SO BE IT.
I'M READY.
THEN DIE!
HOLD... ÷GASP÷... ULFBERHT...
DON'T ...KILL... HIM.
GEIROLF?
I WOULD NOT... WITNESS SUCH A THING... BEFORE I DIE.
WE SWORE OATHS OF FEALTY TO THE... GODS. WHATEVER WE HAVE BECOME...WE ARE **NOT** MURDERERS AND OATH BREAKERS.
FOR HIM. NOT FOR US. WE GAVE OUR WORD... AND HOW WE TREAT HIM IS OUR BURDEN... NOT HIS.
HE **BETRAYED** US. THAT SHATTERS ALL BONDS.

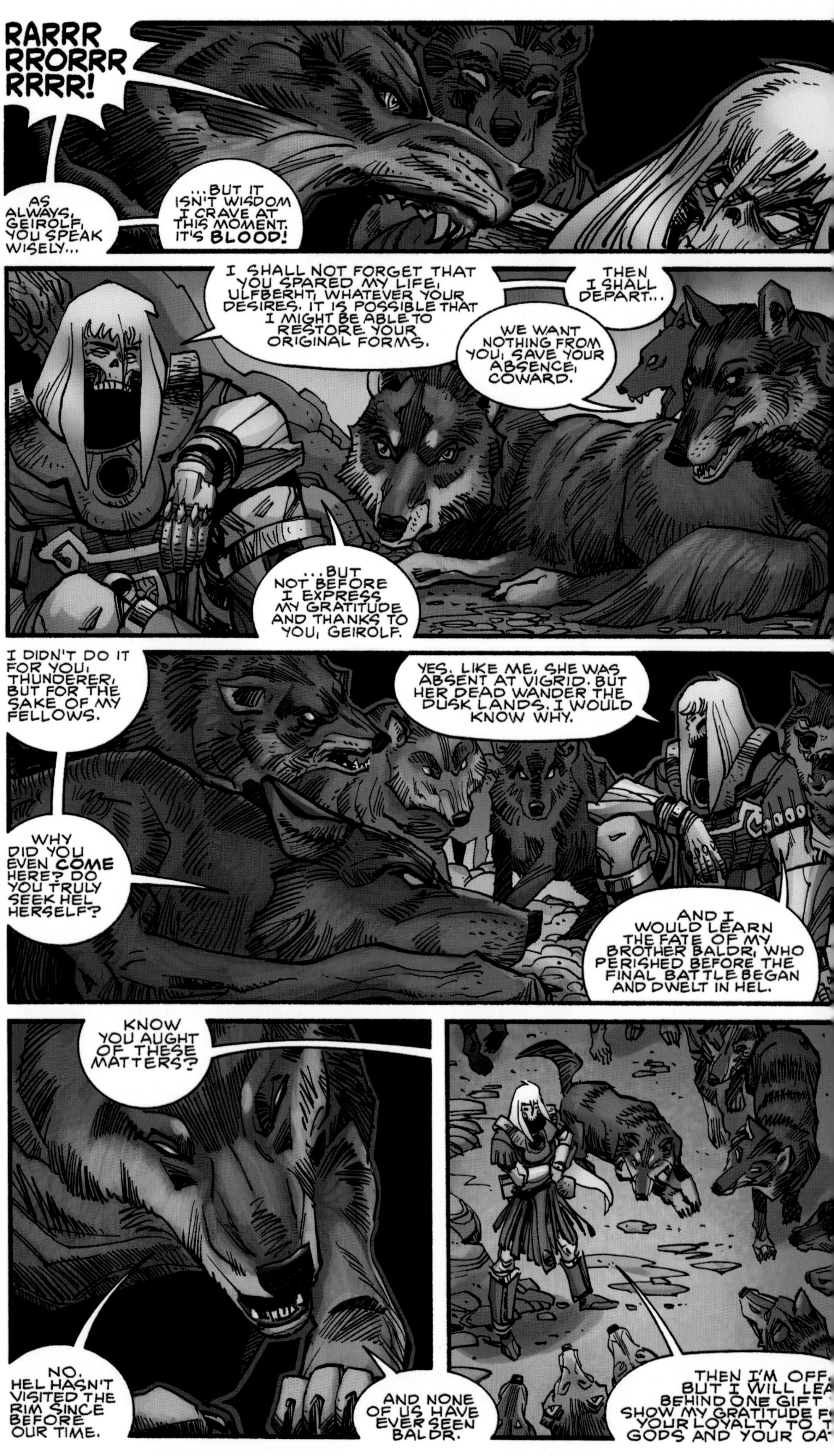
RARRR RRORRR RRRR!
AS ALWAYS, GEIROLF, YOU SPEAK WISELY...
...BUT IT ISN'T WISDOM I CRAVE AT THIS MOMENT. IT'S **BLOOD!**
I SHALL NOT FORGET THAT YOU SPARED MY LIFE, ULFBERHT. WHATEVER YOUR DESIRES, IT IS POSSIBLE THAT I MIGHT BE ABLE TO RESTORE YOUR ORIGINAL FORMS.
WE WANT NOTHING FROM YOU, SAVE YOUR ABSENCE, COWARD.
THEN I SHALL DEPART...
...BUT NOT BEFORE I EXPRESS MY GRATITUDE AND THANKS TO YOU, GEIROLF.
I DIDN'T DO IT FOR YOU, THUNDERER, BUT FOR THE SAKE OF MY FELLOWS.
WHY DID YOU EVEN **COME** HERE? DO YOU TRULY SEEK HEL HERSELF?
YES. LIKE ME, SHE WAS ABSENT AT VIGRID. BUT HER DEAD WANDER THE DUSK LANDS. I WOULD KNOW WHY.
AND I WOULD LEARN THE FATE OF MY BROTHER BALDR, WHO PERISHED BEFORE THE FINAL BATTLE BEGAN AND DWELT IN HEL.
KNOW YOU AUGHT OF THESE MATTERS?
NO. HEL HASN'T VISITED THE RIM SINCE BEFORE OUR TIME.
AND NONE OF US HAVE EVER SEEN BALDR.
THEN I'M OFF. BUT I WILL LEA BEHIND ONE GIFT SHOW MY GRATITUDE F YOUR LOYALTY TO T GODS AND YOUR OA

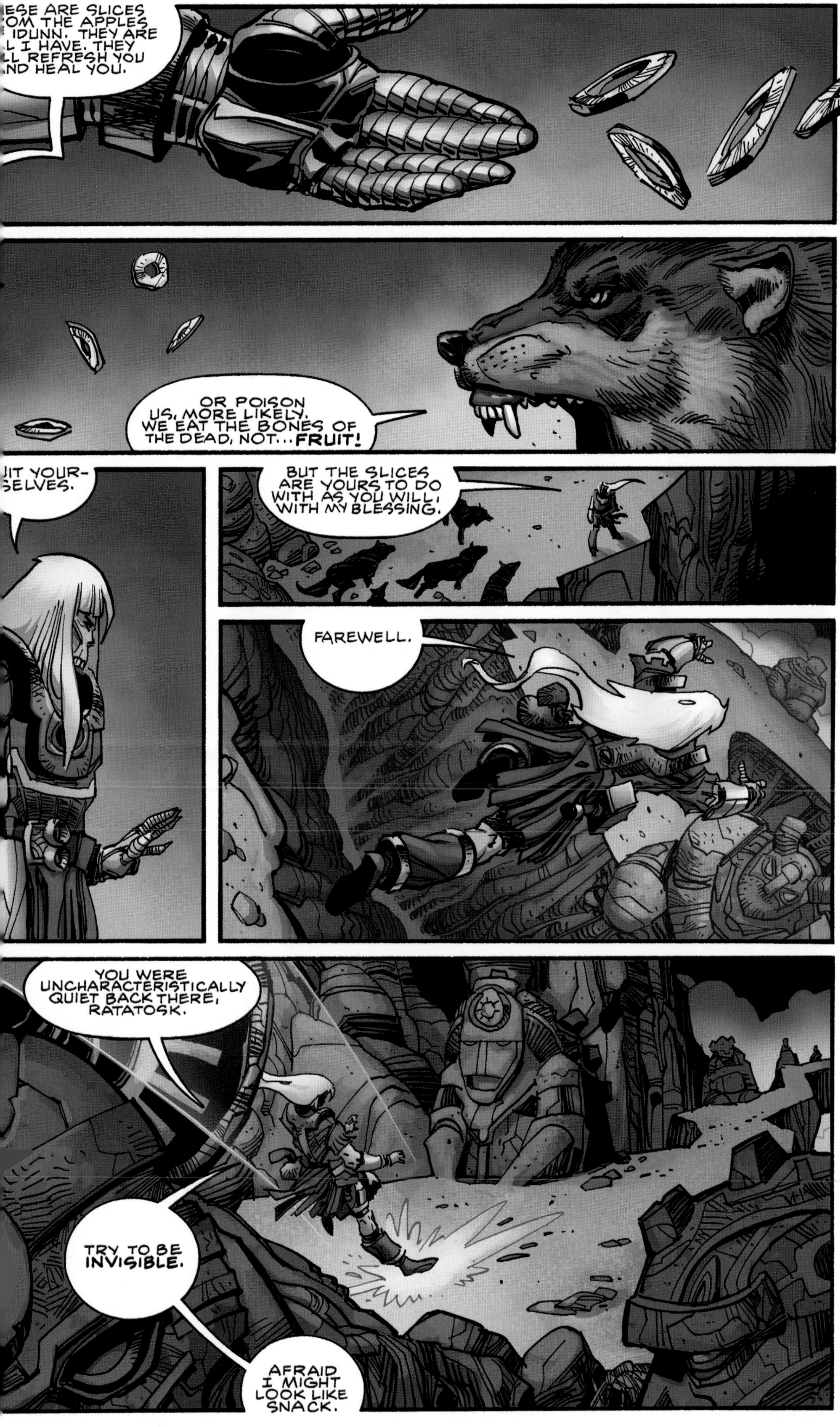
ESE ARE SLICES
OM THE APPLES
IDUNN. THEY ARE
L I HAVE. THEY
LL REFRESH YOU
ND HEAL YOU.
OR POISON US, MORE LIKELY. WE EAT THE BONES OF THE DEAD, NOT... **FRUIT!**
IT YOURSELVES.
BUT THE SLICES ARE YOURS TO DO WITH AS YOU WILL, WITH MY BLESSING.
FAREWELL.
YOU WERE UNCHARACTERISTICALLY QUIET BACK THERE, RATATOSK.
TRY TO BE INVISIBLE.
AFRAID I MIGHT LOOK LIKE SNACK.

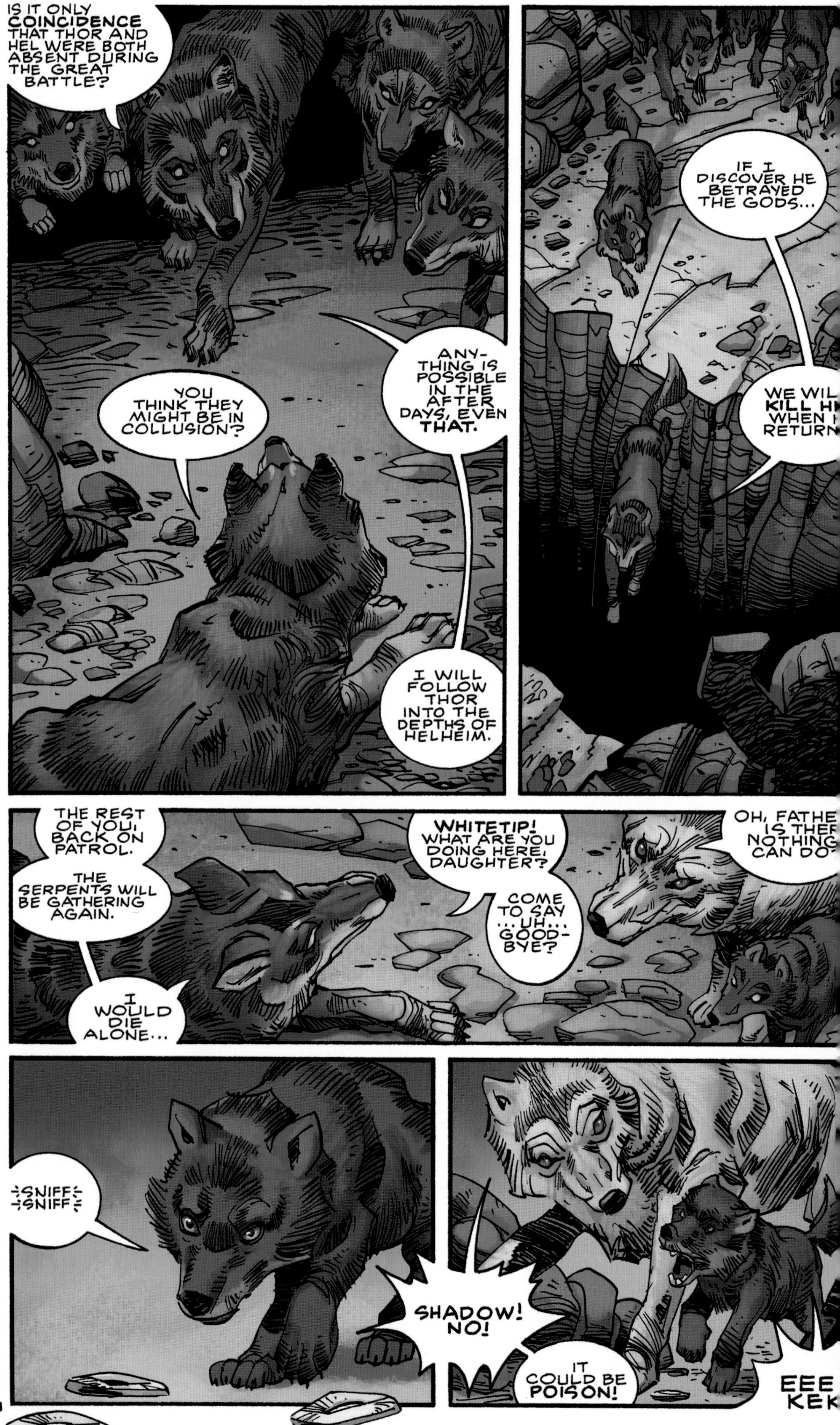
IS IT ONLY COINCIDENCE THAT THOR AND HEL WERE BOTH ABSENT DURING THE GREAT BATTLE?
YOU THINK THEY MIGHT BE IN COLLUSION?
ANY-THING IS POSSIBLE IN THE AFTER DAYS, EVEN THAT.
I WILL FOLLOW THOR INTO THE DEPTHS OF HELHEIM.
IF I DISCOVER HE BETRAYED THE GODS...
WE WIL KILL HI WHEN I RETURN
THE REST OF YOU, BACK ON PATROL.
THE SERPENTS WILL BE GATHERING AGAIN.
I WOULD DIE ALONE...
WHITETIP! WHAT ARE YOU DOING HERE, DAUGHTER?
COME TO SAY ...UH... GOOD-BYE?
OH, FATHE IS THER NOTHING CAN DO
SNIFF SNIFF
SHADOW! NO!
IT COULD BE POISON!
EEE KEK

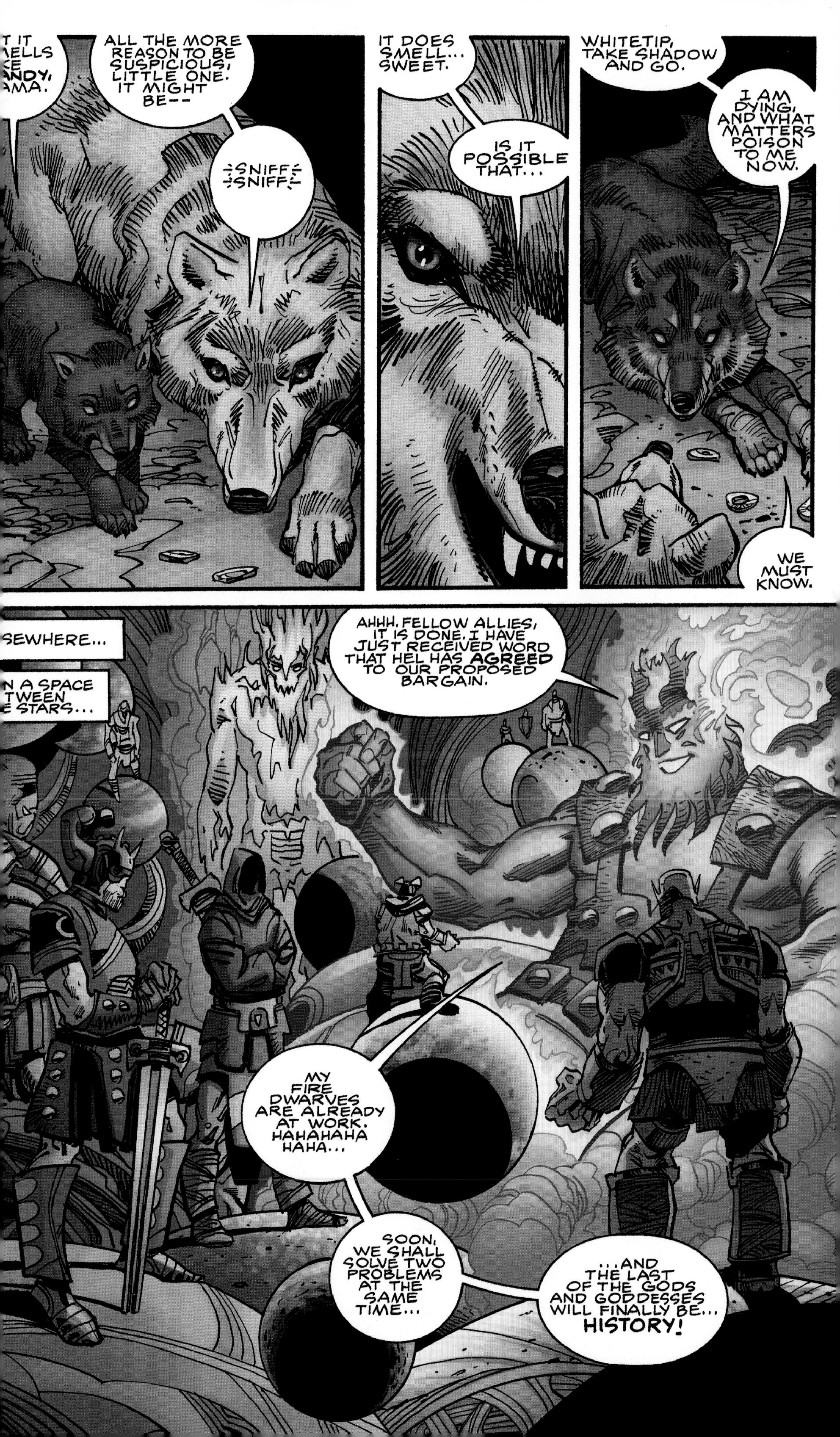
T IT MELLS KE ANDY, AMA.
ALL THE MORE REASON TO BE SUSPICIOUS, LITTLE ONE. IT MIGHT BE--
SNIFF SNIFF
IT DOES SMELL... SWEET.
IS IT POSSIBLE THAT...
WHITETIP, TAKE SHADOW AND GO.
I AM DYING, AND WHAT MATTERS POISON TO ME NOW.
WE MUST KNOW.
SEWHERE...
N A SPACE TWEEN E STARS...
AHHH. FELLOW ALLIES, IT IS DONE. I HAVE JUST RECEIVED WORD THAT HEL HAS AGREED TO OUR PROPOSED BARGAIN.
MY FIRE DWARVES ARE ALREADY AT WORK. HAHAHAHA HAHA...
SOON, WE SHALL SOLVE TWO PROBLEMS AT THE SAME TIME...
...AND THE LAST OF THE GODS AND GODDESSES WILL FINALLY BE... HISTORY!

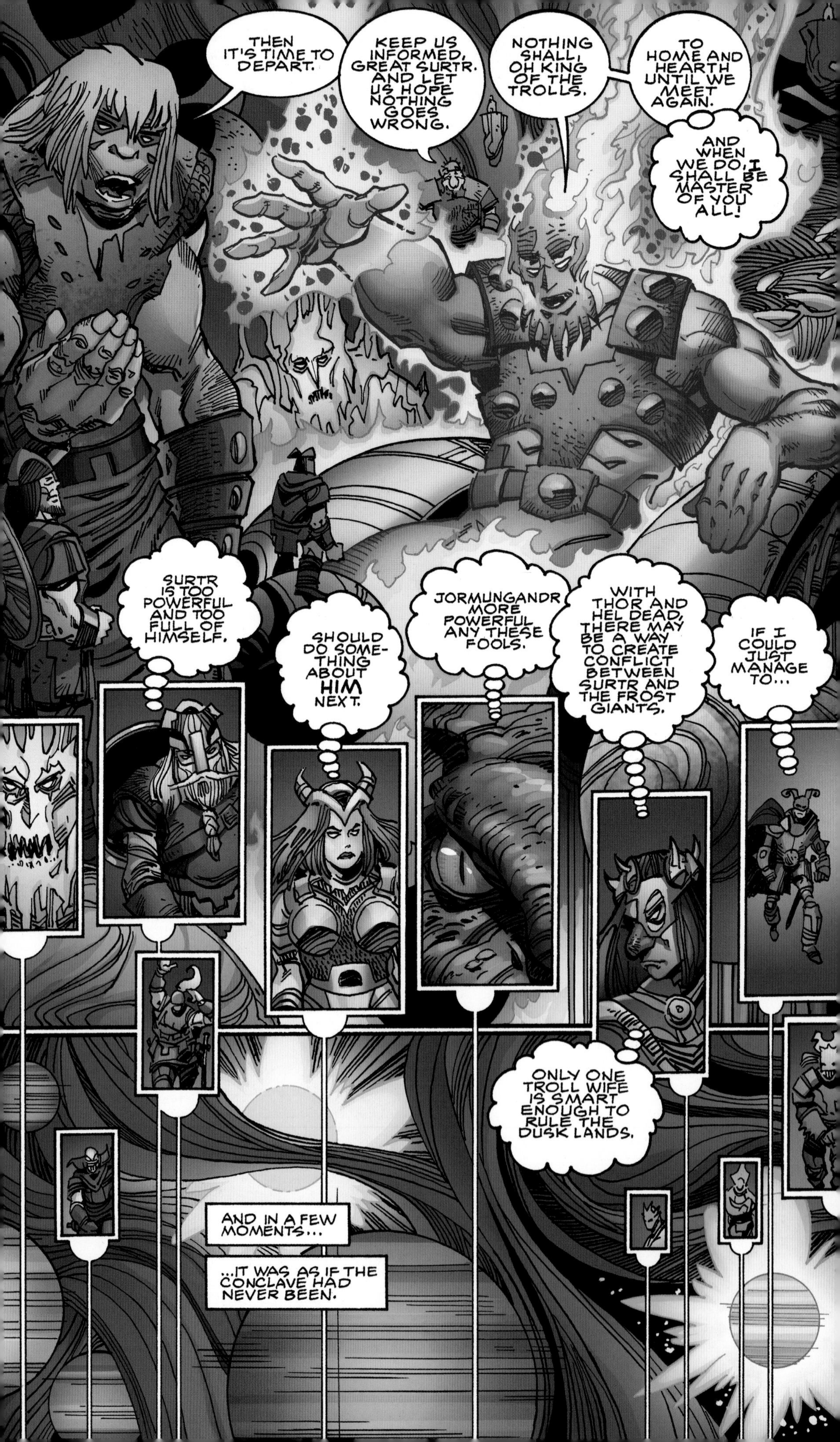
THEN IT'S TIME TO DEPART.
KEEP US INFORMED, GREAT SURTR. AND LET US HOPE NOTHING GOES WRONG.
NOTHING SHALL, OH KING OF THE TROLLS.
TO HOME AND HEARTH UNTIL WE MEET AGAIN.
AND WHEN WE DO, I SHALL BE MASTER OF YOU ALL!
SURTR IS TOO POWERFUL AND TOO FULL OF HIMSELF.
SHOULD DO SOME-THING ABOUT HIM NEXT.
JORMUNGANDR MORE POWERFUL ANY THESE FOOLS.
WITH THOR AND HEL DEAD, THERE MAY BE A WAY TO CREATE CONFLICT BETWEEN SURTR AND THE FROST GIANTS.
IF I COULD JUST MANAGE TO...
ONLY ONE TROLL WIFE IS SMART ENOUGH TO RULE THE DUSK LANDS.
AND IN A FEW MOMENTS...
...IT WAS AS IF THE CONCLAVE HAD NEVER BEEN.

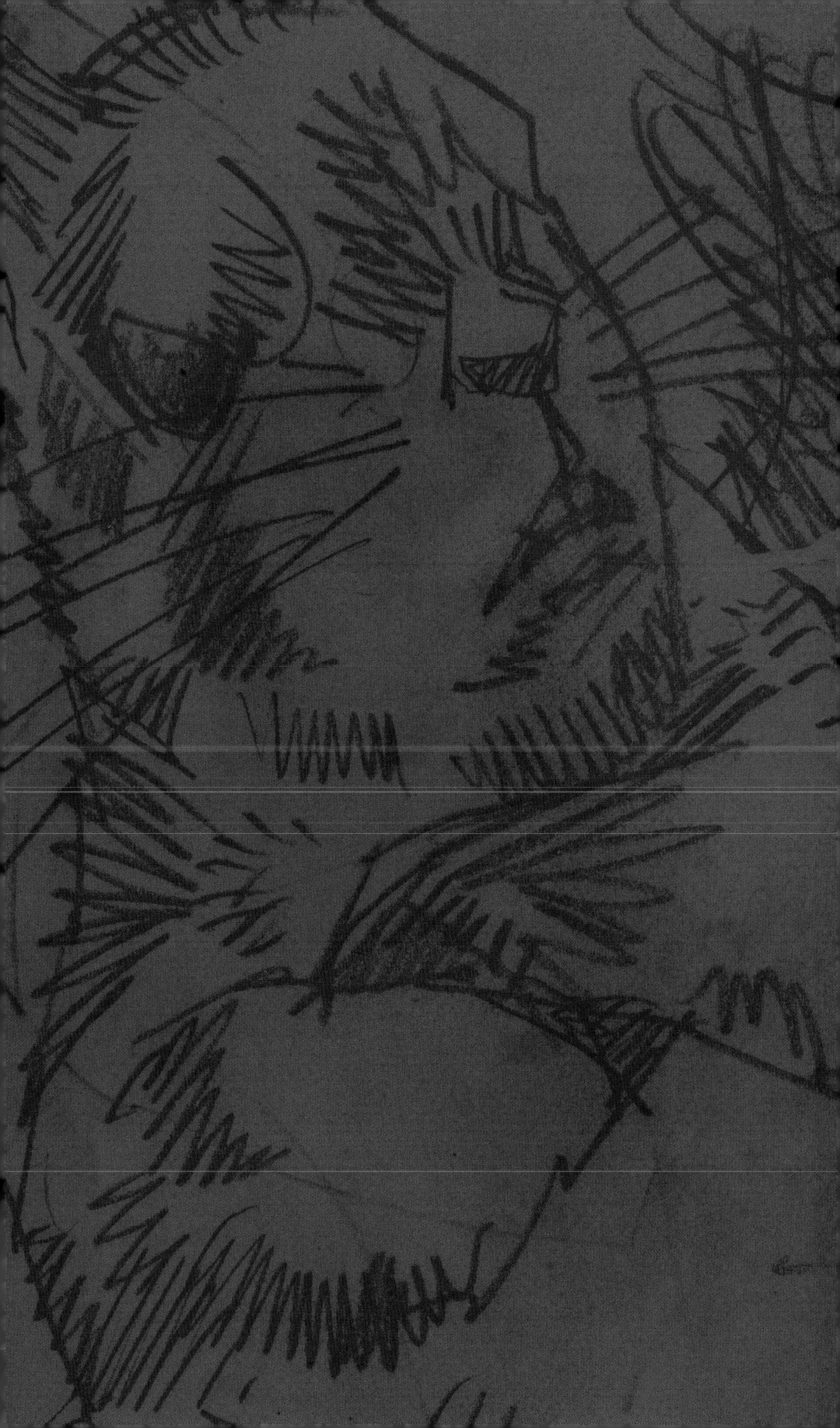

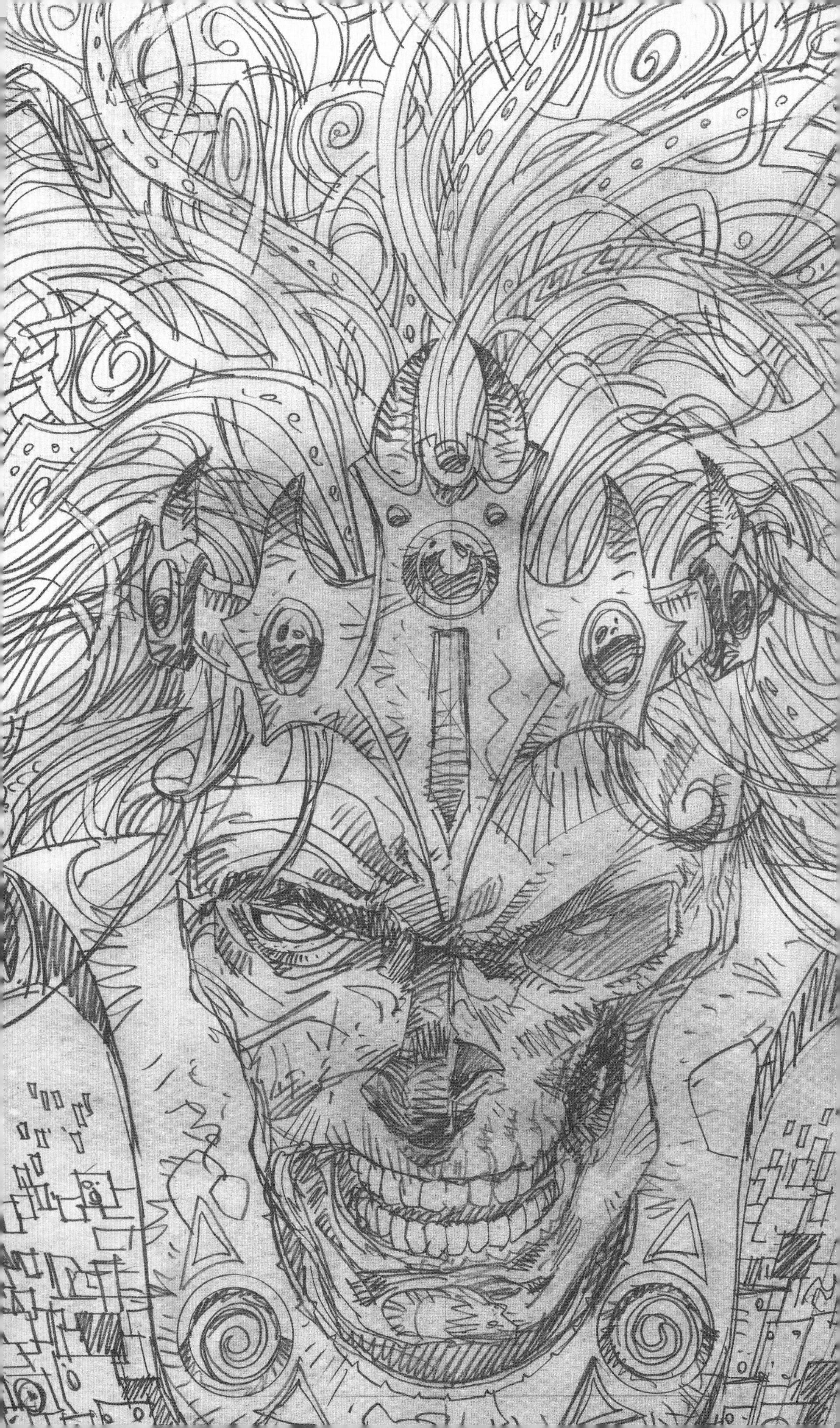

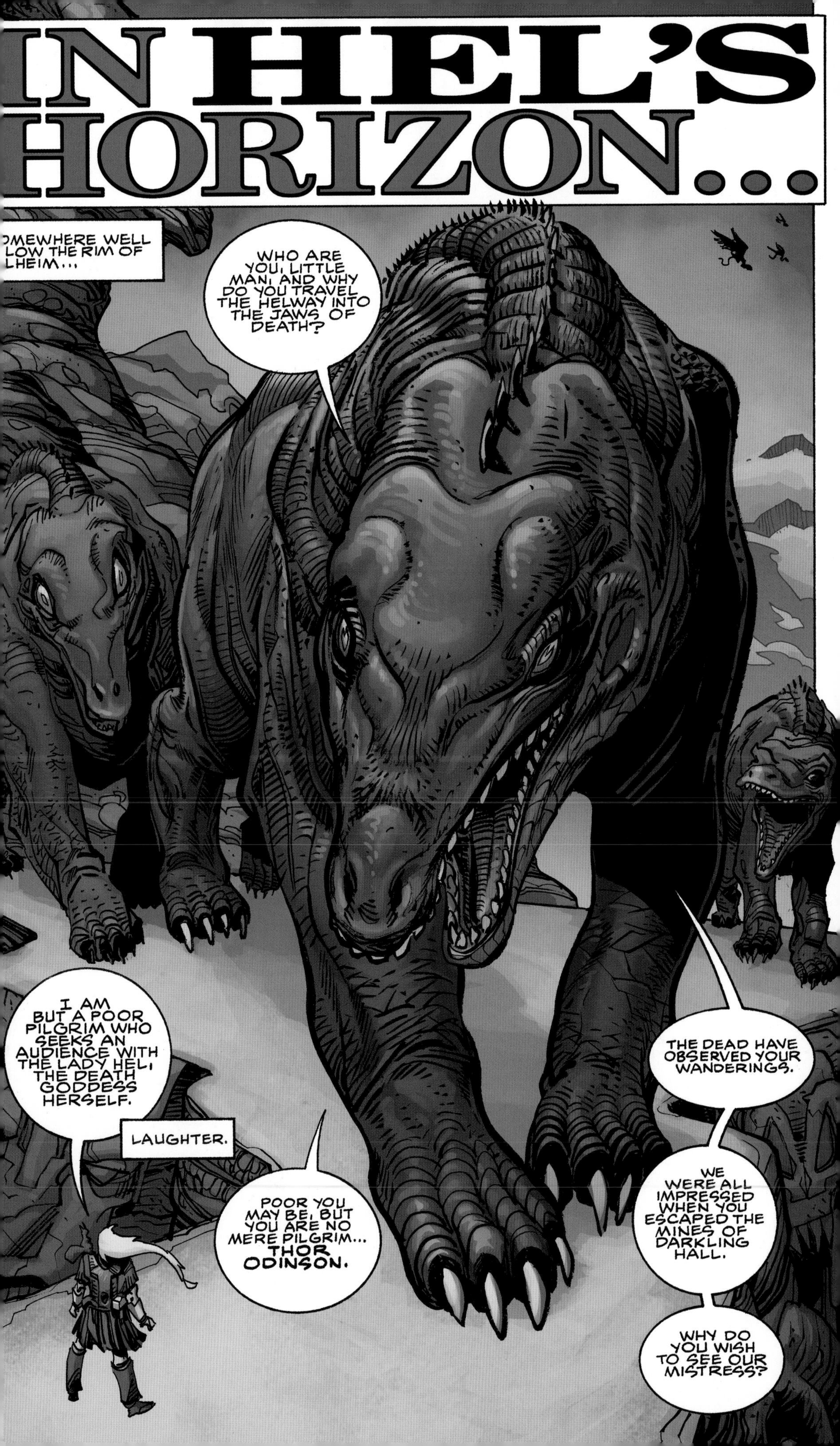
IN HEL'S HORIZON...
OMEWHERE WELL LOW THE RIM OF LHEIM...
WHO ARE YOU, LITTLE MAN, AND WHY DO YOU TRAVEL THE HELWAY INTO THE JAWS OF DEATH?
I AM BUT A POOR PILGRIM WHO SEEKS AN AUDIENCE WITH THE LADY HEL, THE DEATH GODDESS HERSELF.
LAUGHTER.
POOR YOU MAY BE, BUT YOU ARE NO MERE PILGRIM... THOR ODINSON.
THE DEAD HAVE OBSERVED YOUR WANDERINGS.
WE WERE ALL IMPRESSED WHEN YOU ESCAPED THE MINES OF DARKLING HALL.
WHY DO YOU WISH TO SEE OUR MISTRESS?

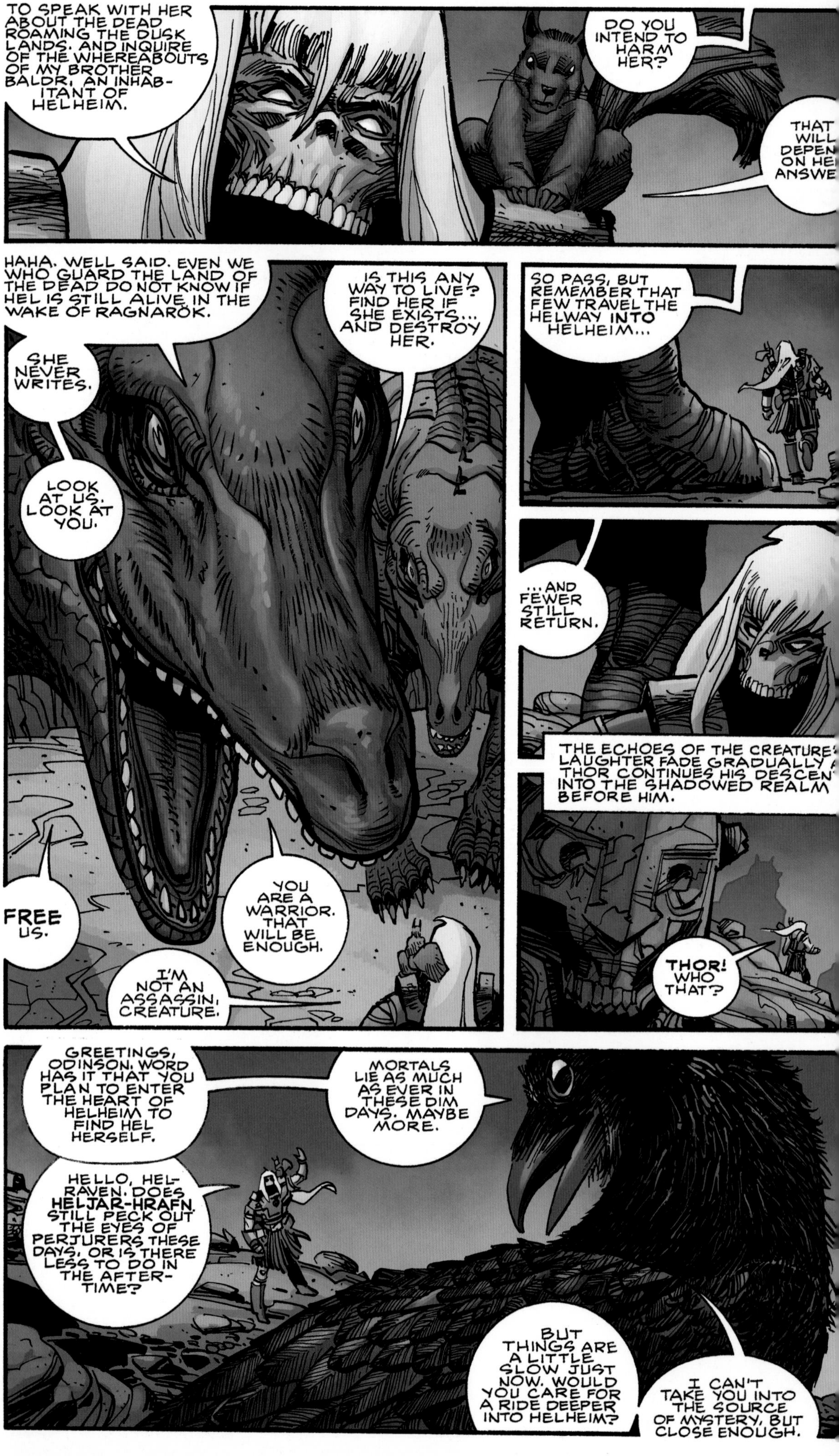
TO SPEAK WITH HER ABOUT THE DEAD ROAMING THE DUSK LANDS. AND INQUIRE OF THE WHEREABOUTS OF MY BROTHER BALDR, AN INHAB-ITANT OF HELHEIM.
DO YOU INTEND TO HARM HER?
THAT WILL DEPEN ON HE ANSWE
HAHA. WELL SAID. EVEN WE WHO GUARD THE LAND OF THE DEAD DO NOT KNOW IF HEL IS STILL ALIVE, IN THE WAKE OF RAGNARÖK.
SHE NEVER WRITES.
IS THIS ANY WAY TO LIVE? FIND HER IF SHE EXISTS... AND DESTROY HER.
LOOK AT US. LOOK AT YOU.
FREE US.
YOU ARE A WARRIOR. THAT WILL BE ENOUGH.
I'M NOT AN ASSASSIN, CREATURE.
SO PASS, BUT REMEMBER THAT FEW TRAVEL THE HELWAY INTO HELHEIM...
...AND FEWER STILL RETURN.
THE ECHOES OF THE CREATURE LAUGHTER FADE GRADUALLY THOR CONTINUES HIS DESCEN INTO THE SHADOWED REALM BEFORE HIM.
THOR! WHO THAT?
GREETINGS, ODINSON. WORD HAS IT THAT YOU PLAN TO ENTER THE HEART OF HELHEIM TO FIND HEL HERSELF.
MORTALS LIE AS MUCH AS EVER IN THESE DIM DAYS. MAYBE MORE.
HELLO, HEL-RAVEN. DOES HELJAR-HRAFN STILL PECK OUT THE EYES OF PERJURERS THESE DAYS, OR IS THERE LESS TO DO IN THE AFTER-TIME?
BUT THINGS ARE A LITTLE SLOW JUST NOW. WOULD YOU CARE FOR A RIDE DEEPER INTO HELHEIM?
I CAN'T TAKE YOU INTO THE SOURCE OF MYSTERY, BUT CLOSE ENOUGH.

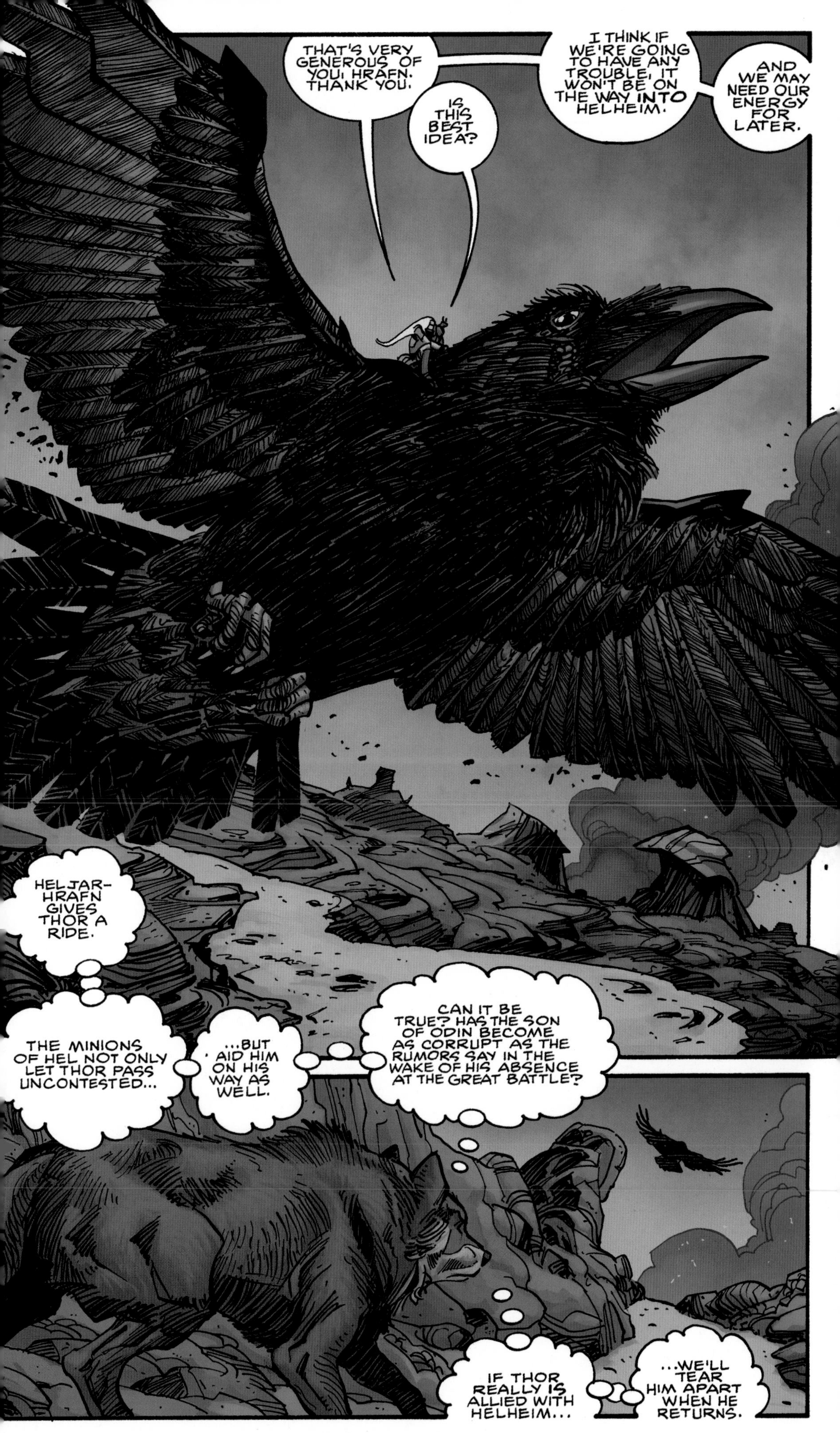
THAT'S VERY GENEROUS OF YOU, HRAFN. THANK YOU.
IS THIS BEST IDEA?
I THINK IF WE'RE GOING TO HAVE ANY TROUBLE, IT WON'T BE ON THE WAY INTO HELHEIM.
AND WE MAY NEED OUR ENERGY FOR LATER.
HELJAR-HRAFN GIVES THOR A RIDE.
THE MINIONS OF HEL NOT ONLY LET THOR PASS UNCONTESTED...
...BUT AID HIM ON HIS WAY AS WELL.
CAN IT BE TRUE? HAS THE SON OF ODIN BECOME AS CORRUPT AS THE RUMORS SAY IN THE WAKE OF HIS ABSENCE AT THE GREAT BATTLE?
IF THOR REALLY IS ALLIED WITH HELHEIM...
...WE'LL TEAR HIM APART WHEN HE RETURNS.

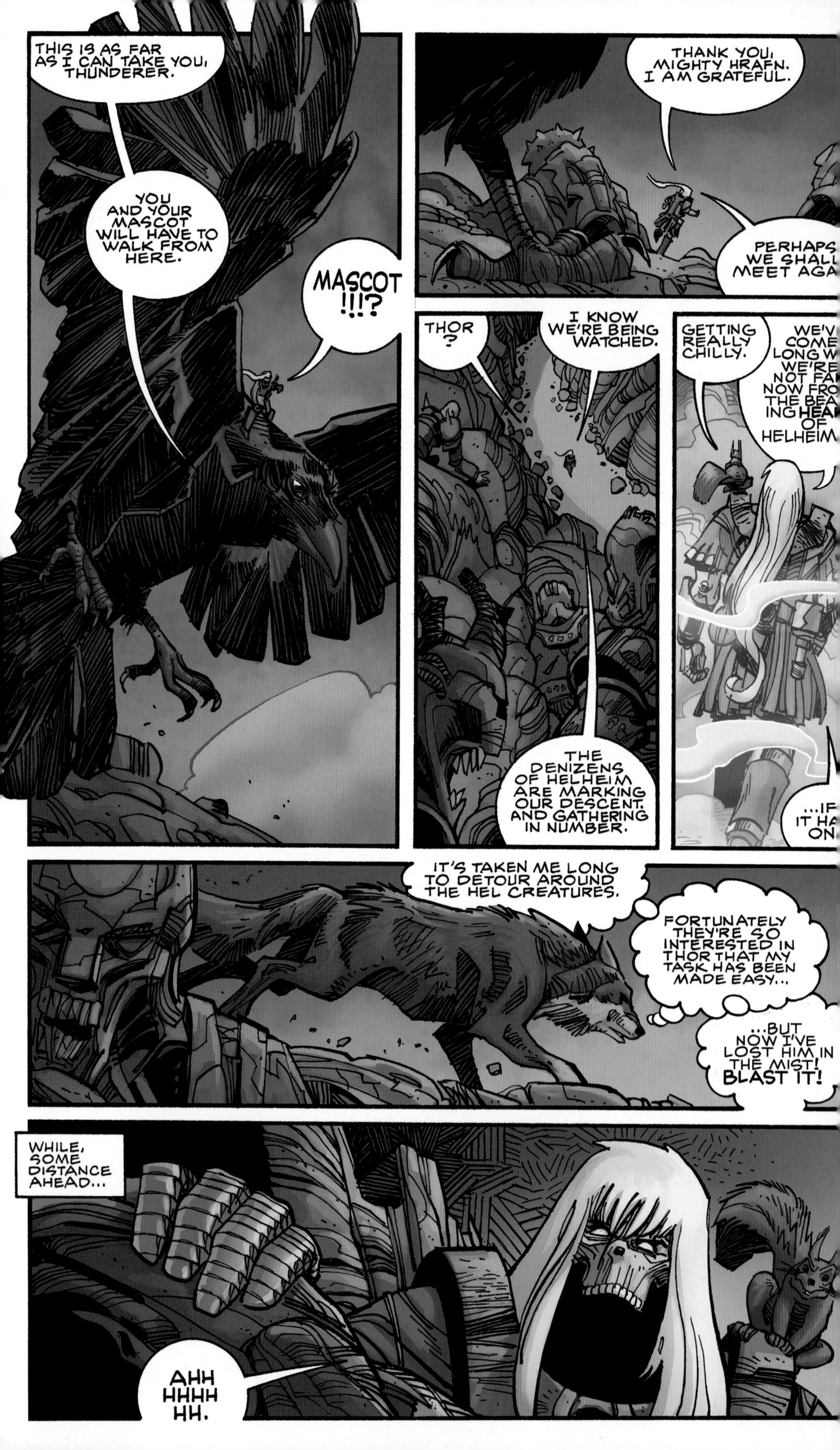

THIS IS AS FAR AS I CAN TAKE YOU, THUNDERER.
YOU AND YOUR MASCOT WILL HAVE TO WALK FROM HERE.
MASCOT !!!?
THANK YOU, MIGHTY HRAFN. I AM GRATEFUL.
PERHAPS WE SHALL MEET AGA
THOR ?
I KNOW WE'RE BEING WATCHED.
THE DENIZENS OF HELHEIM ARE MARKING OUR DESCENT. AND GATHERING IN NUMBER.
GETTING REALLY CHILLY.
WE'V COME LONG W WE'RE NOT FA NOW FRO THE BEA ING HEA OF HELHEIM
...IF IT HA ON
IT'S TAKEN ME LONG TO DETOUR AROUND THE HEL CREATURES.
FORTUNATELY THEY'RE SO INTERESTED IN THOR THAT MY TASK HAS BEEN MADE EASY...
...BUT NOW I'VE LOST HIM IN THE MIST! BLAST IT!
WHILE, SOME DISTANCE AHEAD...
AHH HHHH HH.

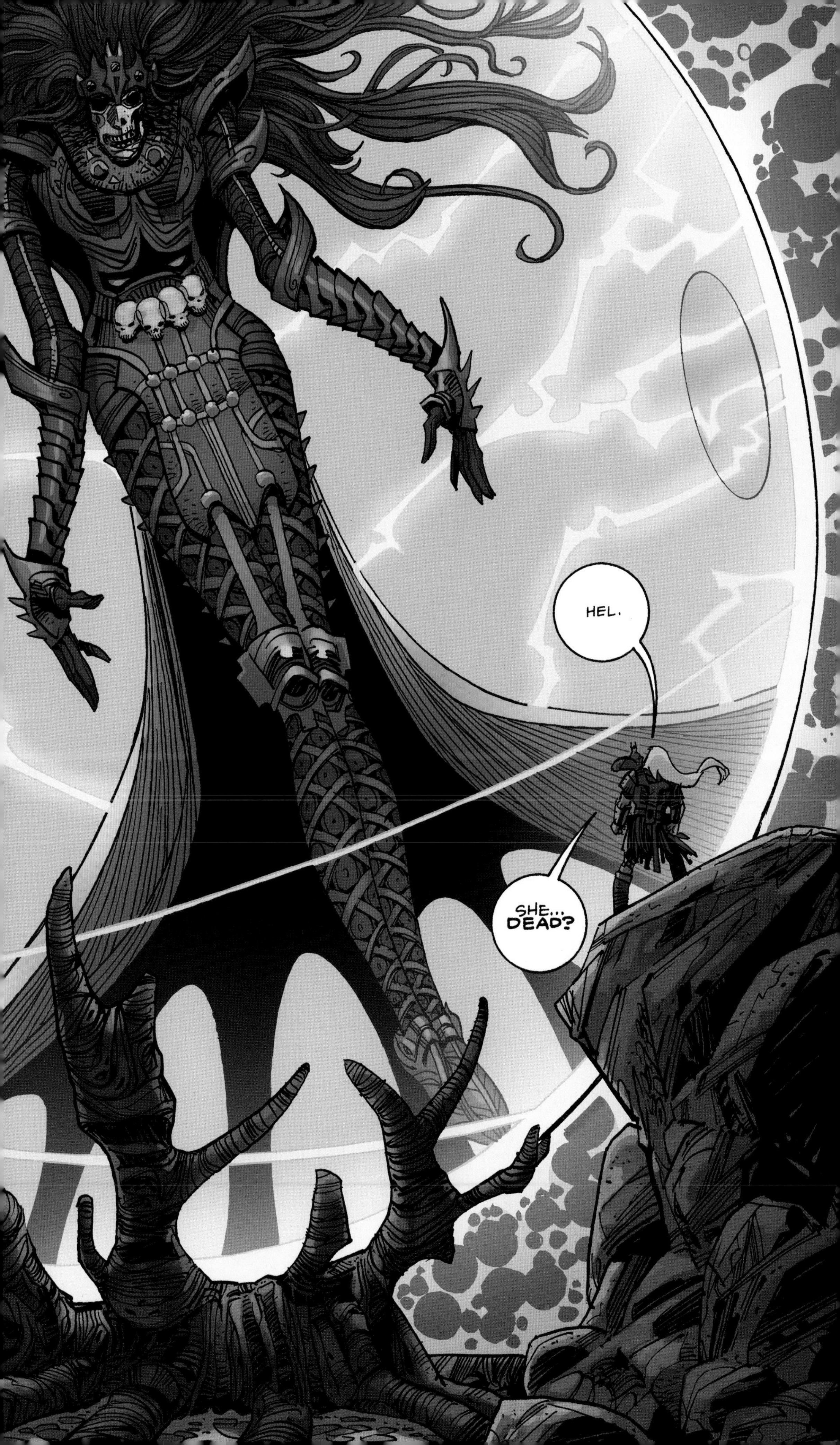
HEL.
SHE... DEAD?

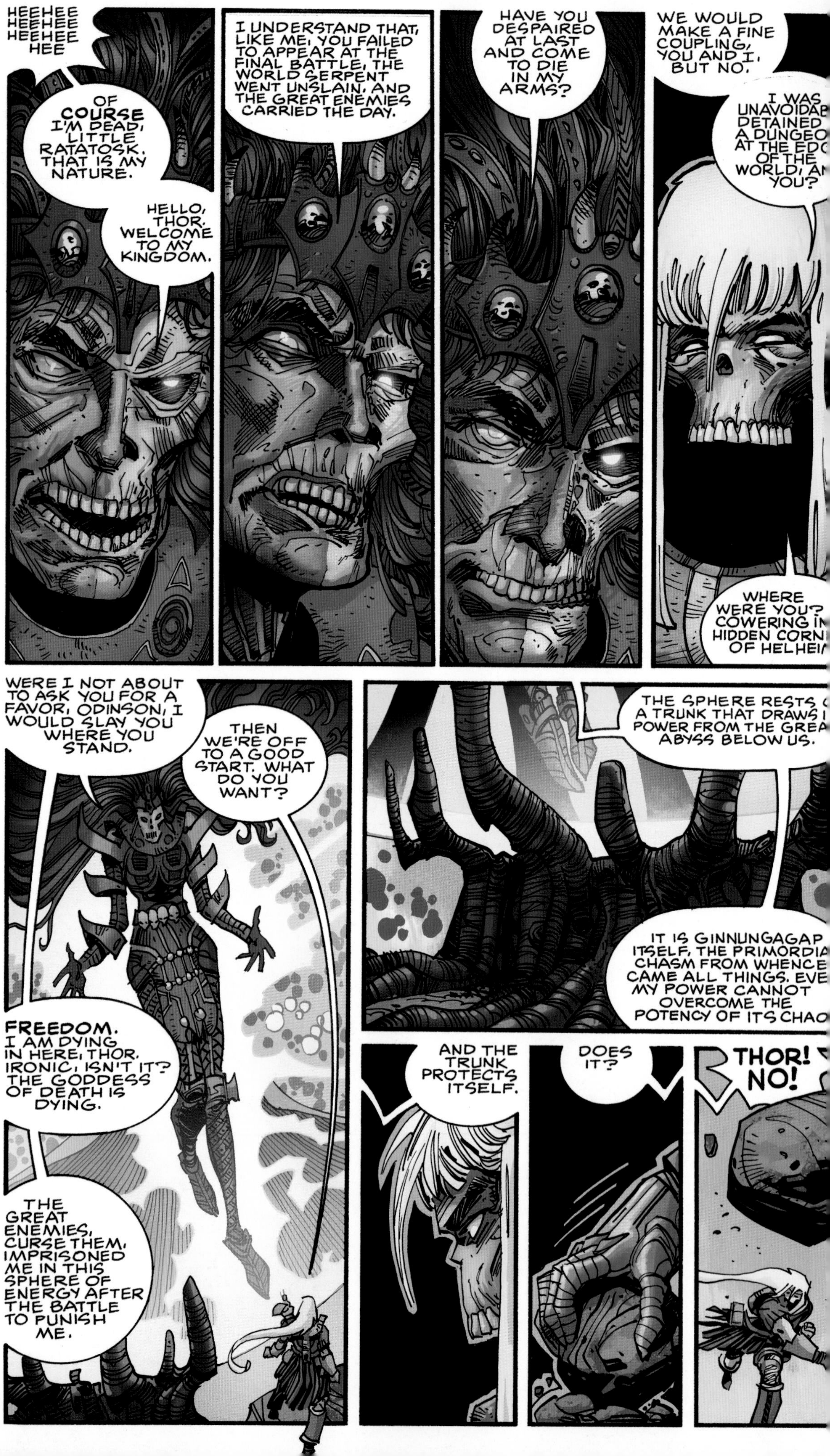
HEEHEE HEEHEE HEEHEE HEE
OF COURSE I'M DEAD, LITTLE RATATOSK. THAT IS MY NATURE.
HELLO, THOR. WELCOME TO MY KINGDOM.
I UNDERSTAND THAT, LIKE ME, YOU FAILED TO APPEAR AT THE FINAL BATTLE, THE WORLD SERPENT WENT UNSLAIN, AND THE GREAT ENEMIES CARRIED THE DAY.
HAVE YOU DESPAIRED AT LAST AND COME TO DIE IN MY ARMS?
WE WOULD MAKE A FINE COUPLING, YOU AND I, BUT NO.
I WAS UNAVOIDAB DETAINED A DUNGEO AT THE EDG OF THE WORLD, AN YOU?
WHERE WERE YOU? COWERING IN HIDDEN CORN OF HELHEIM
WERE I NOT ABOUT TO ASK YOU FOR A FAVOR, ODINSON, I WOULD SLAY YOU WHERE YOU STAND.
THEN WE'RE OFF TO A GOOD START. WHAT DO YOU WANT?
FREEDOM. I AM DYING IN HERE, THOR. IRONIC, ISN'T IT? THE GODDESS OF DEATH IS DYING.
THE GREAT ENEMIES, CURSE THEM, IMPRISONED ME IN THIS SPHERE OF ENERGY AFTER THE BATTLE TO PUNISH ME.
THE SPHERE RESTS O A TRUNK THAT DRAWS I POWER FROM THE GREA ABYSS BELOW US.
IT IS GINNUNGAGAP ITSELF, THE PRIMORDIA CHASM FROM WHENCE CAME ALL THINGS. EVE MY POWER CANNOT OVERCOME THE POTENCY OF ITS CHAO
AND THE TRUNK PROTECTS ITSELF.
DOES IT?
THOR! NO!

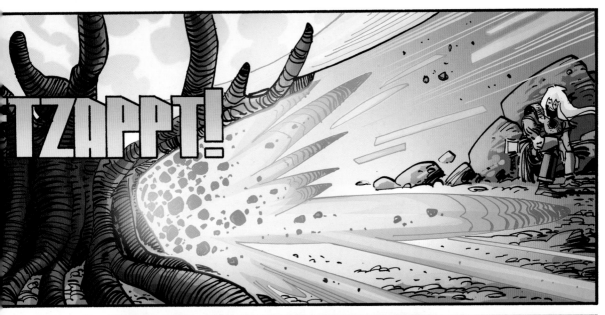

TZAPPT!

THAT ROCK HAD BEEN BIGGER, YOU'D HAVE DIED IN THE BLOWBACK.

AND YOU?

I AM BOTH IMPRISONED AND PROTECTED BY THIS SPHERE.

BUT I HAVE BEEN ILL-TREATED BY THOSE WHO COUNTED ON MY HELP.

"IT WAS **I** WHO ALLOWED THE BUILDING OF THE GREAT SHIP NAGLFAR!

"AND IT WAS THAT SHIP THAT CARRIED THE NUMBERLESS DEAD OF HELHEIM INTO BATTLE ON THAT FINAL DAY OF DOOM.

"MY THANKS WAS TO BE IMPRISONED IN MY OWN KINGDOM, NEVER TO BE SET FREE."

I, WHO WAS ONCE BOTH LIVING AND DEAD, AM NOW COMPLETELY DEAD. MY LIVING HALF STARVED TO DEATH INSIDE THIS PRISON...

...MY DEAD HALF CANNOT BE KILLED.

SURTR DIRECTED HIS CLEVER DWARVES OF FIRE TO FASHION MY GILDED CAGE.

HE IS THE WILIEST AND MOST DEADLY OF ALL THE ENEMIES.

AND BALDR... MY BROTHER?

THE SLAIN GOD YOU WOULD NOT RELEASE FROM HELHEIM...

...THOUGH NUMBERLESS TEARS WERE SHED FOR HIS RETURN?

BE FAIR. I DID SAY THAT IF ONE BEING REFUSED TO CRY FOR HIM, I WOULD KEEP THE GOLDEN ONE.

YOU AND I BOTH KNOW THAT IT WAS LOKI WITHHELD HIS TEARS, HE WHO ARRANGED BALDR'S DEATH IN THE FIRST PLACE...

...BUT I DO CONFESS I WAS PLEASED TO HAVE HIM.

HE BROUGHT LIGHT INTO HELHEIM SUCH AS HAD NEVER BEEN SEEN HERE BEFORE.

HE BROUGHT LIGHT TO ME.

ARE TH STORIE TRUE? DID YOU TAKE HIM TO BED?

I COMFORTED BALDR, AND SHOWE HIM THINGS HE HA NEVER KNOWN BEFORE, MY FINELY WROUGH COUCH OF GOLD

THE CHAINS WERE DECORATIVE?

GROW UP, THOR. HE ENJOYED THEM!

WHAT OF NANNA, HIS WIFE WHO SHARED HIS SORRY JOURNEY TO THIS DISMAL REALM?

A SPINELESS SOP! SHE VANISHED, AND I DON'T KEEP TRACK OF EVERY SOUL IN HELHEIM.

IN MY ARMS, HE FORGOT HER.

"IN THE END, I SENT HIM TO TH DEPTHS OF NIFLHEL, THE DEEPEST PART OF MY KINGDO TO PROTECT HIM.

"NEVER DID I DREAM THE NIN WORLDS WOULD FALL, AND NIFLHEL BE DESTROYED IN A INSTANT WHEN HELHEIM COLLAPSED.

"THERE WE NO SURVIVOR

ENSE THAT WE'RE ALONE HERE IN E PIT OF HELHEIM. UR CREATURES RE GATHERING.

YOU HAVE NO INTENTION OF LETTING ME LEAVE HERE. I SHOULD WARN YOU THAT I HAVE NO INTENTION OF SHARING YOUR BED.

HAVE YOU SEEN YOURSELF LATELY, THOR? YOUR VIRTUE IS SAFE FROM ME. THEY ARE MERELY CURIOUS TO SEE THE **LAST** GOD.

HEEHEE HEEHEEHEE HEEHEE.

ALLOWING THE EATH SHIP TO BE ILT HERE, YOU D A HAND IN THE AYING OF MY ND AND ALL MY WORLD.

I CAN RECALL THE DEAD TO HELHEIM AND FREE THE DUSK LANDS FROM THEIR ACCURSED PRESENCE.

FREE ME, THOR! PLEASE.

THERE AREN'T ENOUGH DEAD IN HELHEIM TO CHANGE MY MIND. WHY SHOULDN'T I LET YOU ROT HERE?

BECAUSE I WILL DO A DEAL WITH YOU, THOR.

AND WHEN I AM RECOVERED, THERE SHALL BE A RECKONING BETWEEN SURTR AND MYSELF.

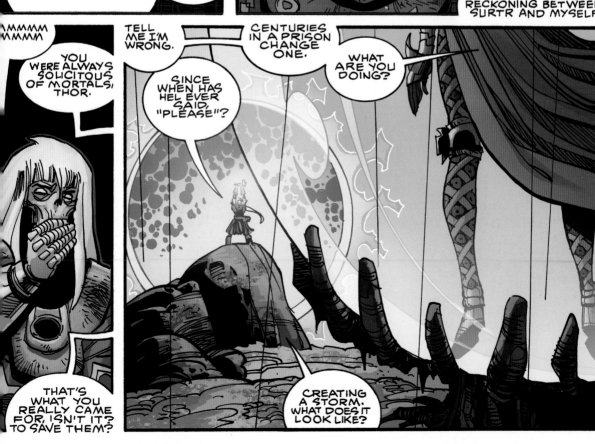

MMMMM MMMM

YOU WERE ALWAYS SOLICITOUS OF MORTALS, THOR.

TELL ME I'M WRONG.

CENTURIES IN A PRISON CHANGE ONE.

WHAT ARE YOU DOING?

SINCE WHEN HAS HEL EVER SAID, "PLEASE"?

THAT'S WHAT YOU REALLY CAME FOR, ISN'T IT? TO SAVE THEM?

CREATING A STORM. WHAT DOES IT LOOK LIKE?

BOOOUM!

IF YOUR CAGE WAS FASHIONED BY SURTR AND HIS FIRE DWARVES, PERHAPS A GOOD RAIN WILL-- WHAT'S THIS?

ENER CABL SECUR YOUR PRISON

...RUNNING ALL THE WAY UP TO THE RIM OF HELHEIM.

SURTR WANTED TO BE CERTAIN I WAS SECURE.

THOR, I BEG OF YOU.

FREE ME.

WE'VE KNOWN EACH OTHER A LONG TIME. HEL. LOKI'S DAUGHTER WOULD NEVER BEG.

BUT IF THE CABLES FETTER YOUR CAGE, WHAT PURPOSE DOES THE TRUNK SERVE?

I TOLD YOU, IT DRAWS ENERGY FROM GINNUNGAGAP

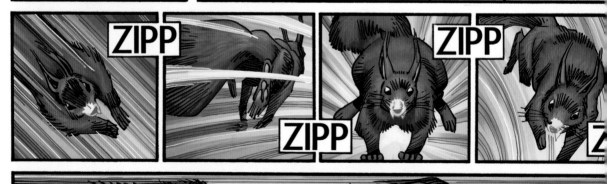

ZIPP

ZIPP

ZIPP

THOR!

THOR!

THOR!

THOR!

THO

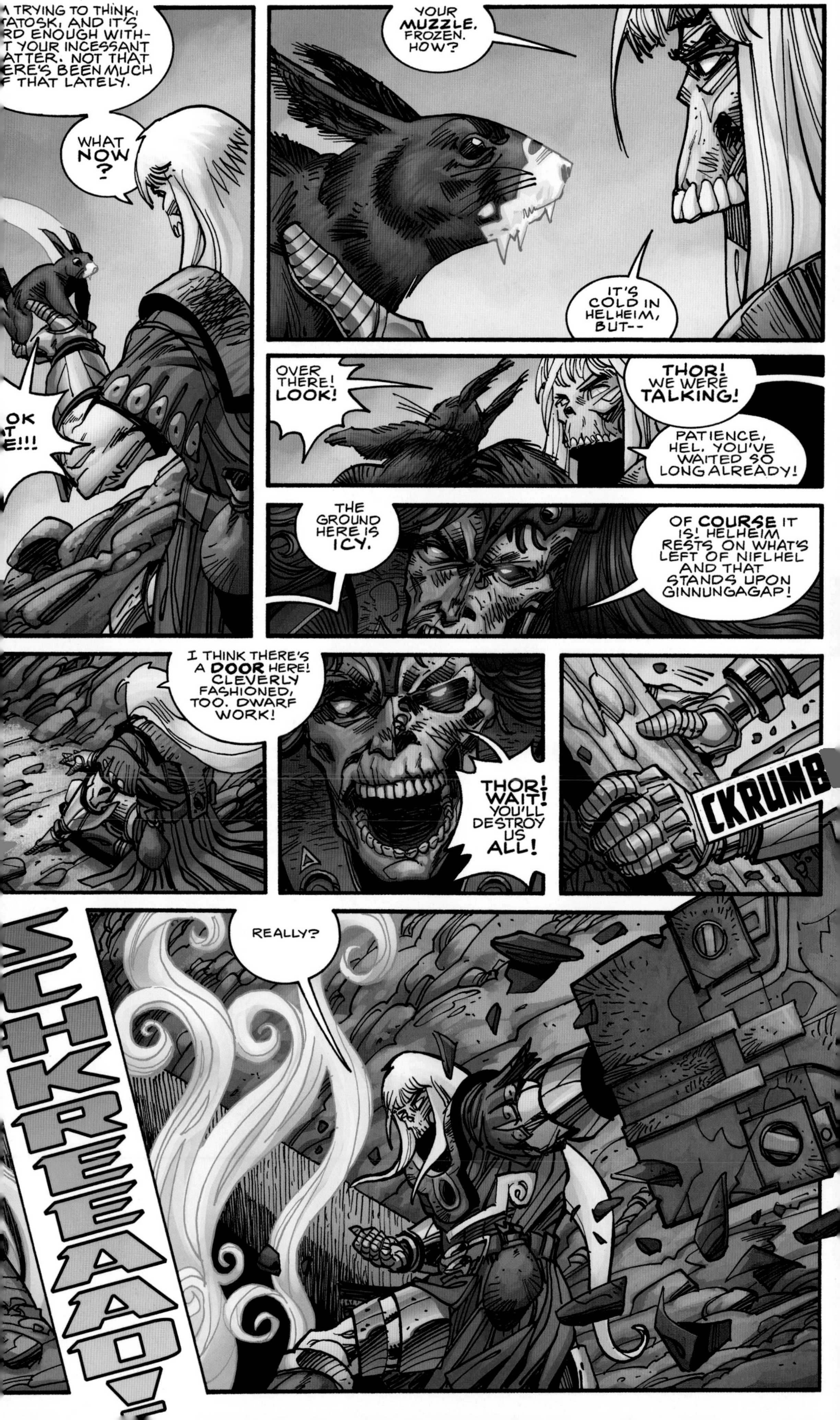

TRYING TO THINK, TATOSK, AND IT'S RD ENOUGH WITH- T YOUR INCESSANT ATTER. NOT THAT ERE'S BEEN MUCH F THAT LATELY.
WHAT NOW?
OK T E!!!
YOUR MUZZLE. FROZEN. HOW?
IT'S COLD IN HELHEIM, BUT--
OVER THERE! LOOK!
THOR! WE WERE TALKING!
PATIENCE, HEL. YOU'VE WAITED SO LONG ALREADY!
THE GROUND HERE IS ICY.
OF COURSE IT IS! HELHEIM RESTS ON WHAT'S LEFT OF NIFLHEL AND THAT STANDS UPON GINNUNGAGAP!
I THINK THERE'S A DOOR HERE! CLEVERLY FASHIONED, TOO. DWARF WORK!
THOR! WAIT! YOU'LL DESTROY US ALL!
CKRUMB
REALLY?
SCHKREEAAD!

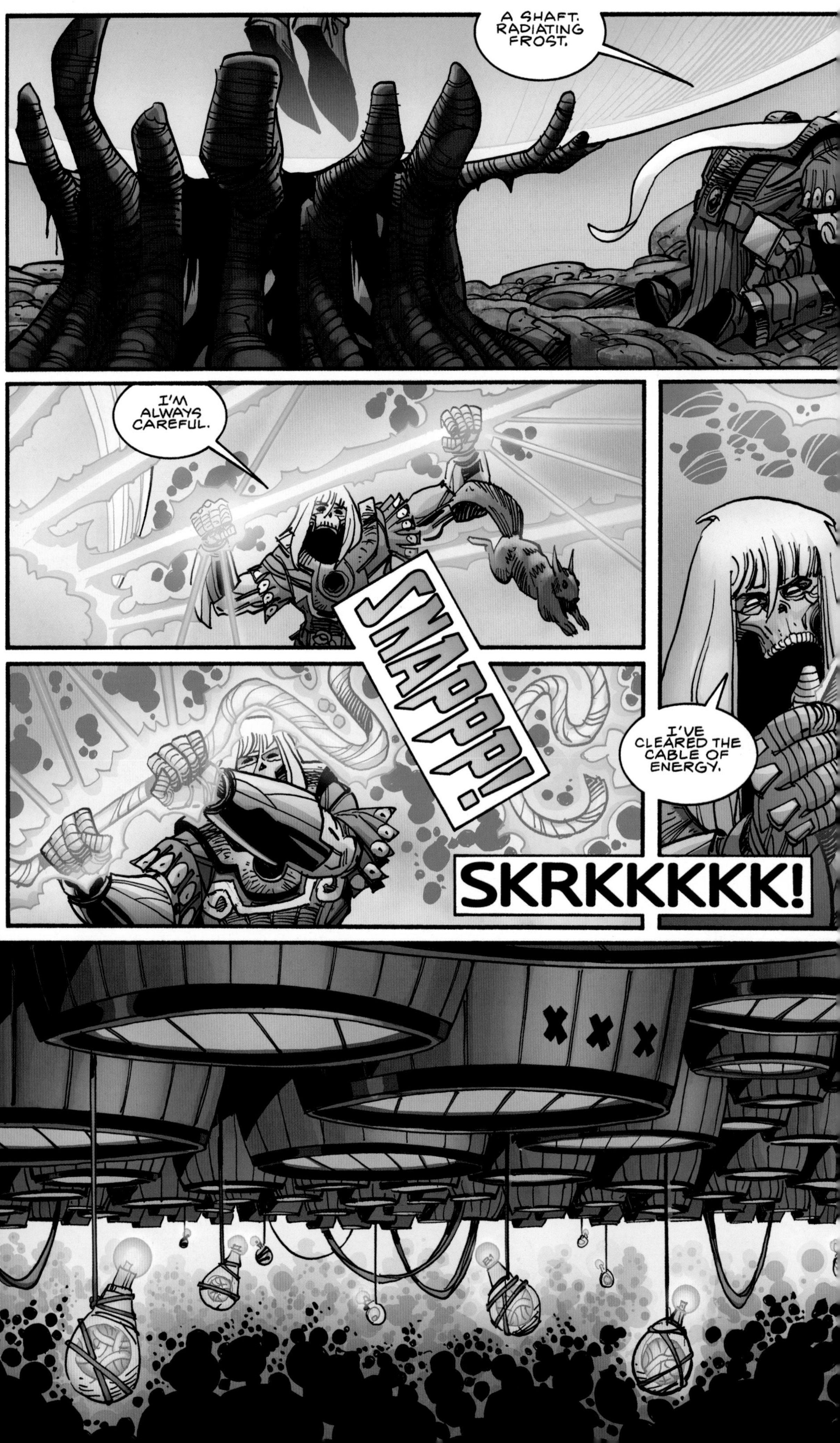
A SHAFT. RADIATING FROST.
I'M ALWAYS CAREFUL.
SNAPPP!
I'VE CLEARED THE CABLE OF ENERGY.
SKRKKKKK!

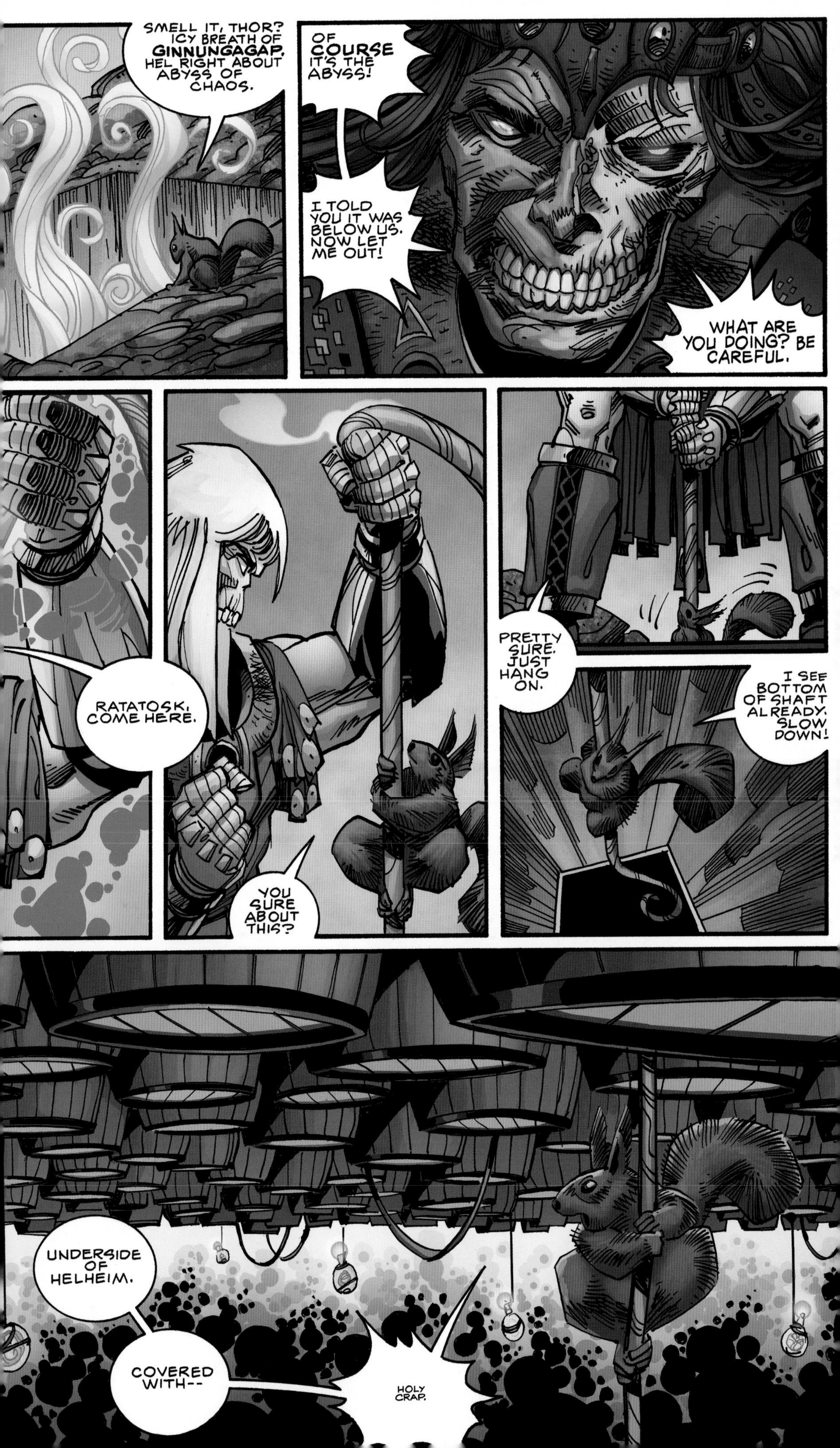
SMELL IT, THOR? ICY BREATH OF GINNUNGAGAP. HEL RIGHT ABOUT ABYSS OF CHAOS.
OF COURSE IT'S THE ABYSS!
I TOLD YOU IT WAS BELOW US. NOW LET ME OUT!
WHAT ARE YOU DOING? BE CAREFUL.
RATATOSK, COME HERE.
YOU SURE ABOUT THIS?
PRETTY SURE. JUST HANG ON.
I SEE BOTTOM OF SHAFT ALREADY. SLOW DOWN!
UNDERSIDE OF HELHEIM.
COVERED WITH--
HOLY CRAP.

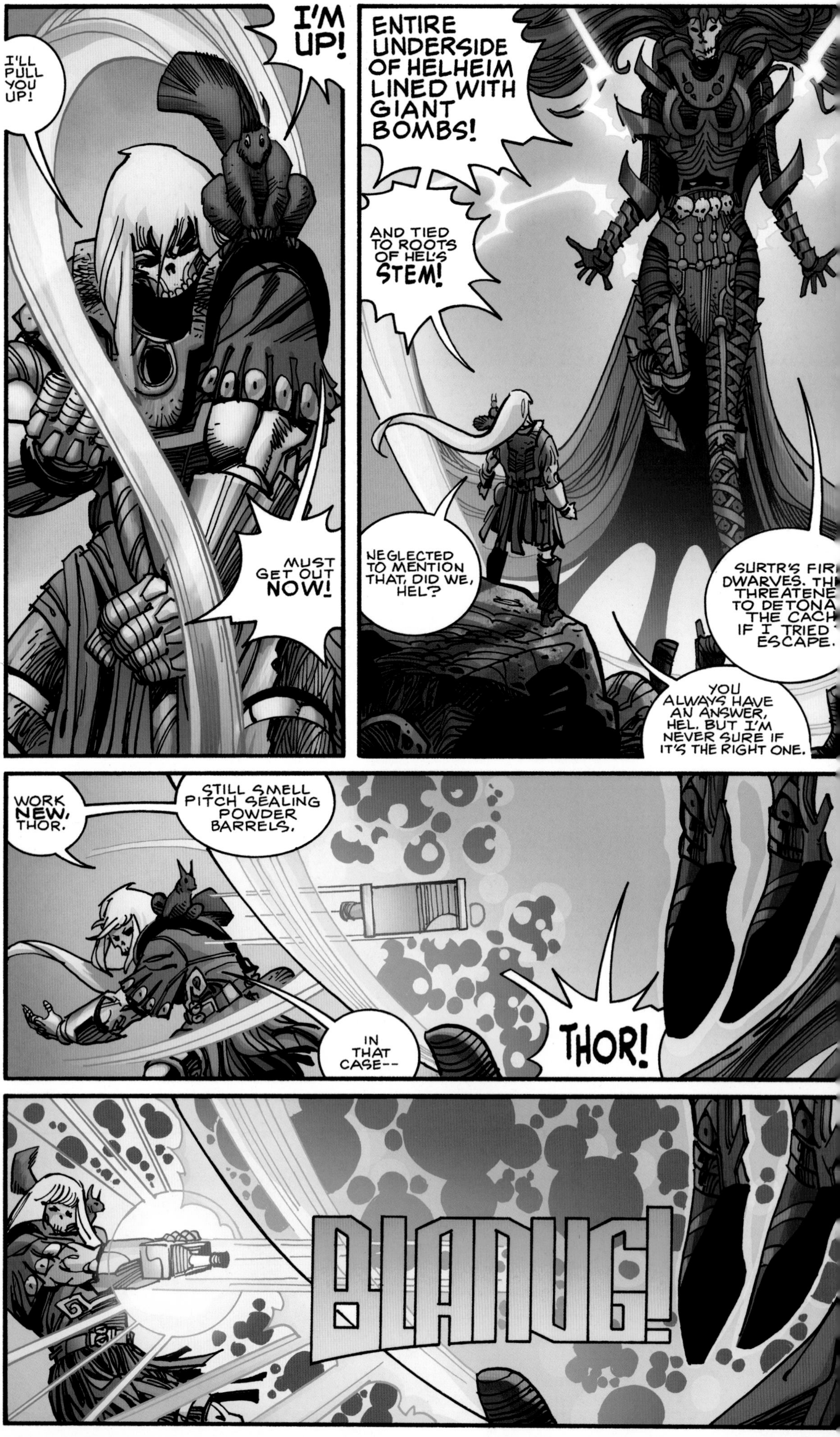
I'LL PULL YOU UP!
I'M UP!
MUST GET OUT NOW!
ENTIRE UNDERSIDE OF HELHEIM LINED WITH GIANT BOMBS!
AND TIED TO ROOTS OF HEL'S STEM!
NEGLECTED TO MENTION THAT, DID WE, HEL?
SURTR'S FIR DWARVES. TH THREATENE TO DETONA THE CACH IF I TRIED ESCAPE.
YOU ALWAYS HAVE AN ANSWER, HEL. BUT I'M NEVER SURE IF IT'S THE RIGHT ONE.
WORK NEW, THOR.
STILL SMELL PITCH SEALING POWDER BARRELS.
IN THAT CASE--
THOR!
BLANUG!

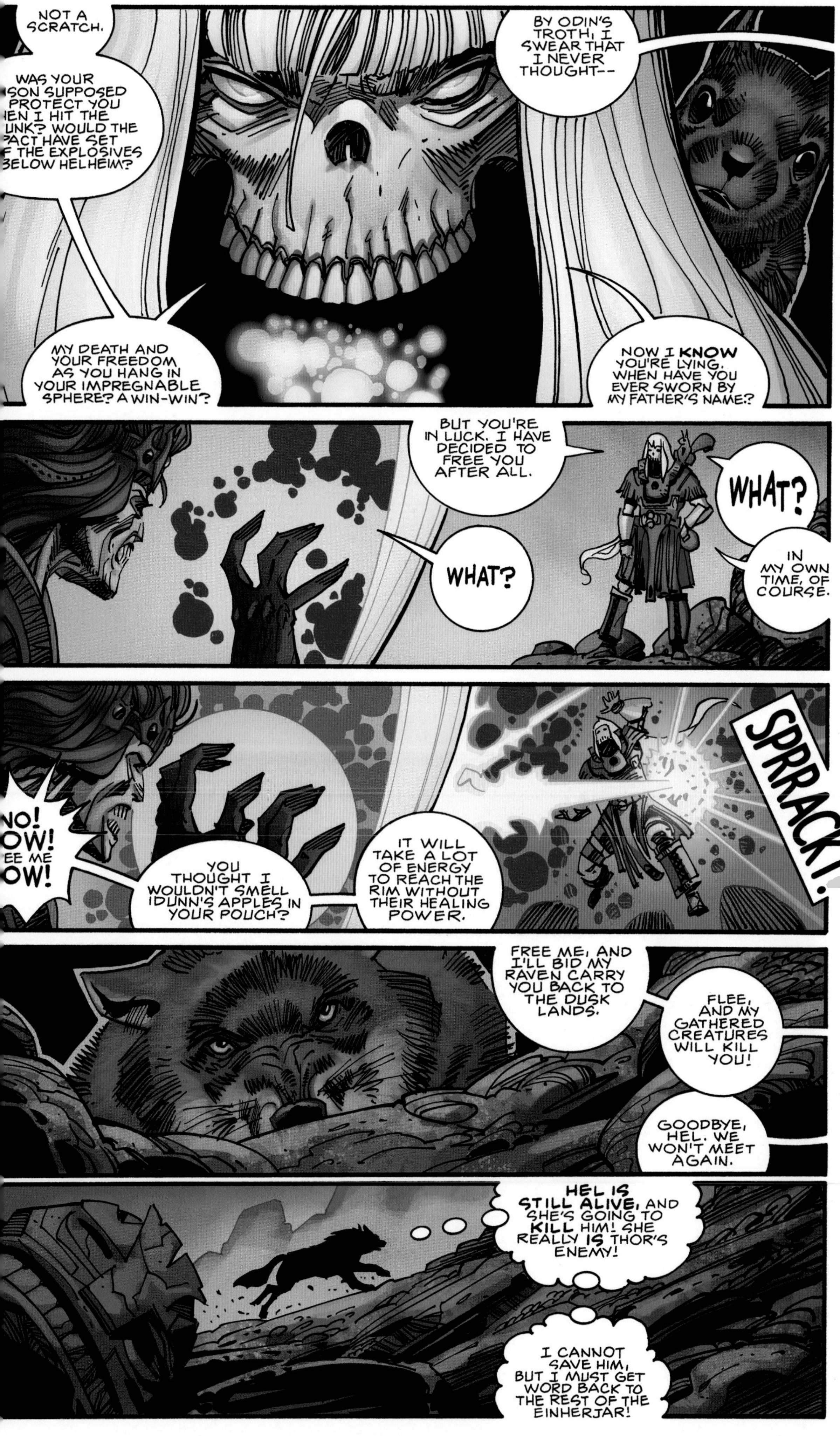
NOT A SCRATCH.
WAS YOUR SON SUPPOSED PROTECT YOU IEN I HIT THE UNK? WOULD THE PACT HAVE SET F THE EXPLOSIVES BELOW HELHEIM?
MY DEATH AND YOUR FREEDOM AS YOU HANG IN YOUR IMPREGNABLE SPHERE? A WIN-WIN?
BY ODIN'S TROTH, I SWEAR THAT I NEVER THOUGHT--
NOW I **KNOW** YOU'RE LYING. WHEN HAVE YOU EVER SWORN BY MY FATHER'S NAME?
BUT YOU'RE IN LUCK. I HAVE DECIDED TO FREE YOU AFTER ALL.
WHAT?
WHAT?
IN MY OWN TIME, OF COURSE.
NO! OW! EE ME OW!
YOU THOUGHT I WOULDN'T SMELL IDUNN'S APPLES IN YOUR POUCH?
IT WILL TAKE A LOT OF ENERGY TO REACH THE RIM WITHOUT THEIR HEALING POWER.
SPRRACK!
FREE ME, AND I'LL BID MY RAVEN CARRY YOU BACK TO THE DUSK LANDS.
FLEE, AND MY GATHERED CREATURES WILL KILL YOU!
GOODBYE, HEL. WE WON'T MEET AGAIN.
HEL IS STILL ALIVE, AND SHE'S GOING TO **KILL** HIM! SHE REALLY **IS** THOR'S ENEMY!
I CANNOT SAVE HIM, BUT I MUST GET WORD BACK TO THE REST OF THE EINHERJAR!

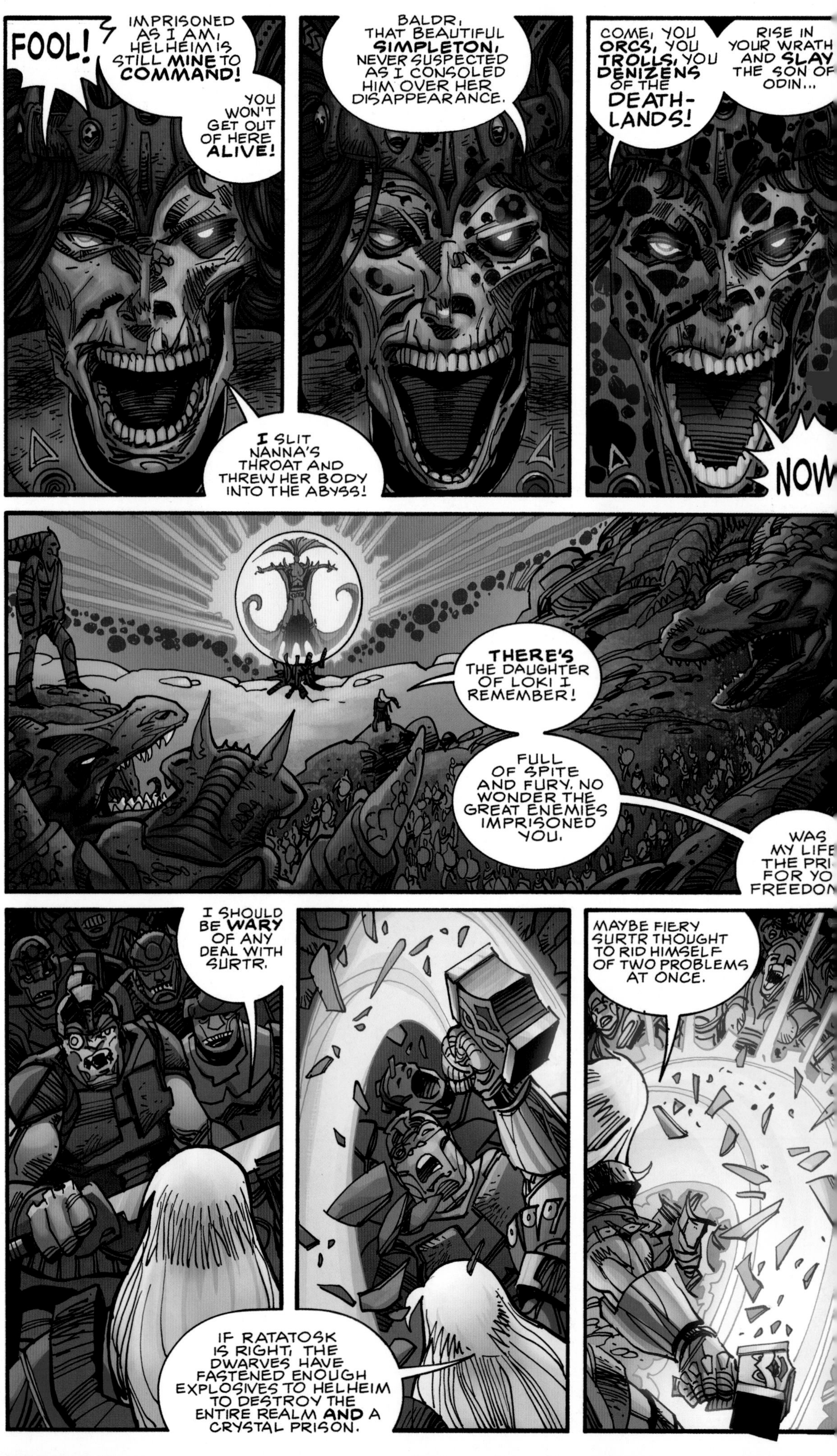
FOOL!
IMPRISONED AS I AM, HELHEIM IS STILL MINE TO COMMAND!
YOU WON'T GET OUT OF HERE ALIVE!
I SLIT NANNA'S THROAT AND THREW HER BODY INTO THE ABYSS!
BALDR, THAT BEAUTIFUL SIMPLETON, NEVER SUSPECTED AS I CONSOLED HIM OVER HER DISAPPEARANCE.
COME, YOU ORCS, YOU TROLLS, YOU DENIZENS OF THE DEATH-LANDS!
RISE IN YOUR WRATH AND SLAY THE SON OF ODIN...
NOW
THERE'S THE DAUGHTER OF LOKI I REMEMBER!
FULL OF SPITE AND FURY. NO WONDER THE GREAT ENEMIES IMPRISONED YOU.
WAS MY LIFE THE PRI FOR YO FREEDOM
I SHOULD BE WARY OF ANY DEAL WITH SURTR.
IF RATATOSK IS RIGHT, THE DWARVES HAVE FASTENED ENOUGH EXPLOSIVES TO HELHEIM TO DESTROY THE ENTIRE REALM AND A CRYSTAL PRISON.
MAYBE FIERY SURTR THOUGHT TO RID HIMSELF OF TWO PROBLEMS AT ONCE.

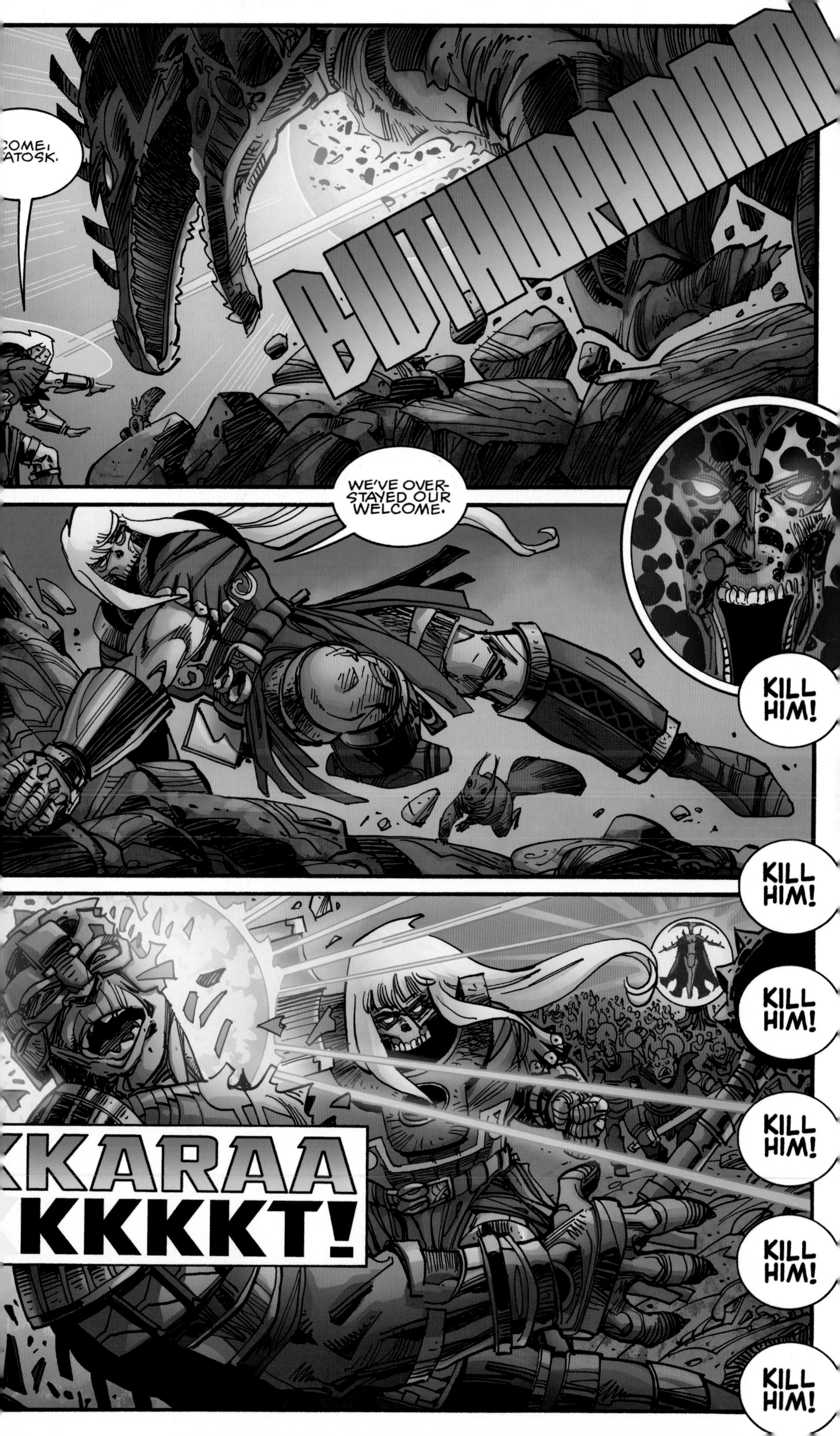
COME, ATOSK.
WE'VE OVER-STAYED OUR WELCOME.
KILL HIM!
KILL HIM!
KILL HIM!
KILL HIM!
KILL HIM!
KILL HIM!
KARAA KKKKT!

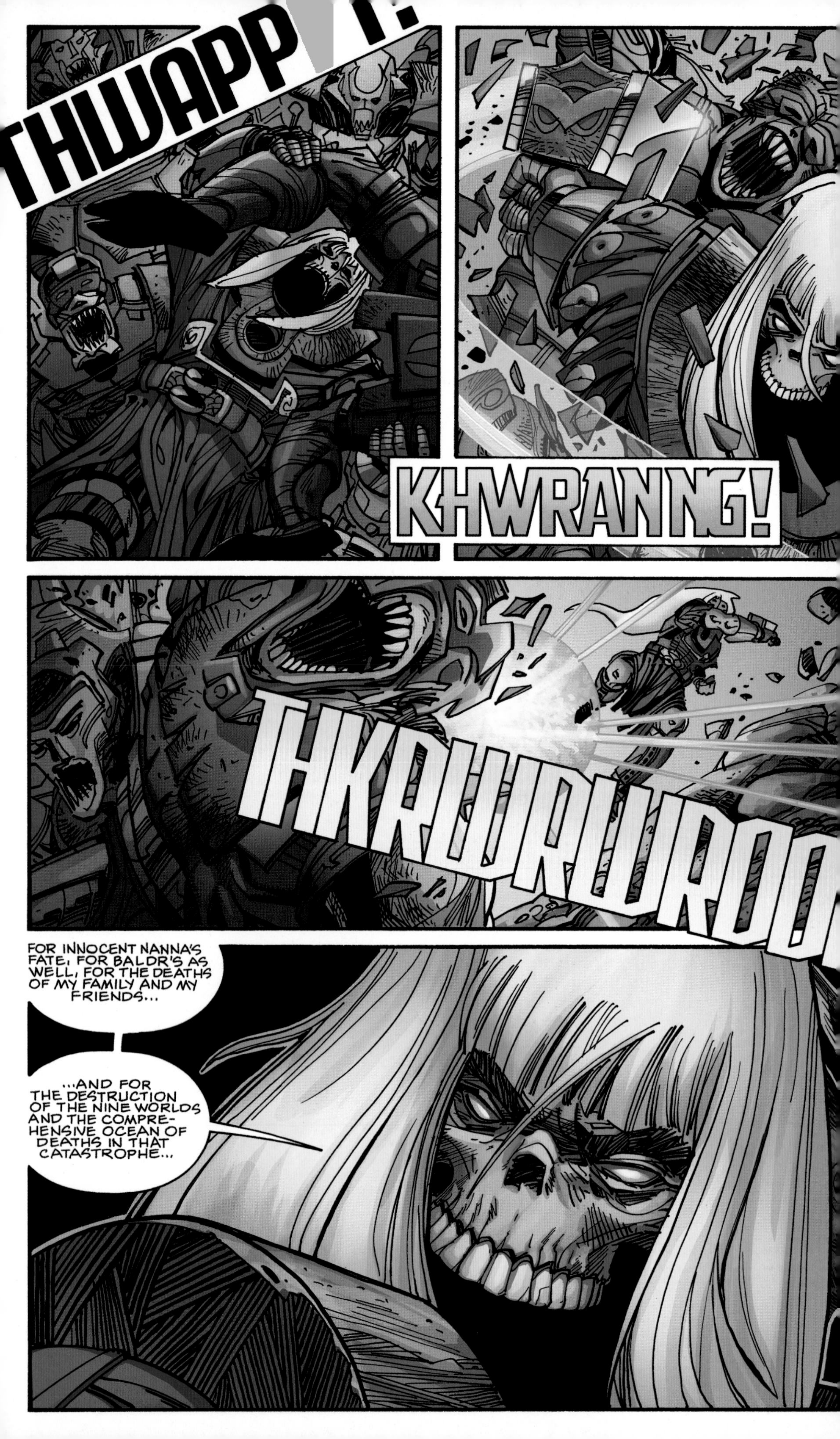
THWAPP
KHWRANNG!
THKRWRWROO
FOR INNOCENT NANNA'S FATE, FOR BALDR'S AS WELL, FOR THE DEATHS OF MY FAMILY AND MY FRIENDS...
...AND FOR THE DESTRUCTION OF THE NINE WORLDS AND THE COMPRE-HENSIVE OCEAN OF DEATHS IN THAT CATASTROPHE...

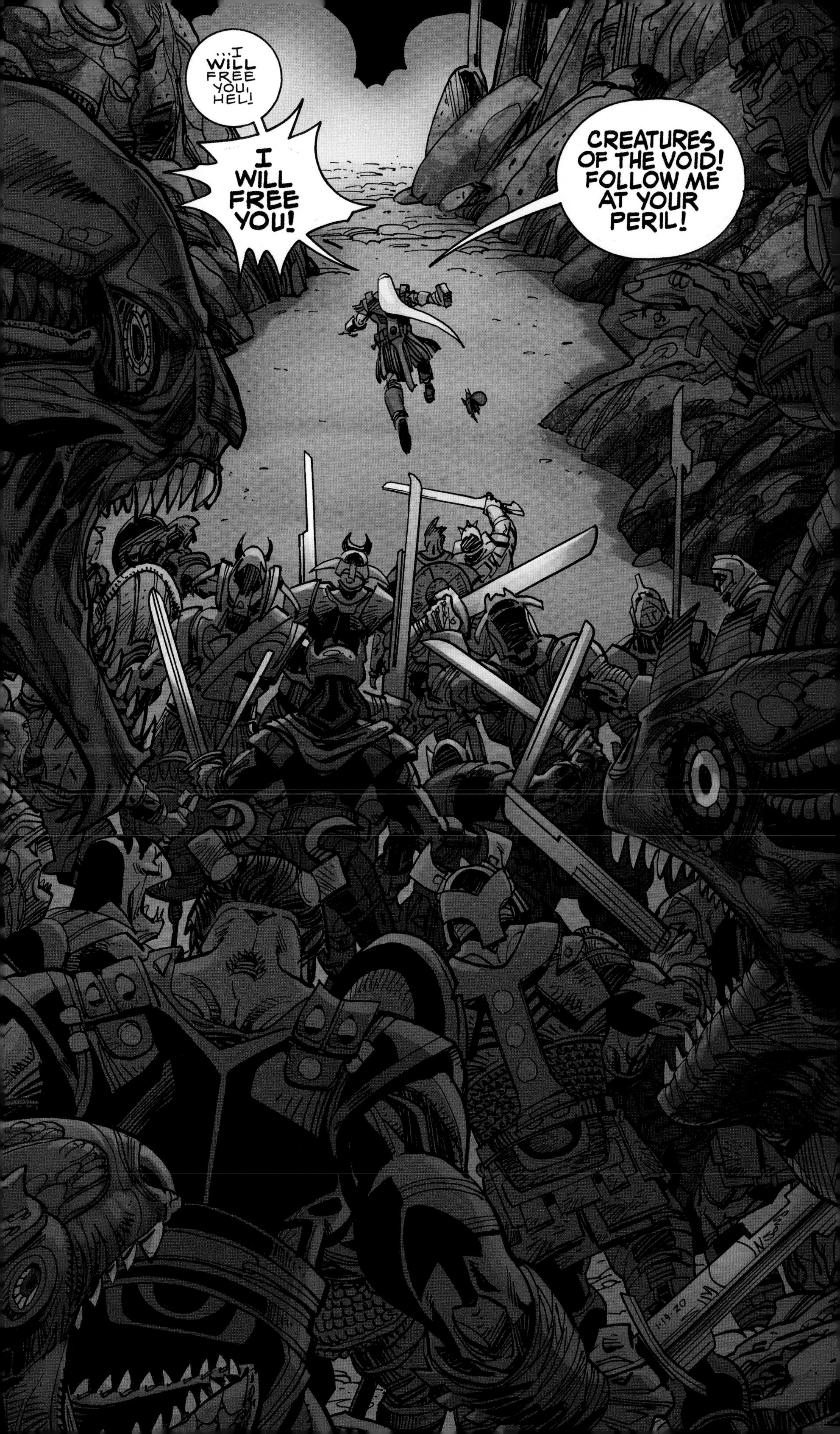
...I WILL FREE YOU, HEL!
I WILL FREE YOU!
CREATURES OF THE VOID! FOLLOW ME AT YOUR PERIL!

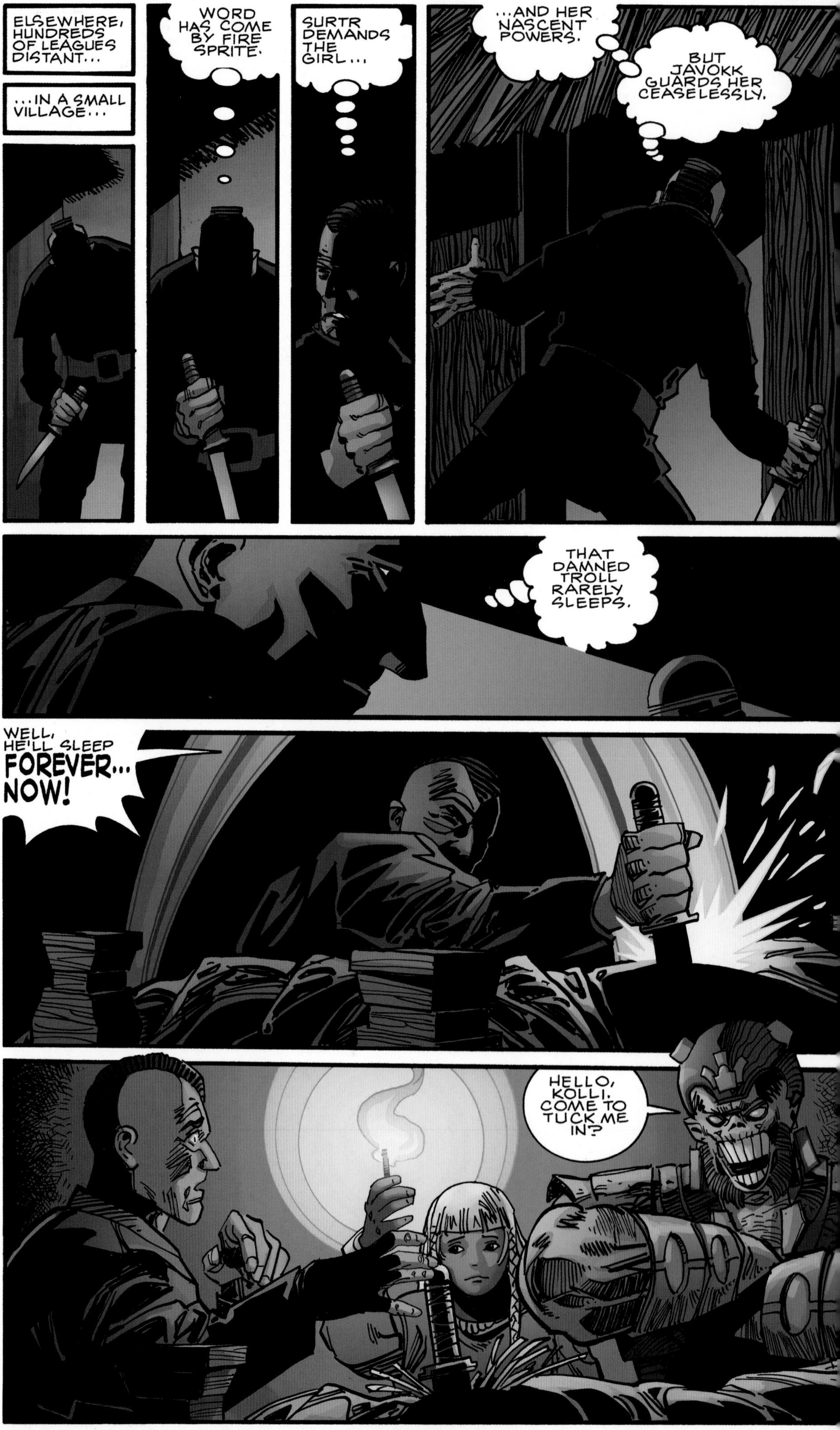
ELSEWHERE, HUNDREDS OF LEAGUES DISTANT...
...IN A SMALL VILLAGE...
WORD HAS COME BY FIRE SPRITE.
SURTR DEMANDS THE GIRL...
...AND HER NASCENT POWERS.
BUT JAVOKK GUARDS HER CEASELESSLY.
THAT DAMNED TROLL RARELY SLEEPS.
WELL, HE'LL SLEEP FOREVER... NOW!
HELLO, KOLLI. COME TO TUCK ME IN?

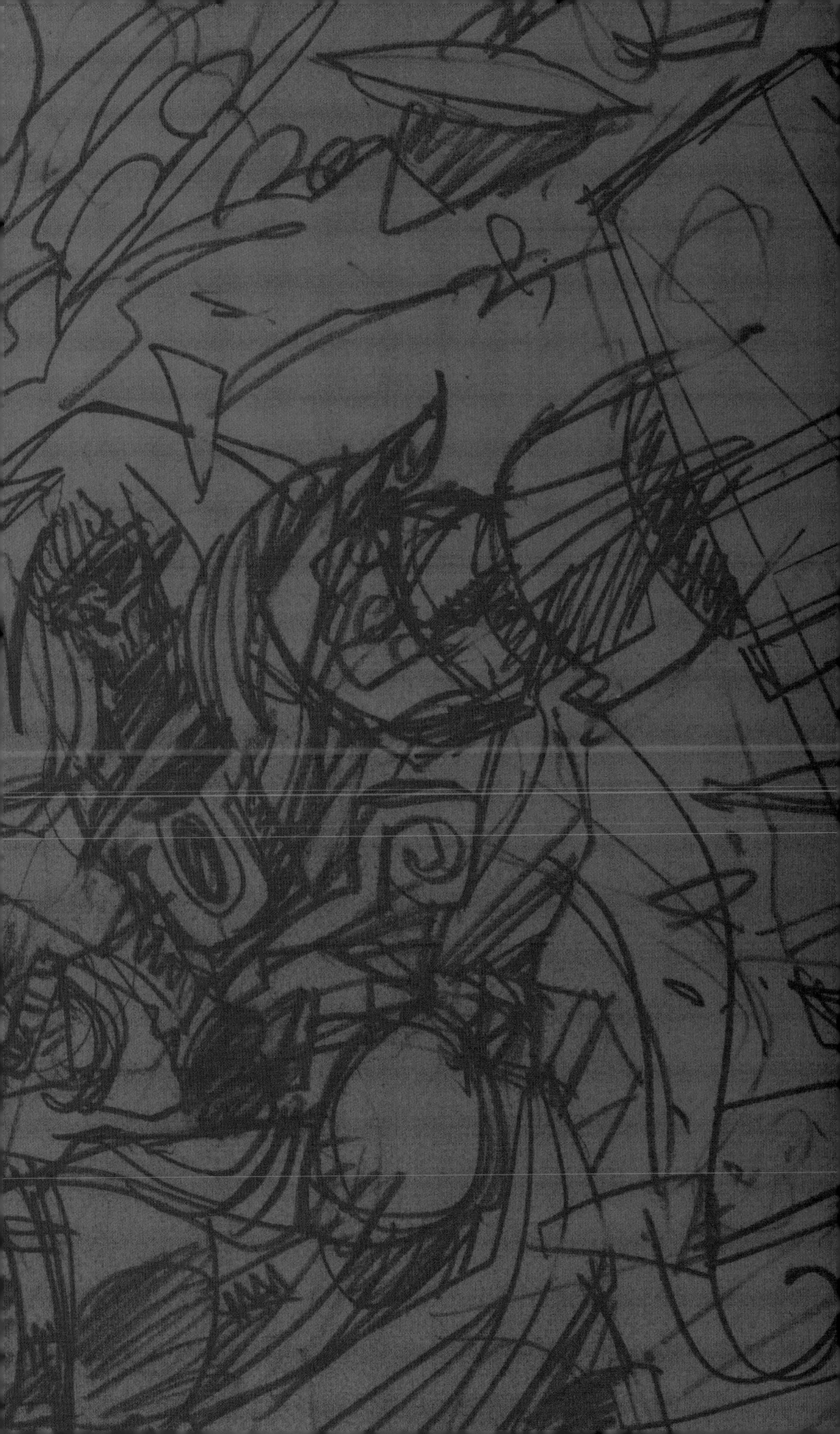

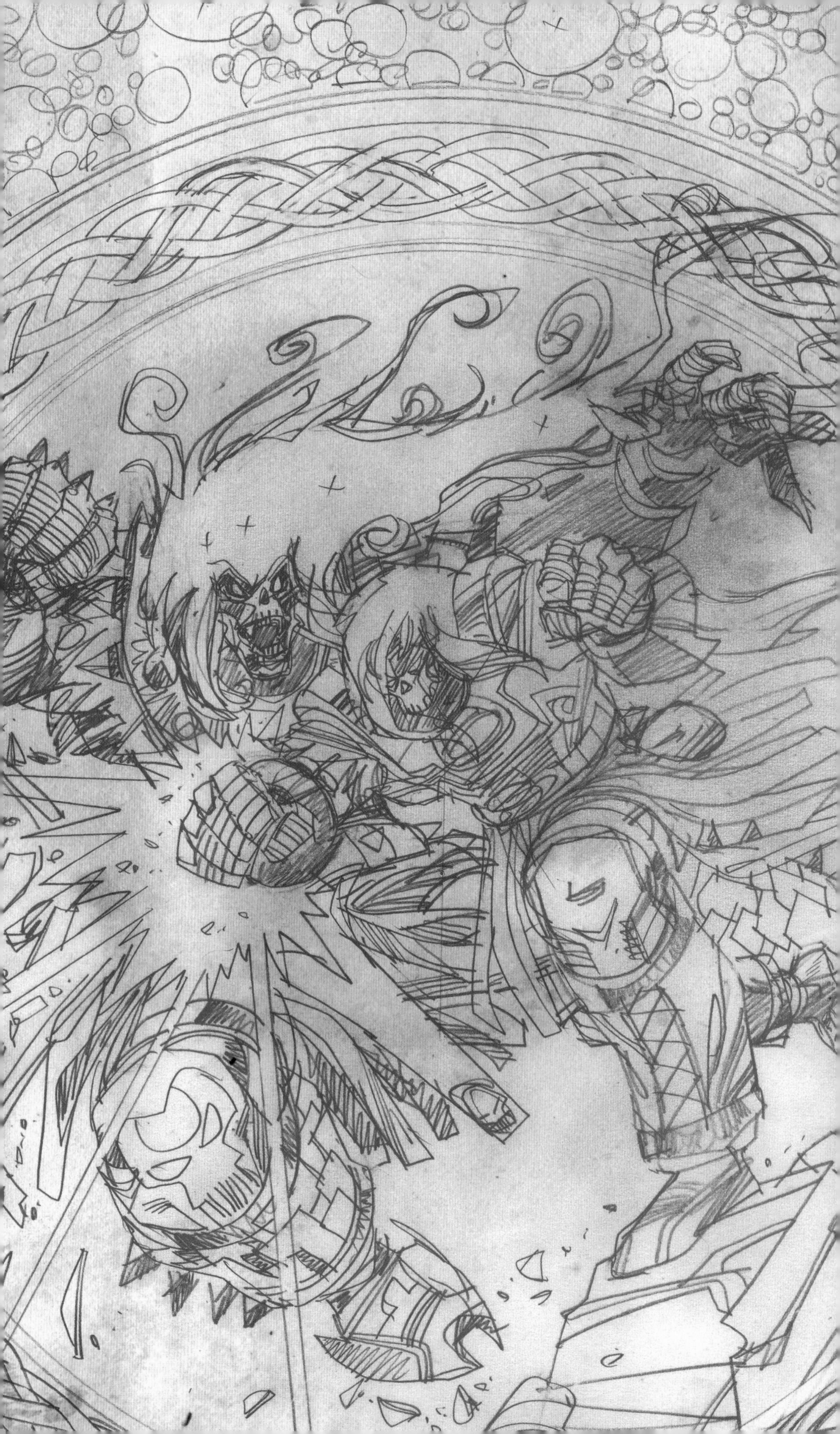

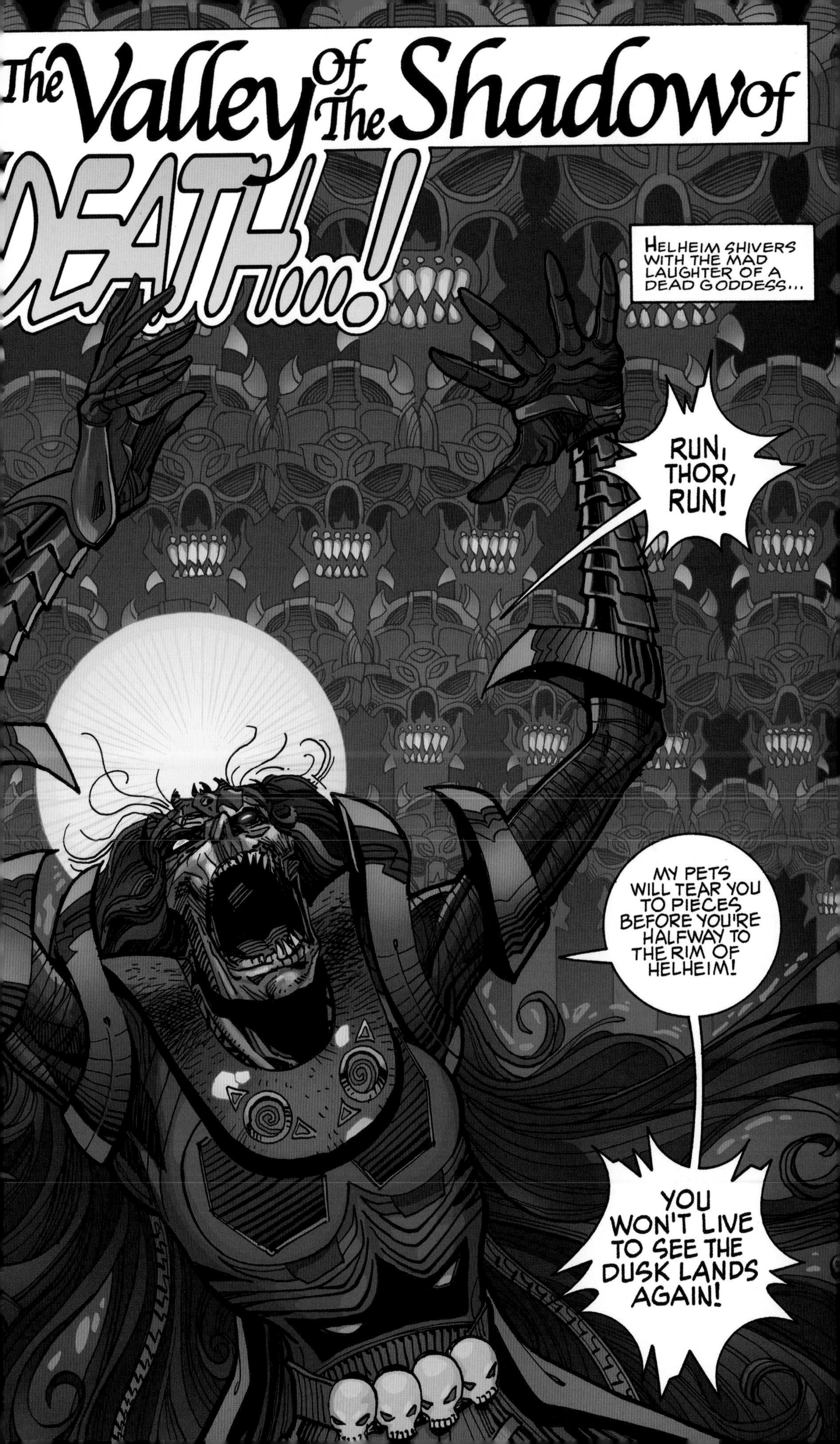
The Valley of The Shadow of DEATH...!
HELHEIM SHIVERS WITH THE MAD LAUGHTER OF A DEAD GODDESS...
RUN, THOR, RUN!
MY PETS WILL TEAR YOU TO PIECES BEFORE YOU'RE HALFWAY TO THE RIM OF HELHEIM!
YOU WON'T LIVE TO SEE THE DUSK LANDS AGAIN!

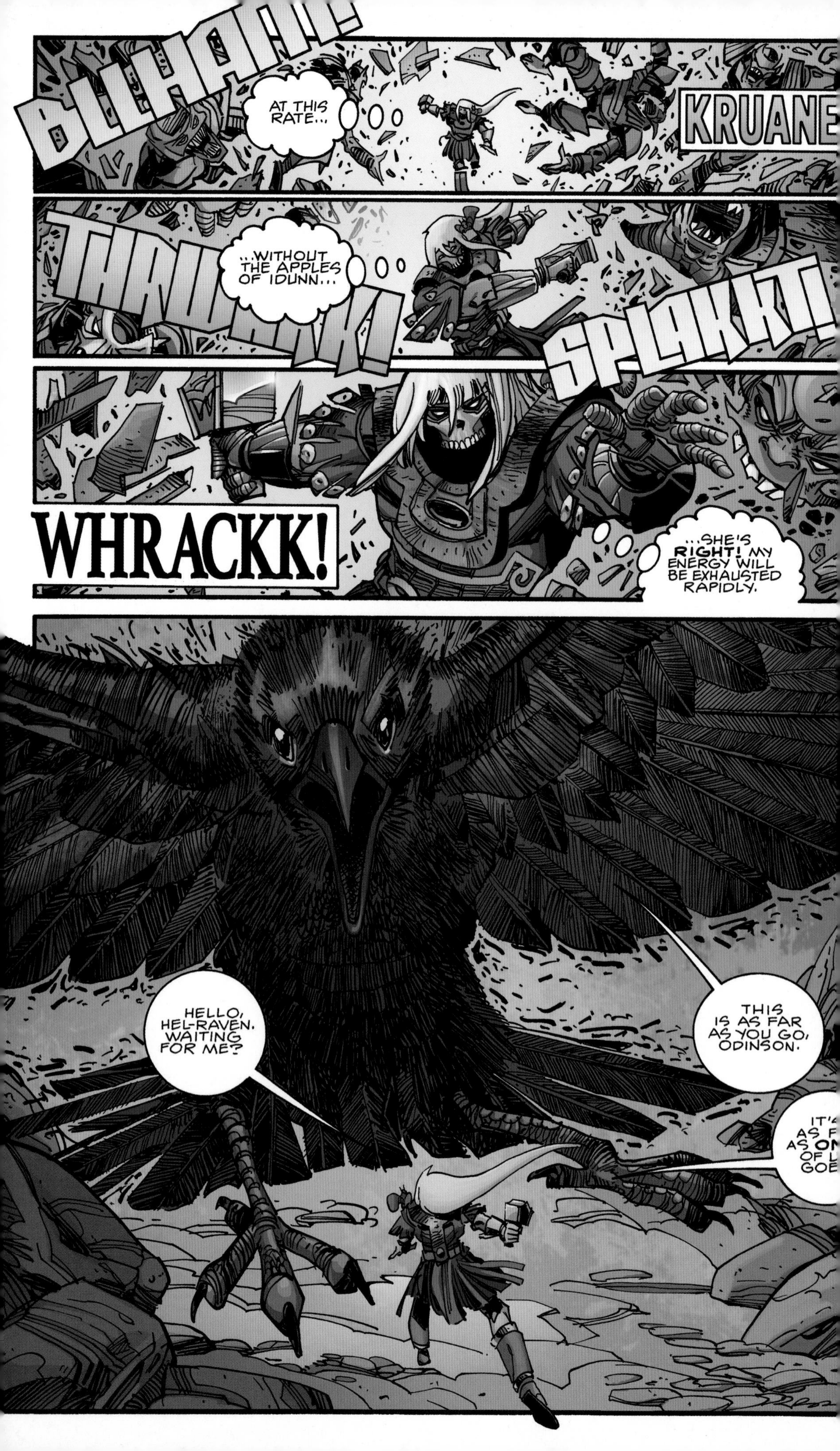
KRUANE
AT THIS RATE...
...WITHOUT THE APPLES OF IDUNN...
SPLAKK!
WHRACKK!
...SHE'S **RIGHT!** MY ENERGY WILL BE EXHAUSTED RAPIDLY.
HELLO, HEL-RAVEN. WAITING FOR ME?
THIS IS AS FAR AS YOU GO, ODINSON.

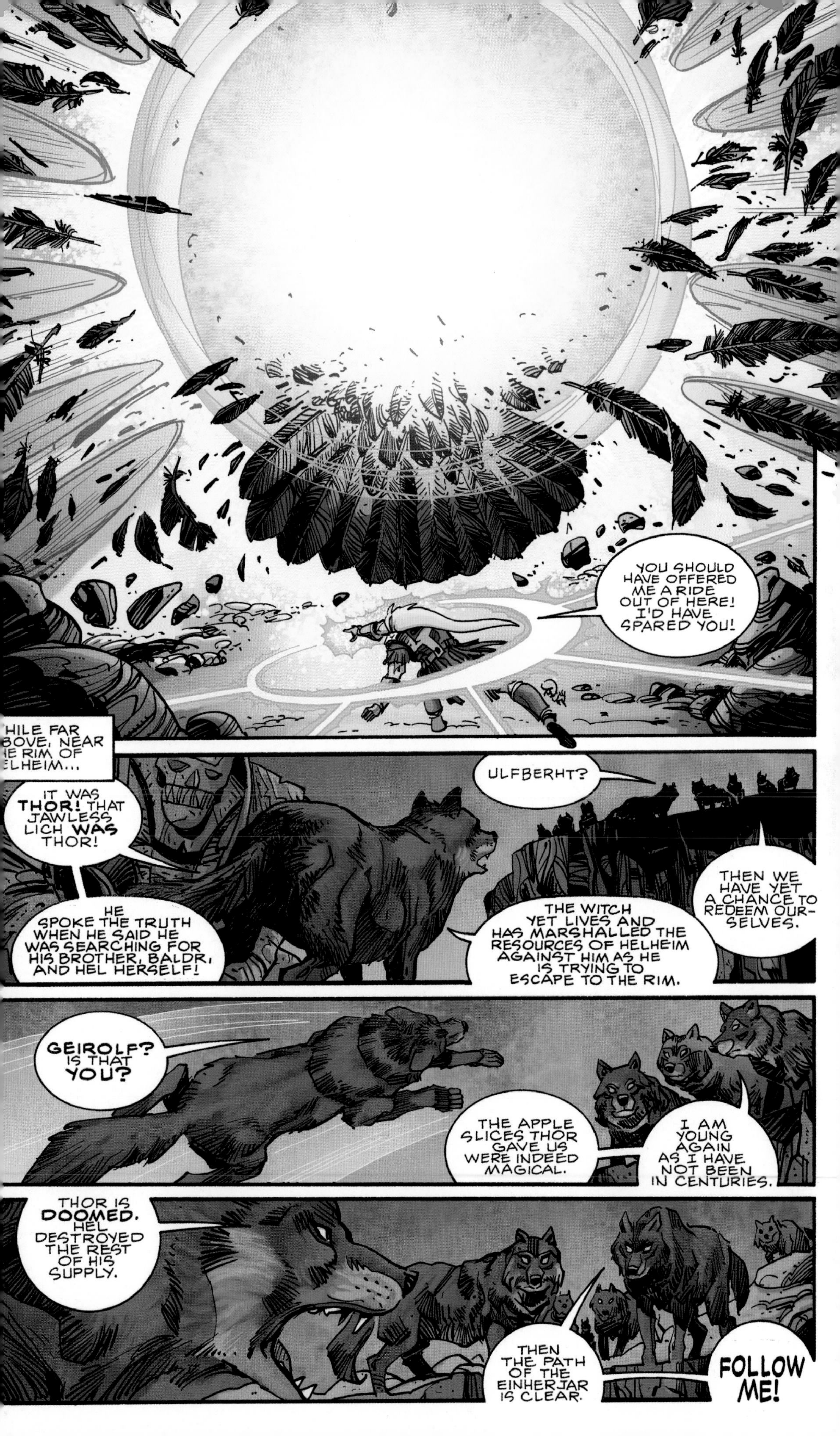
YOU SHOULD HAVE OFFERED ME A RIDE OUT OF HERE! I'D HAVE SPARED YOU!
HILE FAR BOVE, NEAR HE RIM OF ELHEIM...
ULFBERHT?
IT WAS THOR! THAT JAWLESS LICH WAS THOR!
HE SPOKE THE TRUTH WHEN HE SAID HE WAS SEARCHING FOR HIS BROTHER, BALDR, AND HEL HERSELF!
THE WITCH YET LIVES AND HAS MARSHALLED THE RESOURCES OF HELHEIM AGAINST HIM AS HE IS TRYING TO ESCAPE TO THE RIM.
THEN WE HAVE YET A CHANCE TO REDEEM OUR-SELVES.
GEIROLF? IS THAT YOU?
THE APPLE SLICES THOR GAVE US WERE INDEED MAGICAL.
I AM YOUNG AGAIN AS I HAVE NOT BEEN IN CENTURIES.
THOR IS DOOMED. HEL DESTROYED THE REST OF HIS SUPPLY.
THEN THE PATH OF THE EINHERJAR IS CLEAR.
FOLLOW ME!

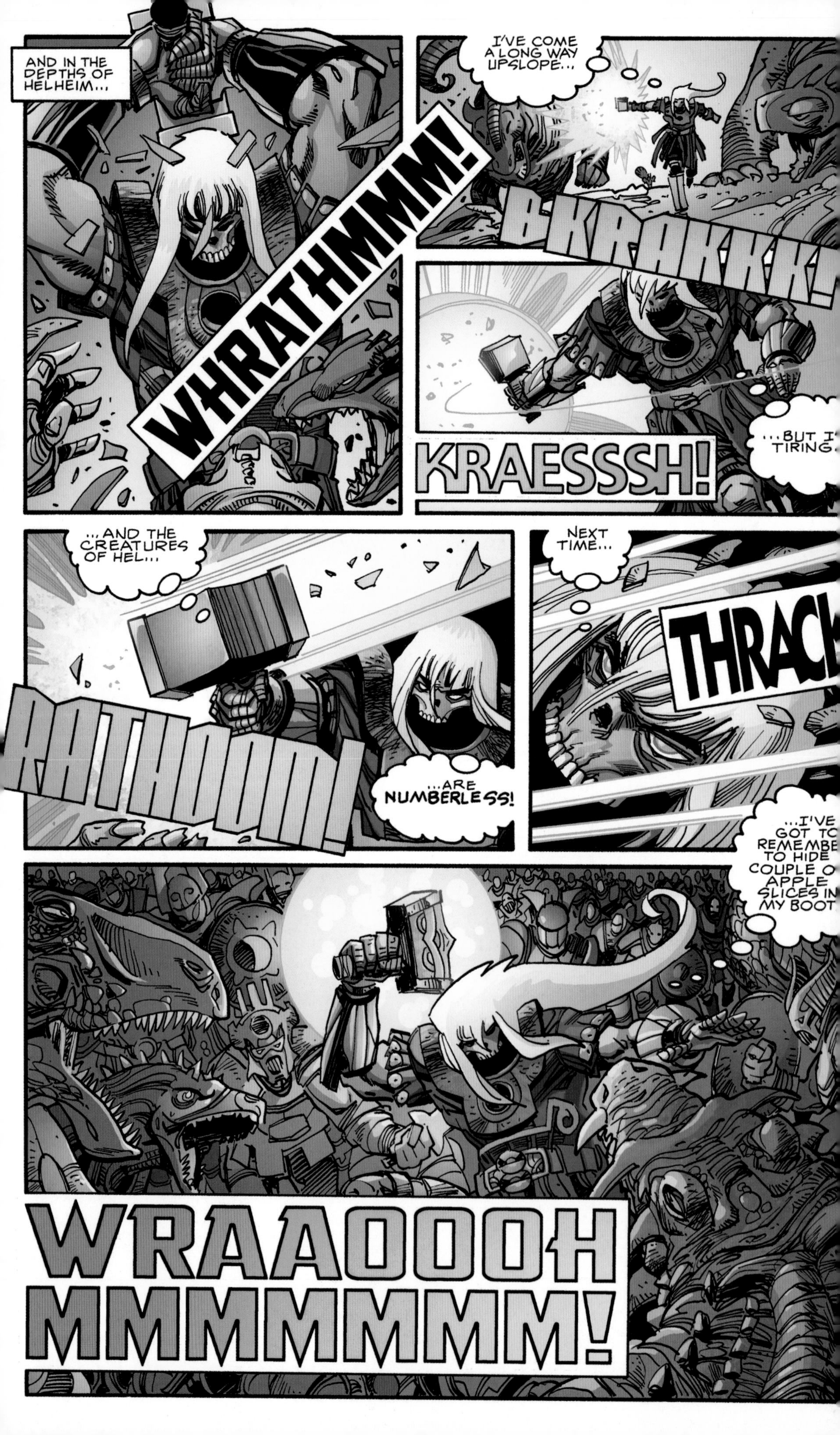
AND IN THE DEPTHS OF HELHEIM...
WHRATHMMM!
I'VE COME A LONG WAY UPSLOPE...
BKRAKKK!
KRAESSSH!
...BUT I'
TIRING.
...AND THE CREATURES OF HEL...
...ARE NUMBERLESS!
NEXT TIME...
THRACK
...I'VE GOT TO REMEMBE TO HIDE COUPLE O APPLE SLICES IN MY BOOT
WRAAOOOH MMMMMMMM!

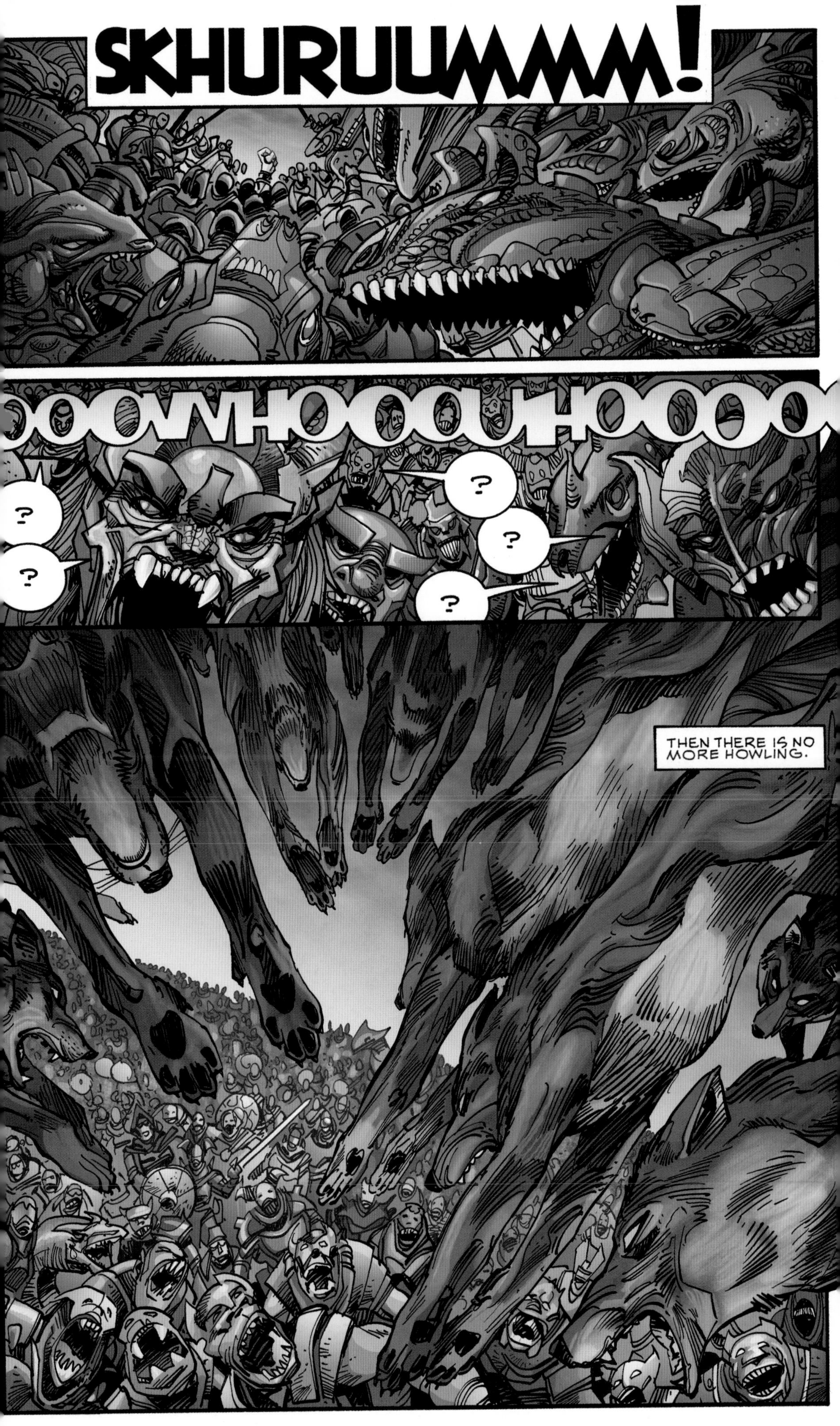
SKHURUUMMMM!
OOOVVHOOOUHOOOOO
?
?
?
?
?
THEN THERE IS NO MORE HOWLING.

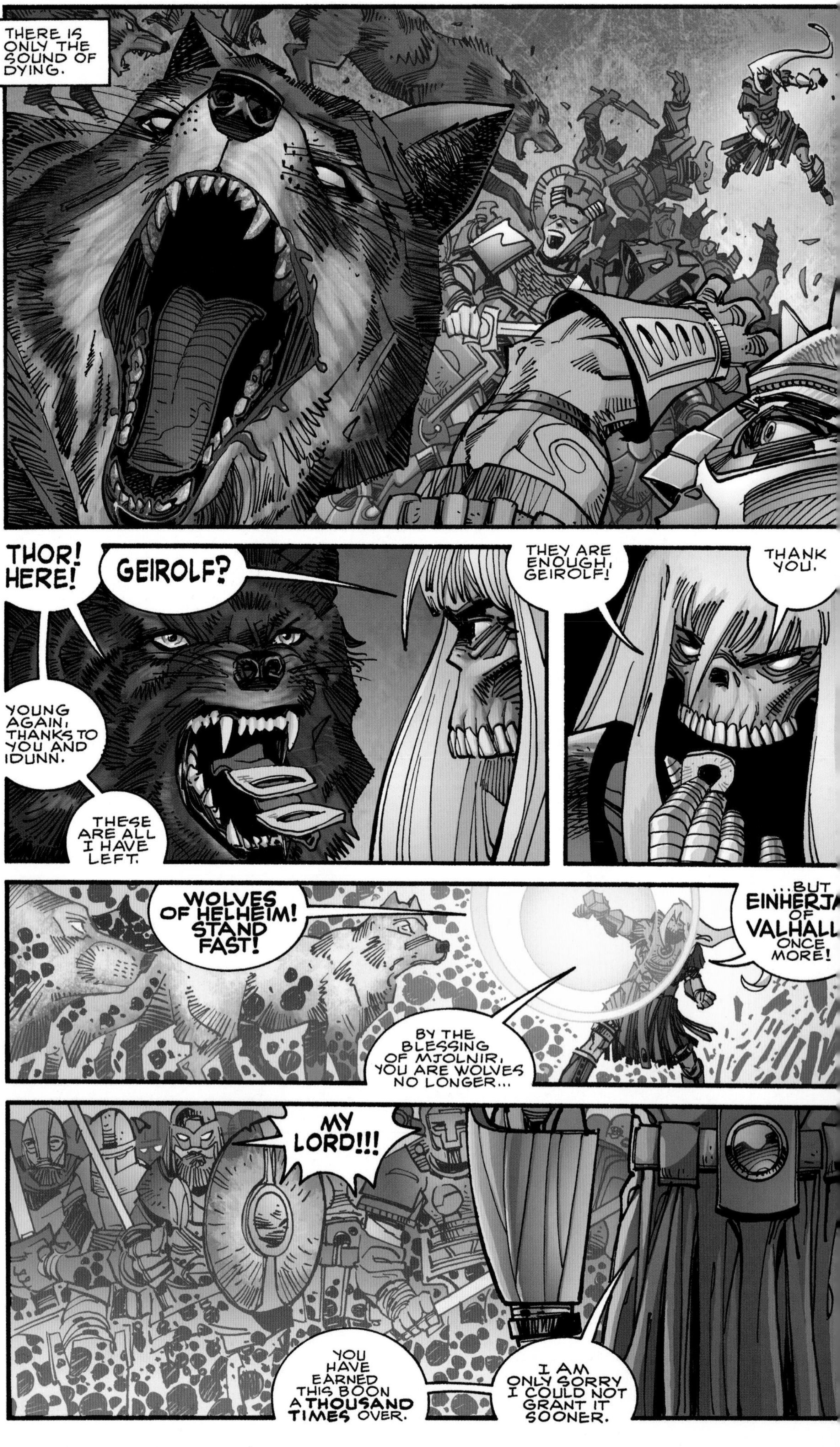
THERE IS ONLY THE SOUND OF DYING.
THOR! HERE!
GEIROLF?
YOUNG AGAIN, THANKS TO YOU AND IDUNN.
THESE ARE ALL I HAVE LEFT.
THEY ARE ENOUGH, GEIROLF!
THANK YOU.
WOLVES OF HELHEIM! STAND FAST!
BY THE BLESSING OF MJOLNIR, YOU ARE WOLVES NO LONGER...
...BUT EINHERJA OF VALHALL ONCE MORE!
MY LORD!!!
YOU HAVE EARNED THIS BOON A THOUSAND TIMES OVER.
I AM ONLY SORRY I COULD NOT GRANT IT SOONER.

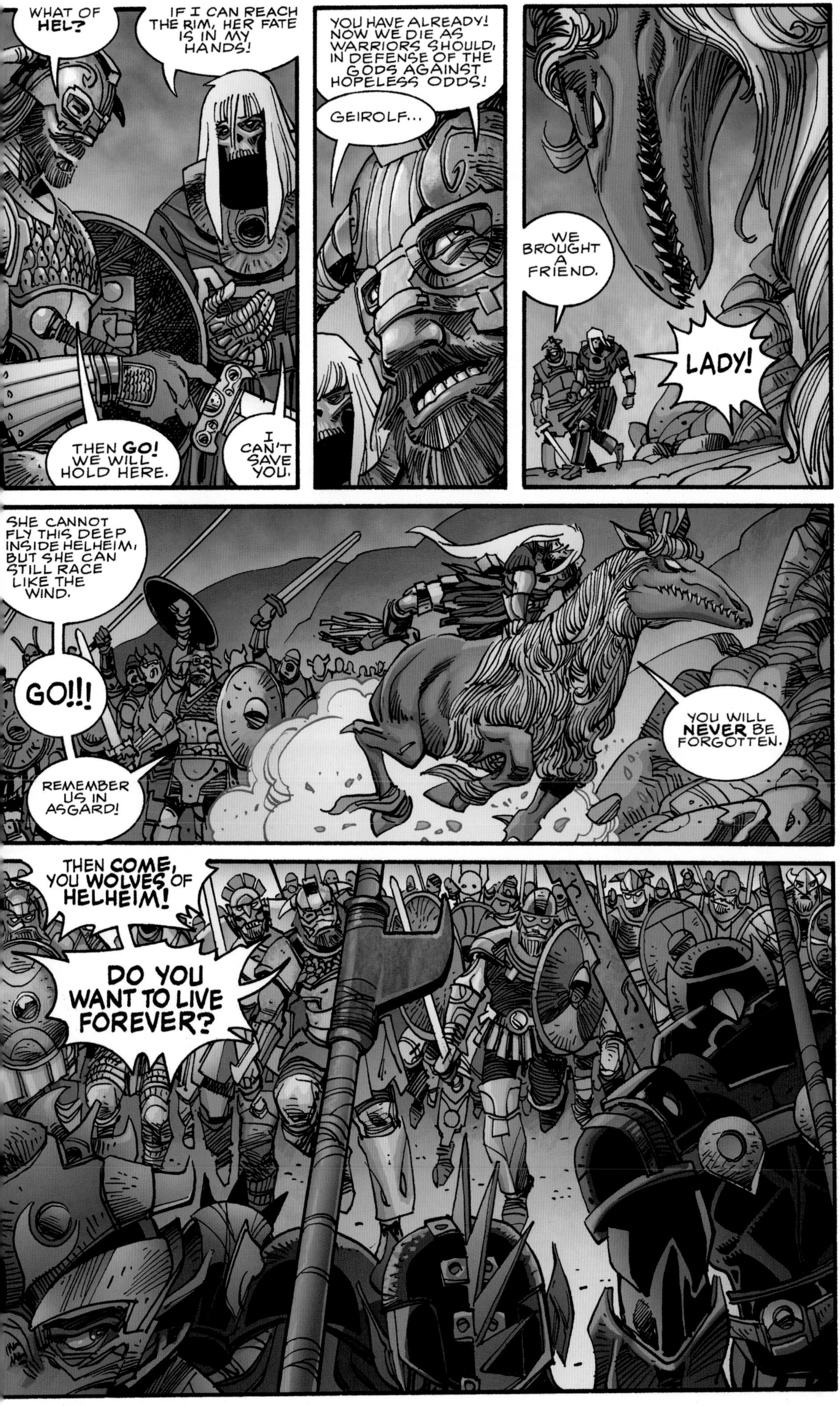
WHAT OF HEL?
IF I CAN REACH THE RIM, HER FATE IS IN MY HANDS!
THEN GO! WE WILL HOLD HERE.
I CAN'T SAVE YOU.
YOU HAVE ALREADY! NOW WE DIE AS WARRIORS SHOULD, IN DEFENSE OF THE GODS AGAINST HOPELESS ODDS!
GEIROLF...
WE BROUGHT A FRIEND.
LADY!
SHE CANNOT FLY THIS DEEP INSIDE HELHEIM, BUT SHE CAN STILL RACE LIKE THE WIND.
GO!!!
REMEMBER US IN ASGARD!
YOU WILL NEVER BE FORGOTTEN.
THEN COME, YOU WOLVES OF HELHEIM!
DO YOU WANT TO LIVE FOREVER?

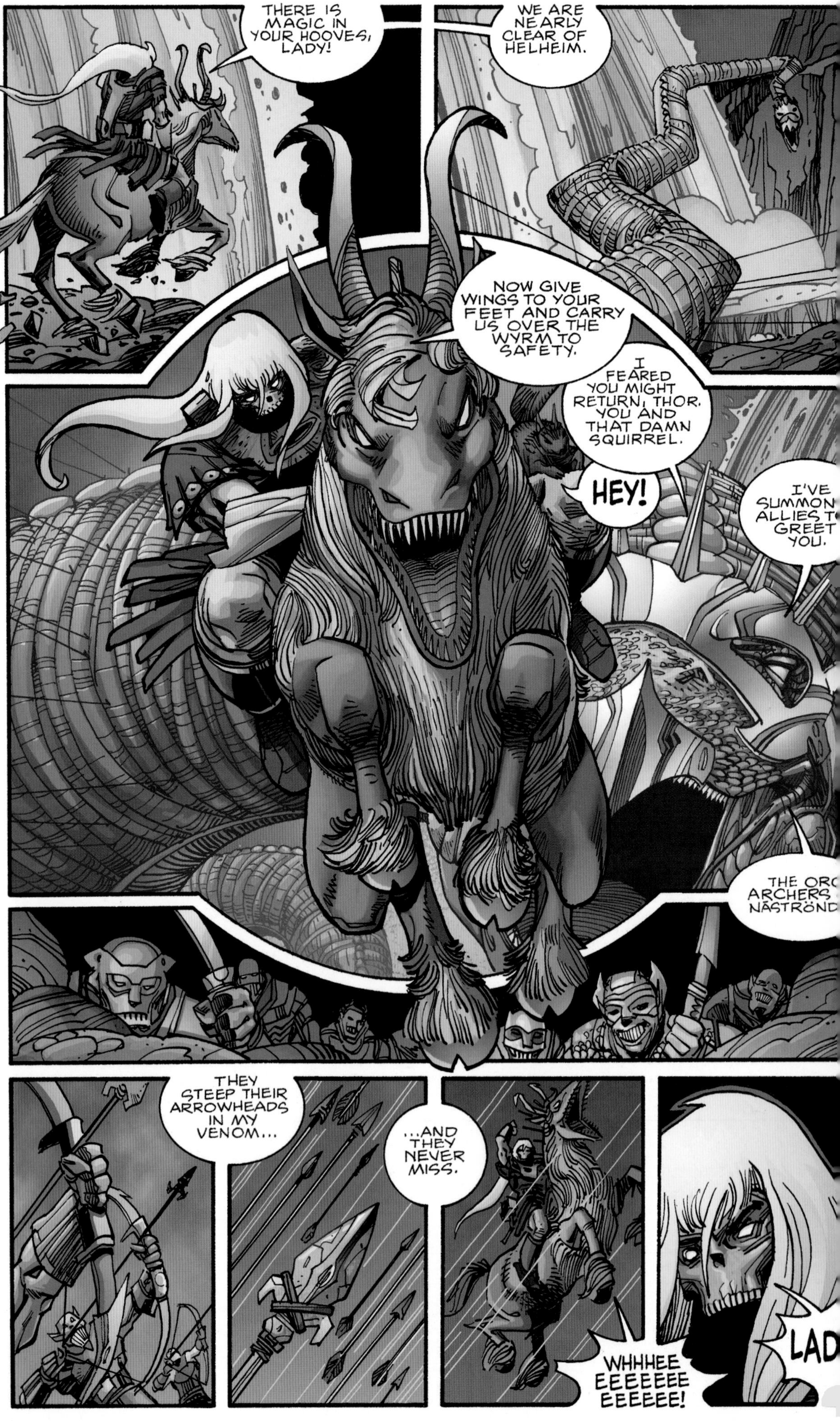
THERE IS MAGIC IN YOUR HOOVES, LADY!
WE ARE NEARLY CLEAR OF HELHEIM.
NOW GIVE WINGS TO YOUR FEET AND CARRY US OVER THE WYRM TO SAFETY.
I FEARED YOU MIGHT RETURN, THOR. YOU AND THAT DAMN SQUIRREL.
HEY!
I'VE SUMMON ALLIES T GREET YOU.
THE ORC ARCHERS NÄSTRÖND
THEY STEEP THEIR ARROWHEADS IN MY VENOM...
...AND THEY NEVER MISS.
WHHHEE EEEEEEE EEEEEE!
LAD

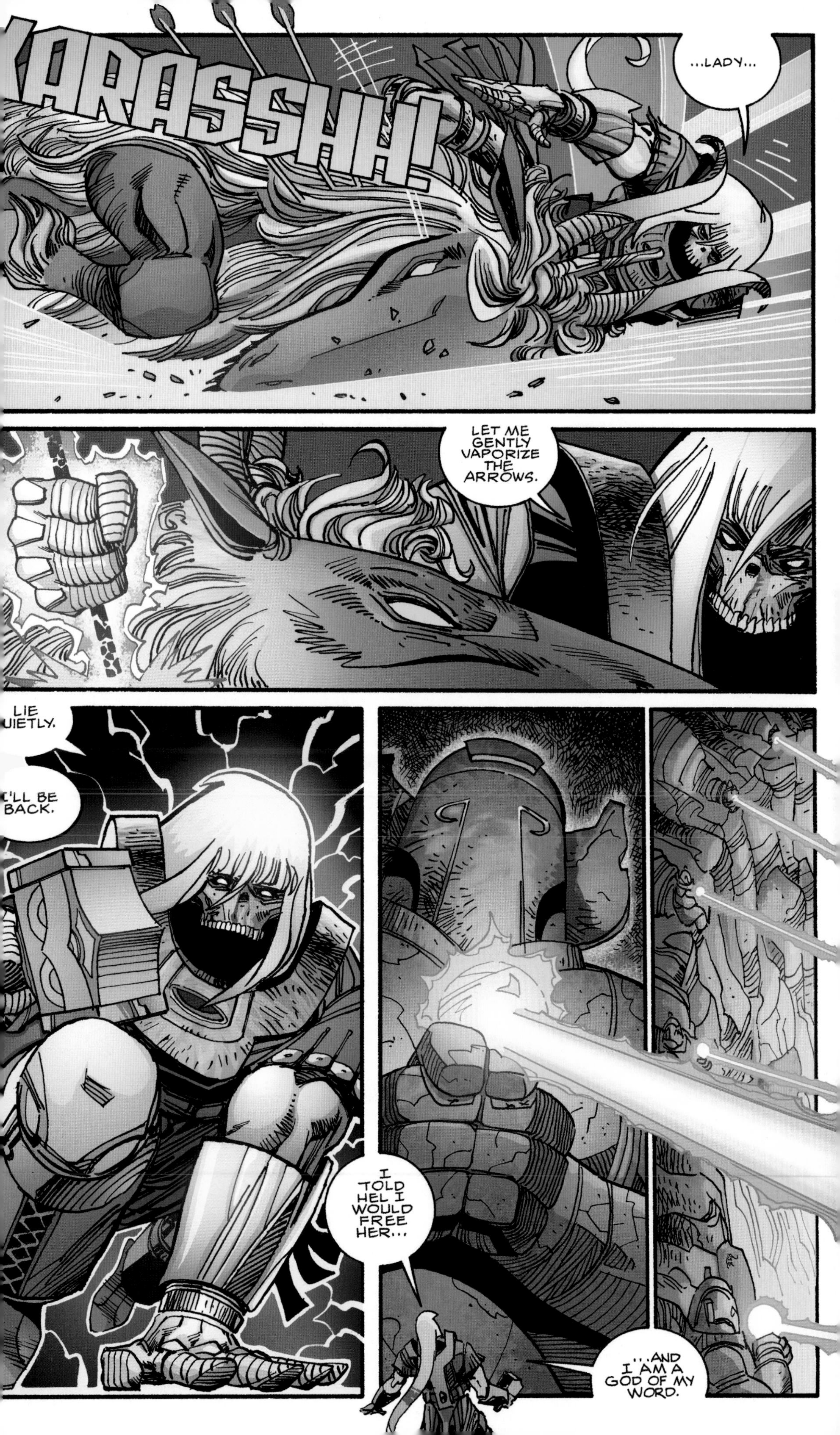
KRASSHH!
...LADY...
LET ME GENTLY VAPORIZE THE ARROWS.
LIE QUIETLY.
I'LL BE BACK.
I TOLD HEL I WOULD FREE HER...
...AND I AM A GOD OF MY WORD.

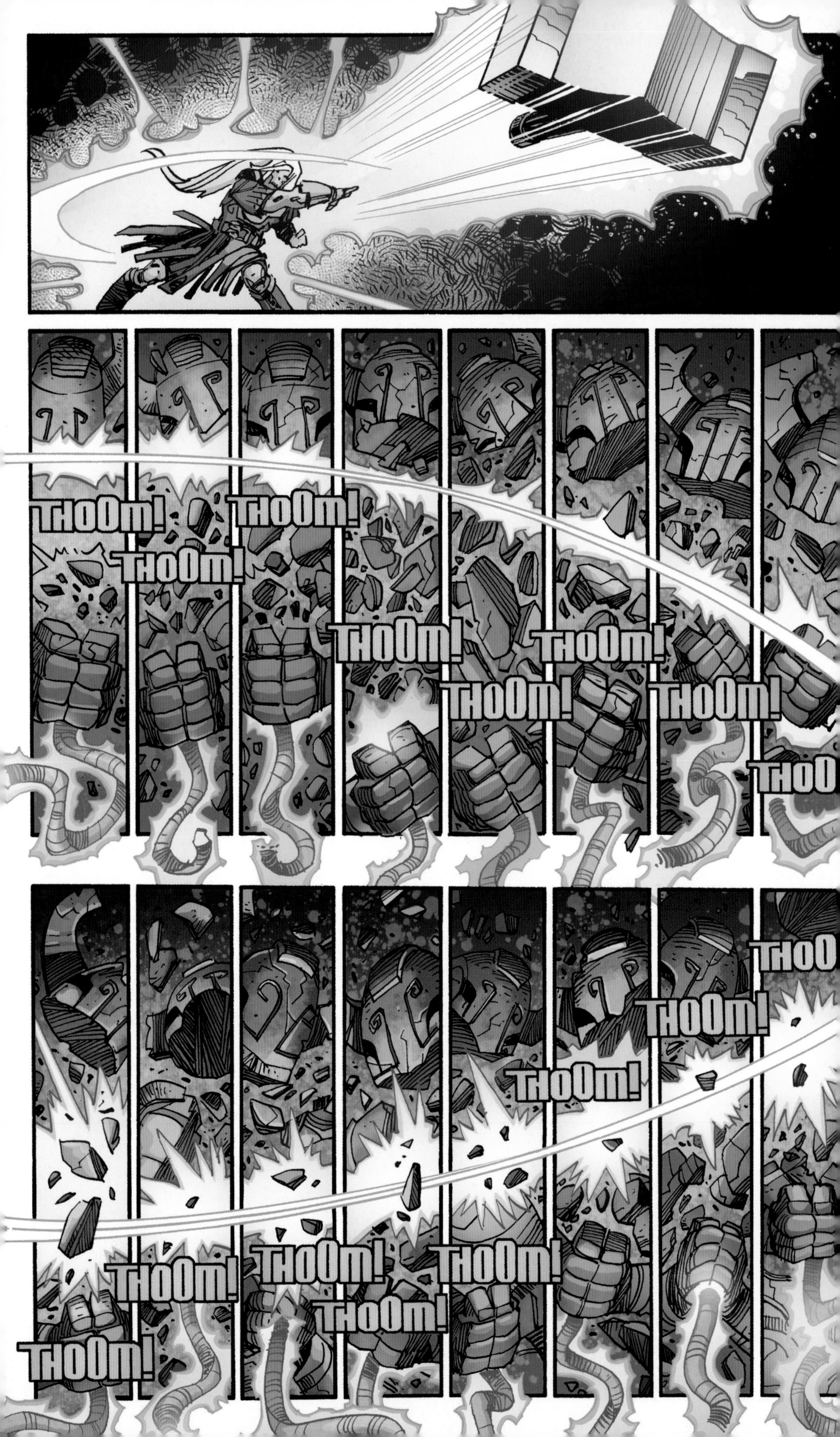
THOOM!
THOOM!
THOOM!
THOOM!
THOOM!
THOOM!
THOOM!
THOO
THOO
THOOM!
THOOM!
THOOM!
THOOM!
THOOM!
THOOM!
THOOM!

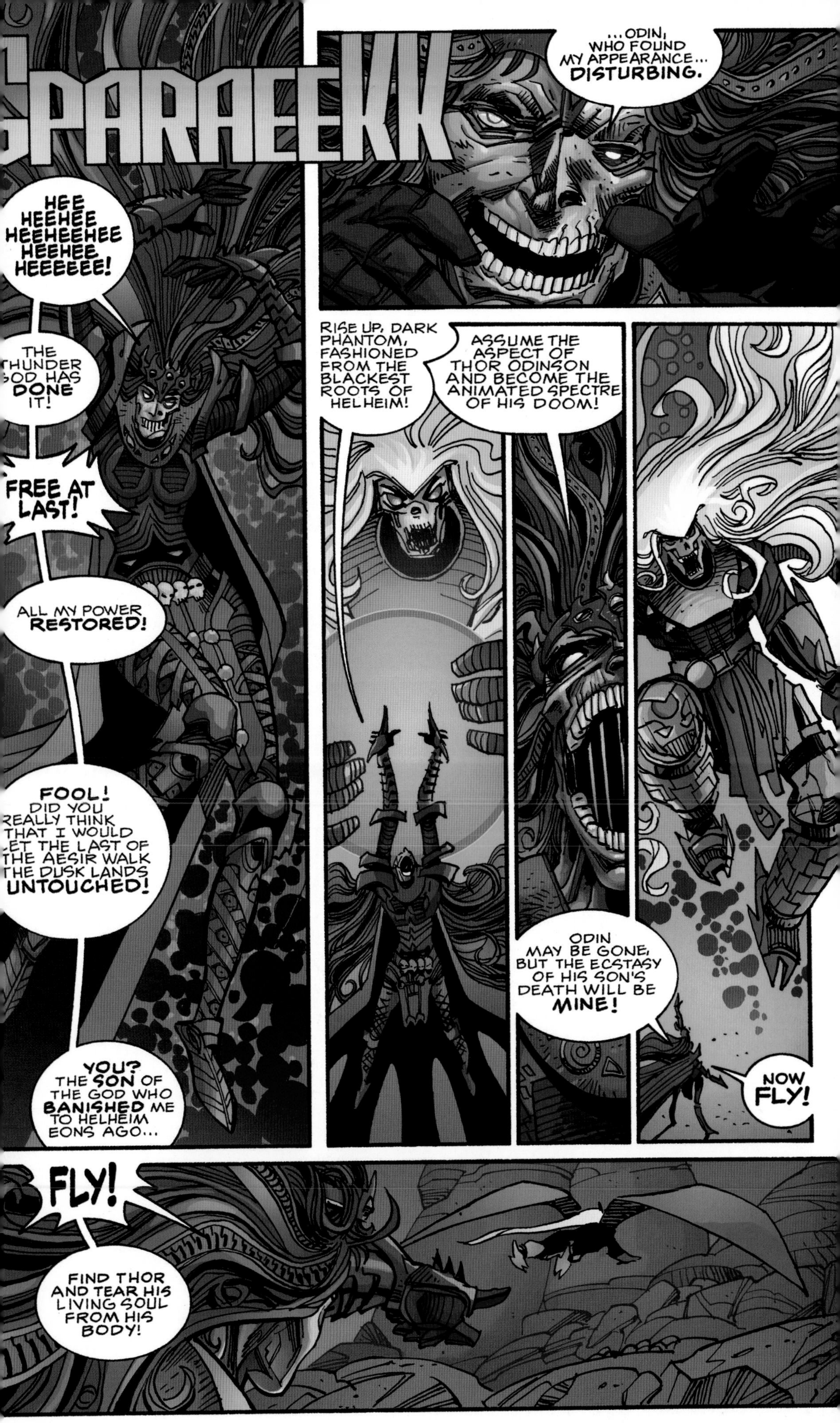
SPARAEKK
...ODIN, WHO FOUND MY APPEARANCE... DISTURBING.
HEE HEEHEE HEEHEEHEE HEEHEE HEEEEEE!
THE THUNDER GOD HAS DONE IT!
FREE AT LAST!
ALL MY POWER RESTORED!
FOOL! DID YOU REALLY THINK THAT I WOULD LET THE LAST OF THE AESIR WALK THE DUSK LANDS UNTOUCHED!
YOU? THE SON OF THE GOD WHO BANISHED ME TO HELHEIM EONS AGO...
RISE UP, DARK PHANTOM, FASHIONED FROM THE BLACKEST ROOTS OF HELHEIM!
ASSUME THE ASPECT OF THOR ODINSON AND BECOME THE ANIMATED SPECTRE OF HIS DOOM!
ODIN MAY BE GONE, BUT THE ECSTASY OF HIS SON'S DEATH WILL BE MINE!
NOW FLY!
FLY!
FIND THOR AND TEAR HIS LIVING SOUL FROM HIS BODY!

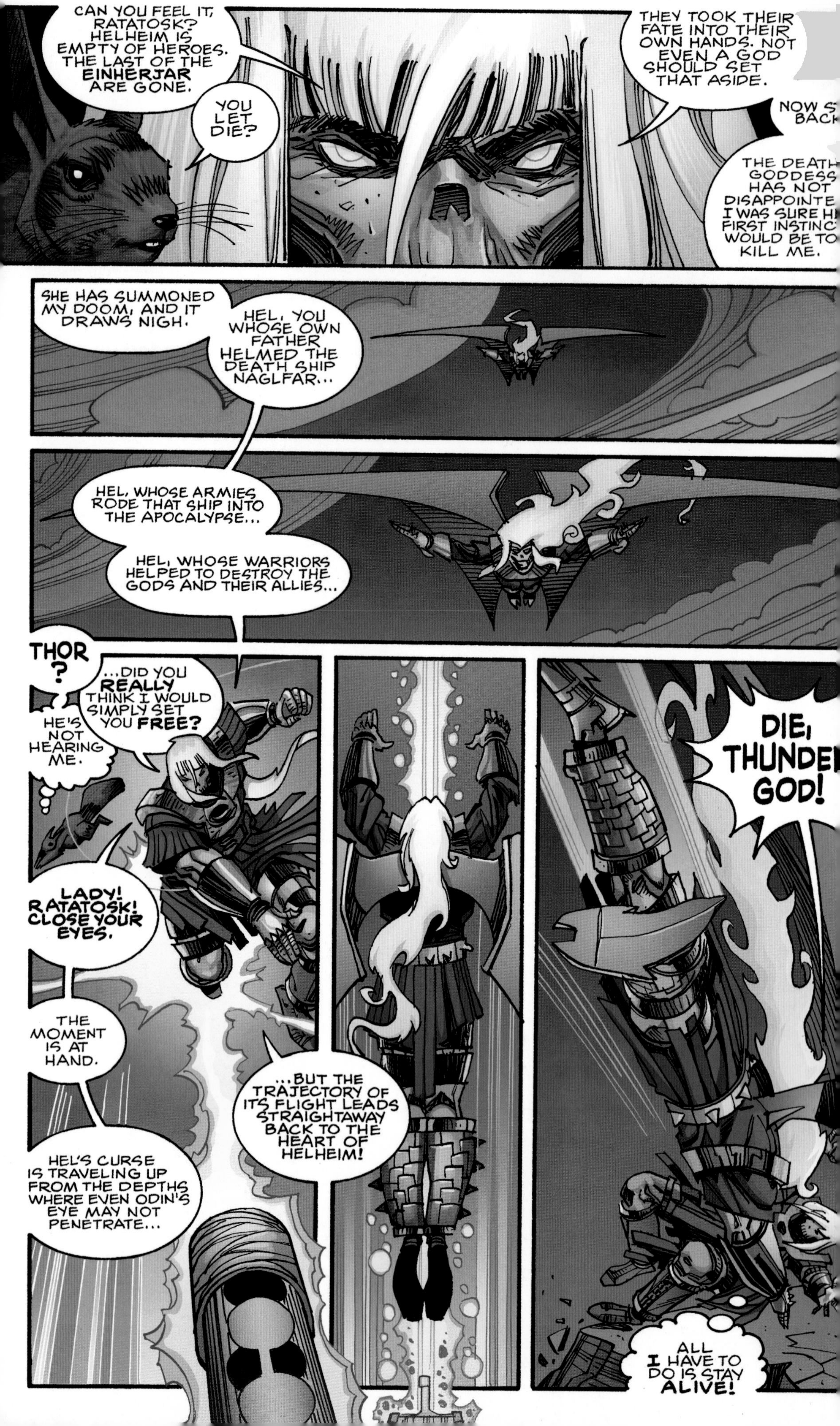
CAN YOU FEEL IT, RATATOSK? HELHEIM IS EMPTY OF HEROES. THE LAST OF THE **EINHERJAR** ARE GONE.
YOU LET DIE?
THEY TOOK THEIR FATE INTO THEIR OWN HANDS. NOT EVEN A GOD SHOULD SET THAT ASIDE.
THE DEATH GODDESS HAS NOT
SHE HAS SUMMONED MY DOOM, AND IT DRAWS NIGH.
HEL, YOU WHOSE OWN FATHER HELMED THE DEATH SHIP NAGLFAR...
HEL, WHOSE ARMIES RODE THAT SHIP INTO THE APOCALYPSE...
HEL, WHOSE WARRIORS HELPED TO DESTROY THE GODS AND THEIR ALLIES...
THOR?
...DID YOU **REALLY** THINK I WOULD SIMPLY SET YOU **FREE?**
HE'S NOT HEARING ME.
LADY! RATATOSK! CLOSE YOUR EYES.
THE MOMENT IS AT HAND.
HEL'S CURSE IS TRAVELING UP FROM THE DEPTHS WHERE EVEN ODIN'S EYE MAY NOT PENETRATE...
...BUT THE TRAJECTORY OF ITS FLIGHT LEADS STRAIGHTAWAY BACK TO THE HEART OF HELHEIM!
GOD!
ALL **I** HAVE TO DO IS STAY **ALIVE!**

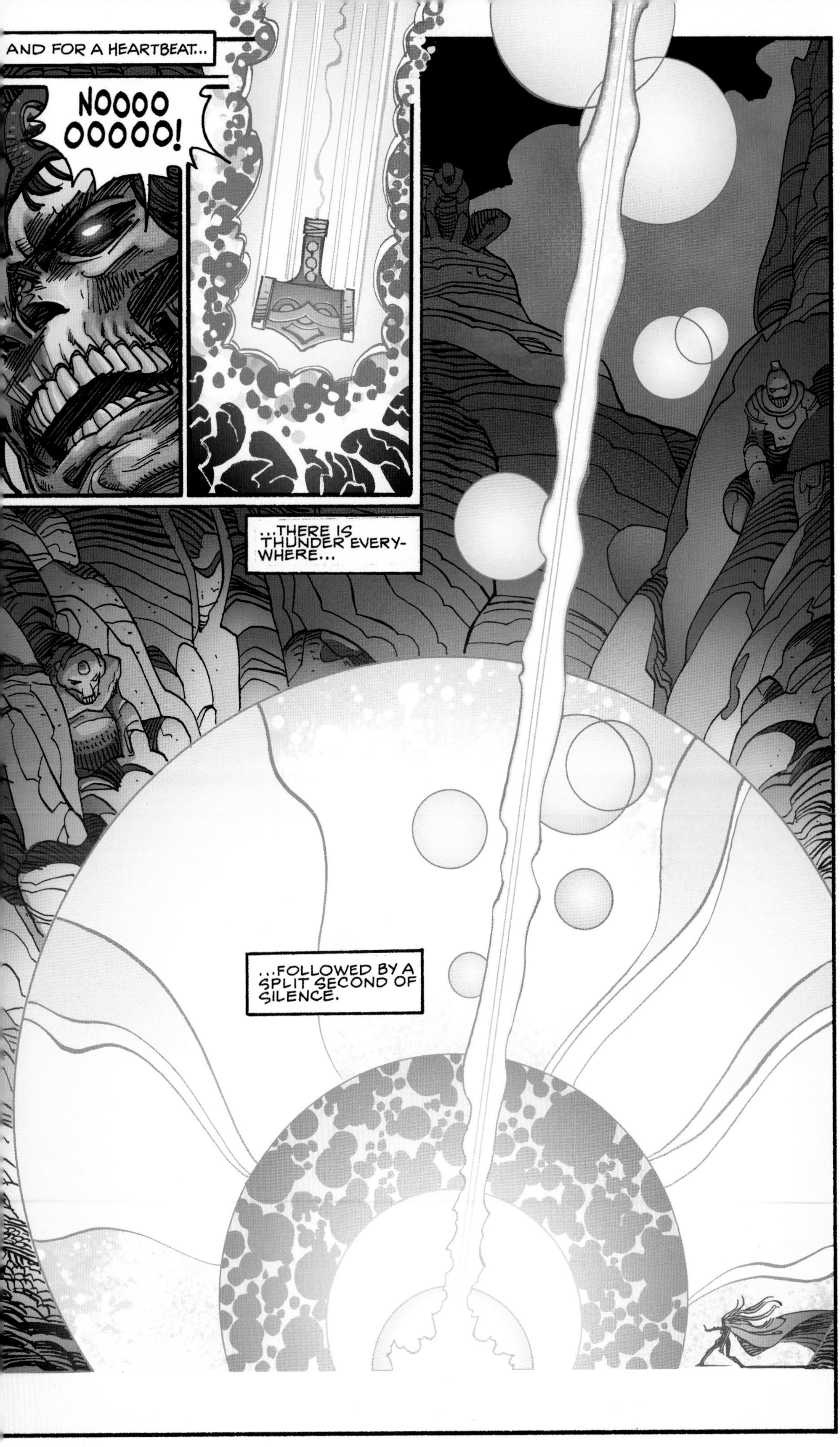
AND FOR A HEARTBEAT...
NOOOO OOOOO!
...THERE IS THUNDER EVERY-WHERE...
...FOLLOWED BY A SPLIT SECOND OF SILENCE.

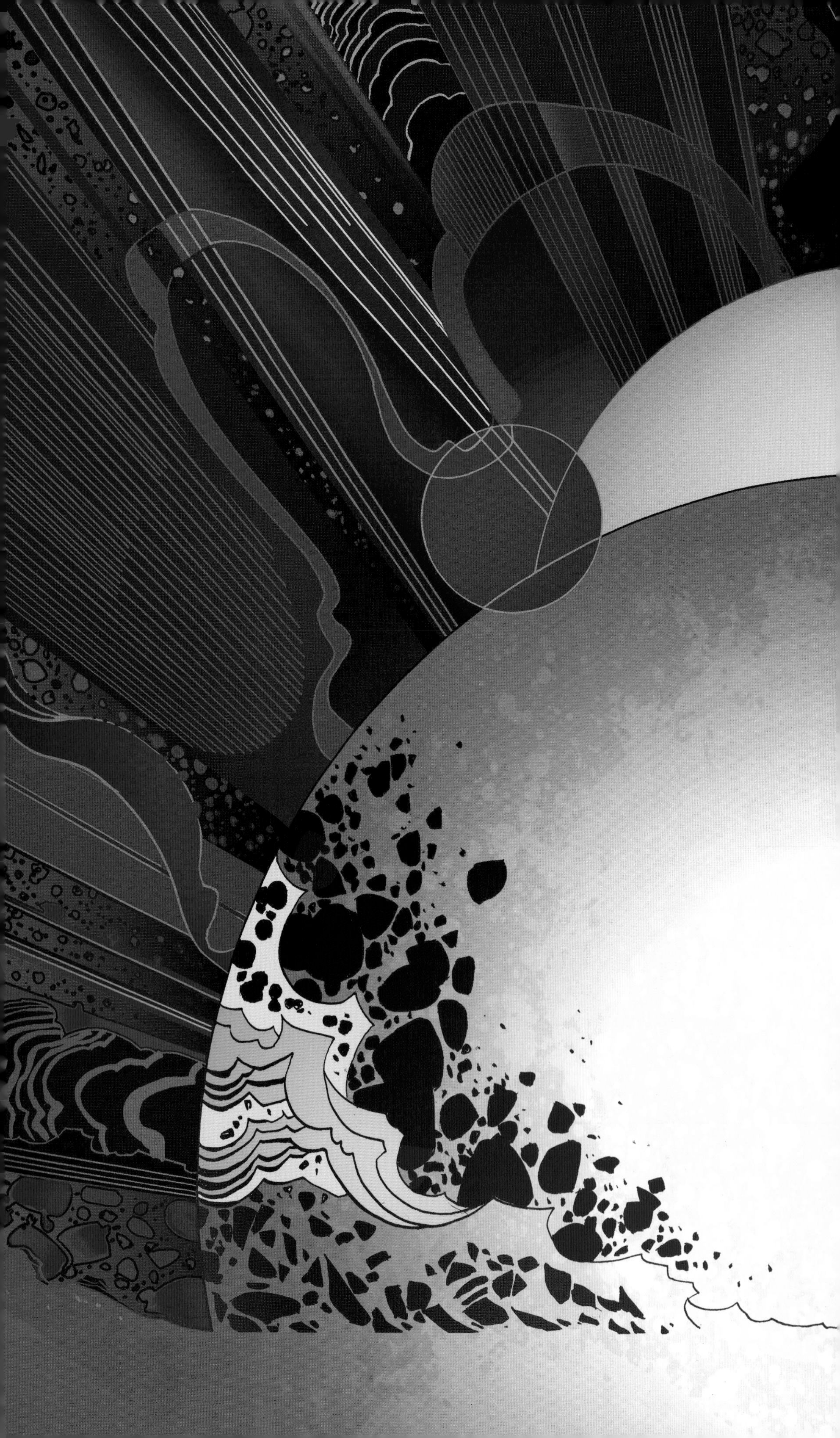

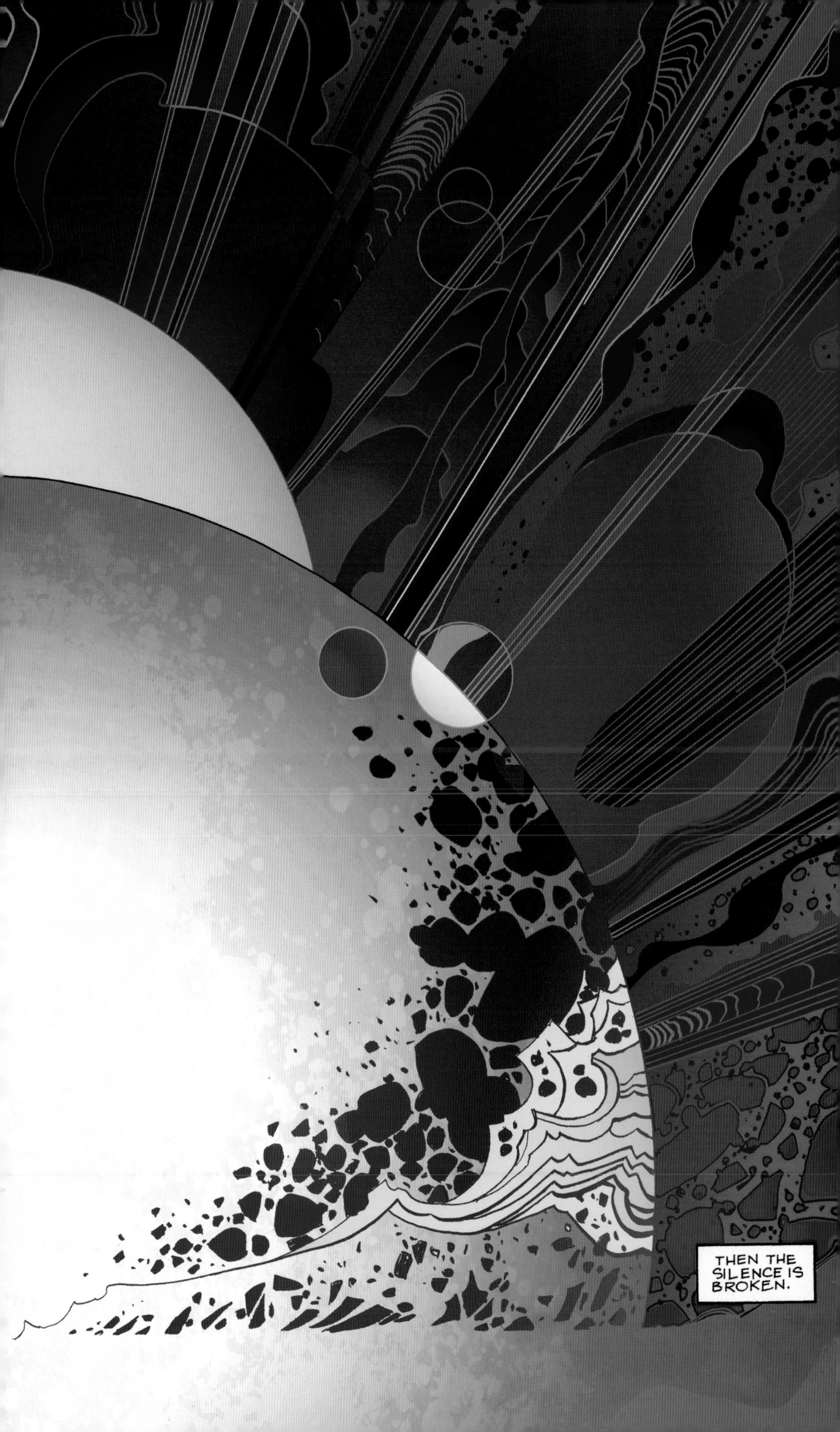
THEN THE SILENCE IS BROKEN.

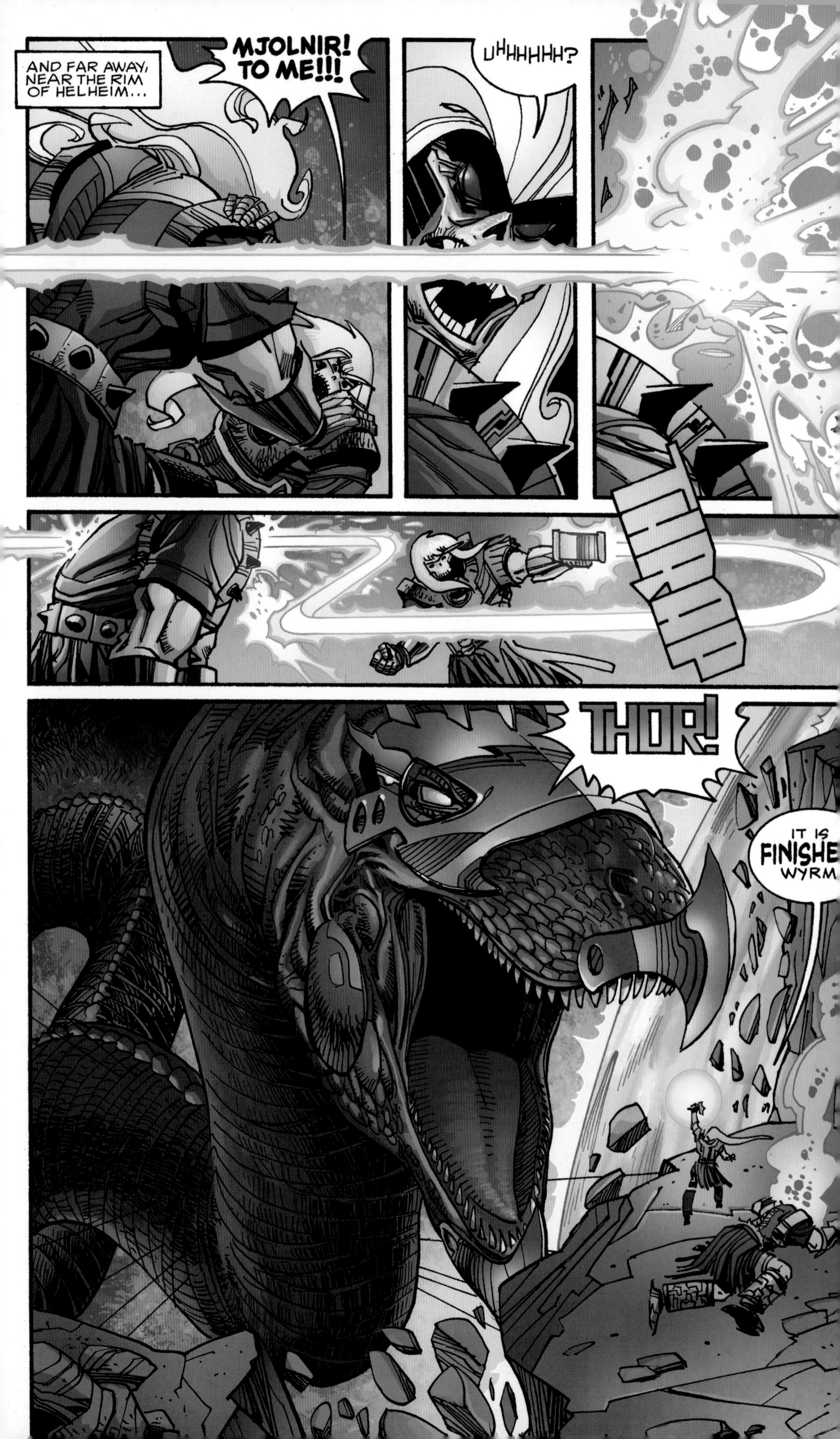

AND FAR AWAY, NEAR THE RIM OF HELHEIM...
MJOLNIR! TO ME!!!
UHHHHHH?
THOR!
IT IS FINISHE WYRM

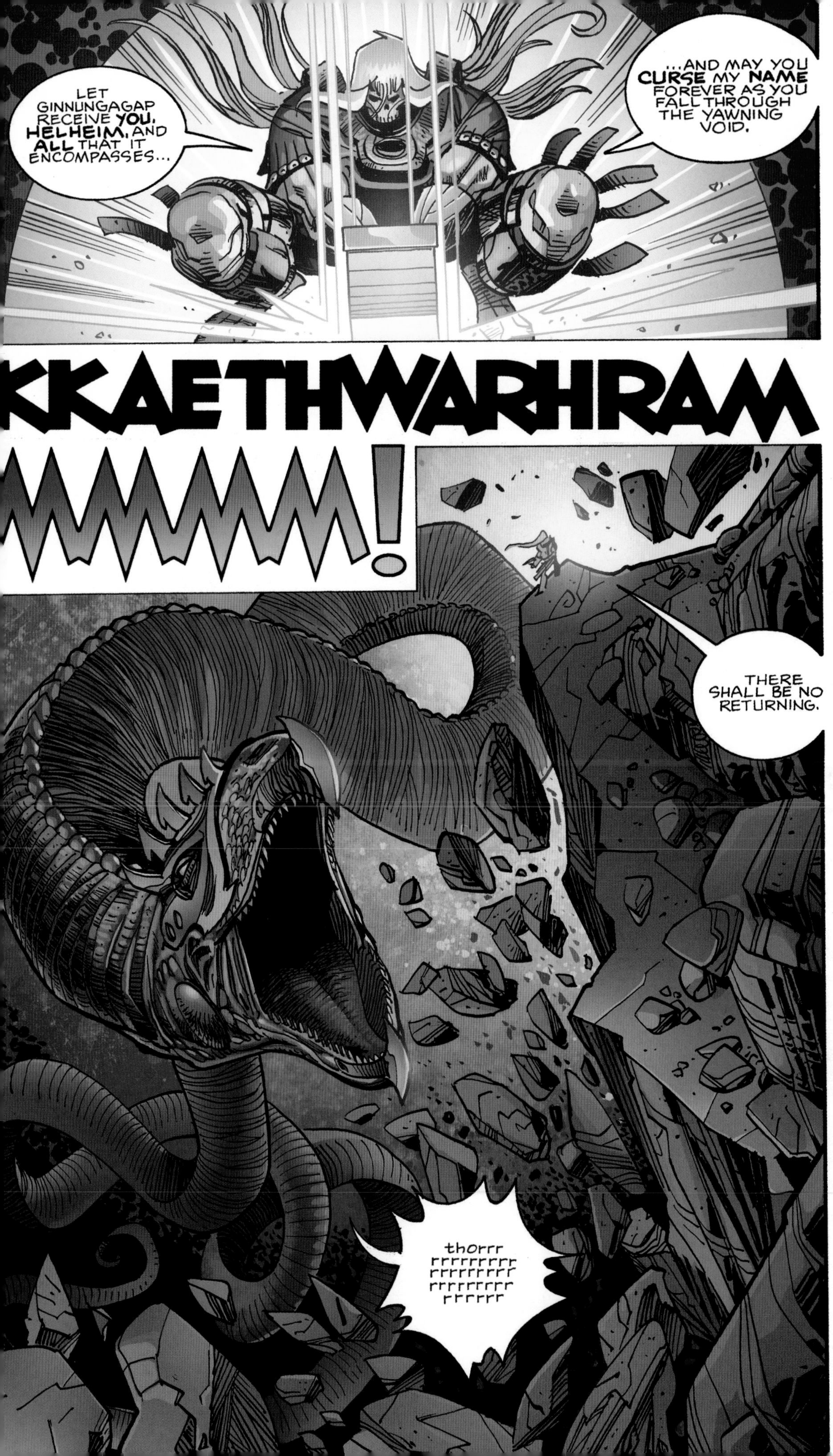
LET GINNUNGAGAP RECEIVE YOU, HELHEIM, AND ALL THAT IT ENCOMPASSES...
...AND MAY YOU CURSE MY NAME FOREVER AS YOU FALL THROUGH THE YAWNING VOID.
KKAETHWARHRAMMMMMMMM!
THERE SHALL BE NO RETURNING.
thorrr rrrrrrrrr rrrrrrrrr rrrrrrrrr rrrrrr

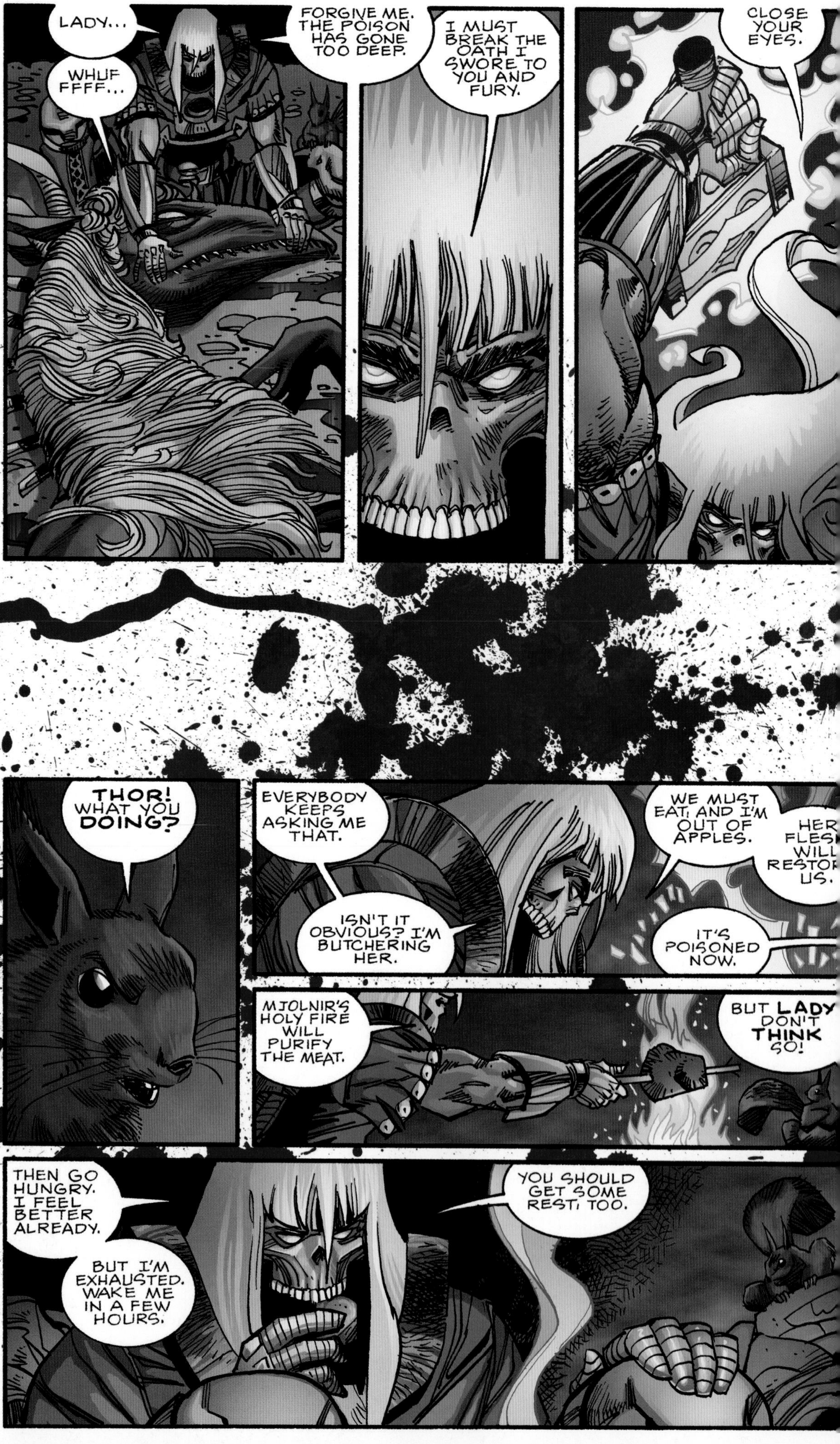
LADY...
WHUF FFFF...
FORGIVE ME. THE POISON HAS GONE TOO DEEP.
I MUST BREAK THE OATH I SWORE TO YOU AND FURY.
CLOSE YOUR EYES.
THOR! WHAT YOU DOING?
EVERYBODY KEEPS ASKING ME THAT.
ISN'T IT OBVIOUS? I'M BUTCHERING HER.
WE MUST EAT, AND I'M OUT OF APPLES.
HER FLESH WILL RESTORE US.
IT'S POISONED NOW.
MJOLNIR'S HOLY FIRE WILL PURIFY THE MEAT.
BUT LADY DON'T THINK SO!
THEN GO HUNGRY. I FEEL BETTER ALREADY.
BUT I'M EXHAUSTED. WAKE ME IN A FEW HOURS.
YOU SHOULD GET SOME REST, TOO.

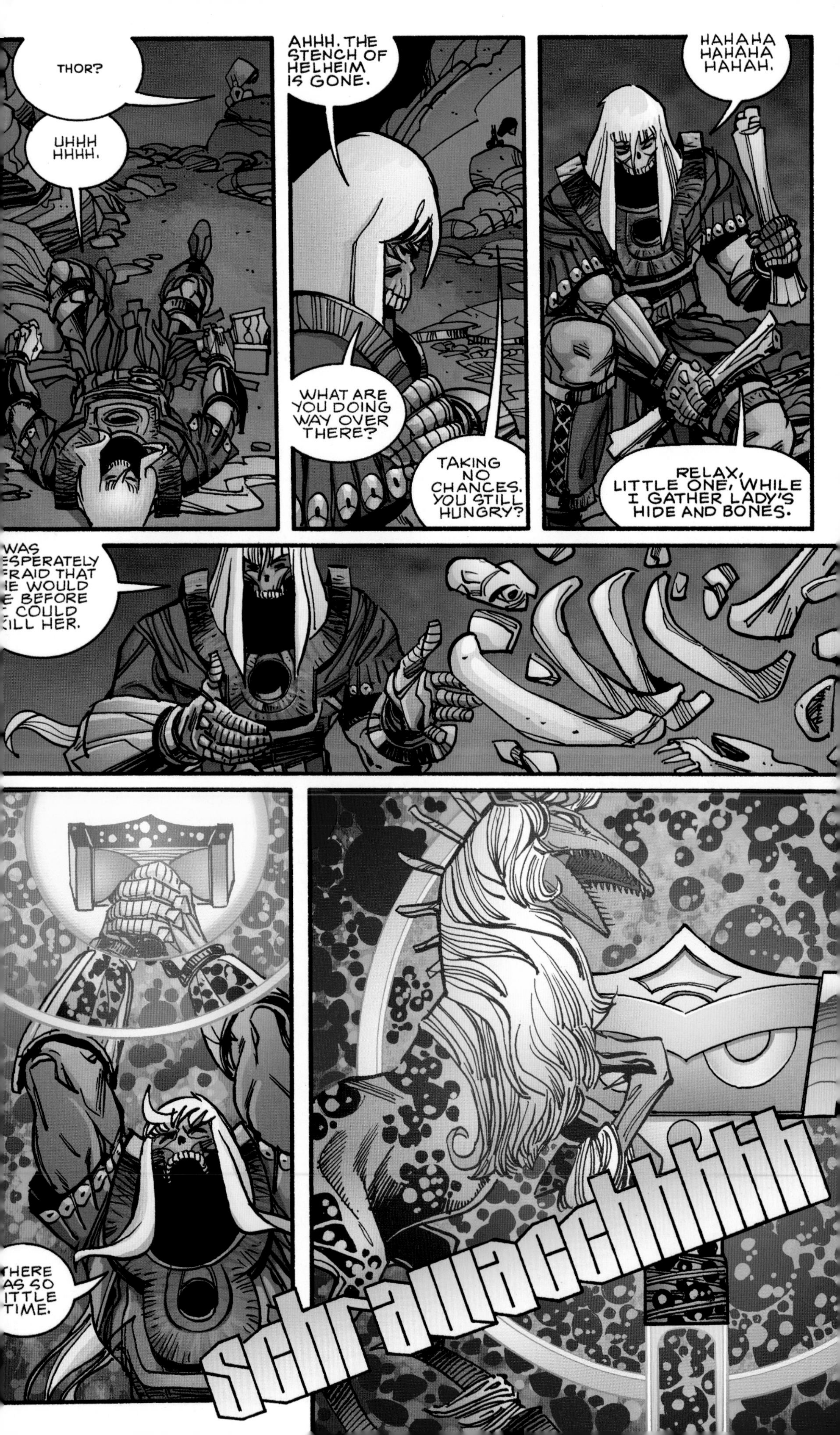
THOR?
UHHH HHHH.
AHHH. THE STENCH OF HELHEIM IS GONE.
WHAT ARE YOU DOING WAY OVER THERE?
TAKING NO CHANCES. YOU STILL HUNGRY?
HAHAHA HAHAHA HAHAH.
RELAX, LITTLE ONE, WHILE I GATHER LADY'S HIDE AND BONES.
WAS ESPERATELY FRAID THAT HE WOULD E BEFORE COULD ILL HER.
THERE AS SO ITTLE TIME.
schrauuacchhhhhh

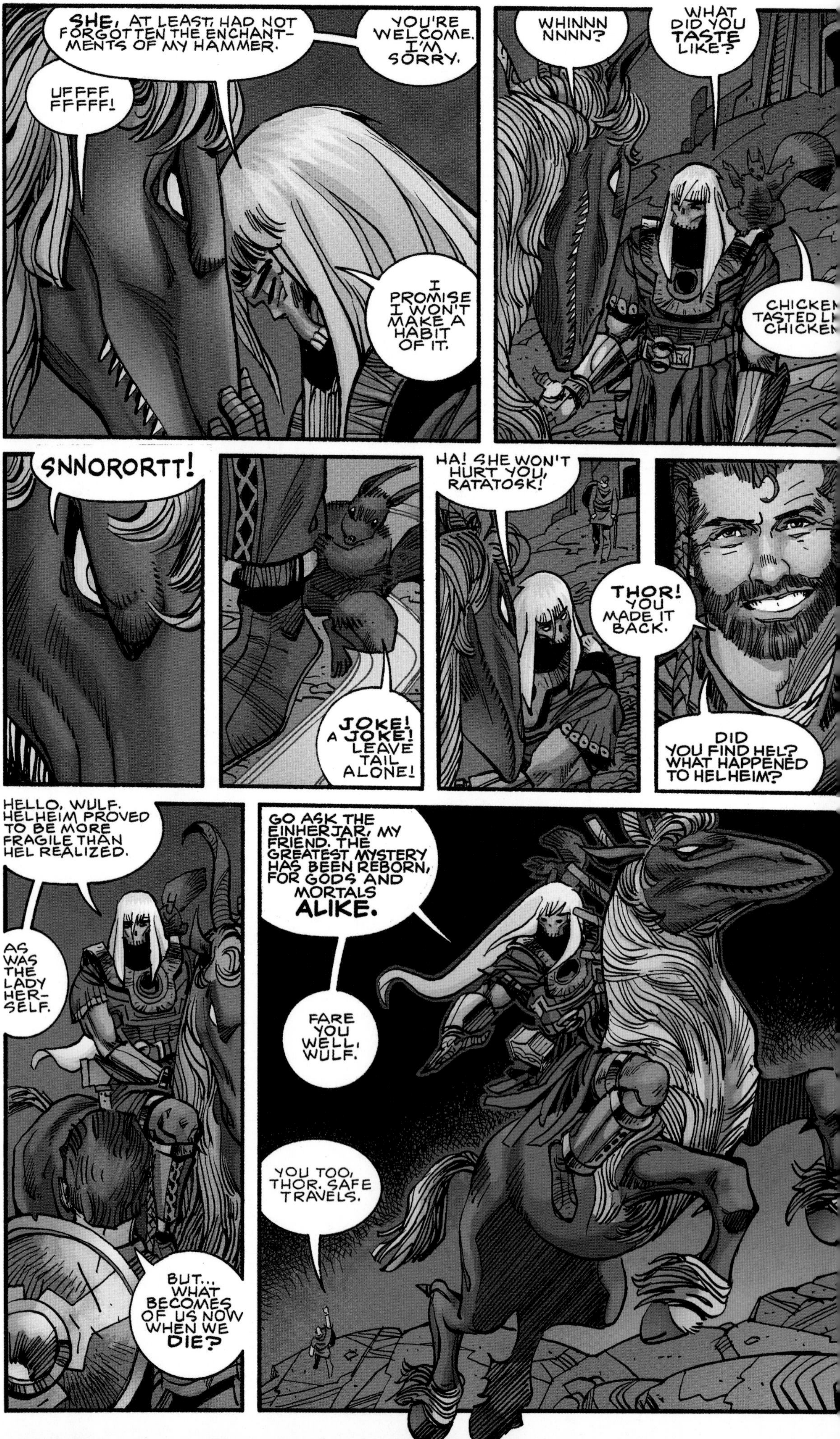
SHE, AT LEAST, HAD NOT FORGOTTEN THE ENCHANTMENTS OF MY HAMMER.
UFFFF FFFFF!
YOU'RE WELCOME. I'M SORRY.
I PROMISE I WON'T MAKE A HABIT OF IT.
WHINNN NNNN?
WHAT DID YOU TASTE LIKE?
CHICKEN TASTED LI CHICKEN
SNNORORTT!
JOKE! A JOKE! LEAVE TAIL ALONE!
HA! SHE WON'T HURT YOU, RATATOSK!
THOR! YOU MADE IT BACK.
DID YOU FIND HEL? WHAT HAPPENED TO HELHEIM?
HELLO, WULF. HELHEIM PROVED TO BE MORE FRAGILE THAN HEL REALIZED.
AS WAS THE LADY HERSELF.
BUT... WHAT BECOMES OF US NOW WHEN WE DIE?
GO ASK THE EINHERJAR, MY FRIEND. THE GREATEST MYSTERY HAS BEEN REBORN, FOR GODS AND MORTALS ALIKE.
FARE YOU WELL, WULF.
YOU TOO, THOR. SAFE TRAVELS.

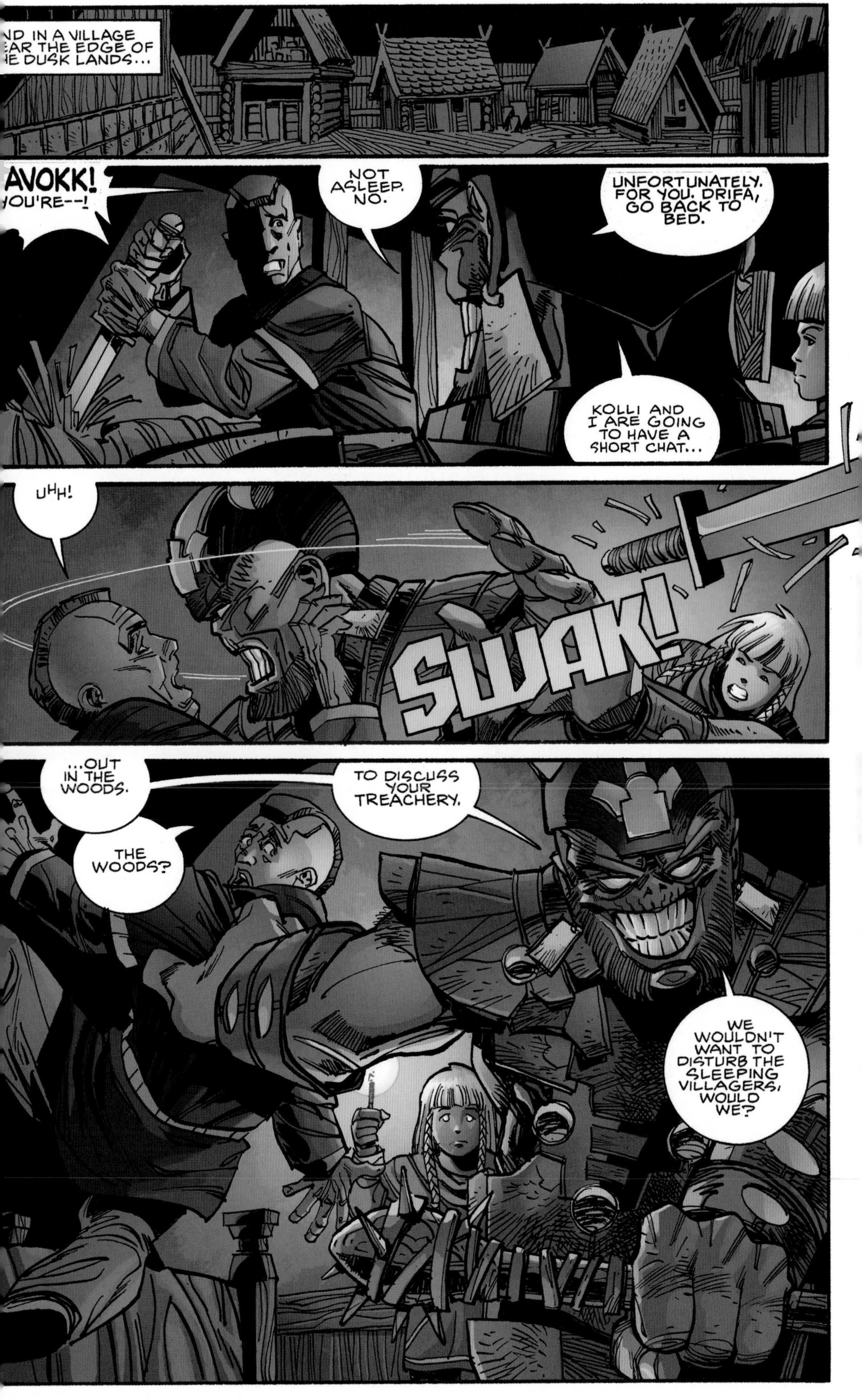
ND IN A VILLAGE
EAR THE EDGE OF
HE DUSK LANDS...
AVOKK!
YOU'RE--!
NOT ASLEEP. NO.
UNFORTUNATELY. FOR YOU. DRIFA, GO BACK TO BED.
KOLLI AND I ARE GOING TO HAVE A SHORT CHAT...
UHH!
SWAK!
...OUT IN THE WOODS.
THE WOODS?
TO DISCUSS YOUR TREACHERY.
WE WOULDN'T WANT TO DISTURB THE SLEEPING VILLAGERS, WOULD WE?

MEANWHILE, AN UNIMAGINABLE DISTANCE AWAY, IN MUSPELHEIM...

THE CONCLAVE ARE FOOLS, SINMARA. WITH THOR DEAD AT LAST, I SHALL ELIMINATE THEM ALL, ONE BY ONE...

...AND IN THE END, I ALONE WILL RULE THE DUSK LANDS.

HAVE A CARE, MY HUSBAND.

JORMUNGAN[D] MAY NOT BE T[HE] SHARPEST OF T[HE] GREAT ENEMIES

...BUT THE WORLD SERPENT POWER I[S] BEYOND BELIEF!

PITY ABOUT THOR, MY LOVE.

4.2.20 SIMONSON

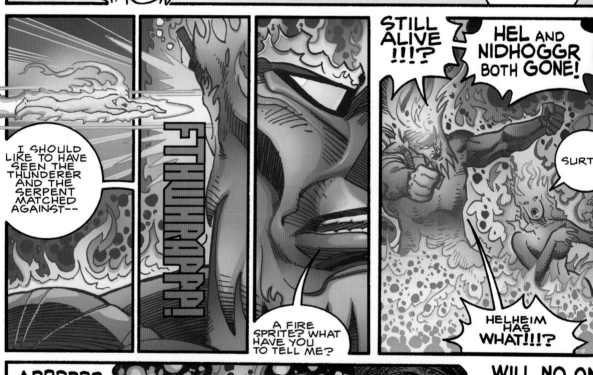

I SHOULD LIKE TO HAVE SEEN THE THUNDERER AND THE SERPENT MATCHED AGAINST--

FTHUHHAH!

A FIRE SPRITE? WHAT HAVE YOU TO TELL ME?

STILL ALIVE !!!?

HEL AND NIDHOGGR BOTH GONE!

SURT[R]

HELHEIM HAS WHAT!!!?

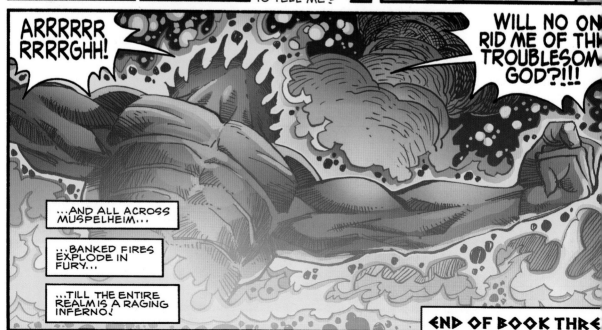

ARRRRRR RRRRGHH!

...AND ALL ACROSS MUSPELHEIM...

...BANKED FIRES EXPLODE IN FURY...

...TILL THE ENTIRE REALM IS A RAGING INFERNO!

WILL NO ON[E] RID ME OF TH[IS] TROUBLESOM[E] GOD?!!!

END OF BOOK THRE[E]

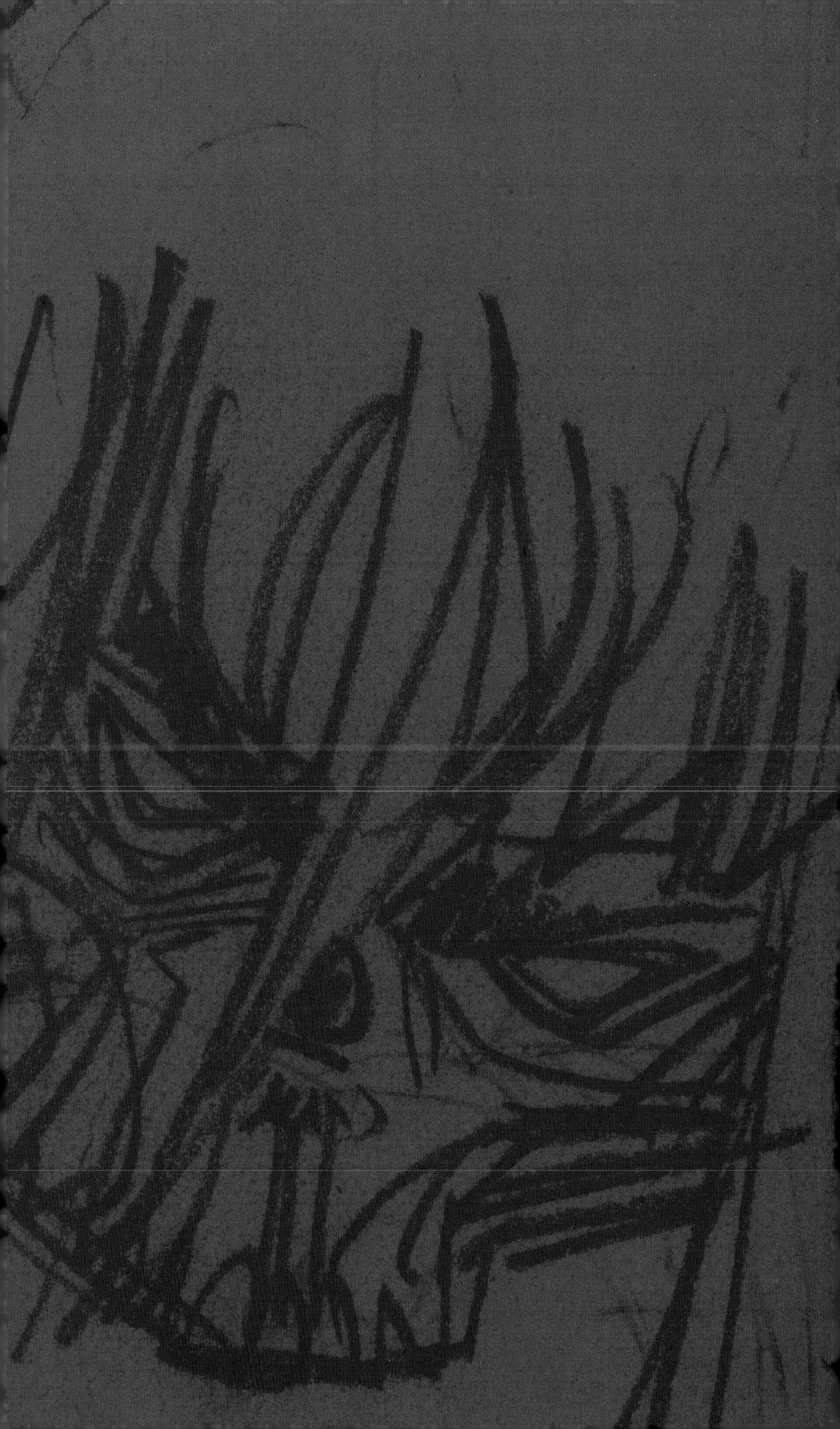

RAGNARÖK

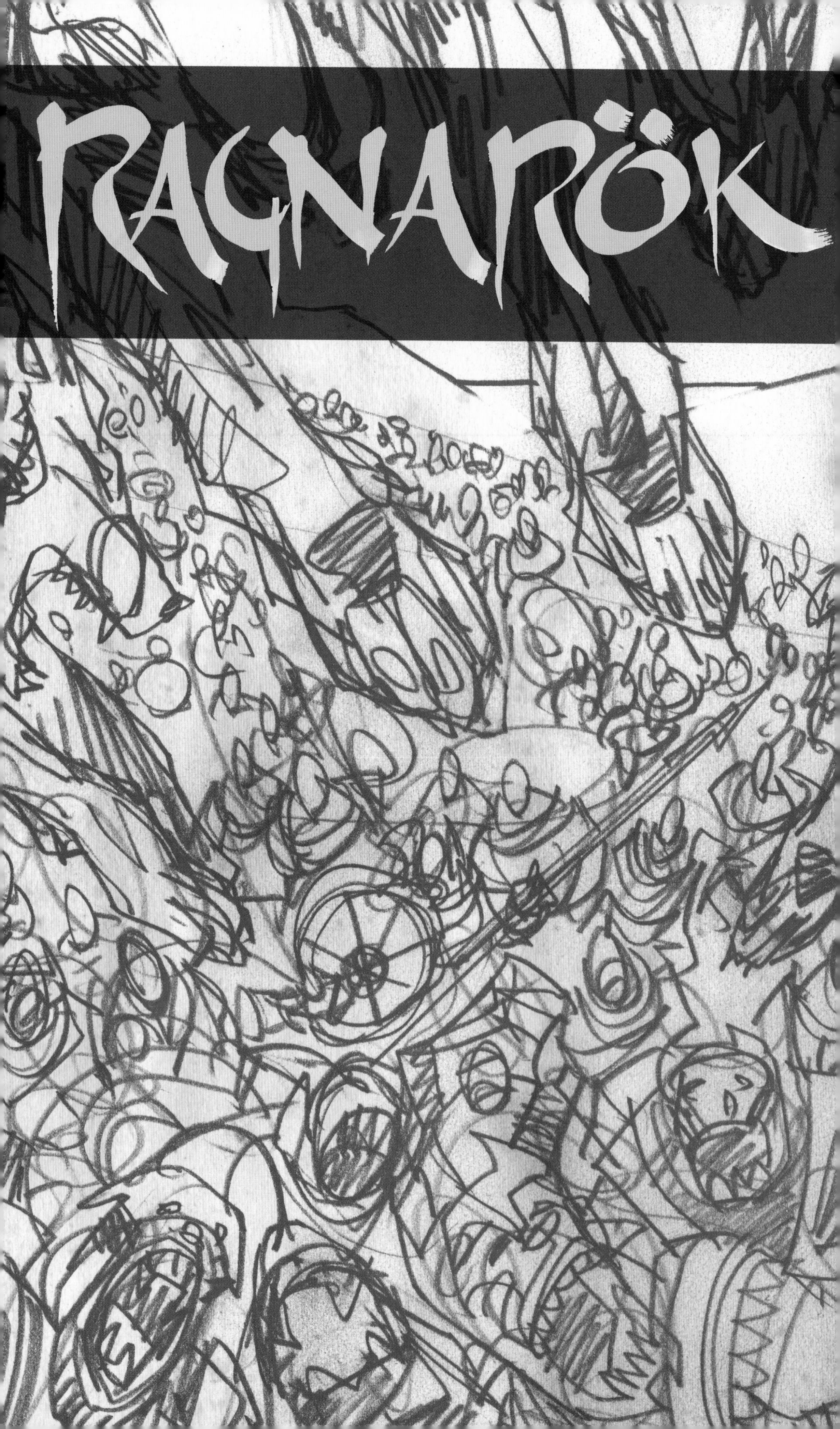

ART GALLERY

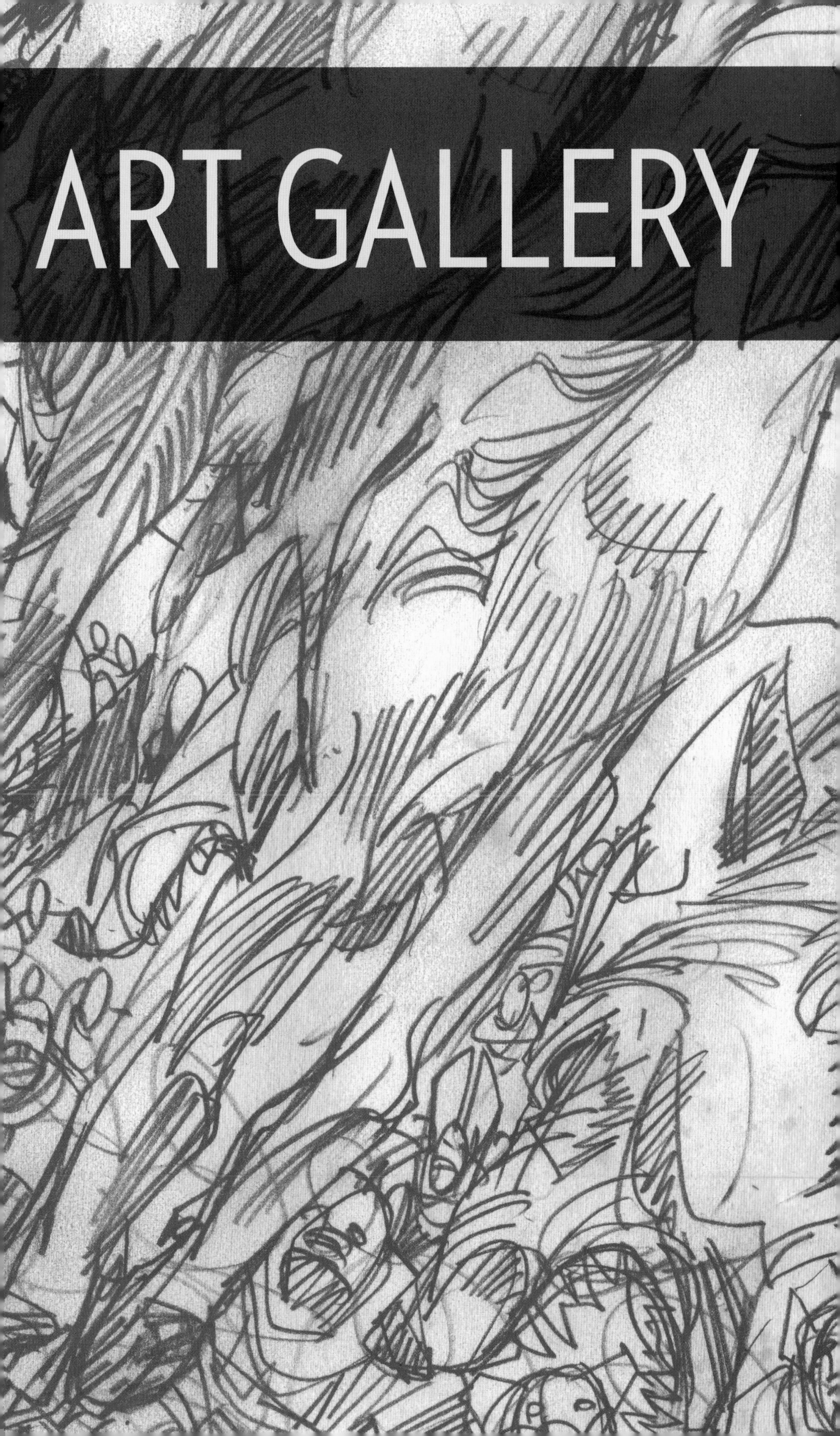

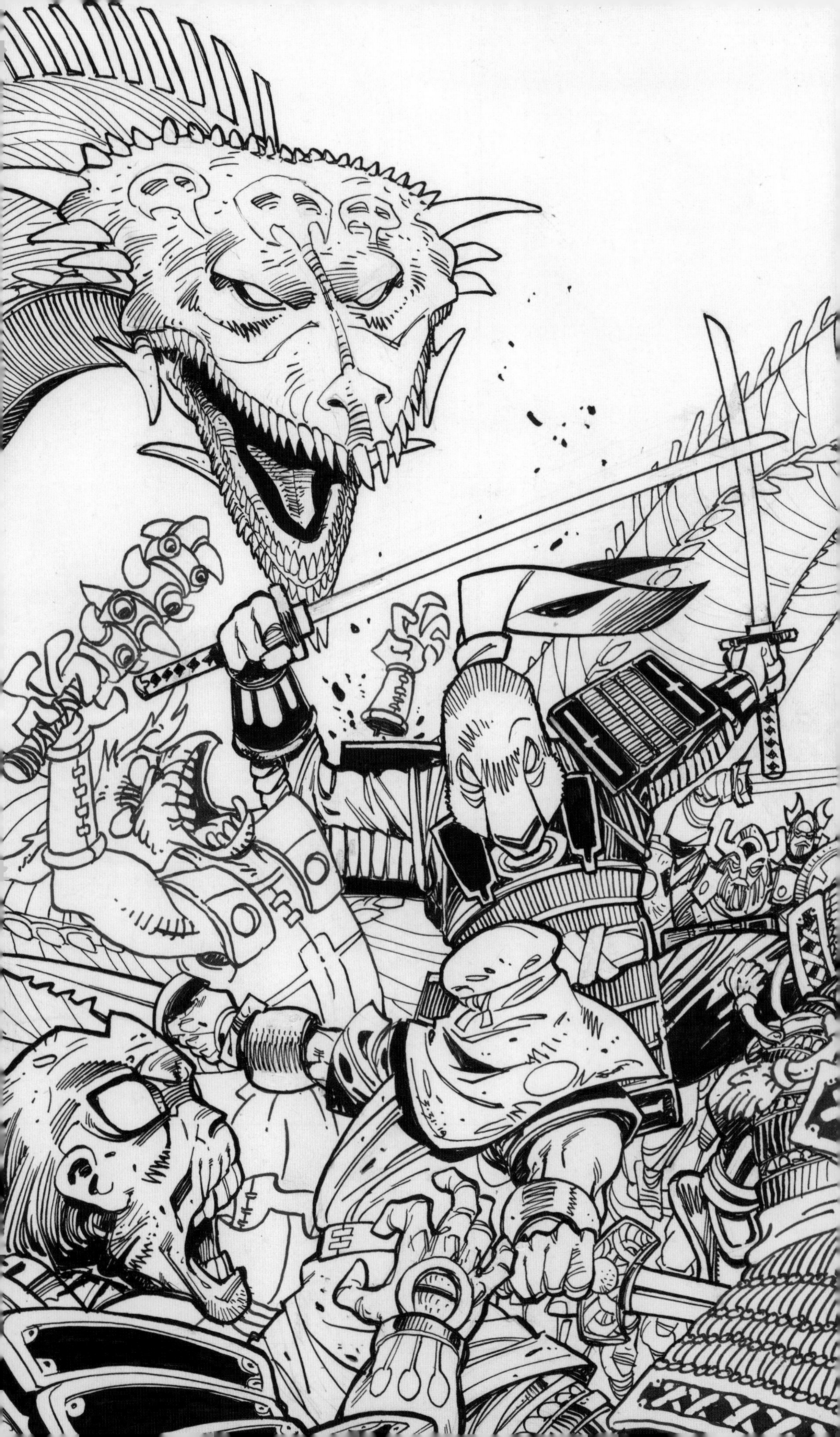

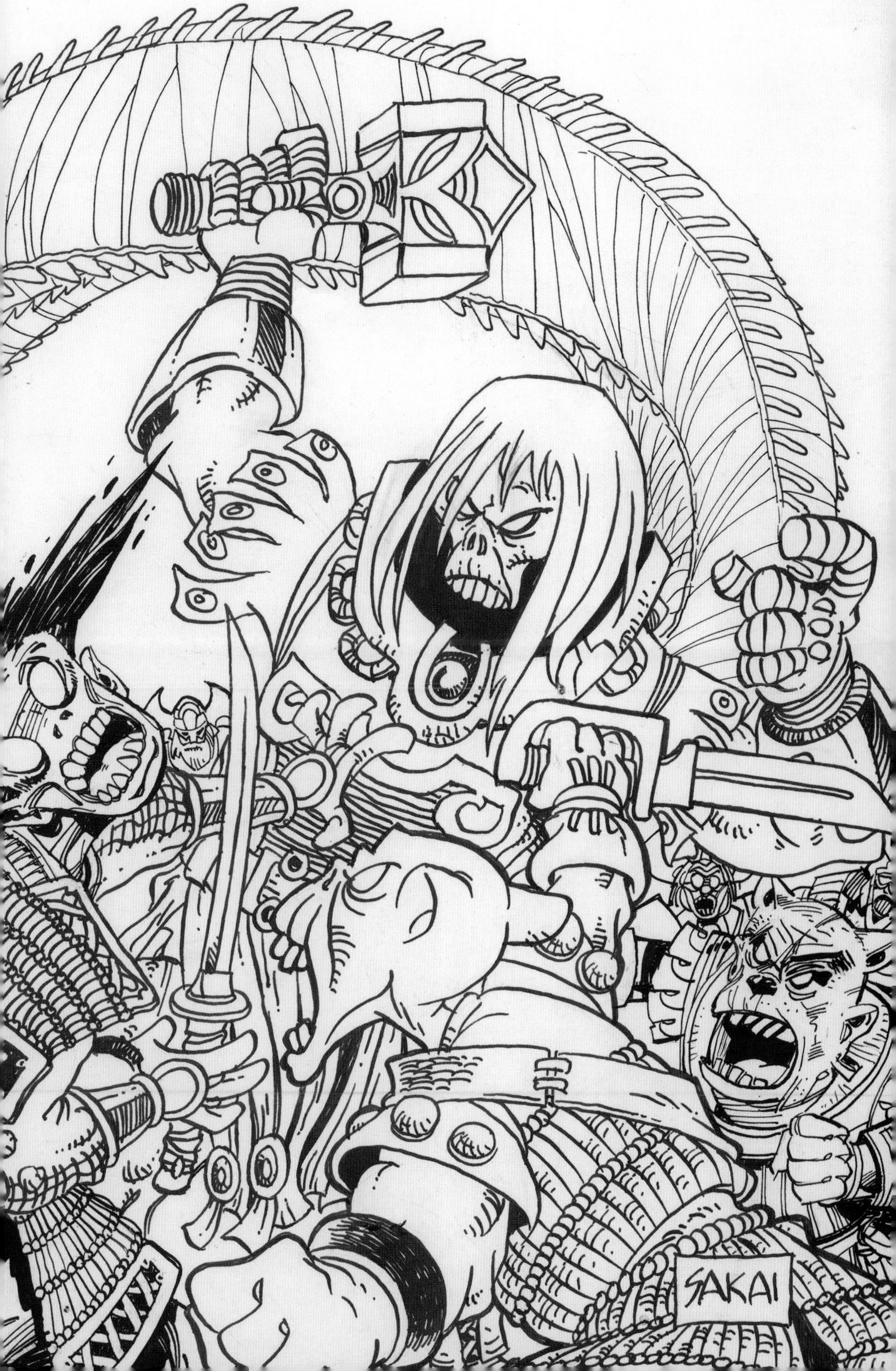
SAKAI

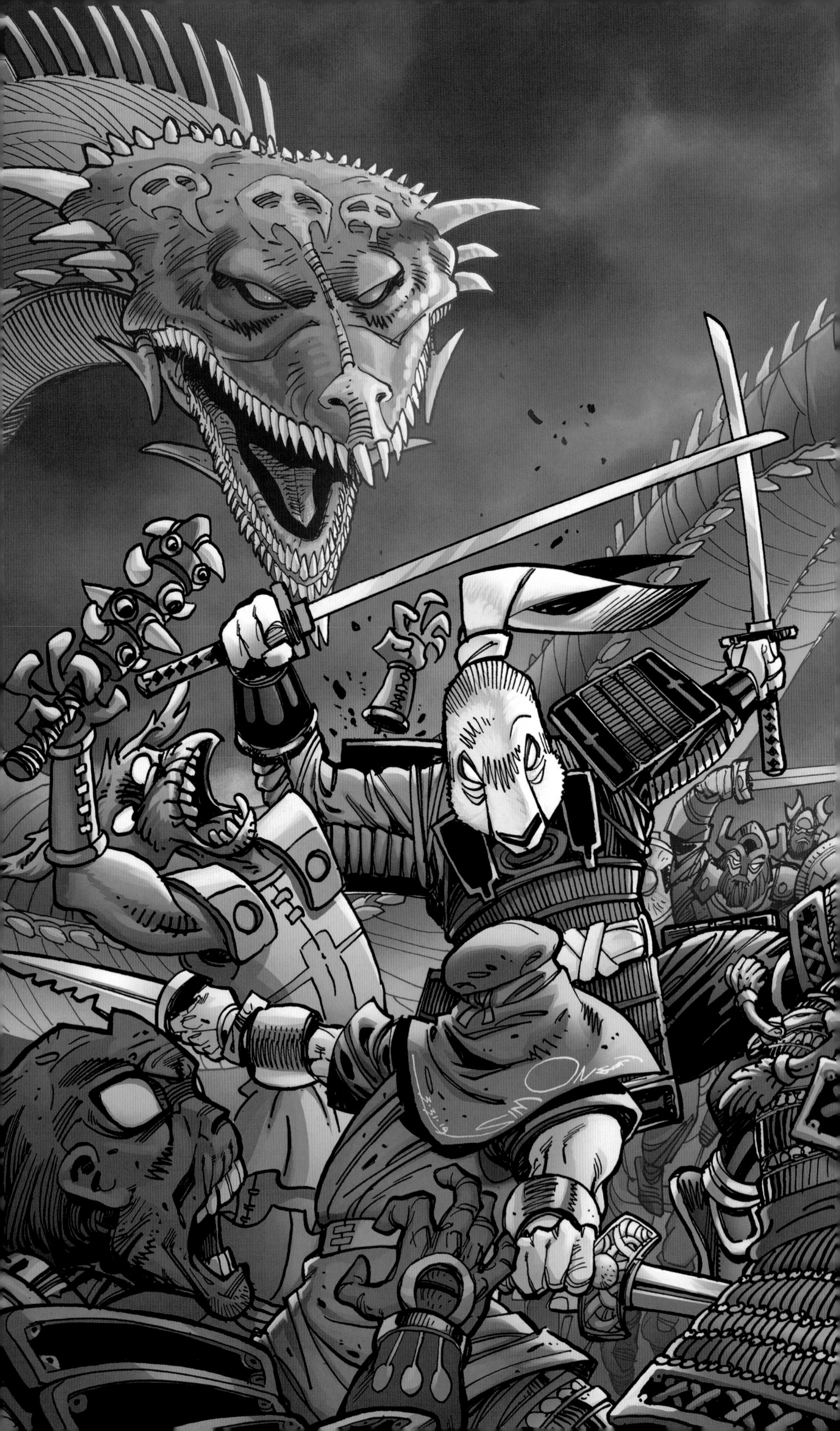

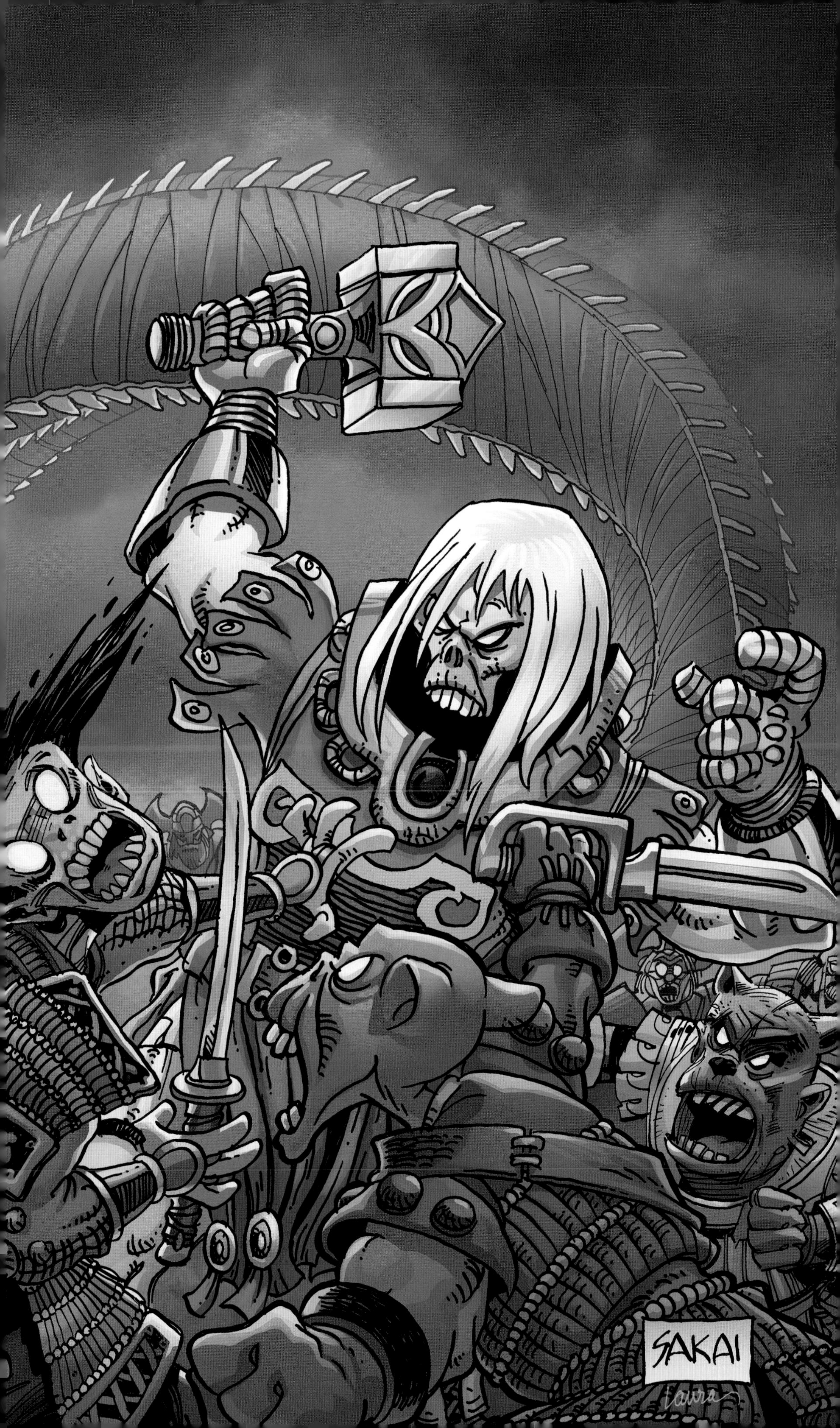
SAKAI

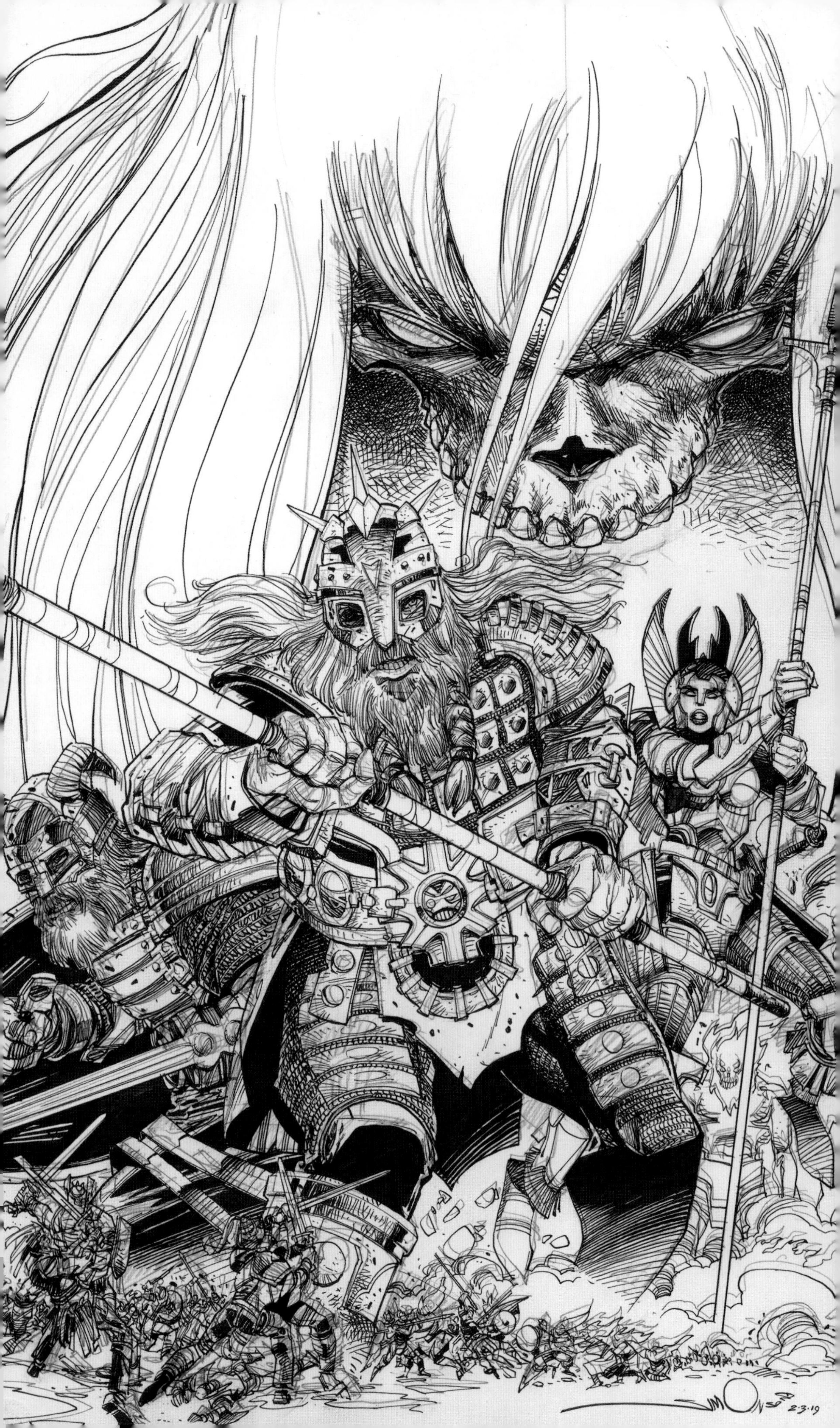

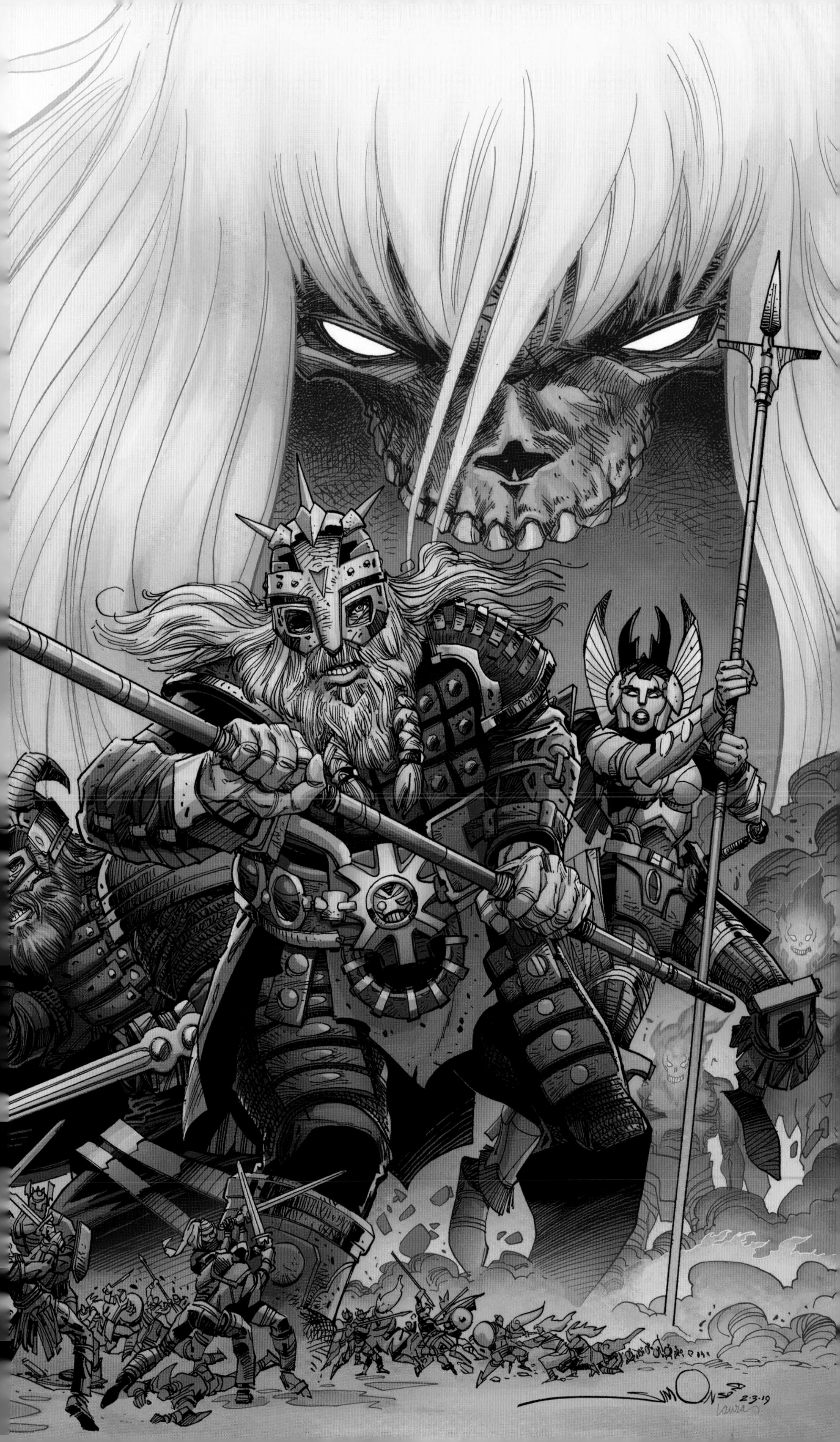
2.3.19
Laura

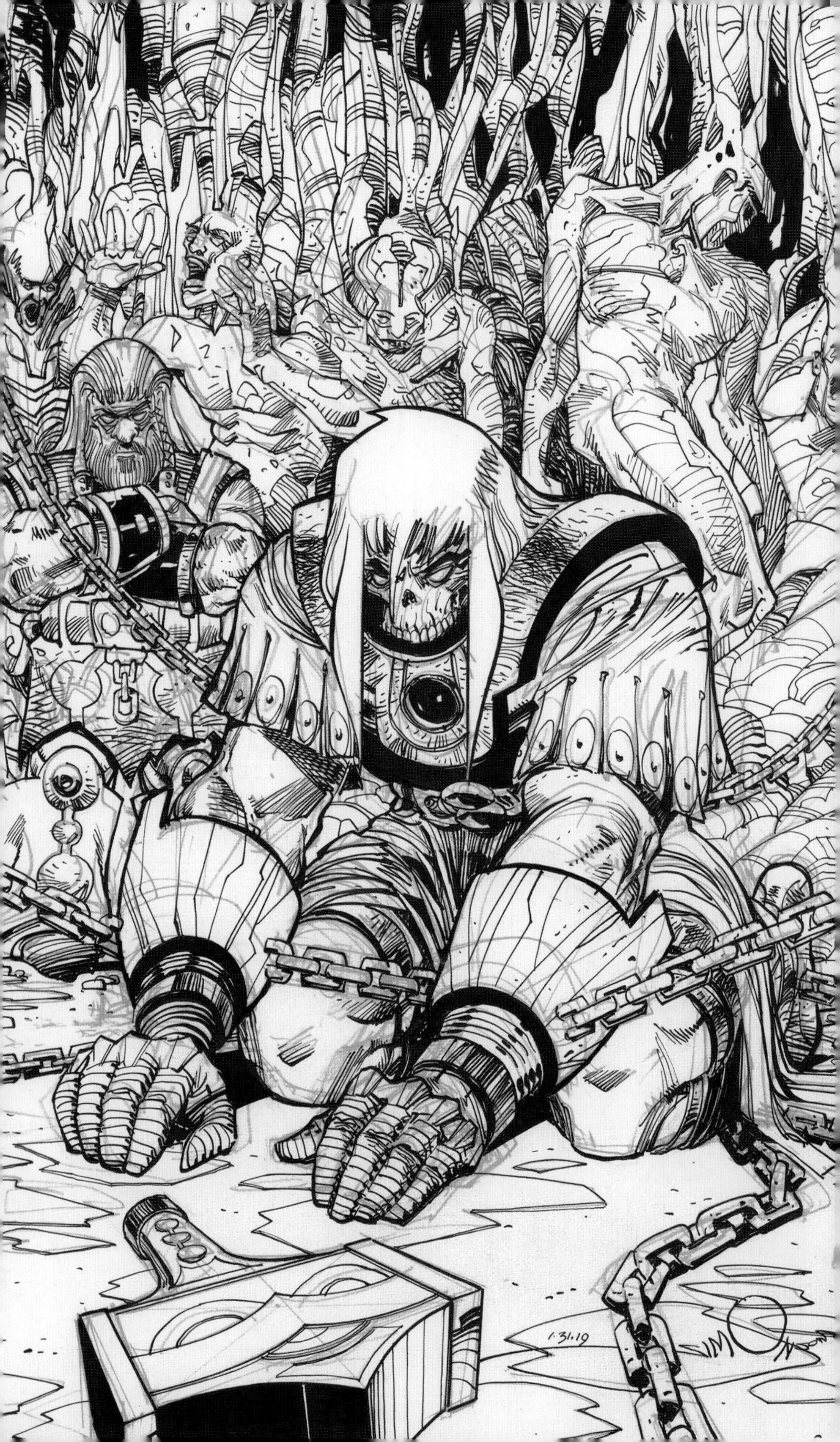
1.31.19

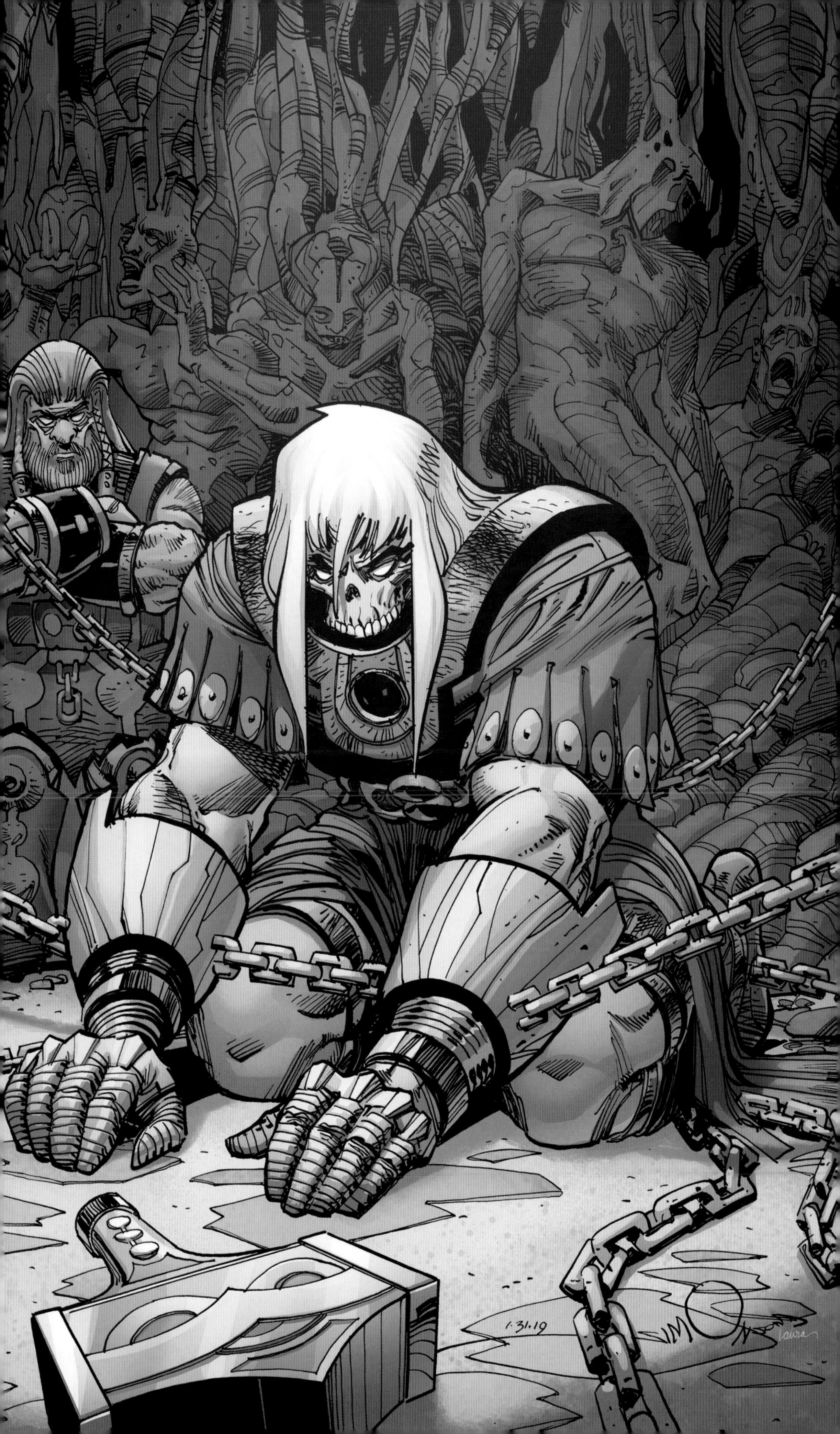
1.31.19

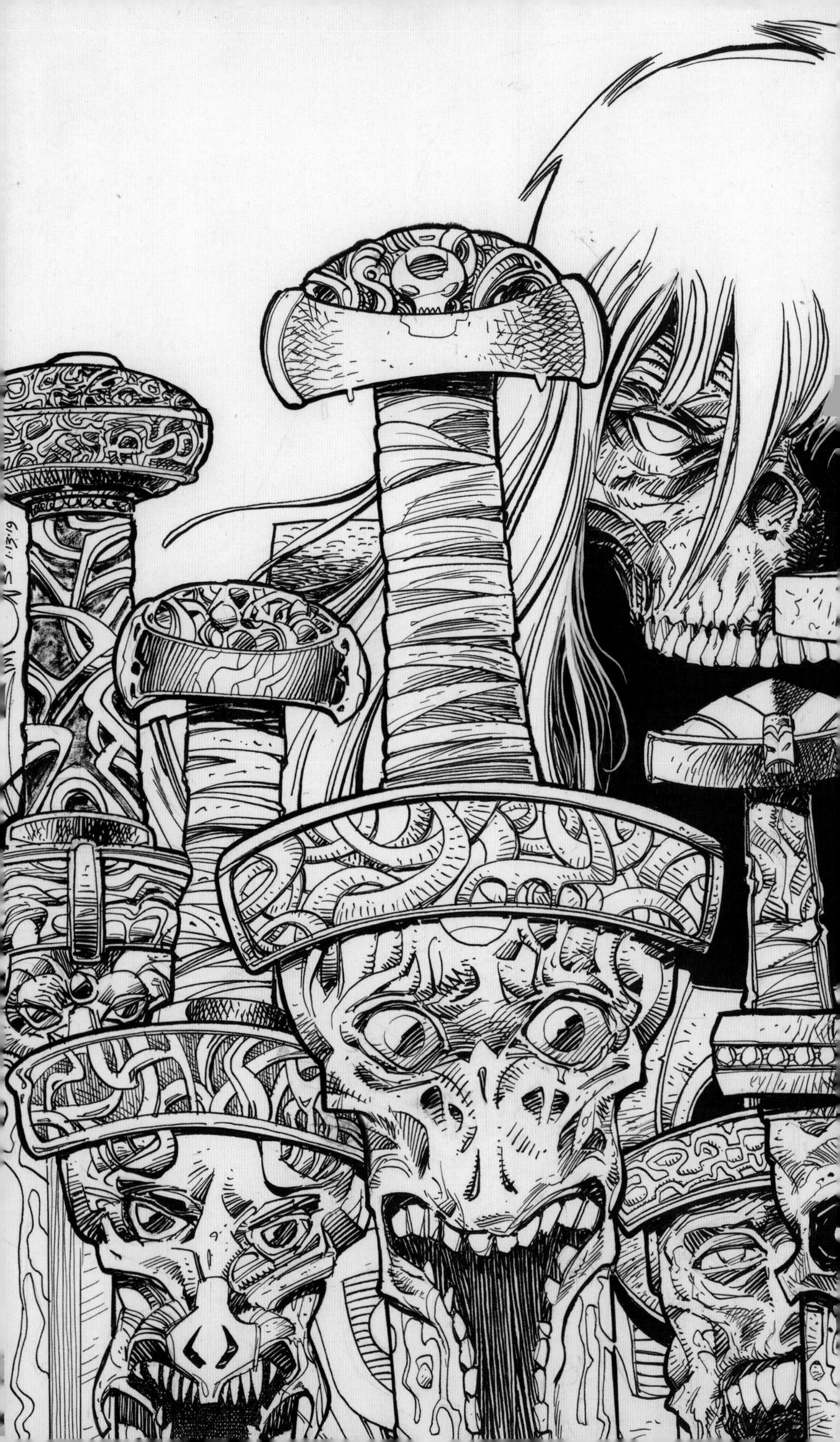

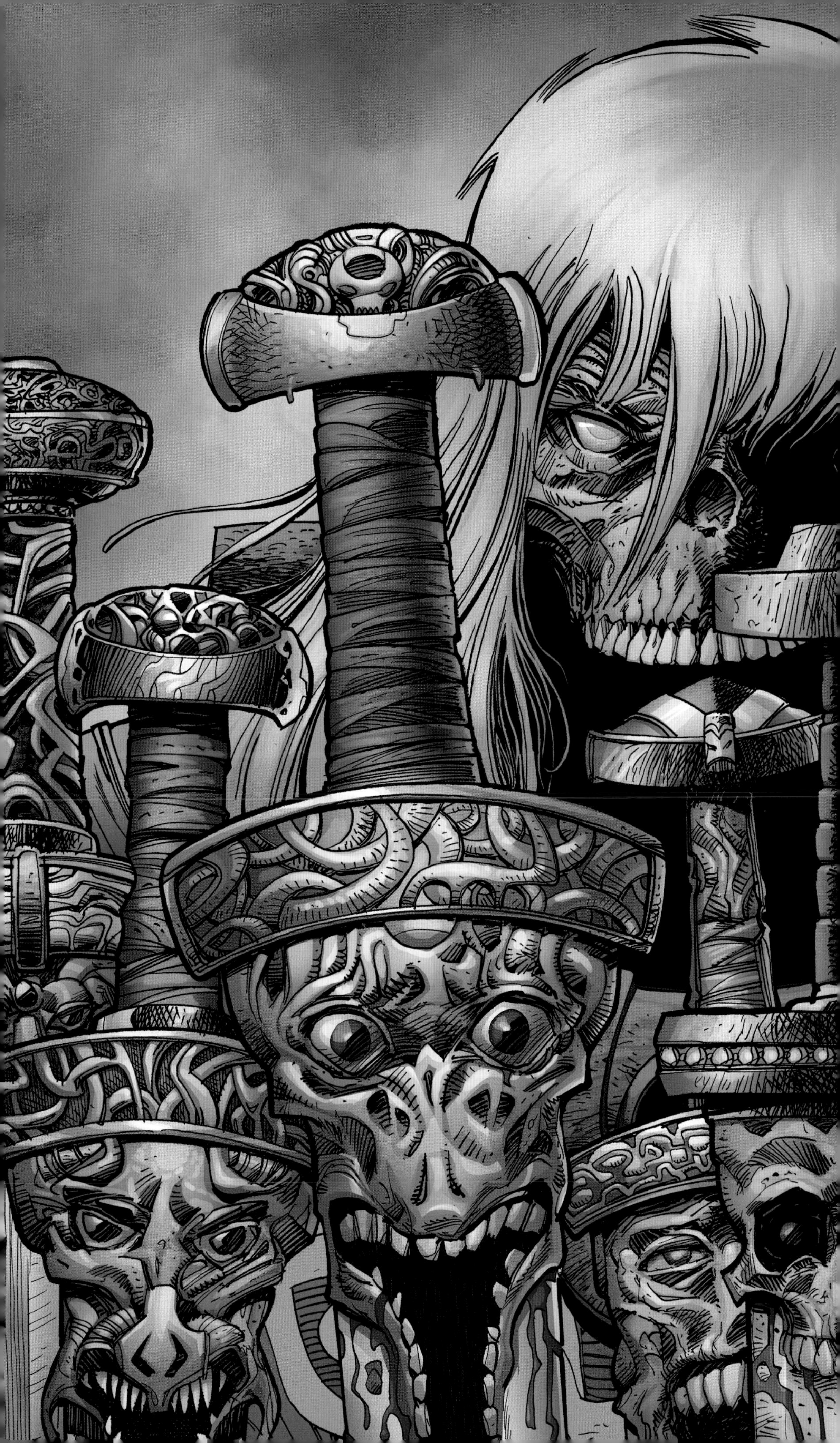

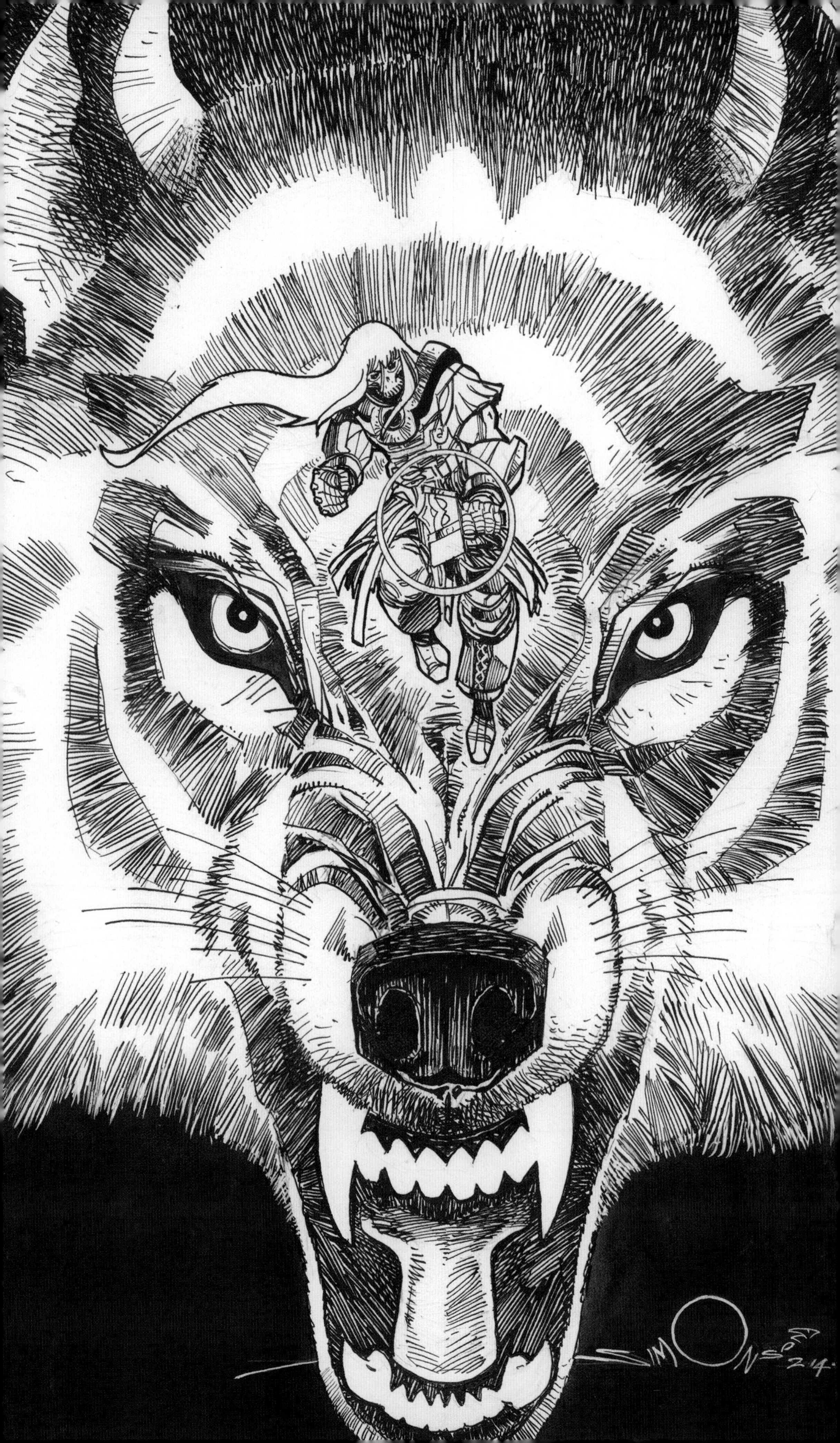

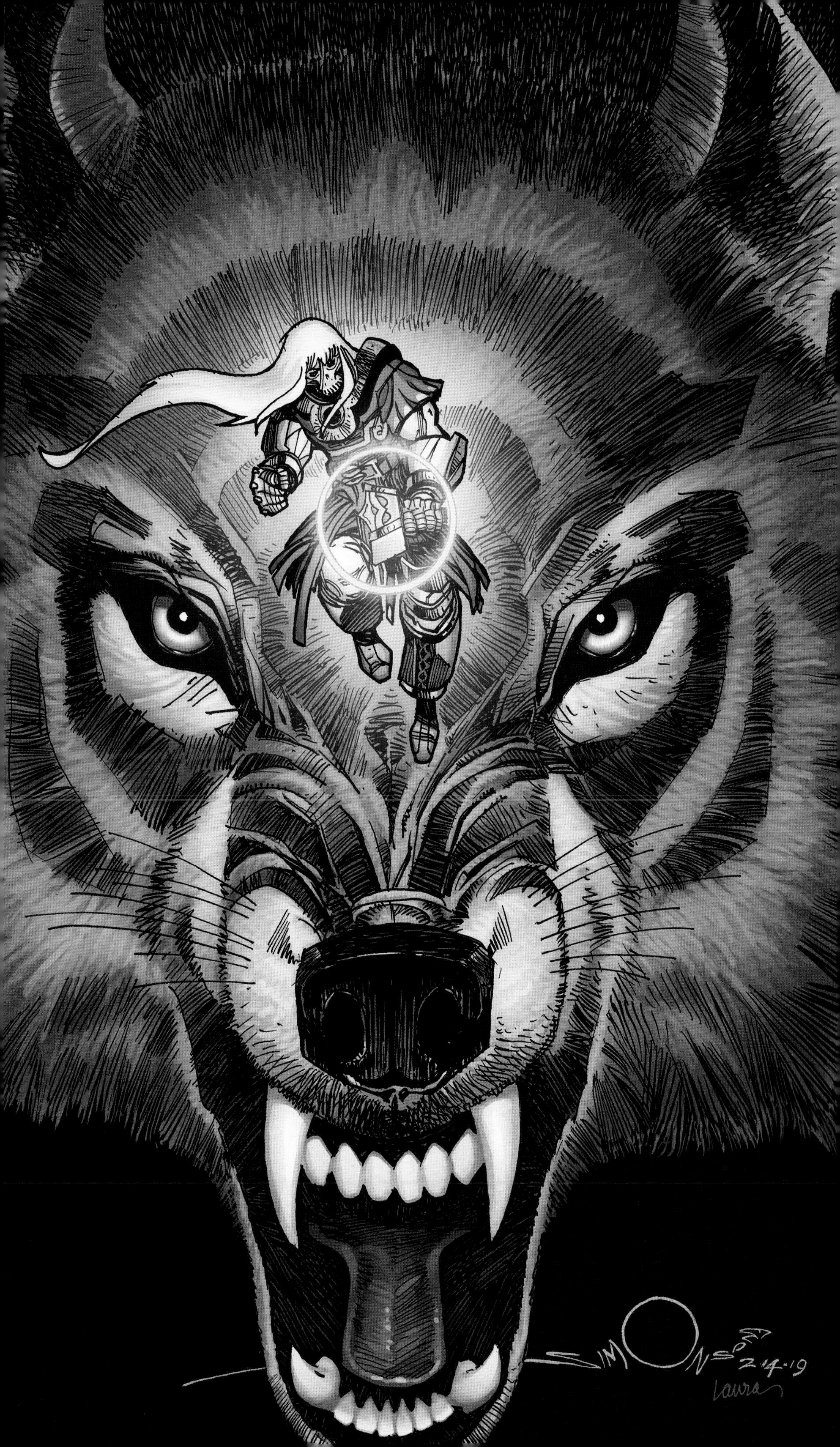
SIMONSON
2·14·19
Laura

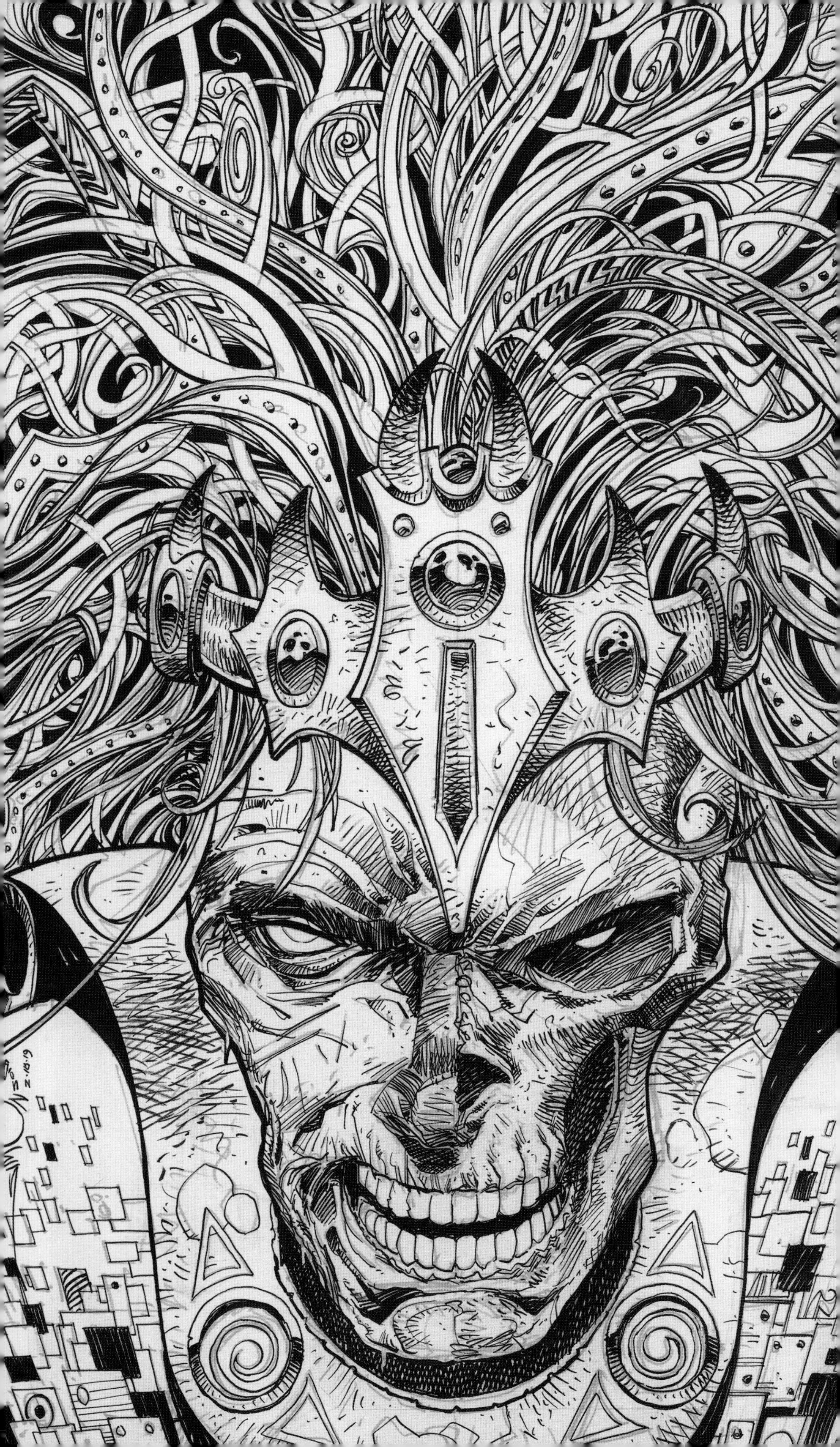

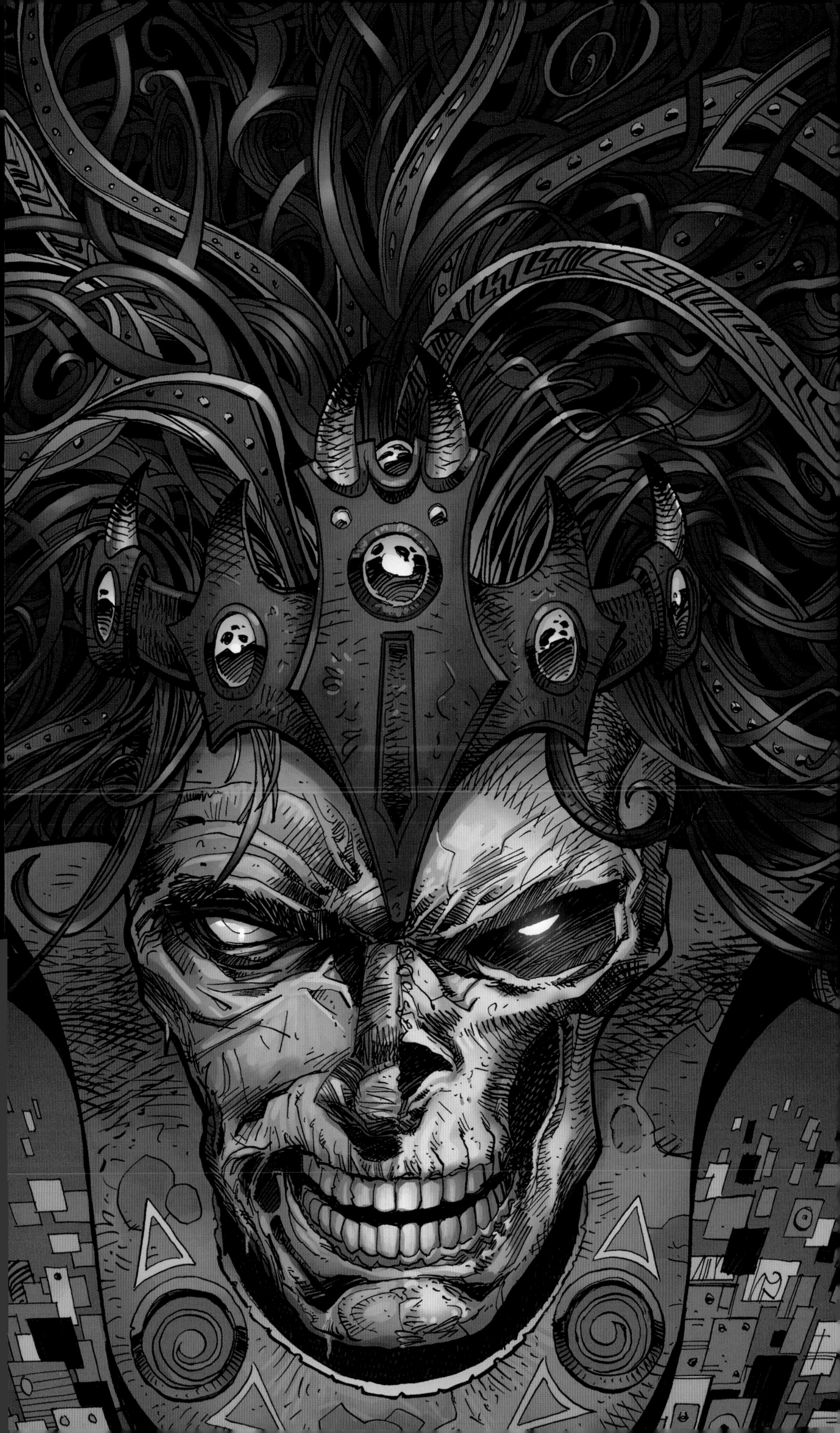

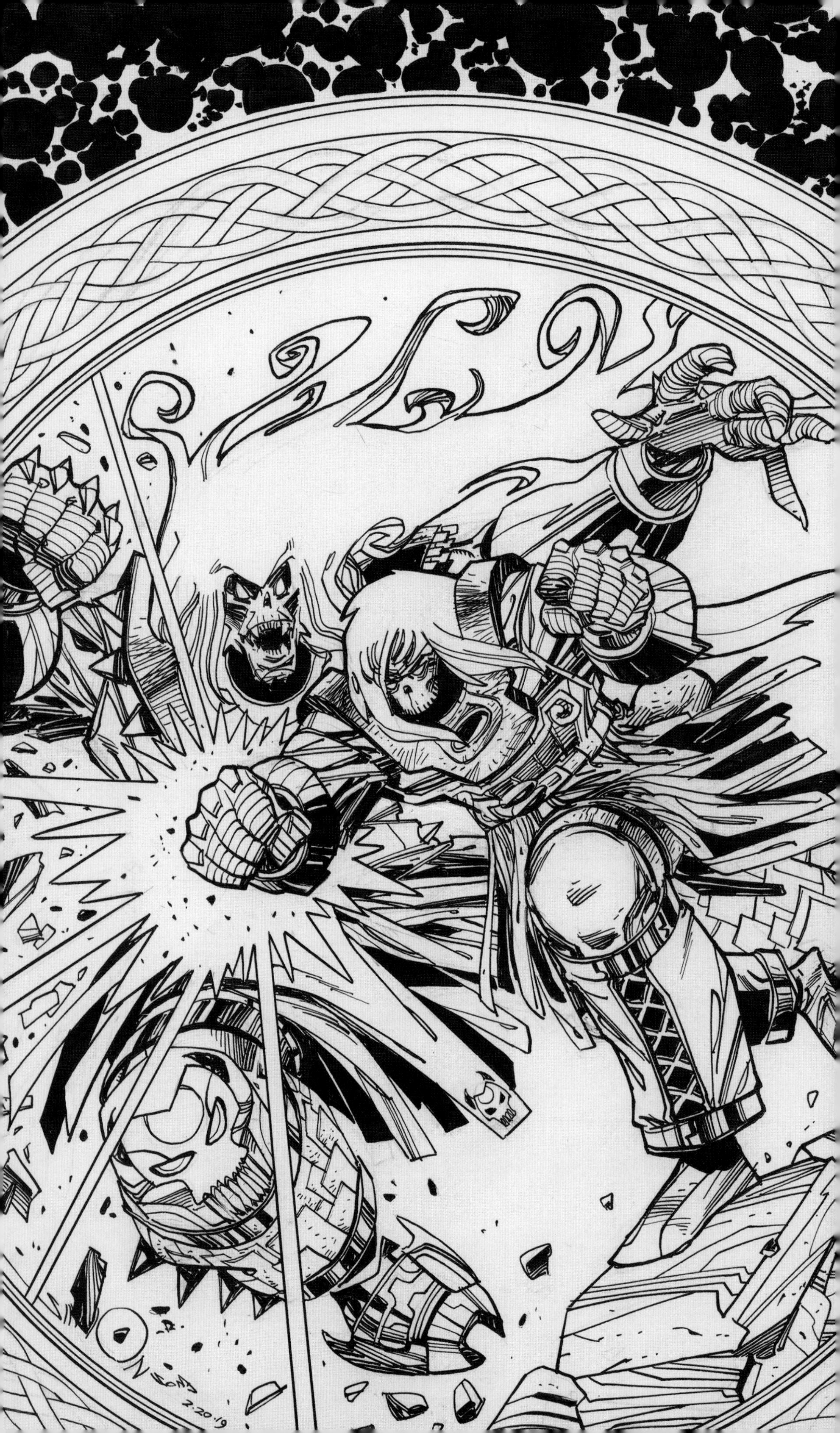
2.20.19

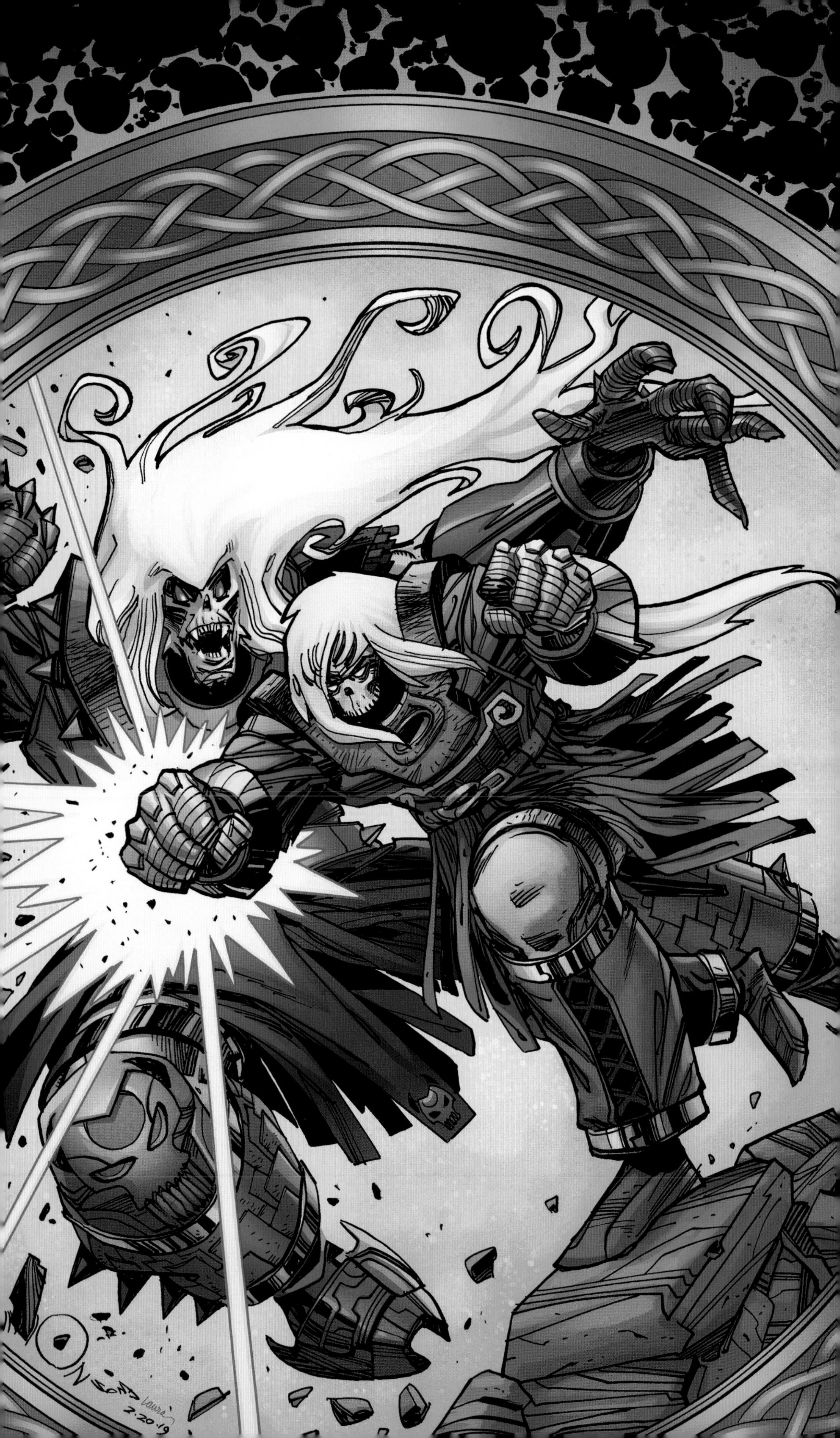

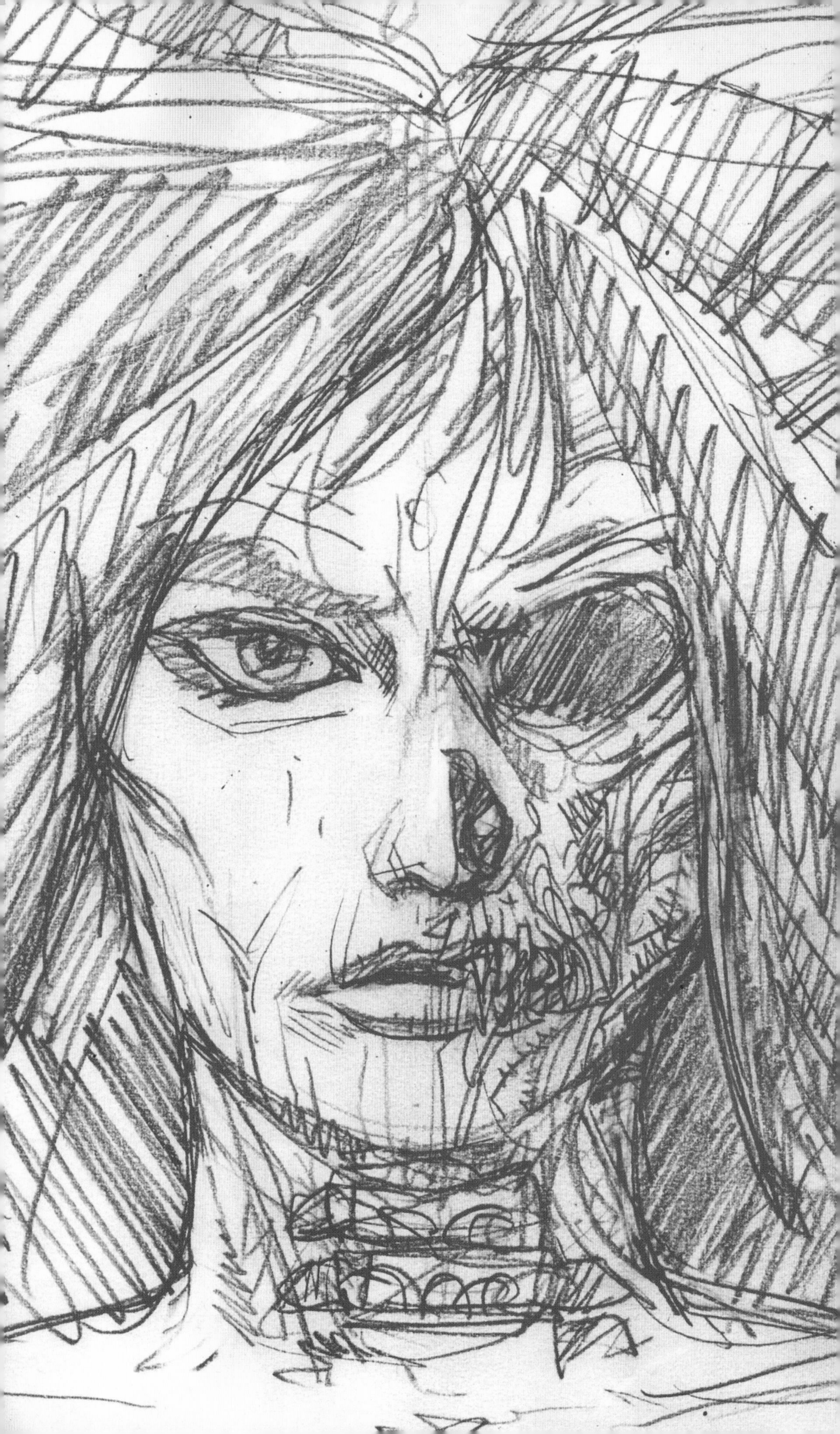

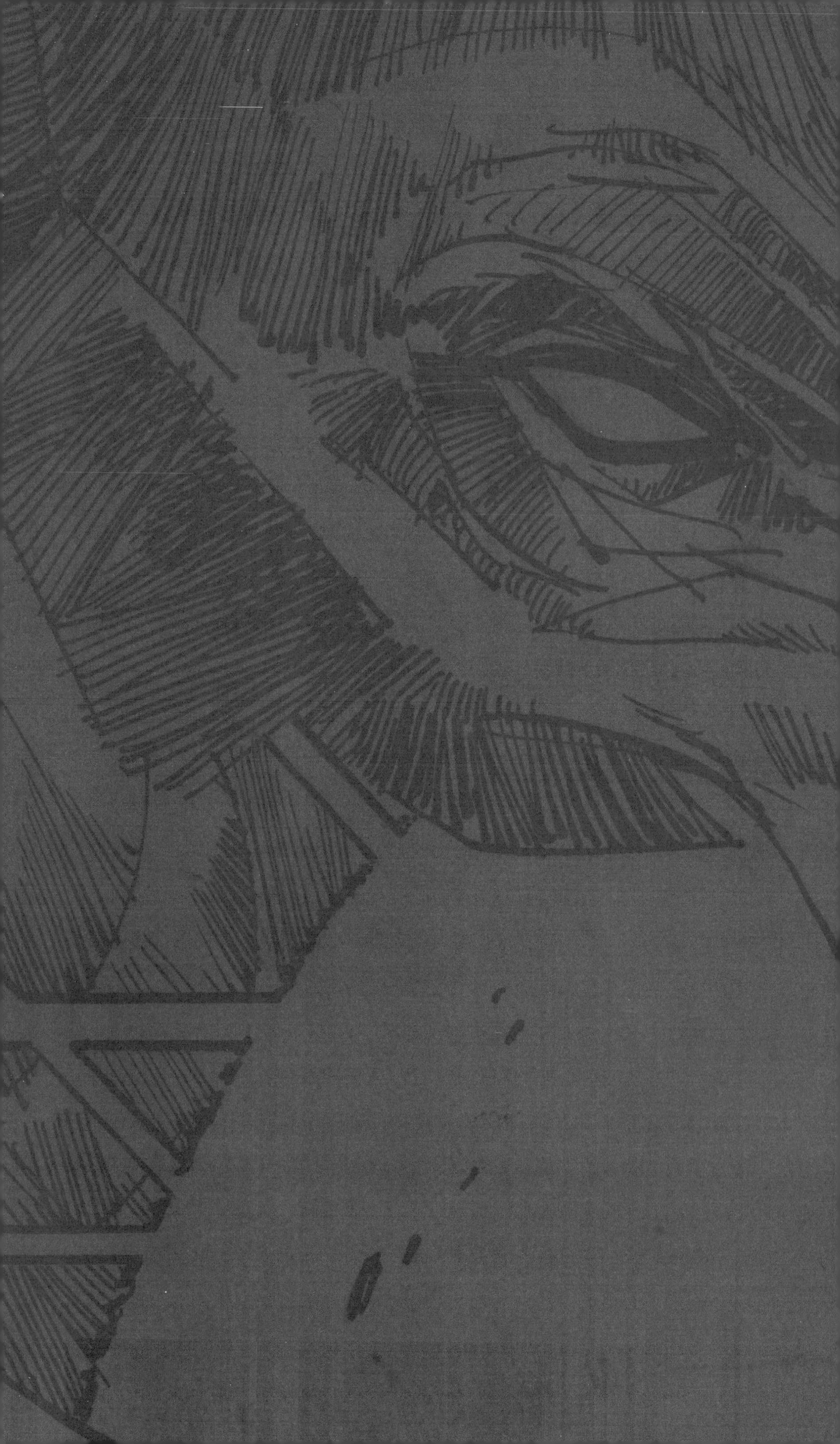